WHISKY FROM SMALL GLASSES

First published in the UK in 2015 by Polygon, an imprint of Birlinn Ltd

This edition first published in the US in 2017 by Aria,
an imprint of Head of Zeus Ltd

9 7 5 3 1 2 4 6 8

A CIP catalogue record for this book is available from the British Library.

ISBN 9781786699053

Aria
c/o Head of Zeus
First Floor East
5–8 Hardwick Street
London EC1R 4RG

www.ariafiction.com

For Fiona, Rachel and Sian

Prologue

Lights sparked and flashed before her eyes. The movement of her limbs slowed as though of its own accord. The pain she had felt was dull now; the panic subsiding. She was aware that her bowels had opened; she no longer cared. Her last emotions were a fading mixture of anger, injustice and overwhelming sadness, the cause of which she could barely recall.

All she was, all she had ever been, was seeping away: her loves, desires, likes and dislikes, the things that made her angry, the things that made her sad, made her laugh, made her cry; now all diminished. Her final moments were descending into a fading abyss – the surreal detachment of the brain soothing its own way to oblivion.

Suddenly, as the light began to dim, the face of a small, blond, blue-eyed child filled her thoughts. Only for an instant did the terrible choking pain, the struggle for breath, the fight to stay alive, return.

PART ONE

I

The body ebbed and flowed rhythmically in concert with the seaweed and flotsam and jetsam trapped in the bay of the low, rocky cove. A Styrofoam cup, a fisherman's glove with three fingers missing, a drinks bottle, the label so bleached by sun and sea that only a hint of its former contents were now discernible, and orange plastic netting which had ensnared a small crab, reluctant to quit the purpose for which it was intended: all of these floated and bobbed in unison with the corpse.

The naked body of a woman lay face down in the water, limbs spread in a lazy 'X' shape. Her skin looked waxy – a horrible cross between yellow and grey, turning black at her feet, hands and the back of her neck. The remains were bloated, consistent with time spent in water. Small areas of her lower back and thighs were gnawed, most likely by prawns, indicating the corpse had spent at least some time further out to sea.

Surprisingly though, and most repellent, were the two bright red ribbons that held her hair in bunches, a hairstyle redolent of childhood and happiness, horribly incongruous with the rotting corpse now souring the sea tang of the mild spring day.

With almost six years' service in uniform, Detective Constable Archie Fraser was new to the CID. So new in fact that he hoped he was surveying the scene on the beach with what could be considered the appropriate degree of professional detachment. A young female PC and the pale dog-walker who had alerted the police looked on with the mixture of abject horror and fascination so common in humanity faced with death; especially of the gruesome variety. A large black Labrador snuffled and pawed at the sand, undisturbed by the corpse.

'Could you put your dog back on the lead, please, Mrs MacPherson?' Fraser bellowed with a confidence he did not feel. It would not be beyond possibility for the dog to catch an unusual scent on the air and wade into the water to investigate its source.

His short time in Kinloch had already been difficult. Only last month his ultimate superior – one Inspector MacLeod, Sub-Divisional Commander – had cause to reprimand him on discovering a young female shoplifter handcuffed to a very hot radiator while her captor answered an urgent call of nature.

'Focus, boy, focus!' MacLeod had shouted in his high-pitched Highland accent. 'The last thing I need is the Discipline Branch descending on me because you've seen fit to roast some daft bint. You're bloody lucky she was too stupid to make the complaint.'

Fraser had noticed how his boss referred to *the* something, in the way a foreigner would; tourists regularly took him for a German or Scandinavian, and not from the Isle of Harris that was his home. A long period of admonishment ensued, after which Fraser resolved to improve in every way and pay many less visits to the Taste of India restaurant.

'Karen, could you come over, please?' Fraser summoned the PC.

She walked slowly towards him, never taking her eyes from the body, in the way a child would, having been asked to pat a snake.

'What's up?' he enquired. 'Surely this isn't your first stiff?' Her doe-eyed nod was barely perceptible. Having worked his probationary period in Glasgow, Fraser was no stranger to dead bodies: murders, drowning, suicides, accidents – occasionally even some natural deaths. All were part of the daily diet of Glasgow's finest. The difference now was that for the time being at least the crime scene was his responsibility. No van full of colleagues likely to appear; the Serious Crime Squad over a hundred miles away; even his DS off sick, laid low with a persistent 'early retirement' back. Right here, right now, he was the senior CID officer on duty in the Sub-Division, in fact the only CID officer on duty in the Sub-Division.

'It's no' jeest that, Archie.' The PC had a strong local accent. 'I mean, this is Kinloch – I probably know her.'

How could he forget? The crime locus was three miles away from one of the most unique places he had ever been to, let alone lived and worked in. Kinloch. The town was situated on a peninsula one hundred and fifty miles away from Glasgow, on Scotland's rugged west coast;

alternatively, miles away from anywhere, as Fraser had come to think of it. Around ten thousand people lived in what could best be described as a modern alternative to the 1950s. Everyone knew everyone else, down to the tiniest detail of family, even personal, life. Sometimes, when working on a case, the young policeman had the distinct impression that everybody knew what he was trying to find out, but of course were never going to tell.

Another symptom of such a close-knit community was an inherent distrust of strangers, including policemen. Fraser's uncle, himself a retired police officer, had advised him always to have friends outside 'The Job', as the force was habitually known to initiates. He believed that because many cops both worked and socialised together, it left them isolated, introverted and out of touch. 'You keep your ear to the ground, son, especially in a wee place like Kinloch,' Uncle Davie had declared sagely. 'I mean, you're never goin' tae find anything oot about these people unless you get out an' talk tae them. Socialise, spend a few bob, buy a couple o' drinks, and you'll see they'll soon open up.'

Archie had mixed feelings about this strategic advice: for a start, Davie had had his ear to the ground, and bought so many drinks, and so regularly, that he was now awaiting a liver transplant. Also, this was Kinloch, a place most definitely apart. However, he thought that some of what Davie had said could be useful. As the town was his first posting as a DC, he resolved to immerse himself in the community. He tried to join the local golf club, though sadly they were full. Unabashed, he tried the local tennis and cricket clubs, both with the same result. He was briefly elated when the town's Gaelic choir had contacted him in the hope he could swell their dwindling numbers; sadly Fraser was about as tone deaf as it was possible to be.

He had tried visiting the local pubs when off duty. Kinloch had a goodly number of such establishments – far too many according to some of the town's more temperate residents. They conformed to small communities within the community. For instance, regulars at the Shore Bar wouldn't consider crossing the threshold of the Royal Borough across the road. Subtly, each establishment catered for a slightly different clientele: rowdy youths attended Pulse, a noisy club bar in the Main Street, while their more cerebral peers became habitués of the Old Bothy, in the square. Roman Catholics preferred the Douglas Arms, while so-called 'blue noses' headed for the Royal. There was a pub that catered for lawyers, doctors and businessmen; another favoured by tradesmen and factory workers; and one hostelry, situated conveniently next to the bookmakers on the High Street, was dedicated solely to horse racing, the 'sport of kings' playing 24/7 on large screens. Jenny's, tucked away in a small back street, was the end of the line. Those who behaved badly enough to be banned from all the other premises – and many had – gravitated there. The 'tick book' was legendary, as were the fights. Locals referred to it as the 'Star Wars Bar', for reasons that were obvious.

Fraser had visited them all. Typically, as he walked into the room the conversation would stop, resuming in a more modulated fashion moments later. People would gradually drift away, leaving the young detective with one of Kinloch's small army of drunks who barely knew nor cared where they drank, as well as a glaring publican, counting the cost of lost customers.

'Can I say something?' Mrs MacPherson said timidly. 'The tide's on the turn ... well, could it ... could she ... not drift back out?'

The young officer had not considered this. 'Right, Karen, time to get your feet wet. We'll need to get her above the water line. Even if we corrupt forensics it's better than her ending up on Islay.'

'Can ye no' dae it yersel', Archie? This gies me the dry boak.' Fraser gently reminded her why she was being paid, and after removing shoes, tights and socks where appropriate, the pair waded into the few inches of water.

'OK, grab her other arm, Karen, and mind and pull gently – we want to disturb this as little as possible.' The police-woman looked doubtfully at the body, but did as she was told, looking away as she grabbed the left wrist, lips pursed in distaste. 'One, two, three ...' They started to pull. To the collective horror of all three on the beach, the corpse, with a great issue of dark fluid and some more solid matter, broke neatly apart, with the deep sucking noise of a plunger working on a blocked sink. Both police officers, having put more effort into their task than required, fell backwards onto the shingle, the top half of the deceased now some two feet away from the rest of the remains.

In a split second, the fetid stench emanating from the newly cleft body induced the dog to stand tall on all fours and emit a mournful howl, as Karen retched copiously over her uniform, still sitting on the shingle where her assistance to the CID had left her. Body fluids seeped darkly into the sand; even the local seagull population had registered the events and were now swirling in a squawking frenzy over the bay.

'Fuck!' Fraser momentarily forgot the presence of Mrs MacPherson, who was herself looking on in disbelief, as though she was waiting for someone to come bounding from behind a rock to confirm the whole ghastly episode was an elaborate joke, of the type played out on late-night TV.

Just then, movement to his right caught Fraser's eye. Three figures were walking purposefully down the beach towards him.

The slight, taut figure of Inspector MacLeod was unmistakable at their head. It took the Inspector a few moments to grasp exactly what was in front of him. One of his DCs was getting up from the sand, leaving the torso of a dead woman, and a PC, who was spewing at his feet. A woman he did not know was sobbing convulsively, while a large black dog happily wagged its tail at the new arrivals. Only feet away, the rest of the body could barely be made out in the badly discoloured water. A sickening stench was all pervasive.

'What the fuck are you doing, boy?' MacLeod's temples displayed throbbing veins. 'In all my years in the police I have never seen the like.'

'I was merely trying to …'

'You were merely trying to fuck things up, as usual.' The Inspector was incandescent. 'Aye, and all our careers along with it. I dread to think what they taught you at the training college. In my day you were shown how to preserve the crime scene, not tear the bloody thing in half!' As though suddenly remembering others were there, MacLeod visibly took hold of himself and addressed the PC next to him. 'Sergeant Shaw, please do your best to ensure that the remains are contained at this locus.' Turning to a stocky man in a well-worn sports jacket with patched sleeves, he said, 'Sandy, are you able to make any kind of examination under these circumstances?' At that he looked towards Fraser with a thunderous glare.

Sandy, whom Fraser recognised as one of the local doctors, ran his hand through greying locks as he surveyed the scene. 'Well, Charles, I can only concur with your accurate assessment.' His accent was straight out of the Scottish public-school system. 'I, too, have never attended such an incident in thirty years of medicine.' He looked at the young DC with a pursed mouth that spoke of nothing but contempt, then leaned over the landed portion of body, rubbing his chin.

MacLeod walked away from the group, gesturing to Fraser to come with him. Once out of earshot, he grabbed the younger man's arm and on tiptoe addressed the DC's right ear with spitting vitriol. 'You listen to me, constable. Since you arrived at my station you've lurched from one crisis to the next.' Fraser could feel his face redden. 'As soon as this sorry mess is over I'll be recommending to HQ that you are not only unsuited to the CID, but to police work in general. Be absolutely sure that the cack will land on your head, not mine. We'll be the laughing stock of the force by tea time at this rate.'

Fraser resisted an urge to grab his superior and fling him bodily to the ground. He was considering what to say in his defence when a shout from the doctor turned both of their heads.

'One for the big boys, I'm afraid, Charles.' The doctor was brushing sand from his trousers as the policemen walked back over to the scene. 'It's murder, nasty business.'

'How can you be so sure, Sandy?' The inspector looked doubtfully at the medic.

'Oh, quite easily, Inspector MacLeod. She has a ligature around her neck.'

2

Detective Inspector Jim Daley reflected on the dispiriting nature of shopping for trousers as he handed his credit card over to the assistant in the fashionable clothes store. In his twenties – even in his thirties – he had been able to maintain a respectable waistline without the deployment of starvation diets or drastic fitness regimes. Now in his early forties – as he liked to think of forty-three – and especially after giving up cigarettes, he felt his stomach now capable of gaining inches overnight. It was not without a little trepidation that he eyed a suit or a pair of jeans he had not worn for a few weeks. Often, trying to get them on, there would follow a desperate tugging at a straining zip, a grunting wrestle with a recalcitrant waistband, a holding in of both breath and stomach, as he fought to get the garment into a position whereby he could move, sit or stand without a trouser button shooting into the air like a misdirected bullet; worse still, without hearing the sickening rip of stitching tearing apart over a more than ample backside.

He had resolved therefore to make a new start as far as trousers were concerned: go out and buy a pair that more suited his thickening frame, regardless of how unpalatable the thought was of having a matching age and waist size. After all, he would get older, diet and join a gym, thus ensuring that these numbers would diverge in an acceptable manner in the near future.

He caught a glimpse of himself in a full-length mirror as he left the shop. Was that overweight, middle-aged man really him? He consoled himself with the fact that he was six feet three and still had his own hair and teeth. Sure, women found him attractive, just not the woman he wanted to, or so it seemed. Tall, dark, getting fatter and older but still handsome – that summed up Jim Daley.

The theme tune from *The Sopranos* jolted him from thoughts of sartorial insecurity to an equally perplexing subject: his wife Liz. She called infrequently when he was at work and he had become used to these calls containing at least a modicum of bad or unwelcome news.

'Hi, Liz. Everything OK?' He always sounded so lame when he had to speak to her unexpectedly. He felt an involuntary frisson of excitement at the sound of the well-spoken, smoky tones.

'Oh, hi, darling. That was quick. Is it OK to talk?'

'Yeah, no bother. I'm actually …'

She gave him no time to finish. 'Great. Just to let you know, Jill wants me to go up to the caravan at Granton for a few days. Anyway, I thought, the weather's nice, and it's not as though we'll be doing anything, so I'm leaving in a couple of hours.'

Daley was used to being presented with a *fait accompli.* He marvelled at the effortless way Liz, again, managed to impart her intention to do as she pleased, while at the same time make him feel as though he was in some way responsible. He attempted a rear-guard action. 'I'll be home about five. We could go to the wee pub for a couple of drinks, or get a curry or something – make a night of it. You could go up to Jill's in the morning.'

Liz's reply was as predictable as it was swift. 'Oh, what a pity you didn't mention it before. She's invited me to dinner tonight as well. Mark has some boring guest to entertain. I've already said I would go. Sorry, darling.'

'Oh, OK,' was all he could muster. He guessed it was true what people said: once a partner had been unfaithful, it was really difficult to regain the trust that was so important in any relationship. And Liz had been spectacularly unfaithful. The first incident – that he knew of – had been with her gym instructor. Sent home early by the force's medical officer after taking a baseball bat across the head during a drug raid, he thought he heard noises as he gained the stairs of their new detached home in the village of Howwood. The vision of Liz on hands and knees on their bed while her paramour worked energetically behind her was seared onto his memory. Suffering from a hair-trigger temper as well as an acute headache, Daley proceeded to render the third party insensible with a swift uppercut, dragged him by the hair onto the small balcony, and despatched him neatly over the railing and into the garden below.

The sight of a naked man struggling to stand up, with what looked alarmingly like a broken leg, accompanied by the shrieks of an obviously frantic woman, constituted more than enough reason for the good people of Howwood to call the police. Eventually, after much pulling of strings and dire warnings regarding the diminishment of his prospects, a deal was done behind the scenes, and Daley – forced to attend anger management classes – was left to resurrect, as best he could, the remnants of his career. Having reached Detective Inspector in his mid thirties, Jim Daley could reasonably have hoped for Superintendent or beyond before retirement. This was now most unlikely. As for Liz, she had vowed undying love for him and tearfully cited boredom and loneliness as an excuse for her behaviour. Although Daley realised he was wrong, his almost cloying love for her saw him take the only action that seemed palatable: forgiveness. Since then, even when close friends and colleagues alerted him to likely dalliances, he chose to ignore them, having neither the strength nor will to do the sensible thing and leave her. Though he would never let her know, he was head over heels in love with her, and, even though he barely believed it himself, was prepared to accede to almost anything in order to keep their relationship afloat.

She said and did all the right things: she showed great interest in him, they made passionate love, declared satisfied happiness, promised unerring loyalty, but all to no avail. Now that trust was absent, only the slavery of obsession remained. Daley was forced to endure the nods and winks of colleagues; the police of course being a small community where gossip was rife. Had Liz been less attractive her indiscretions would probably have gone unnoticed, however, such were the rumours of her wanton nature, every male colleague now reckoned that they had a chance with her.

'Anyway, you know what the traffic's like in the morning.' Liz pronounced 'morning' with that annoying intonation that had crept into everyday usage from Australian sitcoms, as though the knowledge or concept of the morning was something entirely alien to the listener.

The habit annoyed Daley, who hardened his reply. 'Yeah, whatever you think, Liz. When will you be back?'

'Oh, you know me, darling – go with the flow.' He did. 'Anyway, better dash. I've left one of those microwave curries out for you. Ring you later. Love you.' The term of affection was an obvious afterthought.

Daley stood with the handset to his ear for a few moments. So little said, so much left unsaid: it summed up their marriage. He walked back to the car park, made a mental note to get his car washed, then drove to the station.

Jim returned to his office by way of the coffee machine. On reaching the second floor and his shared office he could hear his DS swearing volubly at his computer. 'You know, I'm buggered how they think that getting us tae dae all this typing ourselves is cost effective.' DS Brian Scott was more agitated than normal, which was, indeed, saying something. 'When I joined up you just had tae scribble something doon and wait for some daft wee lassie in the typing pool tae dae the business. Noo, well, I'll tell ye, Paisley's goin' like a fair, while I'm up here learnin' tae be a fuckin' secretary.'

'Ah, DS Scott.' Daley aped the clipped Kelvinside tones of their boss. 'It's incumbent upon us all to integrate with new policing methods.' He grinned at Scott's exasperation.

'Aye, and fuck him tae. It's getting tae be ye need a degree in this shit jist tae dae yer ain job.' Scott was smiling in spite of himself. An IT specialist he most certainly was not; a highly effective, sometimes inspired police officer he most certainly was. His brusque manner and tendency to ignore the rulebook had hampered his progress through the ranks, and he would no doubt end his career as a DS. Daley felt that it was a role tailor made for his gritty determination, and he valued his assistance more than he would ever admit. Simply, they made a good team.

Daley walked to his large paper-strewn desk. A yellow Post-it note placed on top of a mountain of files announced *Numpty wants to see you!* in Scott's bold, untidy hand.

'When did his magnificence call?' Daley enquired, looking up just in time to see Scott's computer screen turn a brilliant blue.

'Oh, just after you left. He's in a right stooshie aboot somethin'. He didna even pull me up aboot whit a coup this place is.' He swung his chair around to face Daley, left hand outstretched in a gesture of disbelief at his computer screen. 'I mean, whit the fuck is this a' aboot?'

Draining his coffee, Daley went over to Scott's desk, where he deftly pressed a few keys on the computer, restoring it to the report on which the DS was working. 'Just how many computer courses have you been on? It must be dozens now.'

Scott's face took on a look of rueful resignation, 'Aye, a few, but you've got tae remember, Jim, every time I get a chance tae go up tae the college it's mair like a break from my dear lady wife. That's a great wee bar they've got there, an', well, by the time ye've sobered up in the morning, ye've well an' truly lost the thread aboot whit the fuck they're on aboot.'

Daley chuckled to himself as he took the lift to the top floor of the building. As the elevator doors swished open he marvelled, not for the first time, at the steep upward curve in the standard of opulence in this portion of the station. Gone was the bare functionality of the other three floors, to be replaced by dark wood panelling, tasteful paintings, picked out by soft lighting and thick carpeting punctuated by tall verdant pot plants. Even the civilian staff were of a more aesthetically pleasing variety; a woman in a tight-fitting skirt wiggled past him in a cloud of expensive perfume that reminded him of Liz.

Behind the closed door the sound of a giggling female was plain. The nameplate read simply: SUPERINTENDENT JOHN DONALD. COMMANDER DIV. CID. Daley knocked loudly three times. After a few moments of mumbled voices, the familiar 'Come' served as an invitation for Daley to enter. He opened the door and stepped inside, straight-backed and confident.

Donald was sitting behind an unfeasibly large desk that made the rest of the office seem shrunken. An attractive woman stood over him clutching a file, looking intently on as the superintendent busily appended his signature to a document.

'Ah, Jim.' Donald's eyes flitted towards him then back to his papers. He gestured airily with his left hand. 'Make yourself comfortable while I satisfy the rapacious appetite for my time this young lady seems to harbour.'

Same old, same old. Jim was used to his boss's eccentricities; at times it felt as though he had worked for this man for his entire career. As a young probationary cop Donald had been Daley's shift sergeant. On his first posting to Paisley CID, as a raw DC, Donald was his DS. Not long after Daley's promotion to DS in A-Division in Glasgow, Donald arrived as the all-powerful DCI. They were once described as star-crossed. He wished they weren't.

The man who sat in front of him now bore hardly any resemblance to the foul-mouthed, overweight philistine of what seemed like a very long time ago. Steadily Donald had ironed out all his imperfections. He stopped drinking, took up running, golf and squash, and consequently lost piles of weight. He spent a great deal of time abroad or under a sunbed, ensuring that his permanent tan was just that. Even his hair had undergone a transformation: gone were the thick black curls cut close to the scalp; now thinning, his gelled coiffure made him look like a hackneyed version of an East End gangster.

His manner had changed accordingly: the harsh accent of Glasgow's East End was now modulated to the clipped tones of middle-class Bearsden, taking him much further socially than it had in geographic reality. His notorious temper was kept in check by sycophancy to superiors or aloof arrogance to those of a lesser rank. Yet Daley had never been in any doubt as to how thin this façade was; Donald was as notorious for his self-seeking ruthlessness as he was respected for being a mediocre police officer who had transformed himself into a truly talented administrator and political mover. The letters BA, LLB after his name bore testament to the hard work and determination it had taken to climb from the mire of a piss-poor childhood to his current middle-class comfort.

Donald signed the document with a flourish, then flamboyantly waved the paper in the air to dry the fountain pen ink he had used. 'Now, Di, don't be frightened to bring in as many papers for me to sign as you want. My door is always open, you know.' He leered at the young woman who nodded dutifully then left the room. 'Now, Jim, sorry about that. Breaking in a new girl, so to speak. One long round of paperwork in here. Now where did I put that ... Ah, here it is.' He lifted a black file from the desk and removed what looked like a number of printed emails. 'Bit of bother in our new dominions. Kinloch, to be exact. There's no point me blustering on, scan these and we'll get on wi' it.'

Daley noticed how the polished edge of his accent tarnished slightly once the secretary had gone. For many, this would have appeared to be an acknowledgement of their shared past; to Daley it was more an indication of how far down he was in the pecking order. Donald obviously felt there was little point in turning on the charm for his senior DI. He opened the file and began to browse its contents. After a few minutes he looked up from the papers and cleared his throat to divert Donald's attention from the copy of *Perfect Home* his superior was avidly consuming.

'Oh, right, Jim. So, there you have it. Bit of a crisis down there in terms of manpower, and experience too. The subdivision is run by a teuchter called Charles MacLeod, a right little shit and the very worst kind of social climber. They have a DS who's no more use than an ornament, and a few eager young DCs. Do you remember Davie Fraser from A-Division? His nephew Archie's there.'

'If he's anything like his uncle, the pubs will be doing a fine trade.' Daley had a sinking feeling in his stomach. Strathclyde Police had undergone yet another phase of reorganisation in an attempt to save money. His division had been amalgamated with what had been the old Argyll Constabulary, meaning that Paisley HQ was now responsible for parts of the west coast of Scotland that few could pronounce, never mind find on a map.

'Quite so, Jim, quite so. Poor man. I think his liver is on the way out. Never met a man who loved a drink more.' Donald looked rueful. 'Anyway, I'm reliably informed his nephew is cut from entirely different cloth.'

Daley hoped so. His experience of Davie Fraser was having to follow him from bar to bar when he was a young cop, watching the man who was supposed to be showing him the ropes steadily becoming more inebriated and objectionable by turns.

'Do you mind me asking what this has to do with me?' He knew what the answer was going to be, but being direct would mean Donald would be unable to dollop his usual helping of sugar onto an unpalatable request.

'Straight to the point, Inspector Daley. That's what I like to hear.'

Daley had the impression that Donald was a bit disappointed, and would rather have had the chance to dish out his usual jargon on 'duty' and 'chances for advancement', the normal precursor to a shit job. 'I need someone there with a bit of experience, to get this solved quickly and prove to those yokels that our way is the best way. Fuck knows, we'll have to get them to toe the line somehow, and this affords us the perfect opportunity.'

'So you want me down there, sir?' Daley moved the conversation away from a lecture on the difference in policing methods between city and county divisions.

'Yes, Jim. In fact, I'd like you down there first thing tomorrow morning. The body is on the way to the mortuary in Glasgow. That prick Crichton will do the necessary this evening at about seven, and I'd like you to be there.'

Daley paused momentarily to take this in. He was being sent to a far outpost of the empire to investigate a murder that could take forever, while the wayward Liz was at the other end of the country doing, well, he dreaded to think. 'I see, sir. What about personnel?' was all he could think of to say.

'I have you booked on the first flight in the morning. You will of course be much better informed after the PM. Take a look on the ground yourself, then we'll decide who we can spare to send down there with you. Take that file, and I'll send anything else we've got downstairs. No doubt we can spare Tweedledum and a few other bodies should the situation require it.' Donald had what could best be described as a strained relationship with DS Scott.

Daley's mind returned to what he had read in the emails: a young woman, ligature, body dumped at sea, and a locus distant from usual amenities. This was not going to be an easy inquiry. 'Have the Support Unit been informed yet, sir?' He was referring to the group of elite Strathclyde officers who specialised in various disciplines now required of a modern police force: firearms, dog branch, crowd control, underwater unit and so on. Daley reckoned the underwater unit would be handy bearing in mind the circumstances of the death.

'Not as yet, Jim. I think it wise to wait until we have some kind of result from the PM, no matter how preliminary. Of course, you realise, in terms of expenditure this is going to be a killer. We've already had a full SOCO team down there. The burden of expense falls to us, the investigating department. I hope you'll bear that in mind when you're on the ground?'

'As you know, sir, cost is always at the forefront of my mind during every inquiry.' Daley smiled, knowing his boss was well aware of his attitude to the bean counters many senior officers had been forced to become.

'Luckily,' said Donald, choosing to ignore the irony of the last statement, 'because this is new territory, so to speak, we are able to introduce a degree of flexibility into our spend. However, Jim, the pot is by no means bottomless. Please take that on board.'

Daley was about to make some sarcastic reply, when Donald continued on an entirely different subject without the need for an intake of breath. He, it seemed, had developed all the skills of the politician. 'And how is Liz? Everything back to normal in that department?'

Daley bridled as a leer crossed Donald's face. Only a few weeks had passed since Liz had flirted outrageously with the superintendent at a retirement party. The couple had rowed late into the night when they returned home, with Liz claiming that she was only trying to advance his career with a little 'networking' – yet another modern term he couldn't stand. Anyway, Donald's body language had made it abundantly clear that 'networking' was the last thing on his mind. The ever loyal DS Scott had administered a left hook to a colleague who had insinuated that something illicit was afoot.

'Mrs Donald and I really must have you for dinner.'

Mrs Daley's more likely to have you for breakfast, Daley thought, somewhat uncharitably.

'Anyway, better get on, we both have plenty to do.' The superintendent stood, hand outstretched. Daley shook it in acceptance of the dismissal. 'Pick up your tickets from Kirsty next door – and don't forget to keep me informed. Don't take any shit off that little bastard MacLeod. Any trouble there and I've got a few tricks up my sleeve. Good hunting, Jim.'

3

It didn't matter how long it had been since Daley's last visit to Glasgow's mortuary: it hadn't been long enough. Part of the training of young police constables in years gone by had included at least one trip to this place to witness a post mortem. Around a dozen pale police officers would huddle around a bluff pathologist, as he hacked, cut, tore and drained, and generally showcased his talents in a way only the most strong of stomach could withstand. Daley had managed not to faint or to be sick, however, he had been in the minority. These incidents were so common that each muppet (as trainee cops were then affectionately known) would be given a paper bag and told to be ready to grab whoever was next to them, in the not unlikely event they passed out. The young PC who had stood next to Daley the first time was so traumatised that she left college that day, never to return.

Things had changed: brushed aluminium sheets replaced the badly grouted Victorian tiles that had served as wall covering; industrial carpet silenced the ominous tread of the cracked linoleum flooring; soft mood lighting illuminated, where once the harsh glow of humming striplights had served to augment a visceral scene of blood, shit and gore.

One thing that had not changed – not in the slightest – was the smell. The olfactory sense being as it is, Daley was instantly transported to his first visit every time he came here. A cloying, sickening mix of death, decay, disinfectant and refrigeration, it was a smell that, no matter how you tried, would be your unwelcome companion, an uninvited house guest, for days on end after departing this Faustian repository of hell on earth.

Not everyone was affected in the same way. Scott slouched along the corridors, untroubled by anxiety or the clammy odour. 'Aye, an' see if he doesna get another centre half – he can forget it.' The DS was expostulating on his favourite subject: Rangers Football Club. 'That fuckin' keeper's fuck a' use an' a'.' From different sides of the west of Scotland sectarian divide, inspector and sergeant usually kept up a healthy banter on the subject of football. At the moment though, Scott found his interlocutor uncharacteristically silent. 'Are ye followin' me, Jim?'

The clatter of a large fire door being slammed shut startled both men and negated the need for an answer.

'Well, well, if it's not the dream team.' The sarcasm was palpable. Another thing was unchanged from the first time Jim Daley had been to the mortuary, and the man was now trying to secure the fire door with one hand as he pocketed a black pipe into a short white coat pocket with the other: Chief Forensic Pathologist Andrew Crichton.

'Still at the pipe, Andy? I dread to think what shape your lungs are in.' Daley walked towards Crichton and slapped him on the back. 'How are you keeping? Surely you must be past retirement age.' He smiled affectionately at the older man.

'One of the advantages of a professional career, Inspector Daley, is that one doesn't have to retire in one's forties and get a job delivering newspapers or doing odd jobs in order to make ends meet.' Crichton was referring to the fact that most junior uniformed police officers retired after thirty years of service. Many would find themselves in rather menial employment, either from boredom or the pressing need to supplement an inadequate pension. In the CID, and from the rank of inspector and above, the situation was different: the higher grades regularly stayed well beyond thirty years in 'The Job'. However, the forces were slowly encouraging ordinary cops to stay on as well, realising that there was truly no substitute for experience.

'Aye, listen tae it.' Scott adopted an expression of mock outrage. 'It'll be nae bother fir you tae get a wee part-time job. That butcher in Kilmacolm's always needin' help, an' think, no reports tae write or fuck a'.'

'I'm so glad those elocution lessons have finally paid off, Brian. Your ready turn of phrase never ceases to amaze me.' Crichton surveyed the DS with a critical eye. 'All that drink is having a devastating effect on your looks too. Good grief, man, you look like you've aged ten years in the last two.'

'Cheeky bastard.' Scott chuckled. 'Anyhow, me an' the boss haven't a' day for this. He's gettin' sent tae the wilds tomorrow.'

'Well, gents, as you can no doubt discern with the use of your legendary detection skills and from the fragrant aroma of tobacco, I have been having a smoke. Really, nothing is sacred these days. My old professor never had a cigar out of his mouth when he performed a post mortem. Now, if you light up within ten feet of the building, you're liable to go down for ten years.'

'Aye, an' you've aye been a stickler for the rulebook, Andy.'

Laughter filled the corridor as they headed for the pathology theatre. Two technicians were working on a body lying on a metal autopsy table. The room itself was dimly lit, however a large bank of lights suspended in a metal frame above the table illuminated the scene with ice-white precision.

'Be so good as to put these on.' An assistant had arrived bearing green aprons, masks and rubber overshoes. Crichton removed his white coat, then headed over to a large metal sink where he rolled up his shirt sleeves and soaped his hands and forearms, operating the taps with his elbows when he was finished. This done, he shrugged on his green rubber overall with a great deal more ease than the two police officers, both of whom had required the help of an assistant.

Now fully kitted out, the trio proceeded to the autopsy table where Daley recognised the blackened, bloated features of the deceased he had first seen on the emails in Donald's office. The body cavity had been exposed; both sides of her ribcage and flesh were pinned back with large stainless-steel clamps. As usual Daley had to suppress an automatic gag reflex. Scott, meanwhile, took in the scene intently, eyes visible over his mask, which was moving in a less than flattering manner as he continued to chew an ever-present piece of gum.

'Aye, you've made a good start, Andy.' Scott's eyes flicked from the eviscerated corpse to the pathologist.

'When I heard who was in charge of this investigation, I thought I'd get the sawing over with before you got here.' Daley could only imagine the broad grin hidden by the older man's mask. 'Right, progress so far … As you can see, we've managed a pretty comprehensive examination of the subject.' Crichton was talking in a more businesslike manner now, rather like a dentist announcing to his nurse which teeth were to be filled. A large microphone hung down above the scene, ensuring no utterances from anyone around the table would be missed. 'At first glance – despite one or two anomalies, which I will come to later – a straightforward strangulation. However, if I may draw your attention to this.' Crichton moved down the corpse to the exposed right leg. 'This mark around the ankle indicates restraint.' He pointed to a band about two inches wide that encompassed the ankle. The skin here was a lighter hue than the rest of the body, which was turning black as the process of putrefaction began. 'However, this mark was left on the body post mortem, so someone felt the need to tie her up even though she was dead.' Without giving the officers time to take this in, or ask any questions, he pulled away the green sheet which had been covering the waist of the dead woman, to reveal a deep black gash that bisected the remains.

Daley could taste bile in the back of his throat.

'Again, after death, the body suffered a major trauma, completed I am told by your colleagues in Kinloch, who saw fit to pull the subject apart like a Christmas cracker.' Crichton looked towards Daley, laughter lines visible above his mask. 'If you need a chair, please just ask, Jim.'

'Very good, Andy.' The inspector changed the subject quickly. 'How – when – could that have happened?'

'If you're asking me to make a wild guess, I would say she was nearly cleft in two by a large, sharp metallic object – a ship's propeller, for example. The wound is precise and clean, which suggests to me a swift slice, rather than the kind of sawing or cutting that would have been required had manpower, or even a tool, been used. I'll have to do more tests on the flesh surrounding the wound. That'll take a couple of days though.'

'Fuckin' hell, this is some mess, Jim. You'd be better takin' Sherlock Holmes doon wi' ye, never mind me.' As was his habit, Scott had displayed his uncanny knack of distilling the most complex of situations down to the lowest common denominator.

'I must admit, in my many years as a forensic pathologist I've never encountered such circumstances. However, as I say, we have a number of lab tests yet to perform: stomach contents, other bodily fluids and so on. She definitely had sex within the last forty-eight hours, but I'll be in a position to tell you more about that after the lab work.'

'What do you mean, Andy?' Daley was curious. He had known Crichton for so many years that he had become used to the nuances of his voice and presentation. He suspected the pathologist had discovered something significant.

'Oh, merely a theory, nothing more. By the time you've had lunch down in Kinloch tomorrow I should be able to give you some answers.' Suddenly Crichton raised his head from the body and looked at the police officers. 'Wonderful place, Kinloch. An old friend of mine lives down there: great fishing, golf, fantastic scenery.' He had a far-away look. 'People are as mad as fuck, though.'

'What are you, a shite tourist board?' DS Scott, straight to the point. 'Once you're done wi' the rough guide, mebbe you can tell us how long she's been deid for.'

'Well, immersion in water has made that more difficult, but I'd say no more than sixty, no less than twenty-eight hours. I'll be able to be more precise within the next day or so.'

'What about her age, Andy? Any distinguishing marks?' Despite the gruesome surroundings, attending the post mortem had whetted Daley's appetite for this investigation. He was intrigued now.

'I was just coming to that. I would say she was between twenty-five and thirty. She gave birth within the last three years or so. Oh, and look at this.' He moved the corpse's right leg. On her inner thigh the letters 'IS' had been tattooed. 'As you can see, not professional – ink and knife job if you ask me – and most unusual for a woman to let herself be disfigured in that way, don't you think, gents?'

For once, DS Scott had nothing to say.

4

Daley hated waiting. He was sure that on his deathbed he would bitterly regret the hours, days and weeks he had spent in the limbo of being unable to do anything while waiting. In this particular instance Scott was fifteen minutes late, and although he would still easily make his flight, he fretted that the time he had added in lieu of any possible delay was fast disappearing. He looked around his lounge, noting that the décor, ornaments, furniture choices – even the photographs and paintings – were really all his wife's work. Not for the first time, he felt like a stranger in his own home; it was an alien environment that bore witness to the tastes and comfort of another.

He remembered being a teenager: the posters on his wall, the black paint that had so infuriated his mother when she had discovered it adorning his bedroom, from floor to ceiling. He had painted his bedroom furniture white: black and white to match his taste in ska music. The music centre, that he had coveted for so long, sat on top of an old chest of drawers that his father had 'acquired', and a Roberts transistor radio dominated his bedside table. The rest of the small space was occupied by an ancient anglepoise lamp and whatever book he happened to be reading at the time. He had managed to cobble together a low cabinet, which contained his records and tapes, all stored in alphabetical order. He remembered making compilation tapes that he gave his father to play on the car stereo whenever they embarked upon one of the epic journeys that were the precursor to visiting some ancient relative. All this had been his pride and joy, an indication to anyone who cared to wonder that he was now an adult who had his own likes and dislikes – his personality encapsulated by a few sticks of rough furniture, poorly applied paint and low-end hi-fi equipment. Nothing special, but his. Even his eventual choice of career had reflected the black-and-white obsession.

Standing now in his expensive home, in one of the well-appointed 'reception' rooms graced with the cream of soft furnishings and contemporary art, a stark realisation that he had allowed his personality to be subsumed by the tastes and whims of Liz dawned. This room – in fact, the whole house – was someone else's stage, a stage on which he was merely one of an ensemble, an insignificant and unaccredited player. He shied away from acceptance of the fact that this relationship was consuming his soul; that his reason for being was increasingly entwined and predicated on his dynamic with an individual he felt he was growing further from every day.

Unnecessarily, Scott was sounding his horn as he drove up the short gravel drive, and bawling, 'C'mon, you! You'll miss that bloody flight if we don't get a fuckin' shift on.'

Daley pushed the front door twice, checking it was properly closed, walked down the three front steps and opened the door to Scott's car. The acrid smell of cigarette smoke hit him like a wave of unwelcome nausea as he eased himself into the passenger seat. 'You know, Brian, this car is a complete health hazard.'

'Fuck me, I'm good enough tae take ye tae the airport, an' a' ye can dae is gie me a hard time. Ye've been a right pain in the arse since ye stopped smoking, d'ye know that?' Scott stubbed his cigarette out in the overflowing ashtray with exaggerated vigour and involuntarily coughed the deep, unhealthy rasp of the diehard smoker.

'See? When you're in the oxygen tent you'll wish you'd done the same as me and given up. How do you think I managed to afford that big plasma TV you like so much?'

Scott coughed out a string of expletives as they drove towards the main road. Daley realised that he had become difficult since quitting fags. He definitely did not miss the hacking cough, the bad breath and the huge amount of money they relieved you of in the course of a year; he hadn't even suffered any noticeable sign of withdrawal. No, his post-smoking self had developed a visceral hatred of cigarettes, something he supposed the body prompted in order to protect this new nicotine-free existence.

Scott broke the spell. 'Mind you met my brother, Willie, at the fitba'?' Daley grunted in the affirmative. 'Aye, well, I'd forgotten he wiz doon there workin' aboot three years ago. He's a sparky, mind?'

'I remember he swears more than you. I didn't think that was possible. Anyway, how did he like Kinloch?'

34

'Fuck me, we had tae wring his liver oot wi' a mangle when he came back. He says they're a' near daft doon there. The wife reminded me last night, you know, when I says I might be goin' doon for a while. A' mad wi' the drink, fightin' their ain shadows, an' close-knit tae. I'm thinking yer in fir a fuckin' hard time wi' that mob, for sure.'

Daley looked out at the leaden sky as he pondered Scott's theories on Kinloch society. Small communities were always difficult places in which to carry out an investigation. However, in a way, all investigations took place within one community or another, whether it be a housing estate, tower block, office or ethnic enclave. Glasgow's Asian and Chinese communities were notoriously difficult to infiltrate, and as for some of the schemes – well, he didn't expect Kinloch could be any worse.

As they neared the airport, large signs announced a change to parking procedures around the terminal buildings. In fact, it was more appropriate to say you couldn't drive anywhere near them. An attack on the airport by terrorists with a car full of gas canisters had put paid to that. As a young cop Daley had worked for nearly six months at Glasgow Airport. In those carefree days all the police had worried about was where they could get a free coffee, or where best to view young holidaymakers as they navigated their scantily dressed way through the terminal. Now, well, things were different. Even here, on Paisley's doorstep, he was aware of a change in attitude. People viewed anyone remotely Asian or Arabic in appearance as a potential threat. The landlord of his local in Howwood had implored him to look carefully at the soles of the shoes of any suspicious-looking passengers. 'Think aboot it,' he said, 'when wiz the last time anybody looked at your shoes when you checked onto a flight? It's obvious, Jim.' Since then Daley had to make a conscious effort not to stare at fellow passengers' footwear. Maybe people were right to be suspicious; perhaps danger was ever present. It was undeniable that the world had changed for good.

Scott dropped him as near to the terminal building as was humanly possible, and Daley made his way along walkways crammed with pale-skinned travellers, chatting excitedly as they made their way into the airport, or their tanned, more subdued counterparts, returning to the greyness of reality from holiday idylls. The scent of cool rain on warm tarmac mixed with the heady odour of aviation fuel and car fumes permeated the air. He'd never liked any kind of terminal building: whether it be train, bus or airport. It was not that they were large, often busy, usually impersonal places; no, it was the air of melancholy that inhabited them. To him, they spoke too loudly of parting, of sorrow: people saying goodbye. Not for him thoughts of a mother greeting a long-lost child, or lovers reuniting; these buildings were filled with a resonance of something coming to an end. Without meaning to, he thought of Liz.

He made his way to the check-in where his boarding pass was issued and his luggage processed. The check-in girl reminded him of the fragrant secretaries who populated Donald's floor of the station. He pondered how many women were passed over for work just because they were not in possession of the requisite looks; life was as unfair as it was ridiculous.

He ambled to the departure gate via a newsagent, where he bought a paper. A quick scan of the front page revealed that, inevitably, the press had got hold of the Kinloch murder story. No doubt he would have to appear at a press conference at some point – something he loathed. He wished he had chosen to wear a different tie and resolved to change it at the earliest opportunity.

Daley couldn't help smiling on discovering that the same girl who had checked him in was now collecting his boarding pass. She noticed his amusement. 'We're a small operation, sir. Everyone has to pitch in.' He detected an unusual lilt to her voice; not the singsong of a Highland accent, nor the upward intonation of the Central Belt – something different, with longer vowels and a more laconic pace.

A bus took them out to the runway. At first he thought they would drive past this mini-plane, until they pulled up and another uniformed flight attendant entered and ushered them from the vehicle towards the aircraft. Daley was normally a confident flier, but he was unprepared for the cramped cabin he now entered, hunched over, walking sideways like a crab. The flight attendant showed him to a window seat on the right-hand side of the aisle. As he adjusted his belt he heard a stream of expletives issuing from two youths who were seated in front of him. The young men were not being intentionally offensive; in the west of Scotland punctuation was gradually being replaced by curses. He and Liz had recently spent a weekend in York, and he remembered being surprised by the absence of swearing. Even the small pub in the Marygate, close to their hotel, offered a warm welcome in an oath-free zone. Along with good beer, it made a pleasant change from the raucous, febrile ambience prevalent in the boozers he frequented.

Momentarily the young men fell silent as a small, middle-aged Asian man was shown to a seat at the front of the aircraft. A snort of suppressed laughter indicated that they had registered his presence. 'Fuck me, Bobby, start saying your prayers. That cunt's probably got a bomb up his arse.' Daley contemplated intervening but was beaten to it by the flight attendant. 'Right you, Camel Johnstone, any mair o' that an' the only arse you'll need tae worry about is yer ain as it bounces off the tarmac when I throw you off the plane. Understand?'

Daley smiled. This was not the type of approach he was used to from airline staff, however it proved most effective as both young men were now quiet and had adopted slightly embarrassed expressions. He had noticed the long vowels again, both from the boys and the attendant; this was, no doubt, the Kinloch accent.

He repressed feelings of claustrophobia as the engines burst into life and the plane began to taxi slowly along the runway. Without warning it rose sharply from the ground, engines straining to get them airborne. Daley's heart missed a beat as the engine noise dropped suddenly when they attained the required height. A grey curtain at the front of the aircraft was flung open, revealing the cockpit where one pilot was seated and another stood hunched with a radio mic in his hand, ready to address the passengers.

'Good morning, ladies and gentlemen, aye, an' you, Camel Johnstone ... We'll be flying at a height of fifteen hundred feet for most of the journey, which will last around twenty-five minutes. The weather in Kinloch is much the same as in Glasgow, so we'll be taking the scenic route over Arran, then down the Kintyre peninsula. If you have any questions, please address them to our lovely flight attendant, Morag. I'm Lieutenant Moran, and your pilot today is Captain Witherspoon. Thank you for flying Scotia Airways. Morag will now take you through the safety procedures.'

As she stood up, the flight attendant obscured the young pilot as he retreated into the cockpit. After jumping involuntarily, she announced perfunctorily the usual list of safety instructions. Daley guessed that Lieutenant Moran had nipped her arse through the curtain, though her expression gave nothing away. He looked lazily out of the window: cotton-wool wisps of cloud floated above a patchwork of tiny fields and the grey snake of roads beneath. Bright sunlight glanced from the silver wing of the plane, making Daley wish he had brought the fancy designer sunglasses Liz had so proudly presented him with at Christmas.

The fields were soon replaced by an iron-grey sea, flecked with the white tips of waves. Daley thought the sea looked out of place; too cold for what was a warm spring day. He shuddered at the thought of the corpse of the young woman floating in this forbidding expanse of water. He had always been wary of the sea; though he swam well, he restricted his aquatic pursuits to indoor swimming pools. The sea seemed too big, too unfathomable, filled with the unexpected and unknown. He had read that humans knew more about the surface of Mars than the hidden depths of the ocean, and it didn't surprise him at all.

His thoughts drifted back to Liz. He had managed to get her on the mobile late the previous evening. Despite ringing since six and leaving several messages, she seemed surprised by his call. The noise of a pub – clinking glasses, loud music, exaggerated laughter – was the backdrop to their conversation. She greeted his news about the Kinloch investigation with the platitudes he supposed she felt were her dutiful responsibility: *I'll miss you ... hope you won't be away long ... oh, the house will be so empty.* All the time he could hear muffled voices and suppressed laughter; it was like a teenager talking to a worried parent from a uni bar while being taunted by friends.

Amongst the conspiratorial mumbles there had been a familiar voice: Mark Henderson. Husband of Liz's sister, Jill. Mark and him had hated each other from the word go. In fact mutual friends would often comment how mismatched both couples were. Mark was more like Liz: haughty, dismissive, immodest, sly, vengeful, superficial, good-looking, and extremely clever. It appeared to many that the sisters had married the wrong men. Jill, though almost identical to Liz in a long-limbed, languid way, had a much more reticent nature. The younger sibling by two years, she lacked Liz's supreme confidence, which, accidentally perhaps, had imbued her with greater empathy and sensitivity. She could almost mirror the role Daley played in his marriage. Mark was a notorious philanderer, having been a more than willing participant in a number of affairs. He worked as a corporate lawyer for an international firm of accountants: two of the slippiest professions under one roof. Who was less trustworthy? The accountant constantly seeking the loophole and the uncrossed 'T', or the lawyer who watched his back?

Daley was fond of Jill. He was able to gauge by the way she looked at Mark how devoted she was, and he sensed the pain and devastation caused by her husband's infidelity. Once, they had spoken about it on a Portuguese beach, sitting in a secluded bay watching Mark and Liz's horseplay in the sea. 'Do you think they've slept together?' Her question was sudden and shocking. Daley realised that he had often wondered the same thing, but he'd done what he always did with unpalatable thoughts about his wife: he banished them. 'No, they're too alike to be attracted to each other,' he had lied. He remembered the quizzical smile that had crossed her face by way of a reply. After that, they had kept their own counsel on the matter, each aware of the bitter unspoken truth and unwilling to grant it the life of acknowledgement.

Jill and Mark did share something that it seemed he and Liz would never have: a child. Beth was their pride and joy. She shared her mother's long legs and easy grace, had her father's round, intelligent face, which framed deep, watchful blue eyes, slightly turned down at the corners. A nest of curly hair crowned her three-year-old head and hung in tangled ringlets when her mother let it grow. She had, as Daley's mother used to say, 'been here before'. Talking fluently before she was two, she combined tireless mischief with quick thought and flawless parody. When Daley visited, she grabbed her favourite Noddy book, climbed on his knee, and demanded to be read to. She chuckled her way through a story with him, mimicking the voices he used for various characters. He didn't envy Mark Henderson his money, his board-level career, big house, fancy car, even the fact that he had probably had his wife: no, he coveted his daughter, dearly wishing that the beautiful little girl could be his own.

Liz, it seemed, had no intention of ever having a child. The five S's she called it: screams, shits, sick, sleeplessness and stretch marks. 'Bugger that. Who in their right mind would want a baby?' Her attitude to children was encapsulated in those few words.

'Ladies and gentlemen, we have just emerged from some cloud cover. Below, you can see the east coast of the Kintyre peninsula.' The uninviting grey sea had been replaced by a low rocky coastline, dotted at intervals with white sandy beaches. To Daley's untrained eye, the landscape looked more verdant than it had twenty minutes before, as though the fecundity of the season was somehow at a more advanced stage here.

'Everything OK?' Morag was making her way up the aisle, tending to her temporary charges, holding a small basket filled with brightly wrapped sweets. Daley had developed a sweet tooth since he'd stopped smoking, something he blamed for his recent weight gain. So, inevitably, as the confectionery was waved under his nose he chose two sweets, being careful to avoid the gold-wrapped toffees that had been responsible for him losing a filling last Christmas.

The chimneys and rooftops of a small town could be discerned now; Daley guessed this was the fabled Kinloch. As though to confirm this, the intercom burst into crackling life once more: 'Ladies and gentlemen, as you can see we are approaching our destination: Kinloch. We will be landing in around five minutes or so. Please ensure that you remain seated and that your seatbelts remain secured.' The buildings below were becoming more distinct; unexpectedly grey, he thought. The street pattern of what looked like tenement buildings reminded him of Paisley. Unlike most seaside towns built around the front, it looked as though

Kinloch's streets were at right angles to the loch around which the town sprawled.

The pitch of the engines changed again as the plane began its descent over an airfield that looked to be only a few fields away from the town. The hangars and other airfield buildings bore a distinctly military feel, though Daley could not see any matching aircraft. From some distance along the runway, a red fire appliance could just be made out speeding towards their likely landing point. 'Ladies and gentlemen, we are beginning our descent into Kinloch Airport. Please remain seated, with your seat belts fastened. May I take this opportunity to thank you again for travelling Scotia Airways and hope that you enjoy your time with the colourful residents of the area.' That had been said with tongue firmly placed in cheek. Daley wondered just how 'colourful' this place and these people could be. In any event he was about to find out.

The plane bumped down noisily onto the runway with a screech of skidding tyres and creaks and groans of the undercarriage, and taxied a short distance to a small terminal building. A green light flashed in time to a dinging alarm from the intercom, indicating that it was safe for the passengers to remove their seatbelts and begin the stooped crab-walk down the aisle and out of the plane.

Morag stood slightly hunched at the exit, handing passengers carefully onto the plane's steps, as an identically dressed colleague stood at the bottom of the stairs repeating this function. The two were carrying on a shouted dialogue in the long vowels he was now sure belonged to the natives of Kinloch. Daley ducked through the exit door and down the few steps onto the tarmac. The tang of the sea was strong. The temperature seemed higher and there was a freshness to the air here. He inhaled deeply, already relishing being away from the stuffy air of the city.

A gaunt man in his late fifties stood in the doorway of the terminal building, examining passengers' identity documents. As Daley got to the front of the small queue, and before he could produce his warrant card, the man held up his hand, indicating that the policeman need not bother.

'You'll be fine, Inspector Daley,' he said in the musical lilt of the Hebrides. 'There's a boy out the front to pick you up.' Junior officers were often described by cops of old as boys. This, coupled with the man's demeanour, led Daley to comment, 'How's retirement treating you?' He smiled knowingly at the man.

'Aye, good, very good, Inspector. Lachie Bain, thirty years before the mast, and heartily glad not to be before it any more.' He held out a large hand for Daley to shake.

'Jim Daley, but you know that already.'

Now it was time for the older man to smile. He had a broad, infectious grin, though Daley suspected that it was not something he did very often. 'Aye, well, as you'll find out yourself, old habits die hard. I saw your name on the passenger list, and anyhow this is Kinloch. The whole town will likely know you're on your way, aye, and why you're here.'

'Like that is it? Looks like a reasonably sized place. I didn't expect gossip to be so rife.'

Bain laughed again, this time tossing his head back in mirth. 'It's the biggest gossip hole this side of Benbecula, aye, and vicious with it. If you ever need a friendly ear,

44

I'm in the bar of the County Hotel about half five most days – after the last flight. Only for an hour or so, you understand,' he said, with a serious look.

'Thanks, I'll certainly remember that, but I think I'll have my hands pretty full. I needn't tell you …'

Bain held his hand up again. 'Och, no doubt you'll not have troubles to seek, but you'll be billeted there anyway. Mind, all work and no play …'

Daley grinned as he headed into the terminal to collect his bags. It was already clear that there were few secrets in Kinloch.

5

A tall, well-built red-headed young man was sitting on the bonnet of what Daley recognised immediately as a CID car.

'Inspector Daley, I'm DC Fraser.' The man held out his hand to greet the senior officer. 'Hope your trip was OK. It can get a bit hairy on that wee plane when the wind's up. Not so bad today though.'

Daley noted the similarities between Fraser and his infamous uncle: while both men were tall, heavily built, with red hair, the young officer in front of him bore no sign of the debauchery that had marked out his uncle. Indeed, he looked like the kind of cop you'd be glad to have at your side going in to sort out a pub brawl in Paisley, not one of the undersized graduates who seemed to be favoured by force recruitment these days. 'Hello, DC Fraser. I used to work with your Uncle Davie. How's he doing by the way? I heard he hadn't been too great.'

'Eh, don't hold that against me, sir. He's on the waiting list for a liver transplant, and I don't suppose I need to tell you why.' Fraser looked ruefully at the inspector.

'Ach, don't worry, son. There's a lot worse than Davie cloaking about,' Daley lied. 'You're getting a bit of a reputation yourself, tearing murder victims in half.' He smiled benevolently at the DC, quite sure that the young man had heard plenty of that particular incident.

Fraser's face turned a deep crimson as he stooped to pick up the inspector's bags and put them into the open boot of the car. 'Eh, would you like to drive, sir? Our boss always insists on driving if he's in the motor.'

'No, no, take the wheel, DC Fraser. This'll be Inspector MacLeod you're talking about?'

'Yes, sir.' Daley noted his colleague's raised eyebrow. 'He has his, eh, routines, so to speak.'

They both got into the car, and leaving the small airport car park, headed along a single-track road. 'How far's the town?' said Daley, remembering to switch his mobile back on after the flight, and noticing, with a twinge of dismay, that he had a missed call from Liz.

'Oh, only about four miles, sir – we'll soon be on the main drag. Have you been here before?'

Daley had only hazy memories of coming to Kinloch on one of the old steamers with his granny, what seemed like a lifetime ago. 'Aye, once when I was a wee boy, so you'll forgive me if I don't remember too much about it.' He put the phone back into his pocket, resolving to call Liz as soon as he got a bit of space. 'How are we doing with this inquiry? Anything turned up?'

Fraser gave a resigned sigh. 'We've done the rounds, sir. Y'know, local fishermen, missing persons, the usual. Nobody seems to know anything. She was a bit hard to recognise with the bloating an' all. What did the PM show?'

Daley smiled. 'If you're worried about your little mishap, don't be. The corpse was nearly severed already, so anyone trying to move it would've had the same problem. Oh, by the way, she had "IS" tattooed on her thigh. Ring any bells?'

Fraser shook his head. Daley could tell he was thinking about saying something but wasn't sure what kind of reception he would get. 'Spit it out, lad. I believe that everyone on an investigation should be allowed an opinion, so don't ever be afraid to speak your mind if you think it's relevant. In this job, the smallest push can topple the most robust wall of silence. Oh, and I get this fireside philosophy from my – our – boss, so take heed.' He winked at the younger man.

'Well, sir, it's just that … well, when you get used to Kinloch, you realise that nothing really happens that the whole community doesn't know about … within minutes usually. I can't understand why we haven't got a lead yet. If somebody was missing, well, it would stand out a mile to friends, family. Know what I mean, sir?'

Daley had of course considered this, however, there were a number of problems: the post mortem had revealed that the body had not been exposed to water for very long, even though the corpse had likely spent time out at sea. Also, by all accounts, the prevailing weather conditions seemed to negate the likelihood of the body being washed up back where it had been. Then there was the strange mark on the

48

ankle, possibly left by a restraint. Maybe he *should* send for Sherlock Holmes.

They were now pulling into the outskirts of Kinloch. He was surprised to note that it did bear a resemblance to Paisley on the ground as well as from the air – but a Paisley from twenty years ago. Four-storey red sandstone tenements bordered both sides of the road; under each one sat a small shop of the type that had all but disappeared back home. In those days butchers, bakers, cobblers, pubs, tailors, grocers, hairdressers, funeral parlours and newsagents could be located on the high streets of every town in Scotland. Now, huge supermarket chains and massive out-of-town shopping malls had all but put paid to the local emporia. Not, it seemed, in Kinloch.

The town was flanked on three sides by hills that stood out starkly against a flawless blue sky. Now they were getting nearer to the centre, Daley noticed that his colleague was being waved at repeatedly, a number of cars were even flashing their lights and sounding their horns – most unusual. Fraser was acknowledging all this in an understated manner, most likely not wanting to make the wrong move in front of the inspector.

'Straight to the office, sir?' They were now at a T-junction, where the good people of Kinloch took the opportunity to stare into the vehicle with undisguised interest. 'Aye, fine. I'll get settled in and have a word with your Inspector MacLeod, then I want to meet the team here. Have you set up an incident room yet?'

Fraser looked anxiously at the Inspector, 'Well, sir, it's been a bit difficult. My gaffer is on the panel … with his back, y'know?' Daley nodded, indicating he wanted him to

49

get on with it. 'Well, Inspector MacLeod said that was your job, sir.' Fraser's embarrassment was plain, his face flushed a beacon-like red.

'Right, how many do we have in CID here?'

'Four, sir, me included.'

'Oh,' was all Daley had to say in reply.

They turned right into what Daley assumed to be the main street of the town, up a hill and towards a structure that looked like a cross between a medieval castle and a Victorian prison. Fraser turned the car through an open gateway and into a car park at the rear of the building.

'Here we are, sir.' Fraser was already getting out of the car. Daley was in the middle of insisting that he was perfectly capable of carrying his own bags when a dapper figure, dressed in the immaculate uniform of an inspector, emerged from a steel security door which led out onto the car park. A full head shorter than Daley, the well-polished peak of his hat was adorned with silver braid. He stopped short, obviously not expecting to see the other two officers.

Daley was the first to speak. 'Good morning, Inspector, Jim Daley. You have an unusual office here.'

MacLeod eyed him suspiciously. 'Daley, yes, of course, we've been expecting you, though why we need assistance from the city, I'll never know.' He had a similar accent to that of Lachie Bain at the airport, though higher pitched and faster paced. The sneering aspect to his face riled Daley immediately, though he tried hard not to let it show. He was irritated that while he had addressed MacLeod with his designation, his opposite number had seen fit only to grace him with his surname.

MacLeod turned on his heel, and held the steel door open with eyes downcast, a reluctant invitation to enter the hallowed portals of his domain. 'Fraser, take those bags to the CID room. Daley, you can follow me.' Fraser took the luggage from Daley with a nervous look. MacLeod was doing his best to stamp his authority over the interloper. Daley refused to descend to his level, so much more meekly than he felt he followed MacLeod to his office, the door of which reminded him of Superintendent Donald's: INSP. C. MACLEOD. SUB. DIV. COMMANDER was picked out in bold, larger than normal letters.

'Sit.' MacLeod's instruction was terse, though Daley did as he was bid, while desperately trying to remember the mantra he had learned in anger management about the man who could keep his temper always winning the argument. MacLeod had removed his hat, exposing a bald head fringed by neatly cropped, silver-grey hair. 'Now, let me make myself clear, I ...'

Daley held up his hand to indicate that he was not listening. 'No, Inspector MacLeod, please let *me* make myself clear.' Maybe some of those classes in temper control had worked, after all. 'In the future when you address me, you will be good enough to use my designation, which is incidentally the same as yours.' MacLeod opened his mouth to speak, but Daley raised his voice, making it clear that he was not finished. 'You may be the Sub-Divisional Commander here, however, I am running a murder investigation, with which I require your every assistance. I'll keep you informed of my requirements as and when they arise, and in turn I'll keep you abreast of the progress of the investigation as I see fit. Now, is that understood?'

MacLeod's face was red, verging on purple. 'Inspector Daley, I really must protest. Here in Argyll we have a different way of going about things. I am ...' Again his words were cut short.

'You are subject to the Force Standing Orders of Strathclyde Police, the force of which you are part. I don't give a shit what passed for organisation here in the old county days. If you have any problems with that I suggest you contact Superintendent Donald, who is ultimately in charge of this operation, and to whom I'll be reporting regularly. I've got him on speed dial ... here.' He handed his mobile to MacLeod, who looked as though he was close to tears as he straightened himself up in his chair before eschewing the offer of the mobile phone.

'Very well, *Inspector* Daley. I will accede to your requests. I have of course my own hotline to a superior.' He smiled wanly, looked down at his desk, and opened a file.

Daley stood up, then leaned forward, resting his large frame on rigid arms. His hands were now fists, knuckles white against the dark wood of MacLeod's desk. 'Fuck me about at your peril, you little prick.' He turned and walked to the door which he opened as if to leave; there he stopped and turned to face his slack-jawed colleague. 'Oh, and I'll be wanting to meet with the local CID officers and two of your best uniformed constables – I'll leave the choice to you – in half an hour. Please see to it. Now, where the fuck's my office?'

Daley sat in the glass box that served as the inner sanctum for the senior officers within the larger CID room. He detested open-plan offices. The lack of privacy, the faux camaraderie, that feeling of enforced togetherness: all of which, in his opinion, only served to heighten resentment and ill feeling amongst ambitious officers, and promote a steep upward curve in the sedentary behaviour of more 'easygoing' colleagues. There was an absolute requirement for a good set of blinds, too. He noted that such had been thoughtfully provided in his box and he pulled and twisted the various cords in turn, ensuring he had at least a modicum of privacy.

He was unhappy that MacLeod had aggravated him so readily, but he felt that their heated first meeting had clarified how he wished to proceed. To that end, he had been shocked to see just how little effort had gone into the operation from the Kinloch CID's point of view. The large clear-boards, on which SOCO images of the victim, locus and eventually suspects were put, were in place but untouched. A computer database had been set up, but had pitifully little input for a case that was already twenty-four hours old. The four young DCs – three men and one woman – had conducted some door-to-door work, spoken to fishermen and other seafarers, and stopped cars at or near the spot where the body had been recovered: in short, they'd done the basics. The local investigation lacked any organisation or impetus: that was what he was here to provide.

Through the narrow blinds he could see them now: four DCs and two uniformed officers. They looked so young. This was, he supposed, the curse of the older officer. He recalled vividly that his initial experience of CID work was one of drudgery: ploughing through endless files, records, bank statements, phone bills, CCTV footage – anything that could provide that crucial piece of evidence to crack an investigation. His opinions or theories had most definitely not been required.

He opened his glass door, and the conversation between the local officers stopped. 'As I'm sure you all know by now, I'm Inspector Jim Daley, and before anyone says it, yes, I do go to the gym daily.' That got a laugh. 'I'll get to know you as we go along. Unfortunately, for reasons of logistics and manpower, we're chasing our tail slightly with this one, however, we seem to be some way along the road.' He walked over to a desk from which he picked up a large manila folder. 'Constable Fraser, if you would be good enough to append these PM images to the second of our boards there in number order. Could you ... sorry, what's your name?' He was looking at the DC, who was standing shyly to one side.

'Dunn, sir, Mary Dunn.'

Daley handed her the pictures of the victim that had been taken by SOCO on the beach. She affixed them to the first clear-board, and then stood waiting for further instructions.

'OK, DC Dunn.' He threw a white marker pen at the young detective, which she caught deftly. 'Please write up all relevant information that we know for sure, such as time, date, method of discovery and so on. Which of you is the computer buff?'

A slight, pale-faced DC, whose pock-marked face gave him the look of a teenager he couldn't be, stuck his hand in the air. 'Me, sir, Neil Cluckie.'

'OK, Neil, you're responsible for updating the database, at least until we can see where we're going with this. I'm sure I don't have to tell you what's required, but I know different investigators have different standards, so in this case I want everything put in there: who we interview, when and why, the statement itself, the opinions of the interviewing officers, feelings. I hope you all know how important feelings and instinct are in this job.' Heads nodded vigorously. He walked over to the window, which looked from their elevated position straight down the sunny main street of the town. The road was busy with cars, the pavements an unexpected throng of people, which surprised him. 'Is it always this busy here? Fuck me, there's over two hundred shopping days till Christmas.'

'It's Thursday, sir,' came the familiar voice of DC Fraser. 'The local paper comes out about ten every Thursday morning. Everyone rushes out to buy it. It's like a local community event.'

'From my brief experience of your lovely town, I would have thought a newspaper was the last thing they needed. Everyone seems so well informed.' Daley was only half joking. Tightknit they may be, but in small communities like this, information changed hands so much that some of it must eventually come the way of the police. He turned back to face his new team. 'Right, let's get this show on the road.'

It took him a couple of hours to get them on track. Cluckie remained in the office updating the database, while DCs Dunn and Keith, another large, agricultural type, were sent to every shop, pub, office and café, in fact anywhere that someone may have heard, seen or been told something of relevance. Daley called the Public Relations Unit and arranged for a press conference to be held in Kinloch the following day.

It turned out that the two uniformed cops had to spell another who was guarding the locus; and in the likely event of the investigation continuing over the weekend, all three would be required to bolster what seemed like a considerable show of strength in the face of the unruly revellers of the town. In short, he was woefully undermanned. He sent an email detailing this fact, along with a short summary of his run-in with MacLeod to Superintendent Donald. Pass the buck – he had enough to do without coping with bruised egos or preening selfishness. He was pretty sure that Donald would appreciate all this.

His next visit was to the harbour master. Now they knew that the body had spent at least twelve hours in the sea, he wanted some idea as to where their victim may have entered the water. 'The harbour master's office is on the pier, right?' This question was addressed to Fraser, whom he had chosen as his local guide and adviser.

'Yes, sir. Do you want to check into the hotel en route? It's on the way.'

'Not just now, Archie. Get one of the uniforms to take my bags down, and tell them I'll want some food later. I fancy a stroll down to the pier. It's a nice day after all, and I want to try and get a feel of the place.'

They left the station, passed the local court and some lawyers' offices, and then headed down Main Street, Kinloch.

'Well, at least the office is close to the court. No excuse if you're late, mind you.' Daley spoke easily with Fraser, sensing that he had already gained the younger man's trust. He felt sympathy for the DC; having to deal with the peccadilloes of MacLeod could not be easy.

'Aye, sir, the town centre is pretty compact. It's mostly over this side of the loch, and mainly residential over the other side. A few shops, a hotel, nothing much.'

'Hello, Inspector!' Two elderly women were shuffling towards them, arm in arm. 'We're all glad you've come down to sort this out. What a dreadful, dreadful crime.' The plumper woman, who was short with round glasses, was doing the talking; her thin, white-haired companion was nodding furiously, drawing in sharp breaths by way of agreement with her friend.

'Thank you, ladies.' Good PR was essential in isolated areas, but it was clear that he would have no need to announce his arrival to anybody. 'I hope that if you hear anything you'll tell my officers – no matter how trivial.' He smiled indulgently at the pair.

'Oh, don't you worry, Inspector, we're well acquainted with your handsome constable. You could say he's a drinking companion of ours. Is that not right, Archie?' The plump old woman smiled broadly at the DC, displaying an assortment of brown teeth in various stages of decay, whilst her companion continued to nod sagely, drawing her breath in as occasion demanded.

Daley wondered just how many shades of red his colleague's face was capable of displaying, as they made their excuses and continued down the street. 'Nothing to be embarrassed about, son. When I was your age I liked them a wee bit older too.'

Fraser turned suddenly, about to reassure his new boss that he only saw the old women in the pub now and then, when, by the look on Daley's face, he realised he was being wound up. 'Oh, very good, sir. Aye, very good.'

The day was warmer still, as it was now mid-afternoon. They made their way through what was now the town's centre, passing the County Hotel where Daley was to be accommodated. Like many others in Kinloch, the building was red sandstone, however a faux Juliet balcony and equally contrived crenellations had been included in the architecture, in an attempt to give the hotel a Scottish Baronial feel. If failing in that regard, it did ensure that the façade was difficult to miss.

As they progressed, they were greeted with nods and hellos. A group of smokers outside one of the many bars regaled them with shouts of 'Here's the cavalry' and 'Fuck me, a proper polis in the toon at last'. Unperturbed, the pair crossed a well-tended roundabout and made their way to one of Kinloch's two piers.

The air was a heady mix of ozone, fish and the diesel fumes emitted by a small number of wooden fishing boats. The raucous shouts of crewmen, radios playing music – all drum 'n' bass – and swooping, squawking seagulls wheeling, diving, made for a din. Daley surmised that their arrival had coincided with the fishing boats landing their catch of the day. He was instantly transported back to his childhood, standing on this very pier with his grandparents: his granny, short, bustling and stout, and his grandfather a thin, almost skeletal figure, tall for his time and dressed in keeping with the period, in an old grey suit, the trousers of which were held up by thick maroon braces. Papa George laughed wheezily as he drew on a Capstan Full Strength. To the young Daley he had seemed like an old man; in fact he was destined not to see his fifty-seventh birthday, his lungs wrecked by years of heavy smoking and a lifetime spent down the coalpits of North Lanarkshire.

Daley walked slowly over to the side of the pier and planted his foot on an iron stanchion built into the side of the construction that allowed boats to affix extra moorings in case of bad weather. Dark, oily water lapped at the jetty. The afternoon was warm, scent laden – almost idyllic. He looked out over the water to the head of the loch, which was about a mile away. His thoughts returned to the investigation and he shivered involuntarily as he turned to Fraser. 'The people here might be a bit dodgy, but the scenery is beautiful.'

They made their way along the pier towards a green building in which the harbour master had his office. A sleek, top-of-the-range Jaguar sat outside the office complex, which was shared with the RNLI and Marine Scotland, as well as other private companies. Fraser led the way through a white door and into a corridor. At the very end, a varnished wooden sign was attached somewhat incongruously to a plain white door, announcing in gold letters: CAPT. A. FLYNN. HARBOUR MASTER. Fraser knocked, and a disembodied voice bade them enter.

Flynn was a small, neat man, dressed in what could be taken for the uniform of a Royal Naval Officer. His shirt was perfectly ironed, as were his trousers, and his shoes gleamed. His cap was a pristine white over a shiny black peak, which reflected a badge embroidered with a golden anchor. He was fair-haired, with a neatly clipped beard. Putting the man in his fifties, Daley wondered idly whether or not both hair and beard were dyed.

The office, which smelled strongly of pipe tobacco, looked as if it had been furnished sometime before the war. A large wooden bureau sat solidly at the end of the room, adorned by a muddle of papers, pens, books and a laptop computer, looking out of time. At right angles to the bureau, facing the window, sat an even older desk which bore further detritus. Next to it, sitting in a basket chair at the desk, an old man with a parchment-coloured face directed his startlingly blue-eyed gaze at the newcomers. His steady, unblinking appraisal gave the impression of great wisdom; he didn't attempt a welcome and remained motionless in his seat.

'Hello, Inspector.' The harbour master held out a meaty, calloused hand. 'Alan Flynn, pleased to meet you.' He gestured the policemen towards two rickety-looking chairs. 'Sorry about the mess. I do try to tidy up from time to time, but bugger me, when I dae, I can never find a bloody thing. So much paperwork in this job, you wouldna believe.'

'I'm sad to say I would believe.' Daley shook Flynn's hand. 'I think the police force could break all records as to the use of unnecessary paper.' He sat down heavily, suddenly feeling tired.

'Just so, Inspector, preaching to the converted. Now, how can I be of assistance to you?'

Daley pondered the contrast between the neat man and the chaos he appeared to work in. 'I have an idea how long our victim spent in the water and I know you've already talked with DC Fraser here' – Flynn was nodding, but looking as though he had something important to say – 'however I'd be most grateful if you could go over things with me.' He lifted his hand palm up, indicating to Flynn that he acknowledged that he was desperate to talk.

'You see, that's just it, Inspector.' Flynn was now standing over the laptop at the untidy desk. 'In my opinion ...'

'I'm sorry, Mr Flynn' – Daley realised just how tired he was – 'as you know, we're conducting what is a murder inquiry. I would be obliged if you addressed your thoughts to us in private.' The old man didn't take the hint.

'Of course, Inspector, how stupid of me. Hamish, I told you the inspector would want to talk to me by myself. Why don't you get up to the fish shed and make sure that none of these rogues are up tae no good? Watch out for that *Lady Kate* mob, they're aye at it.'

The old man sat still, and just as Flynn was about to speak again, cleared his throat noisily. Looking directly at Daley, he began talking in a low, rasping voice that was barely more than a slow whisper. 'Noo, officer, surely a man of your considerable experience can answer me wan question?'

Daley, now getting used to the local drawl, smiled. 'Sure, what would you like to know? Within reason of course.'

Hamish continued, unblinking. 'Ye wid never be able tae guess whoot age I am?' His face suddenly cracked into a broad grin, and he threw his head back and laughed.

Daley said nothing. He knew age to be a very touchy subject with the very old; it was as though they were constantly expecting confirmation of how kind the years had been to them. He was about to say eighty, though he suspected the man to be at least ninety, when Hamish stopped laughing abruptly. 'Seeventy-three, Inspector. Aye, seeventy-three. Noo, ye wirna expecting that, eh?' The broad smile returned to his face, narrowing his eyes and giving him an almost East Asian appearance.

Daley honestly agreed, as Fraser looked on, bemused by the whole exchange. They sat in silence for a few seconds, until Flynn walked over to his elderly companion and took him by the arm. 'Noo, come on, Hamish, these men have a lot on. Let's be having you. Don't roll over, roll out and a' that.'

Hamish got up, slowly but straight backed. He picked up his pipe from the table and began to walk towards the door. When he reached Daley's chair he stopped. Any trace of a smile was gone, and he looked as though he had bad news to impart. 'Fair's fair, Inspector, you gied me a courtesy, noo it's my turn tae dae likewise.' The blue of his eyes was at its most piercing at this close proximity.

Daley smiled. While he wanted to get on with proceedings, he decided to indulge the old man. 'Yer woman, the wan flying doon at the weekend ...' He had everyone's attention now, not least Daley's. 'Weel, you'll need tae make up your mind up wance an' fir a' aboot things. Aye, an' forbye, the man's she's wi', he's no good – no good at a'. Maybes yer passed caring though, eh? But heed this: ne'er let harm come tae the things that ur precious tae you.' With that, he smiled briefly, put his pipe to his mouth and left the room.

Flynn looked embarrassed. 'Just ignore him, Inspector, he's forever making prophecies of doom.'

'It depends how accurate they are, Mr Flynn.' Daley was strangely relieved that Hamish had gone. He had found something about the man unsettling.

'That's the thing, Inspector. He's got a name for it, you know, predicting the future an' a that. His family's a' the same. His grandfaither predicted the Second World War.'

Fraser spoke up in defence of his new boss. 'Och, lots of people predicted that. You just had to have a look at what was happening in Germany at the time. Churchill predicted it too.'

'Aye, no' in nineteen twenty-two he didna, time, date an' everything. They still talk aboot it in the toon tae this day. You must remember, constable, superstition's still strong in wee places like this, especially amongst the fishin' community. Now, gents, take a look at this.' He indicated the laptop.

Daley coughed, anxious to move on. 'Yes, Mr Flynn, back down to business.'

The laptop screen was a live satellite image of the Kintyre peninsula, superimposed on which was a complex swirl of what Daley recognised as isobar lines, and numbers which he did not understand. The map refreshed itself about every thirty seconds. Flynn started typing on the keypad of the computer, with what Daley thought was impressive speed.

'You see, Inspector, I'm now going back over the last forty-eight hours or so. These numbers are indications of tide and direction of the wind. It's quite complicated, takes a wee bit of getting used to, but I wish I had something like this when I was at the fishing myself.' He tapped a few keys and suddenly the image enlarged, showing the area around where the body had been found.

'I recognise this, Mr Flynn. The body was found about here.' Daley pointed his finger at the swirling image, without touching the screen. He was glad he had spent time the previous evening poring over Google maps of the crime scene and the area in general. 'What does this indicate to you?'

Flynn rubbed his beard. 'If you're asking me for an opinion, Inspector, I'll give it freely, but it's only an opinion, mind. Based on what I know of these waters, and the help I get fae this kit, you canna ever be certain what happens at sea ...'

'I understand that you can only give an indication, Mr Flynn. No one's going to question your judgement if it's proved wrong. I really need some idea of how, when and from which direction the body came to end up where it did, and at the time it did.' Daley nodded at the harbour master, who straightened up from leaning over the screen, crossed his arms and pursed his lips. Whatever he was about to say, Daley realised that he didn't really want to say it.

'Well, in my opinion, if the timescale you've given me for this poor lassie entering the water is correct, there is no way possible she could've been washed into that bay by the force of wind or tide. In fact, the opposite. If she drowned in the sound here' – he pointed again at the screen – 'she wid likely be somewhere out in the Atlantic by now, or maybe washed up on the North Antrim coast, aye, or even Donegal. But Machrie Bay – nah, no chance.'

'The post mortem indicated that the body had been gnawed by shellfish, probably prawns – surely they're only present in deeper water?'

'Aye, you're right there, Inspector. There's no such things as prawns in Machrie Bay. Into the Sound, aye: crab, lobster, prawns and langoustines – but definitely not in the bay.

Anyway, we're not talking about a big stretch of water, are we, Mr Daley? If there had been a body floating aboot in it, someone wid have spotted it before. Wid ye not think?'

Daley looked at the computer image. The bay was small. 'So, taking this into account, our victim would had to have been put where she was found? You're saying, sir, that she was dumped in, or spent time out at sea, then was moved into Machrie Bay? Either that, or could she have been dragged into the bay inadvertently by some vessel, Mr Flynn?'

'Aye, it's possible, but mind you, the bay itself is quite shallow. The only craft you get in there are small: lobster boats, pleasure craft and the like. I canna see a vessel like that hauling a body intae the bay without noticing.' He shrugged his shoulders.

'Are there many lobster boats there?'

'Ach, nooadays only six or so. Used tae be a lot mair, aye, an' scallop boats too, but that trade's dead now after the ban. The scallops got infected by sewage. Well, they said they were. If you ask me there was nathin' wrong wi' them. That was my trade, Inspector, scallop fisherman.'

Fraser was frowning, 'I know the fishermen out there, sir, and they don't miss much.'

Daley ran his hand through his close-cropped dark hair. It looked very much as though the body had been dumped in the bay, rather than being washed up there; then there was the restraint mark around the ankle of the victim. 'I take it you have a record of which vessels moor here, Mr Flynn?'

'Of course, Inspector.' Flynn appeared suddenly on the defensive. 'I make sure my books are meticulous.' He looked at Daley and Fraser in turn; the latter had his eyebrow raised at this sudden rush of self-justification. 'Sorry, chaps.' He laughed, eyes downcast. 'A bit of a touchy subject, actually. That's what did for my predecessor, y'see. The place was a shambles when I arrived here.'

Daley looked around, unintentionally making his thoughts clear.

'I know it's untidy, Mr Daley, but I know where everything is.' He reached under a pile of papers on the bureau and pulled out a heavy leatherbound ledger that looked as antiquated as the furniture. 'Everything is here. I've no' had time tae put it on the machine yet, but all the information is up to date. I even log the fishing boats in and out these days. No need to really, since they're moored here permanently, but, well, there's so few of them now.'

'So it's only visiting boats you would normally register?' Daley hoped he was wrong.

'Nah, nah, Inspector, that used tae be the case, but, you know, we're no' all that busy just noo, so I like to keep myself goin', in case somebody takes it intae their mind that I'm no' required, if ye get my drift.' He laughed nervously.

'What about the yachts over there?' Daley pointed at some pleasure vessels moored at a wooden pontoon. There were three small sailboats and a couple of expensive-looking cabin cruisers.

'No, Inspector, they're no' my responsibility. Well, unless somebody breaks the harbour rules, or in some kind of emergency. It's owned and run by a private company – Newell Enterprises. James Newell's the main man.'

'Where can I find him?' Daley took out his notebook, prompting Fraser to do the same.

'Aye, as well as running the pontoon, he has wan o' these big RIBs.'

'RIBs? What's that?' Daley's lack of nautical knowledge was beginning to show.

'Rigid Inflatable Boat, sir.' Fraser's time in Kinloch had not been wasted, 'Big powerful boats – they go like f—' He managed to stop himself.

'He takes passengers on trips, Mr Daley.' Flynn filled the gap. 'He's away on a trip tae Ballycastle with a party o' tourists. He always lets me know his plans – for safety, you understand. He's a nice big bloke. Used tae be a captain in the Royal Navy. A wee bit hoity-toity sometimes, but sure, we all have our faults.'

Daley looked out the window. 'When is he due back? I'd like to have a word with him.'

'No' until tomorrow. They're staying overnight.'

Not to be outdone, Flynn brought his own notebook out of a breast pocket in his shirt. 'Let me see. Aye, due back about two tomorrow. I've got his mobile number here if that's of any help?'

'Yes, please. Take a note, will you, Constable.'

Fraser jotted the number down in his notebook.

'Well, thanks, Mr Flynn, you've given us a lot to think about.' Daley held out his hand. 'I trust you'll keep our discussions to yourself for the time being – not add to the rumours, eh?' He smiled at Flynn, who was now shaking his hand enthusiastically.

'Just so, just so, Inspector. And mind, if you need anything else, just gie me a shout. I'm here all day, and half the night sometimes as well,' he said, somewhat ruefully. The harbour master led them out of the office and to the exit. As he again shook Daley's hand, he looked around to see who could be watching.

Noting Flynn's apparent unease, Daley nodded towards the Jaguar. 'Who belongs to this wonderful beast?'

Flynn looked embarrassed. 'Well, me, actually, just a little indulgence. I'm sure you treat yourself now and again, Inspector?'

'A treat for me is a good malt, I'm afraid I couldn't stretch to anything like this. It must be, what' – he looked along the lines of the car – 'best part of sixty grand?'

Flynn laughed awkwardly. 'Oh no, Inspector, that is to say, I got a good deal on it. I sold my scallop boat when I got this job. A treat, as I said.'

The thought crossed Daley's mind that this was, indeed, a guilty pleasure, judging by Flynn's discomfort. His thoughts were dragged away from the car when his phone rang, and he made his excuses and walked to the side of the pier to take the call.

'Hi, darling.' It was Liz. 'You're a hard man to get a hold of.'

'Sorry, I've been a bit …' As usual she cut him short.

'Listen, I've got some hot news.' She was clearly in a bar or restaurant; he could hear the chink of glasses and the animated conversation of people consuming alcohol. He had learned to beware of his wife's idea of 'hot news', so he listened with no little trepidation. 'Mark has had a brainwave.'

Oh no.

'His company has just bought a helicopter, and he has the use of it if they're not ferrying clients about. Apparently there's a gorgeous golf course down there. So, to cut a long story short, I'm coming to visit you in Mark's chopper, while he plays boring old golf.'

'Mark's chopper' had elicited a guffaw in the background. 'Well, it'll be nice to see you. I've got a lot on though …'

'Never mind that, darling. I'm sure we'll find some time …' There was an exaggerated 'oooh' from those listening in. 'Anyway, got to dash. We'll be down at about lunchtime tomorrow. Bye, love.' With that, the sound of nothing from his mobile, which he was well used to.

Daley felt as though he was being watched, and turned to look down the pier. Standing apart from a group of fishermen, Hamish was staring straight at him. The old man nodded his head and gave Daley a stage wink.

6

Daley was silent as he and Fraser walked back up Main Street. That this investigation was puzzling, there was no doubt. He was also well outside his comfort zone in terms of the location of the case, which surprised him; he had not considered just how different an investigation could be this far away from Glasgow.

His mind turned to his wayward wife. Why was she coming all the way from Granton to Kinloch? He felt sure that all this had been Mark's suggestion. What better than spending a weekend winding up the man he saw as a worthless civil servant, a poorly paid lackey barely worth his consideration? He was grim-faced as he caught sight of his paunch reflected in a shop window and involuntarily pulled his stomach in.

'Any ideas, sir?' Fraser was looking as bemused as Daley felt.

'No. Well, yes and no really. My theory is that our victim was murdered elsewhere, then, for whatever reason, her body was taken to the bay and dumped. Either that, or we are dealing with a truly remarkable suicide.' He smiled wanly at Fraser to indicate that, yes, he was joking.

Inspector MacLeod was getting into a car as they walked to the rear door of the office. On seeing Daley and Fraser, he ducked back out of the car and stood at the open door, his hand resting on the frame. 'Your man has been on from the Glasgow mortuary. You've to phone him as soon as possible.' With that, he got into the car, started the engine and pulled off, taking care not to look at the two CID officers as he passed.

'I take it that's your boss being civil? Well, he can stick his attitude up his arse.' Daley waited as Fraser punched in the security code to the entry system. He was tired and hungry, and he sincerely hoped that Crichton had not uncovered yet more mystifying post-mortem data.

He settled in his glass box, picked up his phone and pressed 2# to enter his voicemail – at least this method was standard all over the force. He heard Crichton's familiar tones, hung up, then dialled the pathologist's direct number. It was six thirty, but Daley knew that when Crichton was working on a case, he might as well throw his watch away. He was dedicated above and beyond the call of duty.

Daley was just about to hang up, when a breathless Crichton answered. 'Dear God, I swear they're making that corridor longer. Give me a couple of seconds, Jim.' Daley heard the clunk of the phone being put down on Crichton's desk, then the rustling of papers mixed with the sighs and breathless oaths of the pathologist. 'Now, Jim, here we are ... Your victim from lovely Kinloch, she had sex with two different men prior to her death.'

'Aye, you said as much last night, Andrew. I thought you had something new. Probably just as well you haven't, this investigation's going to be a bastard as it is. Do you have a DNA profile of the two semen samples?'

'Three semen samples, Jim.'

'You said two, Andy. My memory's not that bad.'

'I said she had sex with two men prior to death. A third man had sex with her post mortem.'

There was a brief silence as Daley processed this new information. 'Necrophilia? Are you absolutely sure, Andrew?'

'Afraid so, Jim. We have highly accurate tests for that sort of thing now. Fascinating, yet macabre at the same time. None of the samples match in terms of DNA, to answer your question.'

'So we're talking about three separate men, right?'

'Yes. The first two within a relatively short space of time – maybe even at the same time – and our third man some eight or nine hours later. Most unusual.' After a few moments of mutual reflection, Crichton spoke again. 'I'll send the DNA profiles to the database, of course. You should get a match, if there is one, early tomorrow.'

'This is a strange one, Andy. A victim, no missing persons, no suspects, and now necrophilia. Anything more on that mark on her ankle?'

'Only that it was made by some rough type of plastic – like that stuff they wrap parcels in these days, but much thicker.'

Daley finished his call with the pathologist. He knew that the possibility of getting a DNA match from the semen samples with someone already on the database was remote. Right now though, it was his only hard lead. The grinding process of checks would continue through the night. A young PC was settling down to check the footage from all the CCTV cameras operational in the town in the forty-eight hour period prior to the victim's estimated time of death. She had contacted all the neighbouring police forces, including the Police Service of Northern Ireland, the coastline of County Antrim being less than twenty miles from where the body had been found. So far, no response.

Daley took his mobile from the inside pocket of his jacket. Within seconds the familiar sound of DS Scott coughing loudly could be heard on the other end of the phone. 'What a way to greet your superior. You sound as though you're on your way out, Brian.'

'Aye, a happy Christmas tae you too. Should you no' be stripping the willow, or whitever they get up tae in Teuchterland?'

Daley smiled. He was tired, hungry and perplexed, but he was realising what a tight team he and Scott had become. He had forgotten all the things his DS would have attended to as a matter of course, until today when he himself had had to make sure all the bases were covered. 'I thought you'd be pleased, a trip to the country at this time of year. Just the thing.'

'No' when you've tae listen tae all the pish I've had tae pit up wi' today. First His Majesty giein' me the pep talk aboot representin' the division. Noo my dear lady bendin' my nut wi' how much she'll miss me, an' how will she manage tae get the shoppin'? Blah blah blah.' Scott told Daley to hang on; muffled oaths were audible as he imparted some more wisdom to his long-suffering wife. 'Sorry aboot that.

She's burst intae tears noo. Ye'd think I wiz headin' off tae Afghanistan. Will you shut up, woman, I'm talkin' tae Jim.'

Daley heard Mrs Scott shouting hello as though there was nothing amiss. 'Have you managed to read the PM report, Brian?'

'Aye, in between a' the shit. Some right goings-on doon there. Lucky I'm comin' doon tae watch yer back.'

'Wait till you meet Inspector MacLeod – he's a cracker.'

'Oh, I've got something for you from on high. I'll gie ye it tomorrow when I get there. Who dae ye want me tae bring? They're all on standby, as ye can imagine.'

Daley thought for a moment. Thinking was getting difficult, so he left the choice of personnel to his sergeant.

'How long dae ye think it'll take me tae get there in a minibus, Jim?'

'Well, hang on.' Daley swivelled around in his chair to consult a large map on the wall behind him. 'Seems as though you're going a long way for a short cut, as you've got to go north before you head back south towards us. One of the lads here said it takes about three hours by car, so I'd guess it'll take you more like four.'

'Aye, OK. Whit's this hotel like?'

Daley looked at his watch. Time seemed to fly here. All he'd eaten were a few sandwiches, and a truly dreadful Cup-a-Soup from the office vending machine. 'I'll tell you when I get there. What time are you leaving tomorrow?'

Scott coughed loudly again, regained his composure, then answered, 'No' before six, so I'll see you aboot half ten. Fuck me, it's like the voyage o' the damned.' After more deeply held opinions about rural Scotland from the DS, and a brief mention of the A4 envelope Scott had been given by Superintendent Donald to pass on to Daley, they ended the call.

Daley went to the toilet. He looked at himself in the mirror as he dried his hands under the inefficient dryer. He was getting grey at the temples, and the flesh under his chin was getting loose. He was turning into his father. At forty-three. How was that happening? He unbuttoned his trousers, able to exhale properly for the first time in hours. After smoothing creases from his shirt-tail, he pulled the trousers back up and buttoned them again with a sigh. He wasn't getting any thinner, despite the paucity of his lunch. Looking at himself side-on in the large mirror, he let his stomach relax again. A large paunch showed over the waist of his trousers. He yawned, as the hunger and fatigue of the day began to take their toll.

Who was this woman? What had happened to her – and why?

Daley and Fraser stood in the County Hotel's reception area. The wide carpeted staircase, the faded gold-leaf banister, the dark wooden panelling and the red-and-gold textured wallpaper gave the impression of an old 1940s cinema rather than a hotel. To their left the foyer was populated with chairs upholstered in red velvet, worn thin by numerous posteriors and redolent of days gone by.

A large glass-fronted box was the obvious reception desk. Sliding windows lay open over a varnished shelf, on which the open register sat beside a large brass bell. Fraser, obviously no stranger to these surroundings, picked up the bell on the desk and rang it enthusiastically, leaning his head into the reception office.

'Aye, aye, gie's a minute.' A woman's voice sounded through a door at the other side of the reception box. 'I'll be with yous directly.' The rear door opened, emitting the distinctive murmur that only a barful of contented drinkers could produce; quiet chat punctuated by short bursts of laughter. Whatever was happening in Kinloch, its citizens seemed to be a cheery bunch.

Daley took in his surroundings. The hotel was strangely familiar; he had first felt this when they had walked past the unusual frontage earlier in the day: the sweet, inviting smell of alcohol mingled with the aroma of freshly cooked food and a strong chemical odour which reminded Daley of his primary school.

A small dark-haired woman in her middle years emerged through the bar door. 'Good evening, officers. How ye daein', Erchie? You'll be wantin' tae check in, Inspector.' Yet again, there was clearly no need for introductions. 'The kitchen will be closing in a wee while, so ye'll have tae order noo. Or I'll get a hell o' a time fae big Wullie, and you'll get nothin' tae eat.' She handed Daley a large brown menu, bound in a leatherette cover and slightly stained by previous diners. 'There's nae beef left, and I widna touch the lasagne since he made it the day afore yesterday. Chicken curry. The fish is always good. Noo, could you fill this in?' She turned an open ledger around to face the men.

Daley busied himself with the usual details, filling in his address as c/o Paisley Police Office and using the number of the Kinloch office as his contact. He slid the ledger back across the desk, along with the menu. 'I'll take your recommendation on the fish. We'll be in the bar. My name's Jim by the way. Do you know if my luggage is here?'

The receptionist reached behind her chair to a wooden board on which were several large wooden keyrings, all bearing the legend 'PROPERTY OF THE COUNTY HOTEL'. 'Pleased tae meet you, I'm sure. My name's Annie. Aye, all your stuff's up in room six, third door on yer left on the first floor.'

Daley and Fraser made their way from reception down the corridor to where the noise of drunken banter was emanating. He had persuaded the DC to have a meal with him; he hated eating alone, and in any case the younger man had had no more chance than his superior of getting a decent meal all day. Fraser had opted for the chicken curry, a choice that caused Annie to raise her eyebrows, though she fell short of making any comment. That they had decided to eat in the bar made her brows arch even further.

Fraser made his way through the frosted-glass door that read 'Public Bar', in an old-fashioned cursive script. Daley followed. The warm smell of alcohol immediately enveloped the officers, though the conversation stopped dead.

There were about twenty customers in all, some standing at a varnished wooden bar, while the rest were spread amongst a number of randomly placed chairs and tables. There was a cross-section of ages, however, regardless of vintage, all the women were seated. Standing at the bar was clearly a male preserve.

'Aye, an' whoot's wrong wi' a' yous?' The formidable Annie was back behind the bar. 'It reminds me o' that werewolf film. Jeest get back tae yer conversations, an' let the officers get their tea.'

A young man at the bar looked baffled. 'Whoot werewolf film dae ye mean, Annie? *Dawn o' the Deid?*'

'Nah, you idiot – *American Werewolf in London*. You know, the bit where they go intae the bar, an' everyone jeest shuts up. Noo get on wi' yer pint, Danny Finlay.'

An elderly woman sitting at a table expressed her opinion that Lon Chaney had been her favourite werewolf to no one in particular, and then drained her glass. Two older men eyed Daley up and down. One of them was wearing yellow oilskin trousers over green Wellington boots, and smelled strongly of fish. 'Yer wasting yer time, Inspector. That poor lassie could be fae anywhere. There's no reason as tae how the sea gies up her dead, no reason at a'.' The man bore the grin of a smart-arse.

Daley reached into his pocket, fetching out his notebook. 'And your name is, sir? I'll take a quick note and get you up to the office for an interview tomorrow.'

The smirk left his interlocutor's face. 'Noo, wait a minute. I mean, I wiz jeest giein' an opinion. I'm no' saying ...' He didn't get a chance to finish his sentence.

Daley had winked at his companions, and they greeted the winding up of their mate with great hilarity.

'Aye, very good, you should see your face, Jackie. Like a skelpit kipper. Fuckin' idiot.'

'Good for you, Inspector,' said Annie. 'Noo, whoot can I get yous?'

'I'll get these.' Fraser reached into his jacket pocket. 'What do you want, sir?'

Daley looked along the gantry; the County Hotel had no mean stock of single malts. He asked for a large Springbank, much to the dismay of his colleague, who took another tenner from his wallet.

'There's a seat at the back there.' Annie served the drinks with a smile. 'That'll be eighteen pound, sixty pence, Erchie. Since it's you we'll call it eighteen.'

He handed the money over grim-faced, and the policemen made their way through the chairs and tables to their seats at the rear of the bar.

Daley had forgotten how expensive Springbank was and offered Fraser some money in compensation, which he refused. 'Well, if you're sure, Archie. I suppose it goes some way to squaring me up after all the drinks I had to buy your Uncle Davie over the years.' The pair laughed, each with their own memories of Fraser's uncle.

The meal arrived without undue haste. Fraser's chicken curry was an unusual shade of green, but it didn't seem to bother him as he took his fork to it with great enthusiasm. Daley's fish on the other hand looked delicious: a large haddock, covered in golden crispy batter, accompanied by marble-sized marrowfat peas, thick, home-made chips – perfectly cooked – a small ramekin of tartar sauce and a huge chunk of badly cut lemon. The Inspector was as hungry as his subordinate, so he tucked in with relish.

'Well, they certainly know how to cook fish in this neck of the woods.' Daley pushed his empty plate across the table. 'What was yours like, Archie?'

The younger man had managed to spill some curry down his tie, which he was desperately trying to remove with a red paper napkin. 'Bloody thing,' Fraser cursed as he examined the stained tie. 'I've only got one other one and it doesna match my suits. Bugger it.'

Daley suppressed a laugh; sartorial elegance was very important to some CID officers. He had known colleagues buy some ridiculously priced suits and shoes, only to have had them torn, burned, stained with blood, soaked in the rain, or a multiplicity of other hazards that faced police officers on a daily basis. For those reasons he had always chosen the cheapest suits on offer; having his own private celebration when one of the big supermarkets began selling them for twenty quid. 'I've got a couple of spare ties in my bag. I'm sure I can spare one.'

Fraser looked relieved. 'Thanks, sir. You don't want to have to buy any clothes here. You'd need to take out a mortgage first, the shops are extortionate.'

'What have you done with your clothing allowance?' CID personnel were given an annual allowance to buy their clothes, which was habitually used to buy golf clubs, a weekend away, a new computer, or on a range of other expenditures that had nothing to do with tailoring.

'Too little to go round, sir.' Fraser was grinning. 'Anyway, I've put on a stone since I've been off the beat, keep having to buy a whole new set of clothes.'

'Tell me about it,' said Daley wryly. 'A few less pints, and a few more hours in the gym, my boy. Take a leaf out of my book.' He smiled. If there was one thing he could empathise with, it was sudden weight gain; even now his belly was protruding over his waistband in a painful and constricted manner – and these were his new trousers.

He signalled to Annie that they were ready for the same again. Annie duly arrived with the drinks on a tray. 'Yous were hungry right enough,' she said as she removed the men's plates. 'I'd keep an eye on the young fellow here. He'll likely be in intensive care by the morrow. Big Wullie's great at plain food, but he canna cook fancy stuff tae save himself.' She smiled at the policemen. 'Whoot time will ye be wantin' yer breakfast? I'm daein' the cooking, so if ye choose continental or jeest a cereal, I'll be o'er the moon.'

Daley ordered a full Scottish breakfast for six forty-five. Annie took a note, pursed her lips, and returned to the bar, reprimanding one of the younger male customers who had just spilled his pint and was swearing loudly.

The police officers finished their drinks. Daley was aware that almost all the customers were either trying to hear what they were saying or throwing glances in their direction every few minutes. 'Time to hit the sack, Archie.' Daley rubbed the bridge of his nose with his forefinger and thumb. 'Keep your mobile on. You never know how or when an investigation like this will pan out.'

They said goodnight to Annie and then walked out into the foyer. A ragged chorus of 'Cheerio-cheerio-cheerio' issued from some of the more rowdy element they had just left behind, closely followed by Annie's now familiar voice leaving them in absolutely no doubt she wanted them to shut up.

Daley said goodnight to Fraser, fished out his absurdly large room key from the inside of his jacket, and made his way up the faded grandeur of the staircase to the first floor. Gaining the landing, he faced a glass-paned fire door, of the type common in schools when he had been a boy. A bright green exit sign shone vividly above it; the transom shuddered to a creaking close as he made his way to room six. He unlocked his room door and pushed it open. Running his hand up and down the inside wall beside the door, he located a light switch, which prompted an overhead striplight into blinking life. The heavy door swung shut at his back.

Facing him was a double bed, which would have been a tight squeeze for two adults, but would do him. It was covered in an old-fashioned candlewick bedspread. The diamond patterned top-sheet had faded from what he suspected had once been a light red colour, to a candy pink. He'd had one exactly the same as a boy. At the side of the bed, a cheap cabinet served as the base for an ancient anglepoise lamp, which looked as though it would snap in two if any attempt was made to change its position.

He sat on the bed as he unbuckled and unzipped his suit bag. In front of him now, and to the side of the door, sat a small pine wardrobe. On investigation, Daley discovered that it contained five metal coat-hangers, and smelled strongly of mothballs. He hung up three suits, a sports jacket, a pair of trousers, and six shirts, and then closed the doors. From another bag, he removed a pair of chinos, a pair of denims, various socks, pants and T-shirts, and arranged them in one of the four drawers of the chest, that sat to the right side of his bed, directly across from a sash window.

Antiquated, the window was adorned with faded, red velvet curtains and full-length net curtains the colour of old parchment. An assortment of dead insects populated the dusty windowsill. The sash window resisted all his strained attempts to get it open. He gave up and stared at the street below, illuminated orange in the streetlight.

To his surprise, one of the old women he and Fraser had met earlier was standing at the bus stop across the road. She looked up at his window and gave a hearty wave, smiling broadly. Daley automatically waved back, and on having done so felt faintly ridiculous. It didn't take long to make friends in Kinloch.

After placing his toiletries on a shelf beside the large Victorian bath and cleaning his teeth, he closed the curtains and switched on the bedside light. Addicted to radio since he was a child, the penultimate item he removed from his luggage was his portable radio-alarm clock. He found a spare socket, plugged it in, set the time, and turned on Radio 4. Finally, he took his copy of Patrick O'Brian's *The Wine Dark Sea* from his case, lay back on the bed, and placed it next to him. It was only then he noticed where the television was located, set well back, on top of the wardrobe. Using the deductive powers for which he was famous, he opened the flimsy drawer of the bedside cabinet and there – sure enough – was a battered TV remote, the batteries held in by peeling black electrical tape.

Daley had a bath. There seemed to be plenty of hot water, and unlike the modern variety, this old bath was deep and wide. He luxuriated in the relaxing warmth for a few minutes. He got out, then towelled himself down, donning the pair of shorts that were his habitual sleeping garment. He lay in the bed. It was a warm night, and the room was stuffy as the window was stuck. He had toyed with the idea of calling reception, but decided against this course of action. Firstly, he thought it unlikely anyone would be about the hotel at that time of night who would actually be prepared, or able to fix it. Secondly, such was the racket of cars going up and down the Main Street, plus the shouts and guffaws of local revellers, he reasoned that the window best remain shut. He tried to concentrate on the discussion programme which was currently being broadcast, but decided it was impossible. He picked up the novel, and admired the cover. Unfortunately, by the time he had found the right page, his eyes refused to obey his brain, and danced over the words. His eyelids began to droop. Leaning over, he flicked the lamp off and turned onto his side. Within moments, he was asleep.

7

He was in a bar, but not like one he had ever been in before. He sat on a bar stool, hunched over a glass of whisky. Behind the barman, on a raised stage, naked women cavorted, using long metal poles as props of phallic seduction. Beside him, a large balding man gesticulated at him with a clenched fist, save for his forefinger and pinkie, which were pointed aggressively in his direction, gold rings visible on the remaining fingers, folded into the palm. All was loud music, shouting and whooping males ...

Awake. Daley realised that the ringtone of his phone had prompted the dream, and for a few seconds he had been in the Bada Bing strip joint. 'Got a blue moon in your eye ...' He picked up the mobile, eyes blurred with sleep and slightly disorientated. 'Daley.'

A woman's voice. 'Sir, sorry to call you so early. It's DC Dunn. I think you better come up to the station.'

'OK. What's going on?' Comprehension was flooding into his brain, replacing the confusing numbness of sleep, but he was still playing for time.

'We've had a report of a missing woman who closely matches the description of our victim, sir. Her husband is here.'

Daley rubbed his eyes. 'Have you told him anything, shown him any pictures of the deceased? Does he know we have a body?'

'He knows that a woman's been found dead, sir. He's a fisherman, lives in Kinloch, but he works out of Dublin on a deep-sea trawler – away for three weeks at a time. It's quite complicated. But no, to answer your first question, we haven't said anything to him. Thought we'd better wait until you were informed. How should we proceed, sir?'

Daley was fully awake now. He looked at his radio-alarm clock: 3.35 a.m. Whatever sleep he'd had would have to suffice. 'OK, I'm on my way. Give me ten minutes. Leave the guy in an interview room until I get there. Get him a cup of coffee or something, but don't tell him anything. I'll talk to him myself ... and you've done well.' He heard a slight sigh on the other end of the line.

'I hope that wasn't a pun, sir.' The line went dead.

Main Street was deathly quiet. There was an unexpected chill in the air, and Daley wished he had packed his overcoat. The sky was a black starry carpet. Light pollution was nowhere near as bad as in the Greater Glasgow area. Unexpectedly he heard a bird squawk overhead, a repetitive shrill note. He resolved to test Fraser's ornithological knowledge later.

The all-pervading smell of the sea provided the olfactory backdrop. He went around the back of the station, keying the security code into the pad on the door that led from the car park. The office was bathed in a subdued blue light. He passed the control room, hearing the intermittent crackle of sub-divisional radio traffic echoing through the corridors, reminding him of his own time on nightshift as a uniform cop.

DC Dunn met him outside the CID offices. She looked tired and slightly harassed. 'Sir, so glad you're here. It's been a bit of a strain trying not to tell this poor guy his wife's probably dead.'

'You sound very sure. What's he been saying?'

They entered an interview room and closed the door. Daley leaned on the table, while the young DC stood stiffly, as though she was about to deliver a speech. 'The guy is Michael Watson. He's a fisherman – deep sea. He used to fish out of Kinloch, but he's based in Dublin now. He works off one of the big trawlers that fish mainly far out into the Atlantic, three weeks on, two weeks off. He still lives here.' She spread her hands over her skirt, smoothing out nonexistent creases. 'His wife and son live here too. Well ...'

'OK, so what do we know about her?' Daley took out his notebook. He was about to interview this man, and he wanted to have his facts straight before doing so.

'She's about the right height, build and age for our victim, sir. He has a photo of her, but what with the bloating on the corpse and the fact that she has dyed blonde hair in the picture, well, it's difficult to tell.'

Daley scratched his chin while he thought, a habit that inexplicably infuriated Liz. 'It's a strange time to report her missing. The reason?'

'Well, his mother's been looking after the wee boy for the last three days. She and her husband have been up the city shopping. They came back early yesterday, couldn't find Mrs Watson, heard about the body being found, and put two and two together. They wanted to wait until Watson arrived before they contacted the police. He arrived from Dublin about two hours ago. His fishing boat had just returned to port. His bosses hired a RIB to get him here quickly.'

'What's his wife's first name?'

'Isobel, sir, Isobel Watson.'

Daley straightened as a knock at the door announced the arrival of DC Fraser. Daley noticed that his hair was sticking up, and he wasn't wearing the curry-stained tie. 'Right, DC Dunn, give me five minutes to get our casually dressed colleague DC Fraser up to speed, then show Mr Watson in.'

Fraser's face reddened as DC Dunn left the interview room. After imparting the facts, Daley had a surprise for the young DC. 'I want you to conduct this interview, Archie. I want to observe our Mr Watson. We'll get a bit of background, then, depending on how it pans out, we'll have to arrange some kind of ID. That won't be easy considering the body's a hundred and fifty miles away.'

'Under these circumstances we normally use CCTV from the mortuary, sir. We only take people up to Glasgow if things get complicated.'

The door sounded again. DC Dunn opened it and stood to the side to reveal a thick-set man, short, with a broad pale face and a shaven head. He was wearing jeans and a T-shirt, his right forearm adorned with a large, blue thistle tattoo, the legend SCOTLAND FOREVER showing proudly in red.

Daley cleared his throat, prompting Fraser into action. 'Mr Watson, please take a seat. I'm DC Fraser and this is Inspector Daley. The young DC was on his feet as he slid a chair back, inviting the fisherman to sit with a gesture of his hand. Both officers opened their notebooks.

Fraser asked Mr Watson if he would mind if they recorded their discussion. He acceded to the request, though he looked uncomfortable. 'Come on, guys.' The accent was pure Kinloch, identifiable in three brief words. 'I'm worried sick here. I want to know whoot's goin' on. Gie's a break, eh?' His eyes were pleading, arms held straight out in front of him, both fists clenched.

'I need a few details first, sir.' Fraser's colour was on the rise again. 'You must understand we have to be really careful in situations like this, so please ...' He pointed at his notebook, an action which saw Watson deflate slightly, some of the tension leaving his shoulders. 'Aye, OK, fire away.' Watson answered the usual round of questions: first giving his name and address, details of his work, recent movements, and how he had heard about the discovery of the dead woman; he then went on to give his wife's details, including a general description, a summary of her personality, habits and so on. Tiring of this line of enquiry, he looked directly at Daley. 'Now, Inspector, jeest be straight wi' us – can I see the body?'

Ignoring his question, Daley had one of his own. 'What was your wife's maiden name, Mr Watson?'

'Sneddon, Isobel Sneddon.'

'Did she have any tattoos? I'm thinking of one in particular ...'

'Aye, on her leg, she had ...' His expression changed to one of grim realisation. 'Aw, for fuck's sake.' He held his head in his hands and started to sob. 'Whoot the fuck am I goin' tae tell the wee man?'

Daley got up and walked to the other side of the desk, placing his hand on Watson's shoulder. The fisherman's body was wracked with sobs. Fraser looked on hopelessly; this was an aspect of police work that he not did like.

'We're going to have to ask you to identify the body formally, Mr Watson.' Daley was calm and authoritative. He knew the value of maintaining a front on these occasions, though he realised that his reaction would have been the same, had anything like this happened to Liz. He felt compassion for Watson, but his job was to find her killer; and now he was sure they had an ID, time was of the essence.

Daley left Fraser with Watson, finding DC Dunn at her desk in the CID office. 'I want you to go and comfort Mr Watson. I think his wife is our victim, but I need to get him to make an official identification.' The young detective was nodding solemnly. 'Once we have that, I want you and a couple of uniforms to go to their house. We'll need to go through everything. I'm leaving you in charge of that. OK?'

'Yes, sir.' She looked suddenly preoccupied, as though already working out some kind of strategy suited to trawling through someone's personal possessions. 'What about Mr Watson? Will he have to be present?'

'Not at the moment. I'll get his permission of course. Now tell me, how quickly can we organise one of these CCTV identifications?'

As it turned out, things took longer to organise than Daley had anticipated. For a start, they had to wait for the Glasgow mortuary dayshift to turn up, which wasn't until seven thirty. The nightshift was there, but they couldn't use the video equipment. And all the problems were not at the other end. Permission from the Sub-Divisional Commander was required before their audio-visual equipment at the station could be used, and MacLeod could not be raised. Daley sent a reluctant Fraser to his home to rouse him.

He had texted DS Scott with the latest developments, and had received a terse acknowledgement in return: *Great. C u soon. On my way.* He had also spoken at greater length to Watson. It appeared that all was not well in their marriage, though Daley had already guessed that. Isobel Watson had apparently taken to going out regularly and, according to her husband, was associating with the underbelly of Kinloch's society, where lots of alcohol, drugs and sex were the order of the day. Watson had described how difficult it was to maintain their relationship when he was away so much; a sentiment with which Daley could empathise, especially since he found his relationship hard to maintain even at close quarters.

On the whole, he found Watson an uncomplicated, even pleasant individual; in extremis he conducted himself with a kind of rough-and-ready dignity that the inspector found to his credit. He had looked carefully for signs of feigned surprise when Watson had discovered that his wife may well be the likely murder victim. He had found none. Nonetheless he had contacted the Garda in Dublin to make sure that his story of being 'deep sea' for the last three weeks checked out.

Daley, Dunn and two uniformed officers were in the station's audio-visual room with Watson, who was sitting forward in his chair, looking exceptionally stressed. A large plasma screen displayed the force's Semper Vigilo logo.

The door burst open, and a sleepy-looking MacLeod breezed into the room, not in uniform, but in a tracksuit with a hooded top, which he seemed to wear uneasily. This leitmotif of youth clashed with his balding head and abrasive manner. 'I can't for the life of me understand what all the rush is about. You're lucky to catch me, I was about to go for my five-miler along Westbay sands.' He looked around, as though this revelation should elicit some praise.

'A courtesy only, I can assure you.' Daley didn't look in MacLeod's direction. 'If DC Fraser hadn't been able to find you, I'd have authorised this myself.'

MacLeod's face took on a look of extreme antagonism. He walked over to the communications unit and picked up what looked like a large mobile phone. After dialling a number and waiting for a few moments he started to speak. 'Yes, Kinloch Sub-Division, authorisation Delta Mike 281165.' There was a pause, and then the screen began to flicker into life. The logo was replaced by a view of the PR room in Glasgow mortuary. A table with small microphones sat in front of three chairs, backed by a brown screen that bore the name of the institution plus the City of Glasgow crest.

Daley saw Watson tense. He was clenching then unclenching his fists, which were resting on his knees, and he sat even further forward in his seat. He looked exhausted. Daley made a mental note to make sure that he sent the fisherman to his parents to try to get some rest once this, the first of many ordeals, was over.

A woman appeared on screen wearing a white coat with three pens arrayed along the top of her breast pocket. Daley recognised her, but did not know her name. She was a junior pathologist, and the inspector recalled Crichton referring to her in what could best be described as less than politically correct terms: in short, even at this hour, her good looks were evident. He saw Fraser's expression momentarily register this fact.

'Good morning.' She spoke in a low, formal manner. 'Mr Watson, could you acknowledge that you are present and can see the screen at close quarters without any hindrance?'

The fisherman grunted a reply and then coughed nervously.

They were communicating through omnidirectional microphones that hung from the ceiling of the Kinloch video suite. 'Could all serving officers present please state their names and designations for the record, starting with the senior investigating officer, then in descending order of rank.'

Daley and MacLeod both started to talk at the same time. MacLeod stopped, his face pinched with rancour.

'James Daley, Detective Inspector, Senior Investigating Officer.'

MacLeod now took his chance. 'I would like to make a point of order, please. You, whatever your name is ...' He didn't give the pathologist a chance to reply. 'I'm Sub-Divisional Commander here, and by rights my name should be submitted first.'

Everyone present looked in disbelief at the short man in the hooded top. MacLeod stood in the middle of the room in an impromptu aisle, formed by the small rank of chairs.

The pathologist however remained unfazed. 'Sorry, sir, the procedure in this matter is clear. The senior investigating officer takes precedence, even to those of a higher rank.'

'Which you are not.' Clearly furious with MacLeod, Daley spoke. 'Please sit down, Inspector MacLeod. I'm sure Mr Watson is finding this hard enough as it is.'

MacLeod muttered something under his breath and retreated to the back of the room where he took a seat.

The remaining police officers gave their details, and the pathologist continued. 'My name is Judy Kelly. I'm Assistant Pathologist in Greater Glasgow.' She walked behind the desk and took a seat behind the microphones. 'Mr Watson, when you are ready, I will begin to show a number of images of the deceased. Please feel free to ask me to stop at any time, if either you can make a positive identification, or you want a break.

'I must warn you that the deceased has been exposed to saltwater for a period of time, which may make her features appear swollen or bloated, so please take this into account. Please say "yes" when you are ready to proceed.' She looked directly into the camera, waiting for Watson's reply.

'Aye, go ahead.' Watson's voice was clear, but ready to break with emotion.

Instantly, an overhead view of a body shrouded in a white sheet became visible on the screen. Only the face and hair were exposed. Daley noted that the sheet was placed high up on the neck, obscuring the ligature marks.

'Can I see?' Watson was peering at the screen. The image zoomed to the face alone. 'Oh, fuck.' Watson looked heavenward, his hands like a child's in prayer. He quickly crossed himself, then bowed his head. 'Aye, it's Isobel,' he whispered. 'She ... she looks different, but that's her.' He hunched over and sobbed uncontrollably.

The pathologist thanked Watson, and expressed her condolences. After a pause she asked Daley to acknowledge the positive identification. The gruesome job was over. The screen flickered back to the force logo.

Daley, sitting beside Watson, had his arm around his shoulder. 'Thank you for that, Mr Watson. I know how hard it must have been. C'mon, let's get you a coffee, eh? Or perhaps something a bit stronger?' Despite the early hour, he was sure that Watson would appreciate a dram.

The pair stood and headed for the door. As Daley opened it, Watson stopped. A shaft of bright morning sunshine pierced the gloom. The fisherman looked to where MacLeod was sitting. 'You're a real fuckin' prick, do you know that?' He turned on his heel and followed Daley from the room.

Daley had his victim's identification, and now the investigation could step up a gear. It was just after ten and he was famished. He had just heard from DS Scott, who was on his way from Paisley and already cursing the state of the rural roads he now had to navigate.

DC Dunn, two uniformed officers, Fraser and the bereaved Watson were now at the fisherman's home. Daley had to arrange a press conference, which he hoped would take place as soon as possible. In these days of twenty-four hour rolling news coverage, he realised that the press conference would go out live. However, in his experience, very few people watched these channels; much better to catch the main news programmes that ran in the early evening. He called the Public Relations Office.

As it turned out, they had been geared up since the previous day, and had already arranged for the press officer designated to this case to contact the relevant news agencies. Daley groaned when he heard who the PR officer was. Pauline Robertson: a woman with whom he had a long and tortured relationship.

Pauline had been a tabloid reporter on one of his first CID cases. In those days, before her Damascene conversion to public relations, she had been the scourge of Strathclyde Police, determined to uncover the corruption, injustice and brutality she was certain beset the organisation. It was a younger Donald who, then in charge of A-Division CID, had persuaded her to take the job in Strathclyde's PR department: 'Fight the demons from the inside,' he had implored her. Of course, once she was tied down to a generous pension plan and an incremental salary structure, and the rest of the benefits attendant with the civil service, such as flexi-hours, job security and six weeks' paid holidays a year, she appeared to lose her zeal for investigative journalism. However, she had lost none of her ability to rile Daley. He was under a lot of pressure here, and because of the isolated nature of the investigation it would have a certain cachet for the press. For now, he put the press conference to the back of his mind.

8

He had been up since three thirty, so, on his way to Watson's home, he nipped into the County Hotel to get a quick shower and change, and hopefully a bit of breakfast.

The smell of bacon and eggs and coffee greeted him like an old friend as he entered the hotel. He saw Annie busy at the reception desk as he made his way across the faded carpet. 'Morning, Annie. Any chance of that breakfast? Say, in fifteen minutes or so? I'm afraid I had a call-out in the middle of the night.'

'Aye, there wiz me, up wi' the larks cookin' the full works, an a' the time the bird had flown.'

'Sorry about that.' Daley smiled at her sheepishly. 'You know how it is in my line of work – duty calls and all that. It's OK, I'll get a sandwich or something in the town.'

'Indeed, you will not.' Annie was adamant. 'There's naebody goin' tae say we canna treat oor guests right in this hotel. No, no' when I'm at the helm o' the cutter.'

Happy that he was going to be fed, he bounded up the staircase and into his room. He had forgotten that there was no shower in his room, so he immediately turned on both taps, and quickly drew a deep bath. He bathed or showered a lot. He had picked up the habit as a young cop, finding the smell of the death and decay he frequently encountered followed him off duty. Bathing at night and in the morning seemed to banish the malodorous taint. He also found the activity invigorating. It was going to be a long day; he needed all the help he could get.

Feeling fresher, he took a clean shirt from the wardrobe, and unconsciously chose Liz's favourite tie. Somewhere in the back of his mind, he remembered that she was arriving this evening with the odious Mark. He sighed quietly to himself. What with the imminent arrival of Scott and his posse, Kinloch was rapidly becoming a home from home.

Downstairs, he sat down to a hearty breakfast – ignoring the fact that this artery-clogging feast would do nothing for his waistline. He devoured the meal, sitting alone in the dining room, with only the local radio station for company.

It was being played over two large speakers attached to the wall above his head. 'Police are still baffled by the discovery of a dead body jeest outside the toon.' The voice was pure Kinloch. 'Noo, whoot is it, Jamie?'

'Weel, I wiz jeest thinking, it wid be a strange kinda thing if the body they found wisna deid. I mean, whoot kinda polis investigation wid cover that?'

There followed much muffled laughter. It most certainly was not BBC Radio 4, but Daley had to admit, it did have a certain charm all of its own. Absorbed in his cooked breakfast and the banter of the *Jock and Jamie Show*, he reluctantly answered his mobile, which displayed Fraser's number.

'Sir, I think you better come over to Mr Watson's now. There's been a development.'

'Well, DC Fraser, you can tell me. What is it?' Daley sounded more impatient than he was, and he grimaced at his brusque tone.

'We checked Mr Watson's house phone, you know, for messages and the like?' Fraser was already sounding maligned.

'And?' Daley was chewing a particularly tasty piece of sausage. 'Don't tell me she's been on the phone. This investigation's strange enough as it is without messages from the dead.'

'That's the thing, sir. We tried 1471 to get the last caller, and it was Mrs Watson's mobile number. Two hours ago.'

Daley looked down mournfully at the remainder of his breakfast, and stuck his fork in a sausage. 'I'm on my way.'

Watson's home was not as he had expected. No low fisherman's cottage, or scruffy council flat. Rather, it was a pleasant bungalow, in a small estate of about ten other properties, situated on a hill with wonderful views of Kinloch's harbour and the rest of the town from a large picture window.

The interior was conservatively furnished, with an expensive-looking Chesterfield-style suite in dark red leather, a large glass-fronted cabinet displaying various items in silver and crystal, and an enormous coffee table centred on a sheepskin rug, which was either artificial or had come from a truly Herculean beast. A CD player was perched on a small table to the side of an impressive gas fire, surrounded by a dark wooden fireplace. On the walls were a couple of Turneresque prints, and above the fireplace a well-varnished ship's wheel. All bore testament to the lucrative occupation of the householder, who was now recumbent on one of the armchairs, his leg shaking up and down in what Daley had already noted as a nervous habit.

Watson was cradling a small silver cordless phone, his expression understandably puzzled. 'I mean, what now, Inspector Daley? It's her number, no doubt aboot that. Look here.' He propped himself up on one elbow as he fished a mobile phone from a pocket of his jeans. After pressing a couple of buttons, he handed the phone to Daley; the screen read 'Izzy', and displayed the same mobile number he had just heard over the house telephone as last caller.

'As you know, Mr Watson, sadly this was most certainly not your wife, and whoever made this call, and for whatever reason, may be able to shed at least some light on what happened to her. However, don't raise your hopes too high. The person who rang may well just have found her mobile. It's a common enough thing to call Home from a phone's contacts list if you're trying to find out who the owner is.'

'Oh, right.' Watson looked towards Fraser, whose face was beginning the now familiar reddening process. 'Sir, I never really thought of that possibility.' He shrugged his shoulders, shifting his weight from foot to foot in an unconscious act of contrition.

'This is a positive development, Mr Watson. We'll trace where the call was made from, and with a bit of luck we'll be able to trace the phone and the caller. Could I have a word with you, please, DC Fraser?' Daley walked out of the house, with the nervous-looking DC in his wake.

'I'm sorry, sir, I ... Mr Watson ... I thought for sure that the call was of importance, maybe from the murderer.' He looked at his feet.

'It's important that we keep Mr Watson onside, Archie. The caller may be our killer. Who knows? We have to keep our suspicions to ourselves though, understand? We'll have the so-called gentlemen of the press descending on us later, and, be absolutely sure, they'll jump on any mistake or unintentional slip. They'll also wind up Watson, so we have to tread carefully. OK?'

'Sir.'

'Consider yourself severely admonished.' Daley now had a smile on his face. 'My DS, Brian Scott, is on the way. Now there's a man who'll be able to show you the finer points of subtle police work.'

As agreed, Watson was taken to his parents' house, a much more modest affair in a housing scheme about half a mile from the police office. Watson's parents were typical of their geography and vintage: Watson senior was of middle height and had probably had the stocky physique of his son when younger, which now had matured into a sizeable girth and jowly face; Mrs Watson, in contrast, was stick thin and birdlike. She fussed over her son as the police officers were shown in by her husband. She had clearly been crying and looked as though she had had little sleep.

After the introductions, Watson's father was the first to speak. 'This is a terrible thing, Inspector, jeest terrible. I mean, whoot kinda person wid murder a bonnie wee lassie like oor Izzy?'

'Don't even speak aboot it, George,' wailed Mrs Watson. 'When I think o' whoot's happened …' She burst into floods of tears. 'That lovely wee boy. What will we say to him, officers? His mammy's deid.' She sat on the edge of her chair, her legs and hands shaking, mirroring the nervous habit of her son.

Daley established that the boy was next door with the neighbours. He would have DC Dunn speak to the child; she had been trained in child protection issues and would be able to couch her questions in a way most likely to gain a response from a boy of that age.

The inspector recalled a seven-year-old girl who had been a successful witness in a murder trial only a few months ago. He had interviewed the girl early on in the investigation, getting nowhere. A properly trained child protection officer had later managed to coax out pertinent information which eventually led to a guilty verdict. He was not going to discount any evidence from this poor kid. 'Could you tell me how your daughter-in-law was when she brought your grandson to stay, Mrs Watson?' he said gently.

'Jeest the same as usual,' she answered, doing her best to regain her composure. 'Done up tae the nines, of course. She wiz obviously away oot that night. Aye, her skirt was halfway up her arse.' She looked up, a look of determination on her face. 'Sorry, Inspector. I jeest wisna happy with the way she … wi' whoot she wiz daein' behind my son's back.'

'Mum.' Watson was clearly reluctant for his mother to discuss his wife's behaviour.

'Mr Watson.' Daley looked stern. 'I need every piece of information that I can get.' He then softened his expression. 'Please let your mother speak.'

Watson got out of his chair and left the room. His father got up to accompany him, but Daley indicated that he wanted him to stay. 'I know this is difficult for everyone, but if we're going to catch the person who did this, I need to know as much as possible about Izzy's life – good and bad.'

'She wiz a lush, Inspector, a lush and a tart.' Mrs Watson jutted out her chin. 'I wiz sick telling my son aboot her. She wiz nothin' but a common slut, an' she wiz leadin' him a merry dance – aye, fir maist o' their mairried life. I couldna stand her. I'm sorry she's deid, but only fir because o' the wee boy.' She looked Daley straight in the eye. Mrs Watson was clearly not as timid as she appeared.

'Margaret' – her husband shook his head – 'whootever she wiz, she's deid. It doesna dae tae talk ill o' the deid, especially when they're family.'

'Aye, an' you were the wan that came back fae the pub every night wi' stories aboot her. No, she wiz no good, Inspector. No good at all. It wid be a lie if I telt ye any different.'

'She wiz a stranger, Mr Daley.' Mr Watson offered this up as an apology for his daughter-in-law's conduct.

'A stranger? What do you mean, Mr Watson?'

'Jeest whoot I say, Mr Daley. She wiz a stranger, she wisna fae the toon. None o' us knew much aboot her. We soon found oot, mind.'

'What did you find out, Mr Watson?'

Watson shifted uncomfortably in his seat. He looked over to his wife, who was only too ready to come to his aid. 'She was from a wee village near Lochgilphead, Inspector. No' a place anybody cares for, no' that I know of anyway.' She had the same determined look on her face, which somehow masked her previously shattered countenance. 'Her mother wiz notorious there too. Apparently she wiz sleeping around when she wiz nae mair than a lassie. Like mother, like daughter. She's a nurse here, wid you believe? I refuse tae be treated by her. Aye, oor poor Michael pit his sows tae a poor market.'

'Do you know anything specific about her background? Did she have any trouble with old boyfriends, for example? We'll have to speak with as many people who had contact with her as we can find.'

'Aye, well, you'll be daein' lots o' interviewin', Inspector. There's nae shortage o' boyfriends, that's fir sure, past an' present. That's why oor son had tae go an' work away.

'He wiz affronted, jeest affronted. An' I tell you, Inspector, in a wee place like this, nane o' your business is your ain, an' whoot they don't know, they jeest make up. No' that there wiz any makin' up needed as far as she was concerned.' She sat back in her chair with a look of vindication, as though she had just managed to rid herself of a great burden.

For Daley, this turn of events was not wholly unexpected, though the scale of Watson's parents' obvious dislike for their daughter-in-law did come as a surprise. Watson himself had given only the slightest indication that he suspected his wife of infidelity. It now appeared as though she was a serial adulterer.

'Janet Ritchie!' Mrs Watson spat the name out. 'Speak tae Janet Ritchie, that wiz her bosom buddy. Another tart: birds of a feather. She'll know a' aboot her carry-on, if anyone does.'

Daley asked a few more questions. Izzy had not given any indication where she was going that night, or who she was going to see. She had assured Mrs Watson that she would be back in time to pick up her son, but when she had not appeared Mrs Watson had put it down to her habitual tardiness, to which she had become accustomed. Only when hours became days did she become concerned.

Apart from Izzy being constantly late, it appeared that Watson's parents were always expecting her to run off with another man. It was only when Mr Watson senior had heard about the murdered woman that they thought of alerting Michael.

With Janet Ritchie's address, Daley took his leave of the Watsons. He persuaded Michael Watson that it was best if he stayed with his parents for the time being. Police officers were currently tearing his house apart in an attempt to find anything pertinent to the inquiry.

A request was made to the phone company about the position from which the call from Izzy's mobile had been made. It would take a few hours.

Daley sent Fraser to find Janet Ritchie, and returned to the police office, where waiting for him was a disgruntled DS Scott with a team of four detectives, including one much-needed female constable.

'That fuckin' road's a nightmare. When you think you're getting here you're still miles away,' said Scott.

Daley decided it best to deflect his right-hand man's obsession with the inaccessibility of Kinloch. He set the small team operational tasks, including the preparation for the looming press conference, and they were told to book into the County Hotel. This organised, he and Scott drove the few short miles to the bay where Izzy's body had been found.

Scott was impressed with the progress that had been made since Watson had come forward. On the way though, Fraser phoned to say that Janet Ritchie was neither at home nor at her work and hadn't been seen for a couple of days by her neighbours. The two detectives exchanged looks. It was possible that Isobel Watson might not be their only victim.

'Aye, it's a bonnie wee place right enough,' Scott mused. 'Beats walking up and down Back Sneddon Street for a living, eh?'

'You know my wife's arriving tonight, with my dear brother-in-law.' Daley changed the subject suddenly.

'That cunt. Whit the fuck do they want?' Scott was, as usual, the soul of discretion. 'I mean, you know, you're kinda busy the now.'

'You know Liz. Anyway, we'll all be one happy family, even though we're far from home.' Daley smiled at his DS.

'You couldna hae a happy family wi' that shite cloaking aboot. Mind you nearly hit him o'er the heid at thon barbecue? I wiz pissing myself … not literally, of course.'

Daley raised his eyebrows at that memory. 'We'll see, Brian. He's out of his own environment, maybe he'll be less annoying.'

'Don't fuckin' bet on it, compadre. If he fucks you aboot again, there'll be a reckonin'.' Scott stared grimly out the window.

Arriving at Machrie Bay, Daley parked the car on the verge. As soon as he exited the vehicle, his senses were assailed by the smell of the sea. The sea was bordered by rough machair, fringed with yellow-blossomed gorse bushes. He often found the loci of certain murders at odds with the act itself. For some reason, finding someone lying with a staved-in head in a grimy block of inner-city flats seemed more fitting than the body of a murdered woman being found at this idyllic location.

The sea was a deep blue; it looked viscous, as lazy ripples made their slow progress to the shore. High overhead, gulls and gannets dived and wheeled over the small bay. Not far from the beach, Daley could see a boat on which two men were hauling in lobster creels, supported by a cacophony of screeching sea birds.

'I think a wee word wi' those guys widna go amiss, Jim, eh?' Scott echoed Daley's thoughts precisely.

The young cop guarding the crime scene pointed out just where the body had been found. Yellow chalk markings left by SOCO were still visible on various rocks. On the shore, Daley kicked at a three-fingered fisherman's glove, as he and Scott took in the scene.

'Do you know these guys out on the boat, son?' Scott enquired of the young PC.

'Eh, aye, sir. It's Bobby Johnstone and his brother, Camel.'

'Camel? What kinda name's that?'

'They call him that because he doesna drink, sir. It's a wee bit unusual here for folk no' tae drink, especially the young ones. I don't even know his real name … just Camel Johnstone.'

'Aye, right. Well, just you use your initiative an' work oot how tae get them tae come o'er here. We want tae talk tae them. Aye, an' it's sergeant, by the way, no' sir.'

The constable apologised awkwardly, then made his way to the waterline, stroking his chin as though deep in thought.

'See, I telt ye, Jim. They're a' half daft—'

'Bobby! Camel! Get yoursels o'er here quick smart! The CID want tae talk tae you!'

The sudden shout made Scott jump involuntarily. 'That's whit you call initiative, son? I could have roared at them myself.'

'Sorry, Sergeant, seems tae have done the trick though.' He gestured over his shoulder to the fishing boat, where one of the men was giving a thumbs-up.

'Great, son. Take the award o' Polis o' the Year. Noo amaze me mair an' find me an' the inspector a cup of coffee. An' don't be wakin' the dead while you're at it.'

They watched as the fishermen attached an empty creel to a rope interspersed with pink buoys, then threw it back into the sea. So engrossed were they with this process that they failed to notice someone heading along the sand in their direction. Not, that is, until he shouted an airy greeting.

'Whit have we got here?' Scott tutted.

On closer inspection, he was a short, stocky man, dressed somewhat colourfully in a yellow oilskin jacket and green waterproof trousers, which were tucked into red Wellington boots. He had thinning grey hair, probably once ginger, swept back over a skull reddened with the sun, as was the rest of his lined, unshaven, jowly face. Daley put him somewhere in his late fifties to early sixties.

'I wonder whit they call him in Kinloch? Joseph, I shouldna wonder. He looks like he had a narrow escape fae a jelly bean factory.' In a rather different tone he called out, 'Hello, sir, how can we help you?'

'Good morning, gentlemen,' the man said breathlessly in a well-spoken accent. 'Allow me to introduce myself: Glynn Seanessy. I presume you are police officers?'

'Yes, sir.' Daley got in before Scott could be sarcastic. 'I take it you're aware of the reason we're here?'

'Oh yes, yes, most unfortunate. I never thought something like that could happen here. I mean, look around – it's glorious. So sad that someone should die here, in such an awful way.'

'May I ask how you know how this person met their death, Mr Seanessy?' Daley tested the man.

'Oh, well, you know, Kinloch rumours – that sort of thing.' Seanessy was now clearly flustered.

'It's OK, Mr Seanessy.' Daley lightened his expression. 'In the short time I've been in Kinloch, I've realised that there are few secrets.'

'Oh yes, just so.' Seanessy laughed nervously. 'It's just … I spend a lot of time on the beach and round about. You know, beachcombing, birdwatching and the like. I'm afraid time's a bit heavy on the old hands now I'm retired. One's little pleasures et cetera. I'm sure you're well aware how it is.'

'No, I'm not, but I canna wait tae find oot,' said Scott. 'I'm counting the days till I retire.'

'Ah yes. I imagine your kind of job is, well, very stressful.'

'You could say that,' said Scott dismissively.

'Well, of course. As I said, I spend quite a lot of time here, so I was wondering if I could be of any assistance. You know, local colour and the like. I'm afraid I haven't any more to offer than that. I wasn't here when the body was found – school reunion, a pain really, but nice to see the old faces.'

Daley could see that the 'local colour' remark was amusing Scott, who was associating the comment with Seanessy's attire. He spoke quickly, before Scott could comment. 'You were at school here, Mr Seanessy?'

'Eh, yes and no. The reunion was back in Cambuslang, where I grew up. But yes, in a manner of speaking. I was a teacher at the local high school here – chemistry – pretty dull really. I'm afraid the stress got to me though. I took early retirement a couple of years ago. I live over there – love the sea – wonderful, don't you think?' He pointed back along the beach to a small whitewashed cottage set back from the shore on the machair.

'A mite chilly in the winter, eh?' said Scott.

'The body was found the day before yesterday. How long were you away?' persisted Daley.

'Let me see,' mused Seanessy. 'Five days in total. I was told about it this morning in the local Co-op. An ex-pupil on the checkout – she knew I lived near where the body was found – looking for gossip probably.'

'So, nothing suspicious in the few days before you left?' said Scott.

'No. Nothing at all. As you can imagine, anything out of the ordinary here sticks out like a sore thumb.'

For appearance's sake Scott took a note of Seanessy's contact details.

'Well, thank you for your help, Mr Seanessy. We know where to find you should we require any ... colour.' Daley made it obvious that that was the end of the conversation by turning round to look at the progress of the Johnstone brothers.

'Yes, quite. You must be busy men … I conduct the odd wildlife tour, if, eh, you ever get time.'

Scott gave him a withering look, and Seanessy muttered goodbye and walked back towards his cottage in a blaze of colour.

'Fuckin' weirdo.' Scott's uncharitable appraisal was no surprise.

'Are you trying for that PR posting again, Brian? Please remind me not to recommend you.'

'Oh, that reminds me, Jim. I've got that letter from His Majesty for you. Fancy envelope, looks mucho official. It's in the glove compartment o' that minibus. Remind me and I'll gie it tae you when we get back.'

The Johnstone brothers were making their way slowly up the beach. They were deep in conversation, a conversation that was becoming heated. They were both of average height with sandy-red hair. However, one of them was muscular with a broad tanned face, while his brother was remarkably slim, his oilskins hanging off his slight frame. He had a sharp, intelligent look, and judging by the body language was very much in charge. Both brothers had the weathered complexion associated with those who spend long hours at sea.

Daley recognised them immediately. 'Gentlemen, did you enjoy your trip to Glasgow?'

The brothers looked at each other, then the thin one spoke. 'Right, I remember you.' He turned to his brother. 'The plane, do you mind, Bobby?'

The thick-set man, now identified as Bobby, scratched his head. 'I canna say I dae, but as usual you'll be right.'

His brother looked at him sharply, and it seemed that the two were about to resume the heated discussion they had been having on the way up the beach, until Scott intervened.

'Whitever, lads,' he said dismissively. 'Now, you'll baith be aware that the body of a woman was found in this wee bay a couple o' days ago. Now if yous were on the plane with the inspector here, I'm thinking that you'll no' have seen too much. How long were you away fir? And when did you leave?'

Scott's ability to get to the point seamlessly always impressed Daley. He reminded him of the men who helped at the fun fair when he was a boy: 'the shows'. Now there was a treat which every child had looked forward to, in the days before a quick hop across the Channel to Disneyland Paris or a run to one of the many theme parks that had sprung up around the country were possible. Despite the obvious excitement of their young charges, these men always looked thoroughly bored with life, spinning the waltzer or manning the dodgems in a perfunctory manner. Scott gave the same impression, conducting the most serious inquiry as though he would rather be in bed, or in the pub – virtually anywhere else in fact. Daley had to concede though, that the approach got results.

The man Daley now knew to be Camel answered. 'We were up at the fitba'. Wish we'd never bothered – the game wiz shite.'

'So you're Rangers fans, eh?' At last, a smile from the taciturn Scott.

'Nah,' Bobby answered with a grin, 'I'm a hoops man, he's the Hun.'

Scott looked bemused. 'But Celtic wirna playing this week. Did you just go fir the trip?'

'Nah.' The grin remained on Bobby's face. 'We take it in turns. Wan week we go tae Parkheid, the next tae the evil empire.' At this his grin turned to a gurn.

'Whoot he means is we don't suffer fae the same level of bigotry here as you lot up in Glesca.' Camel was clearly the more intellectual of the two.

'The next thing ye'll be telling me is that ye all go tae the same schools,' Scott proffered, with a look of scorn.

'Aye, we dae. Nae room for a' that sectarian stuff here, Constable.'

It seemed that Scott had met his match. Camel was as adept at sarcasm as he was with the intricacies of religious division in the west of Scotland.

'Sergeant, son, Detective Sergeant. You've still no' telt me when you left for the game. Just get on wi' it.'

Camel's sharp features lit up with the smile that said 1–0. 'Day before yesterday, on the efternoon flight. We get a hotel deal off the internet, check in, get something tae eat, head tae the game …'

His brother stopped him in full flow. 'I get pished, he helps me back tae the hotel, and we come hame on the flight the next morning. That way, we're back in time for the creels. Nae worries.'

'Do either of you know Izzy Watson?' Daley threw this question in unexpectedly amid the banter. 'Her husband's Michael Watson. He used to fish from Kinloch, works out of Dublin now – a local guy.'

Some cases came to their conclusion on the back of a mere nuance: a gesture, a careless utterance, a facial expression. Daley witnessed what he considered a contender as the smile left the face of Bobby Watson. He lowered his head and looked at his brother.

'Aye,' said Camel. 'Everybody knew Izzy. She wiz, well, very friendly.'

Some of the tension left Bobby's face at his brother's obviously flippant remarks.

'Friendly in what way?' Daley acted as though he hadn't picked up on the implication of Camel's last statement.

'She wiz a whore. She wiz aye gaggin' fir it.' Camel's smile was broad and supercilious. 'It wiz a fuckin' shame fir Mecky, but whoot guy's gonna look a gift horse in the mooth, eh? She wiz a wee cracker.'

Daley let the conversation peter out. In the awkward silence that followed, he watched Bobby as he looked back out to sea, more serious than his brother. Camel simply looked at the two policemen with a fixed smile.

'You keep saying she *was* – why is that?' Daley's expression was blank.

'That's easy. There's been a woman found deid, an' there are polis all o'er Mecky's hoose, aye, an' his mother's hoose tae. I'm a lobster fisherman, no' a polis, but I can still work that oot.' Camel held up a mobile phone, his smile again one of triumph. 2–0.

'What about you, Bobby? How well did you know Izzy Watson?' Daley waited for an answer as the young fisherman's gaze remained on the sea.

Eventually he turned back to Daley and answered. 'She wiz a nice lassie. No' right wi' the drink, but jeest a nice lassie, that's all.' He shrugged his shoulders.

Daley noticed how uncomfortable the young man seemed in contrast to his mocking brother. The pair had very different opinions of Izzy Watson. 'You both seem very young to have your own boat. I mean, can't be cheap – all the kit.' He gestured out to their boat, now bobbing near the beach, the pink and orange buoys to which the fishermen's nets were attached jostling alongside seaborne gulls.

'Oor faither left it tae us when he died.' Camel yet again spoke for the pair. 'I wiz twelve, Bobby wiz ten. Whoot's the point o' school when you've got a career oot here? We baith left the school as soon as we could, an' we've been at this ever since.' His summing up of their lives to date had a precision to it. Even in this brief encounter, Daley could sense that a sharp intellect was at work.

'What did your father die of?' Scott intervened. He and Daley were so used to working together that their interview technique was easily intertwined, each man instinctively knowing what the other was trying to achieve.

'Whoot's that got tae dae with anything?' Bobby was on the defensive.

'The drink,' Camel blurted out, clearly annoyed at the question. 'He drank himself tae death. Aye an' he's no' alone roon' here.'

'I see. And is that why you don't drink?' Daley's question to Camel was direct.

'I can see how you got tae be an inspector. Aye, that's how I don't drink. Noo, if you don't mind, we've got mair creels tae dae ...'

'Just one last question.' Daley wasn't giving in at Camel's request. 'When did you last see Izzy Watson?'

Bobby looked nervous, and tried to give a stuttering response; his brother quickly hushed him. 'Last weekend. She wiz in Pulse, you know, the nightclub?'

'What about you, Bobby? You don't seem as sure as your brother.' Scott was playing the game well.

'Aye, the same. I wiz with my brother the other night.' Both officers noted his uneasiness.

'By fuck, Camel, fir a man that doesna drink, you spend a helluva lot o' time in pubs, eh?' Scott again echoed Daley's thoughts.

'There no' a lot else tae dae here, or has your nose fir shite no' detected that yet?'

Daley saw Scott's face change fleetingly, but he managed to keep his cool. 'You can gie me your addresses, an' the name o' the pubs you drink in, just in case we need tae speak tae you again.'

The brothers shared a house in Kinloch and, as could have been predicted by anyone who knew of the partisan nature of pub-going in the town, spent their leisure time between the Royal, the Douglas Arms and Pulse.

The two policemen watched as they waded out to the boat, started the noisy diesel engine, and went about the business of lobster fishing.

'Someone's no' tellin' the truth.' Scott needed no confirmation from his boss.

The young constable was walking slowly towards them down the beach, carrying two cups of coffee.

'Here, well done, son. Mebbe yer no' such a fuckin' idiot efter a'?'

The constable smiled at the backhanded compliment. 'Got them in the incident van up on the road.'

Scott hadn't thought of that.

9

Back at Kinloch Police Office, Daley was confronted with the prospect of the looming press conference. It was not that he was a particularly nervous performer, or that he was of the shy-and-retiring fraternity. No, rather he was tired of all the experts who would generally mill around before, during and after such an event took place, offering nebulous pointers and pieces of 'useful' advice. Everyone it seemed, from the chief constable to the office janitor, became an expert when the bright camera lights burst into life and the gentlemen of the press arrived. He and Scott had already recognised a couple of red-top hacks in town.

Daley resolved to change tack as far as the press conference was concerned. He had noticed that more and more of these affairs were being conducted by lower-grade officers. It was high time Scott got more used to the limelight. It would be useful experience for him, as well as being a relief for his immediate superior.

Normally, these events were organised by the Superintendent Donalds of this world. They would sit by, faces the picture of gravity, as some poor DCI or DI sweated under the glare of television lights, answering the probing questions of inebriated journalists, always conscious of the dark ranks of their friends and colleagues marking the performance in the shadows, busy formulating an aggravating litany of 'handy hints and tips'. Well, woe betide them today. He looked surreptitiously across the room at his DS as he rifled through a mountain of paper and envelopes, trying to find the one that Donald had entrusted to him to deliver. Needless to say, the air was a particularly bright shade of blue.

'You know, I don't know where the fuck anything goes. I left the bloody thing in the glove compartment, I'm certain.' Paper and brown envelopes were piling up on the floor at his feet; two Paisley DCs looked on disinterestedly as they chewed on bacon rolls. 'Aye, an' you pair can just get off your backsides an' get o'er here an' help me. You wid think we'd been livin' in that minibus fir three years, the fuckin' state it's in. We only got it at six this morning. Get cracking.'

Daley decided that now was not the best time to tell Scott of his decision. Instead, he called Crichton. After a few pleasant minutes on hold listening to Mendelssohn's *Scottish Symphony*, the pathologist's familiar tones jolted him back to life. 'You out for one of those fly puffs on that pipe, Andy?'

'As a feat of detection, that has a certain paucity, Jim. You might even solve a case at this rate. Now, how can I help you?'

Daley watched as Scott threw a banana skin at one of the DCs then answered. 'I'm just wondering if you've had any luck with getting any identifiable DNA from those semen samples? I could really use it just now.'

'Well then, you're in luck.' The pathologist sounded chirpy. 'We extracted successfully from all three. They're being compared with our database samples now. I can't guarantee that we'll come up with a match, but a step forward, what?'

The old-fashioned expression amused the inspector. 'What's the easiest and quickest way for me to get a DNA sample to you for testing, bearing in mind where I am at the moment?'

'In that part of the world, Jim, we usually have the force doctors do the necessary. The chap down there's quite obliging.' He hesitated. 'Can't remember his name for the life of me. May I enquire if this will be a voluntary sample, or one you've managed to get from something?'

'No, just a suspicion.' Daley was shaking his head, even though Crichton could not see him. 'We'll get the sample one way or the other.'

'In that case, my advice is to contact your man down there. Get him to call me first. Some of these hick docs are a bit ham-fisted when it comes to this sort of thing. I'll keep him right.'

Daley had no sooner put the phone down than the door to the CID office burst open to reveal a short middle-aged female dressed in a dark suit, which looked as though it was about to burst at the seams. The jacket was so tight that her ample bosom bulged out of her unbuttoned white blouse. Her hair, cut in a bob, was obviously dyed, as it appeared to be almost navy-blue in colour, and her pale face was dominated by a bright-red lip-glossed mouth. A pair of extra-large sunglasses gave her the look of a malevolent bug, which, Daley reckoned, was exactly what she was.

'Fir fuck's sake,' was Scott's predictable response. 'I didna know they'd given you a long-range broomstick.'

The assembled DCs chortled heartily.

'And I didn't know that the police were still employing deadbeat alcoholics.'

Suddenly Daley wished he had taken the opportunity to speak to his DS earlier. 'Pauline, hello. Pleasant journey?'

The PR officer grunted an unintelligible response, and stood in the middle of the floor taking in her surroundings. She had a large leather bag over her right shoulder, and a wheeled suitcase stood, precariously angled, at her side. 'I see you chaps have been able to replicate the usual standard of organisation, despite the change of venue.' She was looking at the detritus that surrounded Scott. 'Now, I'll need some kind of desk, in this … this shambles. Preferably as far away from him as possible.' She pointed at DS Scott. 'Please, no matter the circumstances, do not be tempted to bring anyone from the press in here. The state of this place would be headline news.' Pauline Robertson had unequivocally made her presence felt.

'Aye, well, just you remember, that while you're prancing aboot wi' a' they chancers, we're busy solving a murder. So keep your opinions tae yersel'.'

Daley reasoned that there was no time like the present, and calmly invited both Pauline and Scott into his glass-walled office. Once his proposal to make Scott the PR liaison offer was made clear, the pair sat in what could best be described as stunned silence.

'I must admit, this is not what I expected. Does no one have anything profane to shout?' Daley's sarcasm was intended to provoke a response.

Pauline was the first to speak. 'I suppose with your newfound eminence, it would be pointless to argue.' Both policemen looked at her blankly. 'Don't tell me you don't know yet? I got the memo this morning before I caught the plane.'

'Oh fir fuck's sake, Pauline, just get on wi' it. Has he got a knighthood or something?'

'Nothing of the kind. So you really have no idea, *Chief* Inspector Daley?'

Daley took a second or two to assimilate the information.

'Of course, that broon envelope His Highness gave me. It must be your promotion. Well done, Jimmy boy,' Scott said, somewhat irreverently, as he stood to congratulate his colleague.

'Yes, congratulations, I'm sure. I'm just pleased I was the bearer of such good news.'

'That's another thing, *Chief Inspector*, how the fuck did she get doon in the plane, and I had tae suffer that fuckin' minibus fir hours on end?' It was clear, as far as Scott was concerned, that very little had changed, and that an elevation to the rank of chief inspector barely warranted a mention.

'Anyway,' interrupted Pauline, 'we better get a shift on. I've arranged this press conference for two o'clock, at the crime scene. Nice day and all that, more chance of getting TV coverage.' She gave both policemen a superior smile.

'So, chop-chop, DS Scott. Most of the work is done, and all you have to do is follow my instructions. Oh, can you read out loud?'

On hearing the beginning of Scott's expletive-rich reply, Daley decided to leave the pair to organise the press conference unaided. He took a few moments to ponder his good fortune. He had most certainly not expected to be promoted – ever, in fact, never mind now. He recalled Donald's assurance that he had something 'up his sleeve', with which to counter the waspish MacLeod. The promotion must have been it.

It changed a lot of things. His operational status would change. He would be forced to pay more than lip service to the bean counting he so despised. And what about his working relationship with Brian? He watched the combustible DS through his glass window, shaking his head, raising his eyes, and finger pointing. Beneath all the repartee, they made an effective team. Would this be their last investigation together?

And what about Liz? She constantly berated him for his lack of progress through the ranks. He knew she would be pleased, but would her pleasure be felt on his behalf, or for herself? He would tell her about it later, after she and Mark had arrived. He didn't suppose that Mark Henderson would give a damn whatever rank he achieved. He saw all policemen as poorly paid, unimaginative functionaries, their careers spent trying to stem the tide of human degradation. Not unlike those who cleaned the sewers or emptied bins; the only difference being they dealt with human effluent. They had talked about it late one night, when without an audience and after a few Highland Parks Mark had become almost human. The contempt he held for any kind of public service was obvious. He had told Daley that he could have done so much better in life, made so much more money – that this would have impressed Liz. Patronising prick.

Daley stood with MacLeod, who appeared to be standing to attention in his well-pressed uniform. The pair had had a brief conversation earlier, when the Highlander had congratulated Daley on his promotion. It was clear he did not intend to call Daley 'sir', merely avoiding the need for its use by addressing him obliquely. They were on the shore overlooking Machrie Bay, where the body of Izzy Watson had been found. Pauline Robertson had persuaded everyone that the beach was an ideal venue for the press conference, somewhere that would stick in the public's collective mind.

Fraser stood beside Scott, who was, in turn, flanked by Watson and Pauline Robertson. The sea fizzed in soft white breakers on the shore behind them. The gulls performed aerobatics in the clear blue sky, their cries adding to what Robertson termed 'a visually memorable happening'.

MacLeod, though, was unconvinced. 'I've never seen anything like it,' he snapped, surveying the scene with a disgusted frown. Television technicians were setting up lights, microphones and cameras. Around thirty reporters, representatives of both the electronic and print media, were present, mingling on the beach in loose huddles, or standing alone with mobile phones clamped to their ears.

One hack sat cross-legged on the sand, typing furiously onto a small laptop. Daley's own mobile rang, and he could see MacLeod's face recoil at the ringtone as he stomped off.

memory, no?' That said, he carried on up to the road, where he got into a marked police car driven by a constable.

'Aye, fuck me, Jim, a nest of vipers here an' no mistake. Is he Norwegian? Me and the wife were there on holiday two years ago, mind? He's a dead ringer fir them.' Scott lightened the mood just as Daley's mobile vibrated again in his pocket. This time it was the office. Camel Johnstone wanted to speak to him urgently.

10

Camel was sitting in one of the interview rooms with his feet up on the table as Daley and Scott entered. Scott casually shoved the fisherman's legs on his way to his seat, nearly forcing the young man off his chair.

'I don't know where you grew up, son – likely in some fisherman's shack – but see where I come fae, ye pit yer feet on the ground. Got it?'

Camel's sharp features accentuated a sneer. 'Aye, whatever. Anyway, I came here tae talk tae your boss, no' you.' His heavy-lidded gaze turned to Daley.

'Well, make it quick, and make it good.' Daley was in no mood for a game of verbal fencing with Camel. 'And if you're here to plead a case for your brother, you can forget it.'

'If ye listen tae whoot I've got tae say before ye accuse my brother, ye might learn something.' Camel was clearly agitated beneath his façade of bravado.

'We're all ears, son.' Scott sat directly across from the fisherman, his arms folded; Daley beside him. The newly promoted chief inspector held his hand out, palm up, inviting Camel to speak.

'Ye might as well know, I wiz havin' an affair wi' Izzy Watson.'

Daley and Scott stayed silent, a tactic they used automatically when someone was embarking on a confession. Often people, burdened by the information they were keeping secret, wanted some kind of confirmation that they were now absolved of the guilt that they felt. In short, if you interrupted a confessor confessing, the well could dry, instantly.

'I must admit, I'd hoped fir mair o' a reaction.' Camel was leaning back, arms crossed, with no trace of emotion on his sharp face. He had clearly come to say what he had to say, and that was it.

'So Bobby's not who we're looking for?' Daley kept his expression neutral. He had misjudged the younger brother's body language on the beach; either that or Camel was making a desperate attempt to save his sibling. Somehow, Daley didn't think so.

'Listen.' Camel sat forward. 'I know you guys will probably have evidence that I slept wi' her the day she disappeared, so why are we fucking about? This has got nothing tae dae wi' Bobby. He just canna help looking guilty, he's always been the same. Jeest let him go. I'm yer man. I promise ye though: she wiz alive an' kicking when I last saw her.' He looked directly at Daley with the unnerving, steady gaze that the policeman had first noticed on the beach that morning.

'So, if you don't mind, maybe you can fill us in on your little dalliance? Where and when did this act of passion take place?' Daley knew instinctively that the fisherman was telling the truth.

'Dalliance? I've never heard it called that afore. If you must know, I couped her o'er the bins at the back o' Pulse.'

'Nae bother tae you, son, eh?' said Scott. 'Never mind a bit of romance an' a' that shite.'

'They ca' it the Honeymoon Suite. It's no' Paris in the spring, but the owner turns a blind eye. An' well you know how it is when passion strikes, boys, or are yous both too auld tae remember?'

Daley rose from his seat and slammed the desk with his clenched fist, an action that Camel was clearly not expecting as he pushed himself quickly back from the desk, an open-mouthed look of astonishment on his face.

'I've had just about enough of your childish sarcasm, son,' roared Daley, the veins now standing out on his neck. 'A woman's lost her life, and a wee boy's lost his mother, never mind her husband, whom you *obviously* don't give a fuck about. Now, I'll give you another chance to answer our questions, this time with the tape on. Remember, son, before we start – right now, after your big confession – you're the prime suspect. So take that fucking stupid grin off your face and try to get yourself out of the mess you're in, or the only crabs you'll be catching will be off some lonely psychopath with a three-day growth and a life sentence. Get it?'

Camel, chastened by Daley's outburst, went on to tell them more about Izzy Watson's life than could have been hoped for. It was apparently not unusual for her to arrive in the club with one man, and then visit the Honeymoon Suite with another. It seemed as though her life was well and truly out of control. Camel confirmed that she was addicted to crack and regularly snorted coke. She paid for this, he said, by acting as a sort of unofficial prostitute, with drugs the reward for sexual favours. He had paid for his romantic interlude at the bins with a wrap of cocaine he had picked up in Glasgow. He also gave the officers an impromptu and extensive list of other men with whom she had similar ad hoc arrangements.

'By fuck, Jim, beasts in the field doon here, eh? Ye wid think it was just a nice wee seaside toon, but they're up tae their ears in illegal drugs and illicit sex. Oor lassie Izzy's been a bit o' a girl right enough.' Scott shook his head, and looked thoughtfully at the floor.

Daley knew his partner was sensitive to his domestic situation, and every now and again – purely because of his inherent lack of tact – would realise that he had said something that was too close to the bone, touching on the marital difficulties of his boss. He wished Scott would forget all about it, but the problem remained, silent and unspoken. He decided to lighten the mood. 'On the subject of wayward women, my dear wife will be winging her way here as we speak, or should I say rotating?' Daley looked at Scott and smiled. 'It's been a long day, Brian. Will you liaise with the local guys and get the rest of Izzy's paramours rounded up? I want to go for a walk for a bit … Clear the head, you know?'

'You do the right thing, boss. If anything exciting happens I'll bell you on the mobile. We'll need DNA fae a' these guys, so I'll bump it upstairs for his Lordship tae sort oot.'

'Aye, do that, Brian.' Daley shrugged his jacket over his shoulders. 'Get young Fraser to help you. He's up at Watson's. He's a good lad, nothing like old Davie, eh?'

'I can tell he's nothin' like Davie cos he's standing up. You go an' get your walk, *Chief Inspector.*' He slapped his friend on the back and grinned. 'An' don't be goin' anywhere near that Pulse, or you'll catch something. I'll mebbe take a wander doon there later and check it oot.' Scott grinned. They were back on easy terms by the time Daley left.

There was a large map on the wall of the CID office, which Daley had consulted when he first arrived. A short distance from the twin piers, there was a stretch of promenade running along the side of the loch towards its mouth. It was here that Daley walked as he mused on the progress of the case so far. The sky was still a cloudless blue, and the fragrance of honeysuckle mixed itself with the ozone from the bay. The everpresent gulls emitted their habitual cackle that somehow, despite its harsh nature, complemented the ambience. The warm sun felt good on his face; if he hadn't been walking he was sure that he could have happily drifted off to sleep.

Izzy Watson's life had been chaotic, and he was convinced that her lifestyle had contributed to her demise. There were, though, nagging doubts at the back of his mind. He didn't seriously think that Camel had anything to do with her murder, but of course he couldn't be sure. The same, he suspected, went for the sixteen guys on the list that Camel had given him. They were all young lads out for a good time. Recreational drugs, shedloads of booze, fast women: yes. Murder: no. The young people he had seen here didn't have the rough, world-weary taint of their peers in the city, where casual and extreme violence had become unremarkable.

The gnawing of instinct continued in his head. He recalled the bunches into which her hair was tied, the red ribbons which stood out so incongruously on the crime-scene images. No one remembered her wearing her hair that way. Why had she suddenly changed her hairstyle? And for whom?

Then there was the friend, Janet Ritchie. Despite having both CID and uniformed officers look for her all day, they had turned up nothing. Nobody recalled seeing her or Izzy after their capers at Pulse. He had officers at the club now, questioning staff and customers. The owner was nowhere to be found. He lived in a flat above the premises that was as quiet as the grave. Daley had toyed with the idea of breaking down the door to the flat, but he wanted to take a look himself before he took this action. At the moment, CCTV tapes made on the night that Izzy had disappeared were being reviewed by two local DCs. Pulse was his next port of call.

On another level, he was revelling in his surroundings. The loch itself was a generous 'C' shape, about half a mile across at its furthest point between one side of the town and the other. On this side of the water, large Victorian mansions spoke of the prosperous times that Kinloch had seen when the sea was the world's highway. He had Googled the town the evening before his departure, and now he imagined the bay filled with small fishing boats, tall masted schooners carrying coal and whisky – the town's main exports – and the general hubbub that such a scene would generate. During World War II the port of Kinloch had seen a brief revival as a strategic base for the Royal Navy. The deep safe harbour provided a welcome retreat from the brutal exigencies of the war in the Atlantic. At that time the population rose to a dizzy 30,000 – the high-water mark of its inhabitation.

As with so many other communities in Scotland, the 1970s and 1980s had brought decline and despair. The fishing industry contracted to virtually nothing; the sea-coal mine, which had tunnelled deep under the ocean near to where Izzy Watson's body had been found, closed. And, of course, attendant businesses suffered a commensurate demise. The thriving shipyard, one that had produced some of the finest fishing boats in Europe, was a spectre of empty decaying buildings on the other side of the loch. The rise in the popularity of Speyside-produced whisky saw all but one of the town's many distilleries demolished. It was the old story: confidence in the area drained away; small factories closed; shops shut; and people moved on. In their wake, a hard core of individuals struggled to maintain what was left of the thriving happy community.

Unexpectedly, a cloud passed over the sun, turning the loch from a shimmering blue to an impenetrable grey. The hills seemed to gather in around their ancient charge. An unseasonable chill rent the air, the squawking gulls quietened, and the town took on a demeanour of black foreboding.

In the distance, the distinctive thud of helicopter blades hard at work could be heard. Automatically, Daley turned to face the noise. A dot, growing steadily larger over the island that sheltered the entrance to the loch, immediately caught his eye. 'There may be trouble ahead …' The words and melody of Nat King Cole's song appeared unheralded in his mind.

He was suddenly aware of somebody behind him. He turned to face the wrinkled visage of old Hamish, his features the same inscrutable mask the policeman had noted in the harbour master's office.

'Well now, Mr Daley.' The old man's voice was a rasping whisper barely audible above the noise of the helicopter. 'That's a day that's changing, eh?'

'Hello, Hamish. You know the weather around here better than me. What do you reckon?'

The old man looked heavenward and took his pipe from the pocket of the green oilskin coat he was wearing. 'There's a storm on the way. Aye, a storm, Mr Daley.' He looked back at the detective. 'That'll be yer wife.'

Daley looked up. The helicopter was now over the loch. There was writing along the side of the aircraft, but he couldn't read it at that distance. He squinted for a moment or two, but gave up. He opened his mouth to answer the old man, but he'd vanished – no sign of him in either direction. Chief Inspector James Daley shivered involuntarily and decided to walk back towards the town. There was still no sign of the mysterious Hamish. Daley reasoned that he had probably taken some hidden route onto the gravel beach.

He was passing a young mother with her baby in a push-chair when his mobile started to ring. It was Liz.

'Hi there, darling! We've just landed, right in the middle of the town. Can you believe it?'

He had seen the helicopter lose height over Kinloch, and had supposed that there must be a landing pad somewhere in the town. He knew that patients from the local hospital were taken to Glasgow by helicopter if their condition was deemed serious enough, and he briefly tried to imagine where such an aircraft could land, using his limited knowledge of the town's topography.

'Hi, Liz. Good flight, I trust? I actually saw you flying over ...'

'Good, Jim, good.' She sounded distracted, and he could hear someone talking in the background. 'Listen, Mark wants to get settled into the hotel. We've a taxi waiting. Can I meet you later? I'm sure you'll be busy right now.' It was amazing how understanding she could be when her plans suited him being elsewhere.

'Oh, fine. Where are you staying?' The halting dialogue of their phone calls remained unchanged.

'We're in some posh lodge about five miles out of town. Mark says he wouldn't like to rough it staying in Kinloch itself. He's been here golfing a lot, darling, and he says the people are, well, rather quaint.' Liz giggled, no doubt prompted by her odious brother-in-law. 'From where I am I can see a little bar overlooking the loch. Hold on, I'll ask the taxi driver what it's called.' There was a brief muffled conversation with somebody who, judging by his accent could only be local, then Liz was back. 'It's called the Island. The driver here says it's the poshest bar in the "toon".' She tried, without success, to affect the accent. 'So, just the place for you and I, love. Meet you there about six?'

'Well, I'll have to see what's happening. I've got something to tell you anyway, so I'll do my best. Will you be alone? I ...'

'Got to dash! This driver's getting himself into a bit of a panic – wants to get home or something. See you at six.'

After the familiar sound of a prematurely terminated phone conversation, Daley slipped his mobile into his trouser pocket with a sigh. He hoped that she would be alone, and he was furious that she was staying at Mark's hotel, and not his. He tried to console himself by reasoning that having Liz underfoot in the middle of an investigation would be a disaster, and that she was better off where she was. But he had just assumed that she would be staying with him. He heard Donald's voice in his head: to assume is to make an ass of you and me.

He banished thoughts of his wife and his superior from his mind, and headed back into Kinloch. The town was quite busy, and looking at his watch he realised that at four thirty, some people might be starting to leave work or head home from shopping. However, come to think of it, Kinloch's Main Street always seemed busy.

It had been a very difficult and long day, but he had time to take a quick look at the nightclub where Izzy Watson had last been seen.

Pulse was situated halfway up Main Street. The windows were glazed with privacy glass, and remembering what Camel had told him of what went on within its confines, he wasn't surprised. A small brass plate to the side of the door was all that announced the function of the building to the public: 'PULSE. Licensed to sell alcohol and tobacco. Prop. P. Mulligan.' It looked like the kind of plaque that might be found outside a private medical surgery or an upmarket legal firm. He pushed open the large black door and entered.

The place was all he expected it to be: an impossibly dim, windowless interior with no natural light to permeate the gloom. A deserted bar with oversized beer fonts was the domain of a jumpy-looking barman, who hastened over to Daley in silent enquiry. A uniformed officer sat with his back to the chief inspector, watching golf on a huge plasma screen at the far end of a lowered area, which formed an obvious dance floor. Cluny, a loud-mouthed but efficient DC from Paisley, was talking into his mobile, and acknowledged his superior with a raise of his eyebrows. A local DC was sitting at a table on the edge of the dance floor, looking intently at a series of black-and-white images on a laptop.

'Hello, sir.' Cluny had finished his call quickly. 'We're just going through the CCTV records. It's taking a while, but we've got sight of the victim now, so we're taking it frame by frame. Anything new on the owner?'

'I was just about to ask you the same question, Chick. He's not surfaced here, then?'

'No, sir, not a peep from the flat. Do you think we should pan the door in?' Cluny was, as usual, anxious to be at the heart of the action, an impetuous characteristic that had got him into numerous scrapes but also had its rewards on a fortune-favours-the-brave basis.

Daley turned to the barman. He was a thin youth, probably still in his teens, with untidy fair hair and a face full of spots. 'Is it usual for your gaffer to be away all day like this? I'd have thought he would have plenty to do while it's quiet.'

The barman made to speak, opening his mouth, without any words coming out. The detective realised he had a paralysing stutter. 'It's ... ac-ac-ac ... actually not that unusual.' The last part of the sentence came at a gallop.

Daley recognised that he was using 'actual' as a trigger word to help initiate speech, a common tactic amongst chronic stutterers. Start speaking with a word that was relatively easy to say, and use it as a springboard for the rest of the sentence. One of Daley's schoolfriends had been a stutterer: Colin Chiveney. He had found it virtually impossible to get words out, and became a target for the ridicule of his peers. Daley had befriended him, and soon discovered that if they were alone, in relaxed surroundings and once they had got to know each other, Colin would begin to talk almost normally. Then, when anyone else appeared, the stuttering would return with a vengeance. He remembered his friend's exasperation and embarrassment.

When he was in his mid teens, Colin had formed a rock band. He was a talented guitarist, using the instrument to express in music what he found virtually impossible to do in conversation. It was then he had discovered something truly miraculous: when he sang or spoke through a microphone, his stutter disappeared. Not only that, he had a fantastic singing voice. Nowadays he played the lucrative Vegas cabaret circuit, as well as session singing work. He was confident, worth several million dollars and only a trace of his impediment remained. The pair had kept in touch, and even though they occupied very different worlds, were still at home in each other's company.

'Take your time, son. I'm Inspector Daley.' He hadn't yet got used to his recent elevation in the ranks. 'Do you have any way of contacting Mr Mulligan, other than those we've already tried?'

The barman looked at the floor, and the set of his shoulders changed, as though he was about to attempt some athletic feat. 'Ac-ac-ac-actually … if he doesn't answer his mobile we … ca-ca-ca …' He shook his head in frustration. 'Actually we canna get a hold o' him.' He looked mightily relieved.

'OK, fine.' Daley looked back towards Cluny. 'I'll just make sure we have a warrant.' He pulled his mobile from his jacket pocket and rang Scott on speed dial. He wondered briefly how you could be a barman with such a severe speech impediment, and then reflected that most of the time in Pulse, no one could hear to converse anyway.

'Hi, Jimbo. Enjoy your walk?' Scott answered brightly.

'I'm at Pulse. Have we got a warrant to break into the owner's flat yet?' He heard a rustling of papers.

'Aye, just arrived fae a local JP a few minutes ago. Dae ye want me to come doon?'

'Aye, good idea, Brian. And bring one of those battering rams. My days of kicking in doors are over.'

'Has your good lady arrived yet? One o' the boys said a helicopter landed on the green earlier – wherever that is.' Scott's curiosity had the better of him.

'Yup, she's on her way to some posh hunting lodge with my brother-in-law. Nice for some, eh?' Daley was glad he couldn't see Scott raise his eyebrows on the other end of the phone. 'I'm due to meet her shortly, so can we get a move on?' He looked at his watch, then sent a text to his wife to tell her he'd be slightly late for their rendezvous at the Island Bar.

Peter Mulligan's flat was a bare, characterless place. There were no pictures on the walls, no framed photographs above the fire, no food in the fridge; in short, it felt as though the dwelling had just been fully furnished, waiting for someone to move in. This was reinforced by the scrupulous tidiness in the flat. Not a thing was out of place: the cushions sat plump on a white leather sofa in the lounge, which also boasted another easy chair and a small TV. A chest of drawers in the bedroom contained the usual array of underwear, T-shirts, jumpers and shirts, all neatly folded and arranged. Even the bed was tidy. It reminded Daley of his time at the police college as a young recruit. As with the army, beds had to be made to an exacting standard of precision, complete with hospital corners and wrinkle-free duvet covers. Some zealots even ironed their beds once they had been made – Daley hadn't gone that far. So it was with Mulligan's place; any inspecting sergeant would have found no fault with it. The clothes in the wardrobe – coats, suits, jackets and shirts – all hung in ordered perfection. Many of the garments were still covered in polythene dry-cleaning covers. There were no personal papers to be found. Come to that, there was not one book, CD or magazine in the whole flat.

'Something's no' right here, Jim. I mean, whit kinda guy has a flat like this, an' at the same time allows lassies tae prostitute themselves doonstairs in the yard? It doesna fit.'

As usual, Scott had summed things up succinctly. Peter Mulligan would have to be traced – as a matter of priority.

PART TWO

I I

She wanted to be able to move her arms, but to her surprise she couldn't. She wasn't doing anything consciously different from any other time in her life when she tried to make them move, but they refused to obey her commands.

She felt numb though. She was cold, very cold, and she knew that the reason for this was being naked. She longed for her recalcitrant limbs to conform to her desire to get off the floor and pull the duvet from the bed around herself. However, nothing could instill even the slightest response from her body.

She was moving her eyes in a slow and random way, a bit like falling asleep as a child. She would get quieter, her eyes would roll, and her granny would lift her from the couch and up the stairs to her bed. It was the only way she could get to sleep. Being left alone in a darkened room conjured up all manner of ghosts – the fears of an overactive imagination, her granny had said. By the time her lids forced themselves closed, those fears receded. She benignly complied with her granny's wishes. It had been so long since she had felt that way. Her head had flopped forwards onto her chest; she could do nothing to stop it. It was so heavy. If she raised her eyes towards her brow until it was sore, she could just about see to the top of the bed. She studied the hand that hung limp over the side with complete indifference, though the blood that trickled down from the fingers and onto the carpet below held a strange fascination for her.

There was noise now. It was like listening to a voice from underwater – another memory from childhood – the swimming pool at school. The screams and shouts of her friends becoming quiet and distorted by the rush and gurgle of the water in her ears. Yes, that was what it was like now, though she was pretty certain she wasn't under water. Something sparked in her mind. Water? Try as she might, the thought would not form.

Then, something else. A change of sound and, out of the corner of her eye, movement: legs, booted feet. A dull prompting. Thoughts through cotton wool. The bed moving. A thud. More mumbles.

She'd had a life-sized doll's head when she was young. A blank canvas on which make-up could be applied, or the hair could be styled. Training, designed to turn fresh-faced little girls into painted, groomed women. That head was looking at her now, though the eyes stared and the tongue lolled from the mouth. She could feel something dripping on her legs. Red rivulets ran down towards her feet, like drops of rain on a window. The head swung from straggly hair held by a black-gloved hand.

She could feel the blood on her legs. She could see the syringe sticking out of her arm, held there by the needle thrust deep into her flesh. She felt gloved hands under her armpits. The scene changed before her eyes, as she was half-dragged, half-lifted from the bed. She tried to focus on the mass of flesh, bone and blood on the bed, but she was pulled away too quickly. She felt her thigh catch on something sharp as she progressed across the floor.

More pain. Her face connected with a hard surface. A dull crack filled her head, as waves of agony consumed her. More mumbling. Something sharp in her behind. A tightness in her chest: this was fear. She was frightened all of a sudden. Abruptly, a rush of noise made her flinch. The cotton wool-filled world had gone. The voice – that horrible voice – so clear now.

She was in a kneeling position, pain from her knees as well as her face. Then a flash of pain she could see as well as feel. Red agony: then blackness.

The bar was a one-room affair. Two old men sat at the long counter, drinking whisky from small glasses. The proprietor – she knew because he had told her – was a looming presence behind the bar, a portly man with a red face and a welcoming smile. She sat at a window seat, looking out over the loch and the road which led from the centre of the town to the Island Bar: 'O'er there,' as her taxi driver had put it. Three fishing boats bobbed in the harbour, while a long low vessel was being loaded with what looked like logs from an orange crane on the faraway pier, the colour of it almost matching the luminous orange of the top half of the lifeboat moored nearby.

Mark had wanted to come too, but she wanted to speak to her husband by herself. She needed to tell him how miserable she was, how much she hated living where she did, how long her days were, how undervalued she felt, how frustrating she found sharing a marriage with a man devoted to a career that could see him drop everything at a moment's notice to go and stare at another mutilated corpse, or try to drag the truth from a low-life scumbag who didn't deserve to draw breath.

She reflected on what loneliness had done to her. Like almost everyone she knew, she had entered married life a starry-eyed optimist: the cottage in the country; the long walks; making love on stormy nights beside a blazing fire. Being possessed by someone so completely that to identify where she ended and they began was an impossible, if hackneyed, spiritual quandary.

The 'cottage in the country' was a dreary detached villa on an equally dreary private estate, in the 'village of the damned' where dozens of identikit women lived identical lives, dressing the same, speaking the same, driving the same cars, and possessing the same ambitions: a good school for Jake, or Jed, or Perdita, or whatever other ridiculous name was currently in vogue; two weeks on a beach in the summer; a weekend in Paris or Prague in the spring; and a skiing trip after Christmas. A new 4x4 every few years, and maybe even a move to a slightly bigger house, on a better estate, in a 'nicer' area where the ambitions were essentially the same though more elevated: a public school for the kids; a more exotic holiday destination; a Porsche Cayenne, rather than a Volkswagen Touareg.

In short, people who would be born, grow up and die with nothing to show for any part of their lives, apart from a reasonably good credit rating and an inheritance for their offspring to fight over – offspring who would themselves embark upon an identikit middle-class existence, while believing themselves to be at the cutting edge of cultured society.

'Would you like another drink? We're in a wee round up here having a wee soirée – I'm on the bell. You're looking pretty lonely over there.' The proprietor smiled effusively as one of the two men turned round from his perch on a bar stool, better to survey her.

'Jeest you stay where ye are, lassie. It's no' a soirée he's thinkin' aboot wi' you. Is that no' right, Big George?' The old man had the bronchial cackle of the confirmed smoker.

It was clear, though, that Big George was not enamoured with his customer's opinions. His face darkened and he glared at the old man. 'Yesss' – the word was an elongated preamble – 'I thought when you lost your job and your wife left you, Dennis, you'd have learned to shut up. Obviously not. Don't worry about him, darling. I like all my customers to be happy. C'mon up, we'll make an evening of it.'

At that, the old man tried to manoeuvre himself around to face her again, however, drink or old age got the better of him, and, after a cartoonish flailing of arms and a desperate grabbing of the bar, he fell backwards on his stool, his head narrowly missing the table where she was sitting.

'Don't worry, darling.' Big George seemed unconcerned. 'If I had a pound for every time I've seen him do that, I'd be able to close up for good, and not have to talk to a barful of drunks every day. Is that not right, Dennis?' He moved as close to the bar as his girth would allow and peered down at his felled customer, who was, by this time, doing his best to get back to his feet amid a torrent of bad language and abortive attempts at balance. 'Hurry up, it's your round.'

'Aye, but you said it wiz your round', big man.' Customer number two looked confused.

'Yes, that's before he fell over and I realised what a fuckin' awful life I've got.' Big George smiled at Liz and turned to the gantry, holding a small glass up to a large whisky bottle. 'You'll be for another dram, Dennis.' That was in the form of a statement.

Dennis, now back on his feet, muttered in the affirmative and fumbled in his pockets for money to buy the round.

Liz wondered idly just how many rounds Big George actually bought his drink-addled customers. Just then, out of the corner of her eye, she saw a tall, dark-haired, slightly overweight man wearing a suit, striding purposefully across the esplanade. Her husband, Jim Daley, was on his way. The flutter in her chest was involuntary.

Daley entered the bar and stood for a moment, his eyes adjusting to the gloomy light. Turning to his left, he spotted Liz sitting at a table near the window. He held his hand to his mouth in a drinking gesture, to which she replied with a nod, pointing at her wine glass.

'Pint of heavy and a dry white wine, please.' Daley was aware that two elderly customers were appraising him from their perches at the bar.

The bartender reached under the counter for a glass, then made his way to the appropriate beer tap. 'Don't tell me you're the lucky man who has the pleasure of that young lady's company?'

The question was impertinent, but glancing at Liz he could see she was smiling, so he assumed she had been made welcome in this odd little bar. 'Yes. I hope you've been keeping my better half entertained.'

'Yes.' The barman spoke as though Daley had just managed to get a particularly difficult question right. 'Unfortunately, as you can see, I don't get the chance to look at many pretty customers in this establishment.' He looked wearily at the two old men at the bar. 'More like the chamber of horrors in this place, with a bit of tapping thrown in, of course. Oh, and hugely stimulating conversation, as I'm sure you can imagine.'

Daley paid for the drinks, telling the barman to put the change into the charity jar, which sat on the bar.

'Thank you, sir, an absolute gent. I'm George, by the way.' He extended a meaty paw over the bar for Daley to shake.

'Jim, Jim Daley. I take it my wife has introduced herself?' He looked back over at Liz.

'Liz,' she shouted with a smile.

Daley took the drinks over to the table and sat down facing his wife. She was as stylish as usual, wearing a tight-fitting, short-sleeved blouse, and a pencil skirt made of faded denim that looked old but was probably brand new and had cost a fortune. The laces from a pair of Roman sandals snaked up her tanned calves.

She observed him with her smoky-blue eyes. His dark hair was not as short as usual, while his top shirt button was undone, as was his habit. He looked tired, and she felt a sudden pang of sympathy – a desire to mother him. She leaned over and touched his hand, looking up at him under her arched eyebrows. 'You look as though you've been up all night, darling.' She stroked his hand absently.

'I have, well, just about. I managed a couple of hours' sleep last night. You, of course, look as stunning as ever.' He didn't know how she did it; even just stroking his hand made his pulse race. 'Sorry I'm a bit late. Did you get my text? It's been one hell of a day.'

'Darling, you work too hard. I've been telling you that forever. The lodge is lovely, by the way. You must come up and have a gander.'

He sat back in his seat, removing his hand from the table and from her caress.

'Aw,' she said, her bottom lip thrust out in an affected pout, 'are you missing me?'

'You might as well know I'm not all that chuffed you're staying with Mark and not me. We might be away from home, but there's plenty of the usual suspects here on this investigation, know what I mean?' He looked straight at her, clearly irritated.

'Oh, I might've known that would be a problem. I simply thought that you and the boys would be in the hotel in the town, and you wouldn't want me there getting in the way. After all, you are working, and this is just a jolly for me.'

Daley had now crossed his arms, and he took a few moments to answer her, during which time he looked out of the window at the loch and the hills behind. 'You know

I can't stand Mark, Liz. You must've realised I wouldn't be happy, you choosing to stay in the lap of luxury with him, while I'm kicking my heels in the local fleapit. Anyway, why can't he bring his own wife? How does she feel about you pair jetting about all over the place? Not great, I'll bet.' He grabbed the pint glass angrily and quaffed a few mouthfuls.

'Oh, we *are* in bad trim.' Liz was now leaning back in her seat against the wood-panelled wall, her smile replaced with a been-here-before frown of bored resignation.

'Liz, I can't stand that cu—' – he remembered where he was in time – 'your brother-in-law, and he hates me, so why jolly all the way down here with him, when you know I'm up to my neck in a serious investigation? Sometimes I feel you're just trying to rub my nose in it – after all that's happened and everything.' He looked pointedly at the floor, his head slightly shaking, as though he was reliving one of her infidelities in high definition.

'Because the chance turned up. Because I needed a break. Because Mark's a good laugh. For all sorts of reasons. You and I need to talk, really.' She leaned over and grabbed his hand, this time holding it tightly.

'If you've chosen right here, right now for my Dear John moment, don't bother.' His face was starting to burn. 'I wondered why you were so anxious to talk to me. I mean, you usually can't be bothered spending more than ten minutes in my presence, and that's in our own house.'

'Me? Me not bother about you?' Her face was a picture of indignation. 'I'm there for you all the time, but you're too busy staring at corpses, or trying to bring about the downfall of some old lag, or whatever it is you call them.'

He looked away again, this time at a painting on the wall: a clichéd Scottish landscape, complete with baying stag. 'Let's keep this civil.' He had lowered his voice, a hunch telling him that the other occupants of the pub were all ears. 'I might have time for dinner or something later, but this is neither the time nor the place for one of our arguments. This town is the mother of all gossip holes, and I'm trying to lead a murder investigation, so I'm quite high profile just now.' He looked at her pleadingly, willing her to understand.

'When are you *not* heading up some investigation?' Liz had no intention of keeping her voice down. 'I remember my poor mother warning me what it would be like being married to a policeman.'

'Oh please, not your mother again.' He raised his eyes to the ceiling.

'Why not? She was right: shit job, shit pay, shit life.' Liz recrossed her legs, folded her arms, and looked resentfully out of the window.

They didn't speak for a few minutes, avoiding each other's furtive glances and eavesdropping on a conversation at the bar about some local who had managed to get his manhood stuck in his zip and was only freed by an emergency flight to a Glasgow hospital – something George found hilarious.

'I've been promoted by the way.' His voice was almost a whisper.

'What?'

He had her full attention now, even though her face was still a mask of anger. 'Promoted. I'm a chief inspector now. I only found out this morning.'

She looked at him for what felt like a long time. She knew how much he wanted career advancement, and she felt guilty that it was because of her that he had appeared unlikely to get it. 'That's wonderful, darling.' Her voice was even now, but she still looked troubled.

'I thought you'd be pleased. It's what you've always wanted. Remember Gabby at the tennis club, or Rachel at badminton? Well, now you can tell them your husband's a chief inspector.' He lifted his glass and glugged thirstily. 'Do you want another?' He took her nod as an affirmative and went up to the bar.

Liz looked at her husband. Those were new trousers, but dreadful, the backside was hanging down towards the back of his knees. She wished he wouldn't shop without her. Somehow though, it was hard to change his level of sartorial elegance; clothes that looked fine in the shop, or online, or on somebody else, immediately developed that lived-in look as soon as he put them on. But he did have something – Jim Daley, her husband. He exuded a raw sexiness that was beyond people like Mark, despite all his success, money and style. He was more, she supposed, like mankind was intended to be, as opposed to the well-groomed, fragrant, slightly effeminate creatures that now inhabited popular culture and the fantasies of women. She smiled at him as he sat down, watching as he put both drinks down then pushed her wine glass across the table. 'I am pleased for you, really. I'm worried what it means for us though, you know? I hardly see you as it is. Will this promotion make things worse?'

Daley looked distracted. 'He's one cheeky bastard.' He lifted his eyes and inclined his head to indicate that he was referring to George behind the bar. 'He's asking if you and I can keep it down to a dull roar, says it's affecting his sensitive customers.'

She managed a gulp of her wine before bursting into laughter. 'Darling, you're a natural comedian, do you know that?'

He began to smile too. Her laugh was so infectious; it was one of the first things he had noticed about her. Her eyes crinkled into mirth, transforming her cool languid gaze into a cheeky sexy grin. She had a dirty laugh too, at odds with her refined façade. As always, he felt the familiar tingle of desire when in her company. He laughed.

Later, they stood outside the bar admiring the loch and the hills beyond, watching their myriad shades reflected in the gently rippling water. Liz breathed in the scented evening air. 'It's so mild. I was quite cold at home, but it's as though summer's come early here.' She looked over at Daley.

'It's because of the Atlantic drift. It comes off the Gulf Stream and warms up the coast. I don't think you'll see many palm trees growing naturally anywhere else in Scotland, eh?' He pointed along the esplanade at three of the exotic trees, as their long green leaves ruffled in the gentle sea breeze.

'Hark at the old sea dog.' She took his arm. 'Shall we meet up later for a meal? How about eight at this County Hotel?'

'Better make it half eight. I'll phone and book in case they shut up shop. I probably won't make it until then. What are you going to do now?'

'Oh, probably just go for a stroll. I can get a taxi back to the lodge any time I want. Mark's opened an account with the taxi company … Sorry.' She noted her husband's face darkening considerably at the mention of her brother-in-law's name.

'Do you still love me, Liz?' The question came from nowhere.

She said nothing for a while, looking out over the harbour. 'Of course I do. It's just, well, it's just that we can't go on living this way. I never see you. I'm lonely, Jim, really bloody lonely.'

He stroked her hair and leaned forward, finding her lips with his.

'Wow, it must be the sea air,' she panted as they quit their embrace. 'I must come here more often.'

Behind them, the door to the bar swung open. 'Here' – it was George – 'you'll be frightening custom away with all that. Folk'll think we're a knocking shop.' He beamed at the Daleys. 'Hope I'll see you both again.'

'After the effect your little town's had on my husband, you'll have to fight me off.' Liz laughed.

'Lucky swine.' George gave Daley a friendly smile and disappeared back inside.

'I liked him.' Liz looked up at her husband.

'Me too.'

They kissed again.

12

Daley felt light, as though some huge weight had been lifted from his shoulders. He often felt this way when things were going well with Liz; all his doubts and insecurities about their relationship seemed to disappear. His irritation with people like Mark appeared worn down, rubbed until almost bare. Almost.

His mood was so good that he hardly noticed the walk up Kinloch's Main Street, and onwards to the office. He eschewed the front door, where he saw a couple of familiar faces lurking about – two journalists from Glasgow. Despite his mood, this investigation was weighing on him: he had a murdered woman, her missing friend, not to mention Mulligan.

As soon as he entered the CID room, Scott got to his feet and ushered him into the glass box that served as his office. 'We've got a lead on the missing woman, Jim.' Scott's voice was conspiratorial. 'Well, it's mair factual to say we've got two leads on the missing lassies.'

'You're sounding very mysterious, Brian. Come on, spit it out. I'm in a good mood, so I can take it.'

'Aye, well, taking it and liking it are two different things, Jimmy boy, as we a' know.' Scott rubbed his chin thoughtfully.

'What? You're speaking in riddles, Bri, it's not like you. Straight to the point, that's what I expect from you.' Daley was half joking when he said this, but he could see that something was troubling his DS.

'First of a', Janet Ritchie was spotted in Tarbert yesterday morning, in a blue Audi A3 that matches the make an' model o' the car driven by oor man Mulligan. That's only aboot forty miles away fae here, so they're either away on a jolly or they're on the run. Wid ye no' think so yourself, James?'

'Let's take one step at a time, Brian. I'm sure people travel away from here for all sorts of reasons, and remember there's only one road out and one road in.' Daley was encouraged by this progress, but he wanted to keep things in perspective. He couldn't fathom why Scott looked so preoccupied by this news. 'Who saw them? Somebody local, I take it?'

'Aye.' Scott retrieved his notebook from his inside pocket. 'A Mr Allan, one o' oor boys spoke tae him in a door tae door a while ago. He knows the lassie cos she wiz at school wi' his daughter. He pulled up beside her in the car park, and she gie'd him a wave.'

'Did she seem OK? Nothing unusual?'

'No. He said she smiled and waved. He didna think anything o' it, but why wid he? I've pit an alert oot fir Mulligan's car, an a' ports an' airport notification, so no' so bad, eh?' Scott looked at Daley with a forced smile.

'Progress, indeed. But you're not telling me the whole story, Brian. What else is there?'

'It's aboot oor mutual friend, Inspector MacLeod.'

Daley felt suddenly relieved. He could take the childish behaviour of the recalcitrant Highlander now that the investigation was taking shape, and especially since he was now senior to him in rank. 'What's the little prick said now?'

'No' so much said, mair no' said.' Again Scott looked evasive. However, the look on Daley's face encouraged him to carry on. 'It's like this ... Davie Fraser's boy, what dae ye ca' him?'

'Archie, and he's Davie's nephew, by the way,' Daley corrected.

'Aye, nephew, whatever. When you went fir your wee jaunt he comes up tae me, sorta quietly like, you know?'

'Yes, quietly. And?'

'So, he says tae me that he didna want tae upset you wi' gossip, but he thought he wid run it past me ...'

'Oh no, has somebody found out what happened between me and that horse? I never touched it.' This was Daley's habitual response to some imagined conspiracy.

'Shut up, you, this is serious.'

'Well, spit it out then.'

'Right. Well, apparently yer man MacLeod has been daein' the business wi' this Janet Ritchie – dirty auld bastard.'

It took Daley a few moments to assimilate this information. 'So, let me get this straight, that wee shit MacLeod's been screwing this woman Ritchie, who's twenty-five years younger than him, and a heavy drug user, and basically a parttime prostitute?'

'That's the kinda thing, Jim.' Scott looked at his boss, waiting for the explosion.

Daley's response was a surprise. He threw his head back and began laughing uproariously. 'Brilliant, Brian, just brilliant. That anally retentive arsehole's in the shit now.'

'I think that's what you call a mixed metaphor, Jim.'

'Ask young Archie to come and see me, would you? We'll nail the policeman formally known as Inspector MacLeod right now.' Tears of laughter were spilling down his face. 'Wait until I tell His Majesty – he might even forget the press conference.'

Scott frowned as he went to find Archie Fraser.

'I know I should've let on earlier – when she was first mentioned in connection with the victim – but you know what it's like, sir. Loyalty and all that shit.' Fraser looked at the floor. Having to reveal that MacLeod was having an affair with Janet Ritchie was obviously weighing heavily on him.

'I just wish you'd told me sooner, Archie, though I don't believe that this will have any bearing on the case. I don't suspect weasel face of any crime, other than a spectacular lack of judgement. I'm going to confront him shortly, and I won't mention your name if you don't want me to, but it would add some weight to my accusation. Are you absolutely sure this is true, son?'

'One hundred per cent, sir. He's been spotted by half the staff. He thinks he's being very clever, meeting her on the West Beach where no one's about. You know what this place is like – eyes everywhere. I got told about it first in the County.' Fraser's colour was high; it was not often that a young cop got the opportunity to get his own back on a senior officer who had been tormenting him for nearly a year, though Daley detected no malice in the DC.

'OK, Archie, I might need a statement from you in the near future. Anyway, we've got more to be worrying about at the moment than Inspector MacLeod's peccadilloes. What are you doing just now?'

'I'm just about to go up to Tarbert with one of your Paisley guys, sir. We'll have a poke about and see if we can find out what Mulligan was up to there. Do you think he's a viable suspect, sir?'

'All we have on him at present is the fact that he's disappeared.' Daley smiled. 'And of course that he's friends with Janet Ritchie, but as we know, that doesn't make you a murderer. I want to find him and the girl pronto though.'

'OK, sir.' Fraser got out of his chair. 'If you're finished with me, I better get on. Folk are champing at the bit.'

Daley watched Fraser leave the office, then he rubbed his hands together vigorously. He had thought of calling Donald as soon as he had found out about MacLeod, but decided to speak to the inspector first. He was a colleague after all, no matter how repellent, and Daley had never been in the business of hanging other cops out to dry – not unless they deserved it. He dialled MacLeod's internal number.

'Hello, Inspector MacLeod.' This guy was formal, even in the office.

'Daley here. I want you to come and see me as soon as possible, please.'

'What?' MacLeod sounded instantly irritated. 'If you want me to run to you like a lapdog now you've got a promotion, you can think again. I'm getting some much needed paperwork done here. I'm still Sub-Divisional Commander, so if you want to speak to me you can report to my office.'

'I want to talk to you about Janet Ritchie. I'm sure I don't need to elaborate any further.'

The line went dead, and within a minute MacLeod appeared in the CID office. He sat down opposite Daley in the chair recently vacated by Fraser. His face was ashen, and he bore none of his trademark arrogance.

'Whatever you've heard is not true.' He looked darkly at Daley. 'This place is a nightmare. If you've got any kind of status at all, they'll come crawling out of the woodwork to try and put you down – fucking bastards. They hate anyone who's not local. You wait, they'll have you in their sights too.'

Daley noted that his voice was even more accented than usual, he hissed his Ss like a spitting snake, his poison the vitriolic hatred of the people he was in charge of policing. 'It wasn't a local who informed me of your – relationship – it was a police officer, if you must know.'

'That big ginger shite, Fraser, no doubt,' he said and muttered some curse in what Daley assumed must be Gaelic. 'I should've despatched him back up the road. He's totally unsuited to the CID. Just you wait till I get my hands on him.'

Veins were prominent on MacLeod's forehead, his fists clenched on the desk.

'You'll shut up and listen to me, MacLeod. I've not mentioned this to anyone other than DS Scott. First, I want you to confirm or deny that you have some kind of relationship with this young woman. Then, if the answer is in the affirmative, I want you to explain to me what the fuck you thought you were doing, and why, when you found out that she was beginning to feature prominently in this investigation, you didn't see fit to come and tell me – like anyone with any sense would have done.'

'It's not what you think, Daley. It's my business. Nothing to do with this investigation at all.' He stood up and thumped the desk. 'Can a man have no privacy in his life?'

Daley got out of his chair too. 'Sit down, MacLeod, and remember where you are.' Furtive glances were already being cast towards the glass box.

Both men sat down, and Daley spoke again, in more measured but no less stringent tones. 'I'm investigating the brutal murder of a woman who was last seen in the company of her best friend, who has herself disappeared. I then find out that the senior officer in the town has been giving her one. You can forgive me for wondering where it will all end.' He stopped and leaned back in his chair, a silent invitation for MacLeod to explain himself.

'You don't understand.' MacLeod's voice was no more than a whisper now, his eyes downcast.

'You're damn right I don't understand, and don't give me the wife-doesn't-understand-me routine.' Daley was beginning to get impatient.

Suddenly MacLeod raised his head and looked right at Daley with his pale blue eyes. 'She's my daughter, Chief Inspector.'

Daley sat motionless for a few moments. MacLeod held his head in his hands, his fingers kneading his balding head.

'May I ask how you end up with a daughter in Kinloch? Apart from the obvious answer of course.'

MacLeod raised his gaze. He looked resigned, tired and unhappy. Daley could see that he was on the verge of tears. There was something else here – something he couldn't fathom. OK, it wouldn't be nice being in MacLeod's position having a daughter with such a chaotic lifestyle, however, it was not unusual for the children of police officers to go off the rails. The son of one of his colleagues was doing time for serious assault, and Brian Scott's daughter had been involved in drugs when she was barely a teenager. No, there was something else going on here.

'I can see your mind working. I know you're a clever detective, Daley, so I don't intend to try and lie to you in any way.' MacLeod's accent was stronger still, a sign that he was under pressure. The same thing happened to Donald when he was stressed; the affected Kelvinside drawl soon took on the guttural twang of Glasgow's East End.

'I can see that something's troubling you, Inspector MacLeod, and if it's of a personal nature then I feel for you, and I'll do my level best to help you, as I would any colleague, but if, in any way, what you're clearly holding back affects this investigation, I demand that you tell me immediately what impact it is having, or is going to have. I realise you'll have loyalties to your daughter, but this is a murder inquiry and Janet is the best friend of the victim. For all I know she may herself be in danger.'

'Do you think I don't know that?' MacLeod shouted. 'I do have some police experience myself, no matter what *you* think of me.'

'I promise you I'll do all I can to keep your name out of this, and that includes informing my superior – on my word, no matter what *you* think of *me*.' Daley's voice was calm. Whatever it was that MacLeod had to tell him, he needed to find out as soon as possible.

'As you are no doubt aware,' said MacLeod, 'my daughter is less than I could have wished for. Her mother and I were close when I was a young beat cop in Glasgow. She was a nurse at the Royal Infirmary.' MacLeod was looking into the middle distance, reliving the past through his mind's eye. 'I got posted up to Oban, I'd never really wanted to work in Glasgow, and I was homesick, I suppose. Anyway, we lost touch. She'd visited me on a few occasions, but she liked the city life. That's why I was so surprised to bump into her here, not long after I arrived. I hadn't set eyes on her for over thirty years.'

'Obviously that wasn't the only surprise she had in store,' Daley said gently.

'No, indeed. She told me about Janet – not straight away, you understand, but after a while. She and our daughter barely spoke. She hoped that when I was introduced to her as her father it may bring them back together. Janet, I learned, had always been a bit of a handful, which is why her mother moved from Glasgow to a village near Lochgilphead when she was young. She thought that rural life may improve things.' He looked at Daley. 'They ended up here because of her mother's work. Do you have any children?'

'No, I don't,' said Daley with no expression, anxious for MacLeod not to lose the thread. 'It must have come as a real shock to you.'

'I don't know what kind of man you are, Chief Inspector, but I had always wanted to have children. My wife is unable to, you see.' His gaze drifted again. 'When I found out I had a girl, well, I was thrilled, despite the difficulties it presented. We all have a past, do we not?' He looked frankly at Daley.

'Did you tell your wife?'

'Therein lies the problem. I didn't. I always meant to, but …' He sounded choked, almost as though he might burst into tears.

'Go on.' No matter how hard these revelations were for MacLeod, Daley had to find out if they were relevant to the inquiry; otherwise, regardless of their nature, they were none of his concern.

'When I found out what a thoroughly detestable human being Janet was, I couldn't bring myself to tell Mary, and possibly ruin our relationship too.' Tears were now in his eyes.

'How do you mean detestable, Charles?' Daley used the man's first name by way of encouragement, letting him know that he sympathised.

'Och, she is all I despise in life: a drug addict, a whore, a fucking opportunist. It didn't take me long to suss her out, let me tell you. A fucking chancer, prepared to open her legs for money or drugs. That's what the only child I have is like. You name it: crack, cocaine, speed, GHB, the works. She's a disgrace.'

'She might be a lot of things, but her record is pretty clean. Nothing for three years. You'd have thought someone with her lifestyle would …' One look at MacLeod answered his question before he had asked it.

171

'Yes, I have covered up for her, I know what you're thinking. She was blackmailing me, her and that bastard Mulligan. I've been a fool, Chief Inspector Daley, a fucking fool.'

'How much have you covered up?' The tone of Daley's voice had hardened slightly.

'Bits and pieces. Turned a blind eye to soft drugs and some of the goings-on in that bar. Nothing serious. You know yourself, the whole world's mad with narcotics. I couldn't have stopped them even if I had the manpower and the courts behind me, which I don't.'

Daley rubbed his face with his left hand. He felt as though he'd been awake for weeks. This was the last thing he'd expected this investigation to throw up. 'What form did the blackmail take? I'm assuming it was pretty bad if you went to such lengths to keep her sweet.'

Silence.

'I'll ask you again, Inspector MacLeod: in what way were you blackmailed?'

'I want your word, Daley – your word – that this will go no further. I promise you, anything I've done has no bearing on this murder inquiry.'

'And?' Daley drummed the table impatiently.

'I had a brief affair – a fling, nothing more. My daugh— Janet found out. The usual stuff: threatened to tell Mary, call headquarters, the bitch.'

'Who did you have the affair with?'

'I've told you that I had an affair, is that not enough, man?'

'You've already told me enough to see the end to your career. I've never come across such wilful stupidity in my life. All you had to do was admit to your wife that you had an affair, and that would've put a stop to the pair of them. You didn't have the balls. Much easier to condone illegal drugs and prostitution right under your nose. Tell me who you had the affair with, or I swear I'll pick up this phone and dial Complaints and Discipline right now.'

When it came, the revelation was enough to rock even the unshockable Daley. 'It was Izzy Watson. Izzy Watson,' he repeated, as though this revelation had come as a surprise to himself. 'Now you know. But I swear to you, I had nothing to do with her death. You've got to believe me, Daley, please. For fuck's sake, man, help me.' MacLeod broke down completely.

'You've got a big heart, Jim, I'll gie you that.' Scott was shaking his head ruefully. 'It was obvious the man wiz a snake, but I didna expect him to turn a blind eye tae drugs dealers an' shagging prozzies.'

'I know it's a risk, Brian, but I don't think he's involved in this murder, no matter what a tit he's been. He's not to leave his house though – he has a pretty good motive after all, so I've stuck a car outside – just in case he thinks the unthinkable. There but for the grace of God and all that, you know?'

'I canna imagine anyone wi' his experience being so stupid. So, he's reporting tae you twice a day until we get this sorted?' Scott looked at Daley with dark-ringed eyes.

'There's no way we can cover this all up, but we can try to get the murder solved, and then he can try to sort out his personal life. Can you imagine what Donald would do?

End of career: full stop. No wonder he was so resentful when I arrived.' Daley rubbed his eyes. What a day, and it wasn't even over yet. He had to meet up with Liz, when he felt more like crawling into bed. 'Get yourself back to the hotel, Brian. I'm meeting herself for a meal. Is everything OK here? Nightshift and all that?'

'Aye, all sorted.' Scott was pulling on his jacket. 'Two o' oor guys, and two o' theirs' o'ernight. Still no sign o' Mulligan or young Miss Ritchie, but they'll turn up. Half the country's looking for them. C'mon, you an' me'll maybe get a dram afore your good lady arrives.'

The bar in the County Hotel was busy. Daley reckoned the good people of Kinloch knew that most of the investigation team were staying at the hotel and there would be a likelihood of juicy gossip to be gleaned over a pint or two.

'The usual, big man?' Scott was already threading his way through the throng of drinkers at the bar, who looked on with the collective interest of a cackle of hyenas.

'Aye, please, Brian, and make it a large one.' Daley looked for a table, and was amazed to find one – the same table he and Fraser had occupied the night before. It seemed like weeks ago to the fatigued inspector.

'A pint o' heavy an' a large Springbank, hen,' Scott shouted at the young girl who was behind the bar. Expensive tastes, he thought as he searched the back pocket of his trousers for his old leather wallet. A tall thin youth was eyeing him from his bar stool. 'Ur you no' too wee tae be the polis?' The young man's slurred words and half-closed eyes bore testament to the fact that he was seriously pissed.

'You're no' too wee tae get a belt in the mouth, you cheeky wee ...' Scott didn't have time to add the expletive.

'Right, that's it, Hughie – oot! And never mind your pint. I've warned you aboot that gob o' yours, an' noo you've had the good sense tae wind up the CID. Well, hell mend ye!' A bustling woman had appeared behind the bar, and was now busy pouring the bemused youth's drink into a sink under the counter.

'Gaun yersel'.' Scott directed this hearty appraisal at the new barmaid. 'Can I ask how you all know I'm the polis anyway?'

'I wiz watchin' you this efternoon on the telly, an' anyhow, you can always spot the rozzers. Is that no' right, Mandy?' She turned to a younger barmaid, who acknowledged this fact with a grunt as she poured a second helping of malt whisky into a small glass from a pewter measure, her tongue sticking out with concentration. 'My name's Annie. I'm kind o' chief bottle washer aroon' here. The drinks are on the hoose by the way – tae celebrate Mr Daley's good news.' She raised a glass and her voice to the new chief inspector who was regarding the scene with mild surprise and no little amusement. 'Allow you, Mr Daley – you've no' been here a couple o' days, an' you've got a promotion. They'll likely make ye a chief constable if ye find oot who murdered that poor lassie.'

'Trust me' – Scott was now collecting the drinks from Annie's colleague – 'that's no' goin' tae happen.'

'Oh, whoot a pity.' Mandy held her hand to her mouth. 'Does that mean yous are gein' up tryin' tae find the murderer?'

'No.' Scott winked at Annie. 'He's never going tae be a chief constable.' He turned and made his way back through the revellers standing at the bar, the drinks clasped in front of him in a manner familiar to any drinker.

'Noo,' Annie addressed no one in particular, 'I widna mind him pumpin' me for information.' She let out a particularly filthy laugh. 'Whoot are you waitin' fir, Hughie? Dae ye want it in writing? Get oot!'

'I see whit ye mean aboot them knowing all your business,' said Scott. 'I mean, how did she know you got a promotion?'

'Because this place processes gossip better than Strathclyde Police. It's just a pity they'll not come forward with information about things that matter.' Daley took a swig of his whisky and worked it around his mouth, better to savour the flavour.

'Ye can hardly blame them' – Scott's voice was almost a whisper – 'wi' that prick in charge doon here. I widna have much faith in the police either.'

'That's another twenty pounds ontae the account, sir.' The taxi driver was parking outside the County Hotel. 'We had tae pick your good lady up doon at the point,' he said by way of explanation.

'Don't worry.' Mark's accent only hinted at being Scottish through his public-school vowels. 'There's plenty to go round, my man.' He turned to Liz, who sat beside him in the back seat. 'Is that not right, darling?'

'No, it is not, and I'm not his "good lady".' Liz addressed the rear-view mirror, where she could see the driver's eyes. 'And I'm not your darling, Mark. For goodness' sake, don't be winding up Jim. We got on fine today, don't spoil it.' She looked from the taxi at the castellated frontage of the hotel. Please don't, she thought.

*

'He's just no' the player that Laudrup was.' The detectives were having one of their habitual discussions on the relative merits of various Old Firm players. Daley was about to answer when he spotted Liz and Mark entering the bar. His eyes were immediately drawn to the open neck of her shirt, revealing her cleavage, and he had the familiar feeling – somewhere between feeling faint and lifting off the floor. A number of the locals had noticed her too, and a couple of lads at the bar appraised her with what they thought was unobtrusive elbow-nudging. She searched the bar standing on her toes, then waved at her husband when she spotted the two men sitting near the back of the room. 'Over here, Mark.' She tugged at the sleeve of his Italian leather jacket as she made her way over to the detectives' table.

Scott eyed her progress. She was a beautiful woman, of that there was no doubt; likeable too, with an easy-to-talk-to manner and good sense of humour. He was sometimes very angry with her though, especially when he saw the negative effect that her actions had on his mate, Jim Daley. A mate: he supposed that was how he saw the big man beside him. They'd first worked together eleven years ago, and had instantly hit it off. Both of them had been detective sergeants then, and while Daley had risen – albeit painfully slowly – through the ranks, Scott had reached the limit of his ability and ambition. He had joined the police to be a policeman, not some kind of diplomatic administrator, drowning in reams of unnecessary paperwork, having to meet quotas on this and targets on that. No, being a detective sergeant was hard enough, and that's where he intended to stay; if he thought about Daley's sudden promotion at all, it was only that he was pleased for him, and that he hoped it would not mean their separation as a team.

Aye, she's bonnie right enough, he thought. He smiled as Liz sat on a small stool across the table from him and Daley. Scott's expression changed as Mark took his seat, with that permanent sneer playing across his lips. That cunt.

Mark Henderson always looked the same to Daley: smug, arrogant, elegant, tanned, fit, tall – around the same height as the Chief Inspector himself – rich, good-looking. The superlatives just went on and on. He had the louche, easy manner of the upper classes and would have looked much more at home at the Henley Regatta, or standing by the Grace Gates at Lord's, rather than here in the faded splendour that was the County Hotel. His family were ancient, if somewhat minor, Scottish aristocracy, and it showed.

'Jim, my good man. How nice to see you again, especially in such' – Mark looked around the room with exaggerated disdain – 'exalted surroundings.' He looked at Scott. 'And with your faithful retainer too – how touching.'

'When can I deck this bastard, Jim?' Scott was smiling, but Daley knew he was deadly serious.

Liz intervened to change the subject. 'Brian, how are you? What a lovely little town this is. It's such a shame you're both here under such sad circumstances.' She smiled her open smile.

'I wouldn't worry too much, Lizzie. Some yokel bint from what I can gather.' Mark was in fine form. 'The taxi driver insisted on telling me all about it. An absolute bore if you ask me.'

'I wisna' aware anybody wis asking you.' Scott was up to the challenge.

Daley wasn't surprised that Mark had turned up, though this didn't stop the disappointment he felt. After a shaky start earlier that afternoon, he thought that he and Liz had been closer than they had been for quite some time. Maybe it had been the change of bar with its larger-than-life landlord, or perhaps just the change of scene. In any case, he had remembered all over again how much he loved her. He was determined to treat the appearance of his brother-in-law as a minor irritation. 'When would you like to eat, Liz?' He leaned over the table and held his wife's hand.

'Asap.' Mark said it as one word. 'I'm bloody famished. Any chance of a decent G and T before we partake in whatever swill there is on offer here?'

'Oh, Mark.' Liz looked embarrassed. 'I thought ...'

'She thought she wanted tae spend some time wi' her husband, an' no' you hangin' on like the posh gooseberry fae hell. Get it?' The smile had left Scott's face as he glared at Mark, who affected not to hear what he had said.

'How territorial these rozzers are, Lizzie.' He got up from the table. 'I'm for a large one. How about you?'

She mumbled in the affirmative as Mark made his way to the bar, shouting impatient 'excuse me's to the locals obstructing his route. Liz gave Daley an apologetic look. 'He just turned up in the taxi. I was walking down by the loch, and the cab just appeared from nowhere. I can't work out how he knew where I was. He's been drinking most of the afternoon by the look of things, and you know that makes him more arrogant than usual.'

'Which is quite a feat,' Scott added quickly.

'Don't worry, Liz. I'll handle this.' Daley had spotted the formidable Annie passing en route to collect another pile of empty glasses. He called her over, and covertly whispered in her ear as she leaned over him.

'Aye, no bother. Jeest you leave this tae me.' She stomped purposefully off to the bar, holding what seemed like an unfeasible number of empties between the fingers and thumbs of both hands.

'What was that all about, darling?' Liz looked puzzled. 'It hasn't taken you long to ingratiate yourself with the locals, I must say.'

Up at the bar, Mandy was just about to relieve Mark of the cost of two large gin and tonics, when Annie appeared with a flourish of empty glasses. 'I'm sorry, sir. I'm in charge here, an' it's my opinion that you've had too much tae drink, so I'll need tae ask you tae leave.'

For an instant Mark looked astonished, as though presented with an amazing fact or a chance encounter with a relative he had thought long dead. Slowly though, the reality of the situation dawned on him. 'Listen to me, I'm a paying customer here, and I will not be spoken to by some … some bottom-feeder who neither knows her job nor her place. Now cut along out of the way while this little treasure serves me with my drinks.' He seemed satisfied with this outburst, and beamed haughtily across the bar at Annie.

'Sir' – Annie was now plainly furious – 'I'll ask you again. Please leave the bar. You've had too much tae drink, and I'm no' prepared tae risk the licence of this establishment by serving you.'

'You listen to me, you dried-up old bitch …' He didn't get the chance to finish his sentence. Three large men stood up from their bar stools and crowded around him. The largest man, sporting the tattoo of a Lion Rampant on his thick forearm, thrust his face so close to Mark's that the lawyer could smell the whisky on the man's breath through the haze of wine and gin he had himself consumed. 'You're talkin' tae my wife. Noo, dae whoot she says 'less I take you ootside an' gie ye a hammering ye'll no' forget. Got it? Arsehole.' He poked a sturdy forefinger into Mark's sternum, forcing him to exhale involuntarily. Mark opened his mouth to say something, but instantly thought the better of it. He turned on his heel, muttered something under his breath, and made his way, red-faced, back to Daley's table, leaving a chorus of coarse laughter emanating from the bar. 'Come on, Elizabeth, we're not staying in this dive to be talked down to by Neanderthals. Let's get back to the lodge and get some decent service.' He put his hand on Liz's shoulder.

Annie's refusal to serve Mark had been more entertaining than Daley had thought possible. He had to admire the gall of the man, simply expecting Liz to abandon her husband, and without protest leave with him.

'Mark, I'm with Jim. We're having a meal.' She looked flustered.

'In other words,' Scott interjected, 'dae whit the lady behind the bar asked you, and dae it before I have you arrested for refusing to leave a licensed premises when required to. Tae pit it mair plainly – fuck off.'

Mark's face was like thunder. He hauled his jacket from behind Liz's chair, making her jerk forward suddenly, almost knocking over her drink. 'Bad choice, Lizzie. Bad choice.' He glared at her briefly, then slung his jacket over his shoulder and strode somewhat unsteadily out of the bar.

'An' don't come back!' Annie shouted through the serving hatch. 'Noo, Chick, whoot are ye for?' She resumed normal service as though nothing had happened. 'An' since when did you become my husband? Dream on, big man, dream on.'

'It's at times like this you really hate the smoking ban.' Liz was breathless as she made her head comfortable on Daley's chest.

'Bollocks, it's the best thing that ever happened.' Daley was stroking her hair absently. They had eaten a shared meal of local lobster – which had been delicious – had a few more drinks, then headed up the grand staircase to his room. 'I'll arrange for you to stay here with me. I'll get someone to pick your luggage up from the lodge tomorrow.' When he didn't get a reply he craned his neck forward to look down at his wife, who was already fast asleep. He lay back, satisfied. They'd eaten, chatted easily, and then made love. She had rejected Mark in an obvious way. There was a warmth between them now that had been absent for such a long time. She looked so beautiful as she lay asleep, her breath soft on his skin. Despite his exhaustion and the stress of his day, he felt strangely content. He thought of Michael Watson. He was sleeping alone.

13

The light streaming through Daley's hotel-room window was of a distinctly more dull quality than before. Liz was still sleeping soundly, despite the restless night he had just experienced. He had been sound for the first couple of hours, but on waking in a cold sweat around two thirty he had drifted in and out of sleep. Thoughts about the case, Mark, his promotion, the body of the young victim, Donald: all had crowded in from his subconscious. Insomnia was something he was used to, especially during a difficult case; usually though, he would consign himself to the spare bedroom at home in an attempt not to disturb Liz. Whether it was the sea air, or the change of scene, he noted with pleasure that she seemed as serene as he could remember. Her auburn hair falling over the pillow framed the soft outline of her face; her long lashes were exaggerated by the fact that her eyes were closed. Her left breast was showing above the top of the duvet, displaying a taut brown nipple.

He remembered last night, smiling unintentionally at the memory of carnal pleasure.

A sudden gust of wind rattled the window. He walked over to it and moved the musty net curtains aside, better to see the street below. Even now, at six thirty, there were a few people milling about, most of them huddled into warm jumpers or buttoned-up jackets; a couple of cars and a bus motored up and down the street. The weather had changed. Looking up, he saw the sky was mostly a light grey with small patches of blue visible. The wind was animating the scene, pushing the cloud along – a constantly changing vista. Even the air smelled different: more about the sea, less of the land. The gulls' cries, carried on the restless wind, echoed amongst the tenement buildings that lined Main Street on both sides. Movement below caught his eye. Annie was crossing the street, waving enthusiastically at him. Shit. It seemed that looking out of the window in Kinloch was a spectator sport. He hesitantly waved back, and then let the curtain fall back into place. He gave Liz another admiring glance as he walked into the bathroom to run a bath.

Shaving in the steam he wondered where the investigation would lead today. He was sure that Mulligan was pivotal in the whole sordid business. MacLeod was merely a hapless accessory – a witless one at that. Still, he couldn't afford to risk his own career in an attempt to cover up for the irascible inspector. Things had gone too far; a crime – the most serious of all – had been committed. MacLeod could at least have done something to curb the drug-taking and casual prostitution that was conducted nightly in Pulse. He had shown little contrition during his confession the day before. Initially, Daley had felt some sympathy for him – the long-lost daughter turns into a newly discovered nightmare – but it had rapidly evaporated on discovering that MacLeod had been more concerned with saving his own skin than atoning for his astonishing lapses in judgement as the area's senior police officer.

Liz slept on as he dressed, brushed his hair, and took a moment to appraise the result of his ablutions in the full-length mirror on the front of the wardrobe. His belly was already doing its best to encroach over his waistband, and peep through the buttons of his white shirt. Maybe he would just have cereal and coffee for breakfast.

Scott was already at his borrowed desk within the Kinloch CID department when Daley arrived. He looked rough: bloodshot eyes, tousled hair and the same shirt and suit he had been wearing the day before. 'Morning, Jim,' he said throatily, rubbing his temples at the same time.

'You look as though you've been on the batter all night, Brian. Did you go to a party after last orders?'

'No. Well, sort of. The lassie behind the bar an' me had a few drinks efter closin' time.' He blinked his eyes and yawned. 'She's a nice lassie,' he said through the yawn.

'Mandy, eh? You're a dark horse, Bri. I'd have thought she was a bit too young for you. I suppose you never know.'

'Nah, no' Mandy! She's a wee lassie for fuck's sake.' Scott reached for a packet of cigarettes on the desk, then pushed them away, realising for the umpteenth time that he couldn't smoke in the office. 'Annie. The manager. Aye, she's quite a character.' His laugh quickly transformed itself into a chesty cough, which he tried to banish in a cacophony of throat-clearing and snorting.

'You try to get that lung up and I'll get you a coffee.' Daley walked out into the corridor where a rather superior drinks machine was located. To his further surprise, a bright-looking Fraser was walking towards him – the antithesis of DS Scott, in a crisp white shirt under a newly pressed suit.

'I'm pleased to see my team are taking this investigation so seriously. Not even eight and my core men are already in place. Do you want a coffee, son?'

Somewhat predictably, Fraser began to beam red. 'Eh, yes, sir. Tea, please, if you don't mind. White wi' two sugars.'

Daley pressed the relevant buttons, fed in the appropriate coins, and, as the first Styrofoam mug began to fill, turned to the young DC. 'I want you to liaise with the nightshift and see what, if anything, happened last night, while I try to sober up our intrepid DS. You're looking pretty fresh this morning. My new tie too, I see.' He smiled benignly at Fraser.

'No bother, sir. I'll get it back to you. Do you think we're getting close with this Mulligan guy? It's all a bit weird, you know, him disappearing an' all. Nothing up in Tarbert last night. People know him because he goes in and out on his boat, but nothing new. Nobody's seen him since our last witness.'

'You know him better than me, Archie. You must've come across him on your travels down here, no?'

'Well, yes and no, sir.' Fraser cleared his throat and moved nervously from foot to foot. 'He wasn't exactly welcoming when I went in for a pint when I first came down here. No' really surprising, when you consider what's been going on in there.'

'More of that later, Archie.' Daley looked rueful. 'He seems a bit of a mystery man, our Peter Mulligan.'

Scott's head appeared out of the CID office. He spoke through a continuous coughing fit. 'It's some guy called Flynn tae speak tae you, Jim ... Says he's the harbour master ... Are you fir taking it, or do ye want me tae deal wi' it? Mornin', son.' He turned to Fraser. 'That's one hell o' a tie ye've got there.' He burst into another paroxysm of recalcitrant phlegm. 'Look after this man, Archie, while I attend to our caller, and bring in the coffee, will you?' he shouted over his shoulder.

Daley picked up the receiver on Scott's desk. 'Good morning, Mr Flynn. Jim Daley here. How can I help you?'

'Aye, guid mornin', *Chief* Inspector. I hear congratulations are in order.'

'Thank you, Mr Flynn. A surprise to us all, let me assure you.' He fell silent, hoping that Flynn had something more to say.

'Oh aye, tae the point, Chief Inspector, tae the point. I thought I wid let you know, there's been a report of a pleasure boat adrift in the Sound. A passing yachtsman called it in to Clyde Coastguard a few minutes ago. If the identification number and description are correct, it's a boat belonging to a ... local man.'

'Very interesting, Mr Flynn, and thanks for letting me know. But I don't see how this affects me, at the moment, at any rate?'

'Oh, well, the cruiser, it belongs to a man named Mulligan. Peter Mulligan. It's just, well, you must have an idea what Kinloch is like now. I'd heard you were looking for him.'

Daley took a few moments to assimilate the information. 'So, what do we do now, Mr Flynn? I take it this vessel will have to be checked out? Obviously I'm interested.' He let Flynn outline the procedure.

'The local lifeboat has been mobilised, Chief Inspector. Would you like to have a police presence aboard? She'll be underway shortly.'

'Oh yes, Mr Flynn. In fact, ask them to give us five minutes. Will there be room for three?'

'Aye, aye, I shouldna think that'll be a bother. I'll speak tae the coxswain noo. See yous shortly.'

The door swung open as Scott and Fraser made their way through from the drinks machine.

'Sorry, chaps, I hope you have your sea legs on this morning. We're going for a sail, and we've got to rush.'

'Eh, sail? Whit are ye on aboot noo?'

'C'mon, Brian. The very thing for a hangover.'

The beverages were placed untouched on the desk as the three men left the office for the harbour, Scott muttering a string of impressive oaths on the way.

The scene on Kinloch's second pier was one of organised chaos. Men in bright orange RNLI survival suits darted to and fro with ropes, life-saving equipment, unmarked boxes and various pieces of technical equipment. The deep throb of a powerful diesel engine added tempo to the scene, even blocking out the ubiquitous cries of the gulls that gravitated to the harbour in search of food from the meagre assembly of fishing boats.

Flynn was standing by the lifeboat on the quayside as the three detectives pulled up in their unmarked car. He was wearing a robust-looking fleece with HARBOUR

MASTER emblazoned in bold gold lettering over his chest. 'Gentlemen, guid morning. Yous have picked a fine day for a sail. Hang on there, and I'll introduce you tae the coxswain o' this fine vessel.'

Daley recalled how thick his accent was, and just how neat the harbour master was too. The white of his cap contrasted sharply with the gloom that had now descended over Kinloch despite the continuing strength of the strong breeze. He noticed also that Scott looked a pale grey colour as he stared over the side of the quay to the loch below; itself a more dark, impenetrable shade than in the last couple of days. 'All right, Bri? You're looking a bit green about the gills there.' He slapped his old colleague vigorously on the back, inducing another coughing fit in the detective sergeant.

'Are ye sure ye need me here, Jim? I mean, I'm sure I'd be better employed back at the ranch, you know? Cover for you?'

'No, don't worry, Brian. Just enjoy the trip. I've got a feeling about this.'

'Well, if you're sure, boss,' said Scott, looking doubtfully at the restless water of the loch.

Fraser was on the phone to one of the DCs who comprised the day-shift investigating team. They were busy ploughing through the mountain of records, interview statements, CCTV footage and other nebulous strands of the investigation, which had, as yet, yielded little positive information. The young DC had been assured by one of the lifeboat crew that they were unlikely to lose mobile signal on this trip, and in any event they could be contacted via the boat's radio system, or internet comms link, should anything vital arise. He felt a bit foolish. When Daley had asked him questions about the character of the locals, he hadn't been much help. He clearly wasn't paying enough heed to the surroundings he found himself in. Sometimes Fraser felt that Inspector MacLeod was not merely torturing him with jibes about being hopeless and unsuited to his current position; perhaps there was some truth in it and he did lack the intuitive qualities necessary to be an effective CID officer. He tried to banish these thoughts from his mind as he walked over to the DCI and apprised him of the status quo back at the station.

Scott eyed the whole situation with something more than trepidation. He had drunk much more than was good for him the night before, which was not an unusual occurrence. However, he was more used to assuaging his hangover with a greasy fry-up followed by a couple of pints of coffee; certainly not taking to the high seas, an element on which he had never been comfortable. He knew enough about the sea to realise that the agitated quality of the waves here in the harbour was likely to be much worse when they reached the Sound. He stroked the stubble on his chin as a seagull, swooping low over the assembled throng, deposited a large watery shit on the shoulder of his jacket. He turned to his colleagues, who were already in the first throes of mirth. 'If any of yous says this is lucky, I'll stick my toe up yer arse.' Moments later, he saw the funny side himself, laughed ruefully and strengthened his resolve ahead of his impending nautical odyssey.

A rotund, ruddy-faced man appeared, sporting the grey-and-orange survival suit of the RNLI, augmented by a peaked officer's cap similar to that worn by Flynn.

'This is John Campbell, coxswain of this fine vessel,' announced Flynn. 'Born on the seventh wave, eh, Johnnie?'

Ignoring this warm introduction, Campbell held out his hand. 'Which one of you is DCI Daley?' They shook hands and exchanged introductions, Scott somewhat less enthusiastically than his superior. 'Ah, young Fraser. I hope you're still working on your court technique. Poor effort the last time we met, don't you think?'

Both Daley and Scott looked confused. Fraser explained: 'As well as being lifeboat coxswain, Mr Campbell is also a local lawyer.'

'C'mon, old chap. Managing Partner of Campbell, Hope and Mason, Solicitors, Notaries Public and Estate Agents. Though since the demise of poor Stuart – Mason, that is – the property side of our business is sadly on the wane. Now, would you slip on these waterproofs and lifejackets' – he indicated to a crewman carrying an armful of garments – 'and we'll make haste to sea, don't you think?' With that he breezed off, shouting a request to another member of the crew, who hurried off to do his master's bidding.

'I'd expected some auld sea dog tae be daein' the job. This guy's mair like a coxcomb than a coxswain.' Scott was clearly unimpressed.

'You know, you never cease to amaze me,' Daley addressed his DS, who was still trying to remove the bird dropping from his jacket with a white tissue, the name 'County Hotel' emblazoned upon it. 'For a man who never reads a book, where do you find words like coxcomb?'

'Well, that, Jim, would be telling.' Scott winked.

Flynn, clearly put out by Campbell's dismissive attitude towards him spoke up. 'Aye, in days gone by the lifeboat wiz manned by fishermen. Usually the auldest skipper got the job o' coxswain. Generations o' families served afore the mast. No' noo.' His face spoke volumes. 'As ye know, there's precious few fishermen left, and those that are wid rather be in the pub during their spare time than hangin' aboot on call for the lifeboat. Pity, really.' He stared into space wistfully.

'Whit next? Lawyers takin' tae the sea? I'll tell you this, I've never been impressed wi' a lawyer in my life. I hope he knows whit the fuck he's daein'.' Scott's question was querulous.

'Oh aye, he knows whoot he's daein' a' right, he's an officer in the RNR tae. The Royal Naval Reserve.' He answered their blank looks at the acronym. 'The trouble is, nowadays being on the lifeboat's mair o' a middle-class thing, like a badge o' honour. A' these posh buggers have yachts, an' they're a' jostling fir a place on the boat. Wan o' the toon's other solicitors is involved tae, he's the deputy cox. But believe it, or believe it no', they'll no' sail on the boat thegither. It's a wile carry-on, right enough.' Campbell shook his head in apparent disbelief. 'Right, gentlemen, let's be having you. On and out, on and out.'

'I'm no' goin' tae enjoy this one bit,' moaned Scott as Flynn helped him to clip his lifejacket on. 'Nah, no' in the slightest.'

The bridge of the lifeboat was much more high-tech than Daley had expected. Two black high-backed seats that wouldn't have been out of place on the space shuttle dominated the front of the cabin. An impressive array of dials, levers and LED screens, along with two large computer monitors, faced John Campbell and his deputy, who were, Daley assumed, responsible for steering the boat. Behind them, on a lower seat facing the side of the craft sat another crewman, staring at a huge monitor, which to Daley's untrained eye was displaying similar geographical information to that he had seen in the harbour master's office.

The three police officers, now thoroughly out of their comfort zone, held on grimly to chunky handrails. Other members of the crew moved about the vessel with the easy gait of those accustomed to the rolling nature of sea craft.

'As you can appreciate, gentlemen' – the coxswain's voice was amplified via loudspeakers built into the bridge – 'we are unable to ramp up the power until we're out of the harbour area and clear of the loch. As soon as we pass the island there' – he gestured airily with one hand – 'we will be able to take her up to forty knots plus.'

'Aye, just fantastic,' Scott mumbled, his face now bordering on a shade of lime green.

Daley leaned forward to peer out of the bridge windows. The island at the mouth of the loch looked like an oversized bread roll. He could see that the water beyond looked choppier, and he suppressed a smile as he sneaked a look at his DS clinging manfully to his handrail.

Campbell's voice boomed out from the loudspeakers. 'Now, from the position reported earlier this morning, I reckon that it will take us around thirty minutes to locate the craft. I must warn you that the weather is deteriorating somewhat, and once we get beyond the island it might get a tad rough, so I may have to ask you to take a seat and get strapped in. I'll see how we go.'

They were now level with the island. Daley could see what he thought was a sheep grazing halfway up what appeared to be a sheer cliff and mentioned it to Campbell.

'Too much time spent in the city, my good man. That sheep's a mountain goat. Ancient beasts, you know. Probably introduced to this area by the first hunter-gatherers. Fascinating! Run wild now, of course. Ah, hang on, chaps!' He pushed a large lever located in front of him. The tone of the engines changed; they could now be felt through the steel floor of the vessel. The prow of the lifeboat rose into the air as the trim altered, and they began to pick up speed more rapidly than Daley thought possible at sea. Of course, his experience of the ocean was mainly confined to the Clyde steamers of his childhood and the odd Channel ferry or trip on Mark's yacht. This feeling was much more exhilarating, even though the boat was now bouncing through the waves, shaking up those onboard like ice in a cocktail shaker.

He saw Campbell lean over to the man beside him, who began to unbuckle his seatbelt. 'As I expected, the swell here's a bit lively. Gareth here will help you into the chairs behind you, and get you strapped in. The last thing I need is a lifeboat full of injured bobbies.'

The crewman helped them into the seats located just behind the bridge in a wide corridor. As he strapped Scott in, Daley noticed the DS whisper in the ear of the lifeboat man, who smiled and disappeared, only to return a few moments later with something that looked like a small cardboard potty, the type provided for elderly patients in hospital.

Scott contemplated the receptacle for a few seconds, then retched violently into it, splashes of vomit dotting his orange lifejacket. Fraser, sitting next to him, wrinkled his nose in obvious distaste and leaned away from his colleague, in case he too benefited from the return of last night's over-indulgence. The smell of stale alcohol filled the vessel.

'Fuck this' seemed an adequate summation of events as far as Scott was concerned, as he wiped his face with a large paper hankie provided by the attentive Gareth.

'You all right, mate?' Gareth's English accent was discernible through the general hubbub.

'I'll tell you when I'm back in Paisley, son,' was the pallid policeman's reply.

The engines suddenly quietened, and the lifeboat slowed perceptibly. Daley turned in his harness and looked towards the bridge where Campbell was unbuckling his seat belt.

'Unscheduled stop, gentlemen,' he said as an aside to the three trussed policemen. 'Have you met Hamish, our local seer?'

'Oh yes.' Daley nodded vigorously. 'I don't understand, though. What does he have to do with all this?'

'He's just waved us down. I'm going to have a quick word with him. He's got a working boat, keeps his hand in with crabs, shellfish and the like. Do you want to come up top and see what he wants? It won't take long. He's a good old buffer – knows much more than people think.'

'Of that I have no doubt.' Daley was struggling to unfasten his belt. 'I'll come with you.'

Scott was rubbing his forehead with his left hand, still looking deathly. 'If yous don't mind, I'll jist stay here an' try and stop my guts from ending up in a bucket.'

'I'm OK, sir.' Fraser was still keeping a considerable distance between himself and the DS. 'I don't want to abandon a colleague in his time of need.'

Daley released himself from the bonds of his safety belt and followed Campbell up a small gangplank and out onto the deck. Light drizzle brushed his face. The sea was a deep grey colour, and he could see a bank of darker sky to his left, just above the horizon. The water lapped noisily against the sides of the lifeboat, as a much smaller vessel chugged slowly towards them in a blue pall of diesel fumes. It looked like a large rowing boat, onto which a square wooden cabin had been incongruously grafted. The registration number KH213 was painted in peeling black letters on the prow of the craft. Hamish's head popped up from beneath the cabin canopy, his tanned face distinctive under a well-worn Breton cap.

'Ahoy there, Hamish!' Campbell shouted from the bow of the lifeboat. 'What can we do for you?'

The engine fumes from the venerable vessel caught Daley in the back of the throat, and momentarily he thought he might retch. He swallowed, took a deep breath and allowed the nausea to pass. The sensation of movement on the lifeboat was much more pronounced than he had ever experienced at sea, and he was glad that Liz's presence in the County the previous evening had ensured that he hadn't over-indulged.

Hamish threw a coil of rope at the lifeboat, which Campbell caught in the casual manner of the accustomed sailor. 'Mornin', Mister Campbell, Chief Inspector. How yous daein'?'

'Fine, Hamish, fine.' Daley noticed how Campbell, despite being a Scot, pronounced the name with a flat vowel, in the way of the Scottish upper classes; an unconscious imitation of their social peers south of the border. 'More importantly, what can we do for you, old chap?'

For a heartbeat Daley thought the old fisherman wasn't going to answer; he wondered if he had even heard the coxswain. Slowly though, Hamish turned his head, and seemed to be sniffing the air. 'Aye, there somethin' no' right, Mister Campbell. Can ye no' smell the taint in the air?'

Campbell raised his head, as though he too was about to carry out an olfactory assessment. He stopped though, thinking better of it. 'What do you mean, Hamish? None of this mystic stuff. Have you seen something? We're here to find a small cabin cruiser that's been reported to be drifting unmanned off Thomson's Point. Have you spotted it at all?'

'No, no, canna say that I have. But ye don't need tae see the moon tae know it's there, dae ye noo?' Hamish flashed the huge beaming smile Daley had first noticed in the harbour master's office.

'Eh, what do you mean exactly?' Campbell looked confused.

'It's a black day, that's a' I'm saying. Ye can feel it in the air.' He raised his head and sniffed, as though illustrating the point. 'Aye, an' the weather's fair comin' in tae.' He turned to Daley. 'I'm willing tae bet you'd still rather be cuddled up tae that lovely wife o' yours in bed, eh, Chief Inspector?'

Daley was stuck for words, however, Campbell saved the day. 'Well, we have to get on, Hamish, and judging by that sky and the weather report we've just taken off the satellite, you'd be well advised to head back to Kinloch now. I don't want to be diverted to come and rescue you, too.'

Daley, who admittedly had little knowledge of nautical etiquette, thought Campbell was being a little high-handed. However, he should have realised that the old man would have a response to this.

'I've spent mair time on the wan wave than you have experience on the sea. Aye, an' I don't need any fancy statalite neither.'

'I'll leave you to be the judge of that, but don't say I didn't warn you. Come on, Chief Inspector, we'll get back underway, and leave this old sea dog to his tricks.' Campbell waved perfunctorily at Hamish and stomped off towards the bridge, with Daley following in his wake. The detective turned round to bid Hamish a farewell. The old man was standing proud at the wheelhouse of the small boat, his hand raised in a middle-fingered salute.

'No' you, Mister Daley. No, no' for you.'

Daley was being strapped back into his seat as he heard the loud chug of Hamish's boat sailing away from the lifeboat and towards Kinloch.

Their vessel was soon ploughing through the waves. From what Daley could see through the bridge windows, heavy rain had started to fall, and the yawing motion of the boat indicated that the sea was much more restless than it had been when they left Kinloch harbour.

Presently, Campbell announced over the tannoy, 'By my reckoning, gents, it will take us about another ten minutes to reach the last known location of the vessel we're looking for. However, such is the fickle nature of time and tide, we are already on the lookout for her. As soon as we find anything, I'll give you a shout, and then you three will come into your own.'

Scott shouted over to Daley, 'I wisna expecting tae be chasing the wreck o' the *Hesperus* when I got up the morn'.' He still looked bilious. 'First that fuckin' press conference, noo this. It's like that Japanese game show – you know the one where they stick scorpions doon their troosers and suchlike. Aye, an' before you get any ideas, you're no' pitting any dangerous insects anywhere near me, never mind my troosers.'

Their laughter was stopped in its tracks by a sudden slowing of the engines and Campbell's voice over the tannoy: 'Gentlemen, we have reached our objective.'

Daley released himself from the harness and walked forward to the bridge of the lifeboat, where Campbell was speaking into a radio microphone. 'Vessel, *Russian Gold*, this is Kinloch lifeboat. Is there anyone aboard?' Daley could see no movement on the small cabin cruiser.

He looked at the coxswain, who tried again. '*Russian Gold*, if you can hear me please show yourselves. We are making ourselves fast to your port side, and will board unless we receive confirmation that all is well and that your vessel is appropriately manned. Over.'

Nothing. Daley gave Campbell a questioning look. 'OK, Chief Inspector, we've fulfilled our legal obligations. There's no response from the vessel and we're now at liberty to board, as I feel she may be a hazard to other shipping. Charlie, signal my intent to Clyde Coastguard, please.' His crewman busied himself on the radio, while Campbell extricated his considerable bulk from his seat.

'So, how do you want us to proceed, Mr Campbell? This is still your domain, after all. Though I'll ask you and your crew to disturb as little on or in the boat as possible, in case it turns out to be a crime scene.'

'Of course, of course. By the same token, I must ask you and your officers to follow my instructions as far as gaining this vessel is concerned. We'll get you some more suitable footwear for a start.'

The ever helpful Gareth appeared with a selection of bright yellow Wellington boots. The three officers donned the boots, and followed Campbell out on deck.

The sky was a lowering grey, and although the sea was not showing itself in angry breakers, the swell was making the thin line of the horizon skew in an alarming way. A light drizzle had already coated their waterproofs. Scott's hair had been pushed back from his face, and was now standing in salt-and-pepper spikes from his head. Fraser was looking at the grey water between the two vessels as three lifeboat men – one of them now on the deck of *Russian Gold* – secured ropes between the lifeboat and the cabin cruiser.

'I'll take the lead, Chief Inspector. I'm technically in charge of both vessels, unless, of course, something happens that should ensure that I relinquish that charge. The lads will secure both vessels as soundly as possible, but I should warn you all that getting down onto her deck will be tricky in these conditions. Are we good to go, gents?' He looked at the three detectives, who showed various degrees of acknowledgement. Scott, unsurprisingly, looking the least willing.

The main problem was that the cabin cruiser was a much smaller vessel than the lifeboat, which meant that each man would have to be lowered from boat to boat, as well as across a gap which, regardless of how well the lifeboat crew had made their lines, changed in width and height quite rapidly.

Campbell explained: 'I'm afraid that we can't lash her right to our side, as we'll end up doing damage to both vessels. Do you follow?' Daley nodded. 'What I recommend is that you watch me and then try to replicate what I do.' With that he made his way to the lifeboat's safety rail, stiffly hefted his left leg over it while leaning on a stanchion, then with equal lack of poise repeated the process with his right leg. 'Now,' Campbell said hesitantly, as he stared at the gap with concentration, perched on the narrow ledge between the safety rail and oblivion. 'One judges the pitch and roll …' He leaned forward, hand outstretched towards the grim-faced lifeboat man below. 'And … off !' He jumped clear of the lifeboat, while making a desperate attempt to grab the hand of his crewman below. Unfortunately, he misjudged his jump, the rapidly rising swell having propelled the smaller vessel upwards and towards him more quickly than he had anticipated. Despite the valiant attempts of his colleague to arrest the fall, Campbell's large bulk hurtled onto him with some force, ending with both lifeboat men writhing on the deck clutching various parts of their anatomy, to many grunts and oaths.

'Fuck me.' Scott eyed the scene with a furrowed brow. 'I'm no' in a hurry to replicate that. If that's the best he can dae, how the fuck am I goin' tae manage?'

'Are you OK, Mr Campbell?' Daley enquired of the stricken coxswain, who was now being helped to his feet by his unfortunate crewman.

'Ah, harrumph.' He brushed himself down. 'Well, you get the general idea. Who's next?' He looked up at the policemen.

Jim Daley was not one to shirk the responsibilities of rank, so he stepped over the rail, positioned himself on the ledge, and looked down at the ever-changing gap. It reminded him of the penny falls he had played at the fair when he was young. Trying to calculate the optimum time to insert a two-pence coin in order that it would fall at the back of the pile, prompting the outpouring of financial reward. He had always been quite good at it. He held his hand out towards the crewman and took the leap of faith.

He had always prided himself, despite his size, on being relatively graceful; he was a good dancer and golfer, and motor skills picked up during these pursuits saw him land squarely on the deck. He breathed out in silent relief.

Fraser managed the jump with some aplomb, judging the rise and fall of the vessels relative to each other perfectly. He landed on deck sure-footedly, barely requiring the assistance of the crewman.

Next, Scott. Daley caught him muttering something about Fraser being more like Rudolf Nureyev as he concentrated on the job in hand. 'Are yous ready?' He turned to Gareth, who was giving advice at his side, and then, without warning, he jumped. Not the exaggerated stride that the others had executed with varying degrees of success, but a full-blown spring, head first, towards the smaller boat. He landed, somewhat fortuitously, on the large bulk of the coxswain, and for the second time in a couple of minutes, the corpulent solicitor struggled on the deck of the cruiser, Scott on top of him muttering a sentence

devoid of anything but expletives. 'Well done, Detective
Sergeant Scott. You reminded me a bit of a Rangers striker
there – beautiful dive.'

Campbell, now back on his feet again, gave the remaining
lifeboat crew the thumbs up and surveyed the deck of the
cabin cruiser. 'Typical of its class, Chief Inspector. This is
the flying bridge.' He gestured at a level above the main
deck, which housed a large wheel and was bordered on
three sides by a slanted windscreen, giving it the look of an
expensive open-top sports car. 'Now, here' – he pointed at
a low door located on the base of the bridge – 'is the access
to the lower cabins: heads, bunks, galley, that sort of thing.'
He pushed at the door with the toe of his boot. It swung
open with a high-pitched squeak to reveal a precipitous set
of steps leading to the inner cabin, which was out of sight.
'Be my guest, officers.' Campbell made a sweeping gesture
with his outstretched hand, as though showing them into
his own home.

Daley grabbed the handrails and gingerly lowered
himself down the steps, the unfamiliar footwear making his
descent difficult. Already, a sixth sense was telling him all
was far from well. A few steps on, he realised why.

The body of a woman was slumped forward on hands
and knees over a table which was bolted to the floor. She
was kneeling on an upholstered bench that served as a
dining chair. She was naked apart from a bra, which had
been torn in two and hung from her shoulders by its straps.
Daley noticed her hair was tied back in a ponytail with a
thick white bobble.

The cause of death was sickeningly obvious. The handle
of a stout wooden walking stick protruded from her anus,

and had been inserted there with such force that a huge amount of dark congealed blood was visible down the backside and legs of the victim, and also in pools on the bench and the cabin floor below. Daley reckoned that the walking stick had been forced almost two feet into the body of the dead woman.

'Only police officers down here, please,' Daley shouted. He didn't want Campbell and the crewman to witness or trample over the gruesome scene with their big boots.

'Have you found something? What the fuck?' Scott was now just behind his boss.

'Careful, Brian. Archie, come down here, will you?' The DC was descending the stairs. Fraser looked at the woman's body, and then he and Daley edged around the pool of blood on the floor to look at her face. Her head was left-side down on the Formica table, her eyes wide open in an expression of abject horror; more dark thick blood issued from her mouth and pooled on the table.

'Sir, that's Janet Ritchie.' Fraser was as white as a ghost.

'Are you sure, son?'

'Yes, no doubt.' He turned away from the scene, desperately trying to swallow down the gag reflex.

'Go back up and get yourself a breath of air.' Daley nodded to the DC. 'See if you can get a mobile signal and let me know. Don't tell our lifeboat friends anything right now, or news of this will be back in Kinloch before we've had a chance to speak to the office. OK, on you go.' He watched Fraser make his way back up top.

'Fuck, Jim, that's some mess.' Even Scott, the hardened detective, was horrified by the level of violence on display.

'I've a feeling there's more. Come on, Brian.' The two detectives walked towards a narrow wooden door. Daley took a hankie from his pocket and turned the handle. They found themselves in the sleeping cabin. On a double bed with raised sides lay the body of a man, stripped to the waist. His left arm had blackened due to a tourniquet having been applied just above his elbow. A large hypodermic syringe was still attached to his forearm, its needle thrust deep into the darkening flesh.

Peter Mulligan. It was not the first time either of the officers had attended a heroin overdose victim, but it still shocked. The man's bowels had emptied, and his head lay in a pool of his own vomit – the normal physical manifestations of a body desperately attempting to rid itself of the poison destroying it. A raw black gash ran along the neck of the victim. The corpse had been decapitated, then the severed head put back in place as a macabre resolution.

'It doesna' get any prettier, Jim.' Scott held his hand over his nose. 'What are these marks?' He pointed to the victim's chest, where the man's chest hair had been singed away, leaving small brown burns to the skin.

'Taser.' Daley bent down low over the victim, without touching him. 'He's been tasered. I remember being on a tactical weapons course a few months ago, and they asked for volunteers. You know that bastard Phil Anderson from the crime squad?'

'Aye, he's a right prick.'

'Well, they asked for volunteers, so he stuck up his hand and they tasered him. Took him the rest of the day to recover. He had two wee marks exactly the same as this on his stomach where the electrodes had attached themselves. Our man here's been tasered, then the overdose has been administered, no doubt about it.'

Scott peered at the corpse. 'They're no' long deid, either o' them. Whit dae you reckon, Jim? A few hours?'

'Something like that. Late last night maybe.' He stood up, almost hitting his head off the low cabin ceiling. 'We'll have to get forensics down here pronto and secure the crime scene. How the fuck do we do that out here?'

'Can these bastards in the launch sail oot the Clyde? I've never heard aboot it if they have.'

'I'll have to get a hold of the supreme leader – he's going to love this. Give Fraser a shout, Brian. See if he's managed to get a signal.' Scott ascended the steps gingerly, to be met by coxswain Campbell at the top.

'Just what's going on, Sergeant? This boy won't tell us anything. I have a right to know. After all, I'm still in charge of this little party. So come on, spill the beans. If it's legal consequences you're worried about, remember I'm a lawyer.'

Scott looked at him unimpressed. 'The *boy* you're referring to is a detective constable, and your being in charge has just come tae an' end. Have you got a signal, Archie?'

Fraser, still looking green, was making his way towards them from the stern. 'Aye, comes and goes a bit, but it'll do.'

'I have a satellite comms link back on board. You can use that, but first you must tell me what the fuck's happening.' Campbell was doing his best to sound emphatic.

'This boat's a murder scene.' Scott suddenly looked weary. 'For the time being, however, I don't want anyone from your lifeboat phoning hame tae tell the missus – is that clear? The chief inspector will take charge from here.' Scott looked to the heavens. The weather was deteriorating fast. His face was already soaking and the cabin cruiser was beginning to pitch and roll alarmingly, despite now being tethered at both bow and stern to the much larger lifeboat. 'What's the likely forecast, Mr Campbell?'

'Grim, Sergeant. I've just had an alert from Clyde Coastguard – we've got a storm warning. I strongly advise we tow this vessel back to Kinloch before it becomes a Herculean task. Do you understand?'

Scott went back below. 'The weather's getting bad. Yer man says we've got a storm on the way, and he's advising us tae head back tae Kinloch wi' this little boat o' horrors in tow. What dae ye think, boss?'

Daley thought for a moment. It was unlikely that there would be anything gained by maintaining the vessel in her current location. Even from his limited knowledge, he realised that the evidence would be at risk with a storm brewing. 'OK, Brian, tell him to make arrangements to tow us in as soon as possible. I'll need to get a hold of Donald, and we'll have to get Flynn to find us a berth somewhere on the harbour where the whole of Kinloch can't see what's going on. We'll have to have somebody down here for the duration too.'

'Young Archie says he's got an intermittent signal on the blower. Campbell's got a satellite phone.' Scott shrugged. 'Your call, James.'

Daley chose the satellite phone on the lifeboat, and after another undignified scramble from one vessel to another, made the relevant calls.

Flynn, back in Kinloch, assured him that *Russian Gold* would be away from prying eyes on the second pier where the lifeboat itself was moored, which was currently closed to the public for health and safety reasons. The harbour master told him that the Royal Navy sometimes used the berthing for dignitaries coming ashore from warships moored further out in the loch and that the health and safety notice was merely a ploy – 'anything to keep the locals at bay'. The harbour master also promised to provide plastic sheeting to cover the boat and help to preserve the crime scene.

With that in mind, Daley, having failed to get hold of Donald despite numerous attempts, alerted forensics. They were going to send a helicopter to Kinloch within four hours. As an afterthought, he contacted the PR department. After the disastrous press conference, he would have to grasp the nettle and face the cameras himself. The brutality of these killings, plus the link with the existing inquiry, would ensure that this would be a national story.

He rubbed his eyes wearily; he was still standing on the lifeboat bridge, while her crew prepared to tow *Russian Gold* back to Kinloch. The sea was swollen, but steady. The storm that Campbell had predicted had not yet materialised, though the sky to the west looked dark and forbidding, reflecting the detective's mood.

One murder could be anything: a personal vendetta, revenge of a cuckolded partner, or, as was often the case, pure bad luck on the part of the victim, caught up in a whirl of fatal circumstances, without premeditation. The brutal killing of three people with close personal ties was another beast entirely. Ritchie and Mulligan had not just been killed, they had been slaughtered. It was not impossible that sex had been the motivation, although even in this sordid world the level of violence shown in these murders was exceptional.

There was a cold, professional feel to what had taken place on the boat, which chilled Daley to the core. These murders could be the work of one sick individual, or a clear warning sent out by organised crime – signals that did not require too much interpretation. The connections to drugs and the underworld were already there.

'OK, Chief Inspector, we're ready to get under way.' Campbell was at his side. 'Let's hope the weather holds.' He gave a few orders, and the powerful engines throbbed into life.

14

'Can you tell us how the couple on the boat died, Chief Inspector?' The reporter held a large microphone to his face, with what looked like a dead hamster affixed to the end.

'No comment, at the moment.' Daley was flustered, and not just by the reporters who swarmed around him as though he was a hunted celebrity. No, he was furious that within an hour of their arrival at Kinloch with the cruiser *Russian Gold*, the press had begun to descend on the town's police office. Someone had talked. The reporters were all aware that two bodies had been found on the vessel, and they were pressing Daley to confirm that they were those of Janet Ritchie and Peter Mulligan, which, because he had not had the chance to contact the next of kin, he steadfastly refused to do.

To make matters worse, Superintendent Donald was on his way, with a senior PR consultant in tow. At least, Daley reasoned, Donald would, in his usual fashion, attract the attention of the press like bees to honey.

Because of the unwanted media attention, they had been forced to close the large gate which guarded the rear car park at the station. The gate creaked open enough to allow Daley and Scott entry, leaving the three constables who had the unenviable task of closing it again to their business.

'Bastards,' Scott intoned just within earshot of the reporters. 'Some bugger on that lifeboat must have spilled the beans. My money's on that pompous arsehole, Campbell. What d'you reckon?'

'I'll set our beloved leader on him. That'll give him something to get his teeth into, and keep him out of our hair.' Yet again, he hadn't had the time to eat anything since breakfast, and his stomach was groaning balefully. Lunchtime had come and gone.

'I'll be trying tae stay out o' his way efter that press conference. It seems like a hundred years ago now.' Scott looked reflective as Daley punched the security code into the door-entry system.

'Sir' – a young constable met them inside – 'Inspector MacLeod is asking for you. He's, well, quite upset?'

Daley winced at the intonation. 'Where is he, son?'

'He's in his own office, demanding to see you the minute you get in.'

'Tell him tae stick it up his arse,' Scott spat.

'No, it's OK. I'll go and see him in a minute. Tell him I'm on my way, son, will you?' Daley turned to his DS. 'Remember, Brian, Janet was his daughter.'

MacLeod was sitting behind his desk, his uniform replaced by a garish golfing jumper, replete with a large diamond pattern on a pink background. He looked tired and drawn, and had none of the arrogance so evident when they had first met.

'I'm sorry, Charles, I've not had a minute since ...'

'It doesn't matter, not now. Lord knows, she was hardly without sin herself.' His Highland accent was strong. 'Did you know, Chief Inspector, my father was a minister in the Free Church?'

'No, I didn't.'

'He was ashamed enough of me.' He looked directly at Daley. 'I drank, smoked, liked women – all the things he hated most. I had to get away from him and his moralising. That's why I joined the police.' He looked out the window, down onto Kinloch's Main Street. 'He died fifteen years ago. I wasn't there. In fact, I'd only seen him a few times since I joined up, but he left me a letter.' He opened one of the drawers in his desk and took out a pale blue sheet of paper covered in what looked like faded fountain-pen ink. 'Aye, no wonder you're looking. One page – one page from my dying father.' He put on his glasses and started to read. '"You have been an affront to me, to my church, and to my beliefs. Mark my words, as ye sow, so shall ye reap. You too, Charles, will feel the shame that I have felt, and the pain. You are, and have always been, a wicked man. May the Lord forgive you."'

MacLeod looked up, removed his glasses. 'Not much of a goodbye, eh?' There were tears in his eyes. 'I wondered for years what he could mean: when I met my dear daughter, I knew.' He looked down at the desk, his tears falling on the bitter epistle sent by his dying father.

Daley stayed silent for a few moments, not quite knowing what to say. 'I'm sorry' was all that seemed appropriate. He knew that he would soon have to tell the broken man in front of him of the horror involved in his daughter's death; for now though, he decided to leave it. He got up to go, to leave MacLeod alone with his thoughts.

'If you could indulge me for a short while longer, Chief Inspector. I know you are a busy man, but I have something to say that you need to know.' He massaged his eyes with the forefinger and thumb of his right hand. 'Janet and Mulligan were involved in the supply of drugs. Even though I turned a blind eye, as you know, I still investigated the matter. I know what you're thinking' – he was responding to an incredulous look from Daley – 'but please hear me out.'

'OK.' Daley sighed heavily. 'You'll appreciate that I have my super on his way, as well as a triple murder to solve, with precious little to go on.'

MacLeod nodded. 'The drugs were coming from the Baltic states – on a fishing boat from Latvia, to be precise.'

'*Hence* Russian Gold?'

'Aye, just so, just so. The pattern was regular. Mulligan knew I was getting wise to him, so he berthed the boat at Tarbert and sailed from there. Then the Latvians got a taste for the high life. They started to come into port themselves – drink and women, you know. I may have been misguided, but I did what I did for all the right reasons, in my head at any rate.'

Daley again found it hard to feel angry with the inspector, who cast such a pitiful figure. 'You must know Donald will destroy you for this?'

MacLeod nodded absently. 'No pension, no job – who knows? Maybe even a spell inside? Shame, affront and pain. Do you see? My father was spot on.' He paused. 'The boat from Latvia, it's due in tonight, well, the early hours of tomorrow morning. I've checked with Flynn. She's called *Koba*. But be careful, Chief Inspector. From what I know of these men, they're ruthless: ex-Russian military and KGB. For them, fishing is merely a hobby.'

Daley stood up. 'I don't suppose you'll tell me how long you've known this?'

'You suppose right. Here, take this, I'll not be needing it.' He threw his warrant card at Daley, who made no attempt at a catch, stepping over it as he left MacLeod's office.

'I canna believe that, man. I mean whit can ye say? He knows aboot the supply o' drugs by the crew o' a foreign fishing boat, aye, intae his ain community, an' he does nothin' aboot it. Do you think he wid have ever taken any action?' Scott looked at Daley in disbelief.

'Who knows, Bri. But I don't think we have to look too far to find out how the purchase of Pulse was funded. I've got the forensic accountants coming down to audit everything. It kind of makes sense now. You know, the way his flat was: impersonal, nothing in it, sterile. I very much doubt that our man is even really called Peter Mulligan. There's certainly nothing to identify him in his effects.'

The two fell silent. The case was proving far more complex than they could ever have imagined. They now had three murder victims, investigations into prostitution, illegal drug-taking and possession, and as if that was not enough, international drug trafficking. Daley was sure that false accounting and money laundering would be added to that list once the accountants had done their work.

Needless to say, any chance that Daley could cover for MacLeod was now impossible. The inspector would be lucky to keep his liberty, never mind his job. He knew he would have to be straight with Donald, whose arrival was imminent.

'So run it past me again, Jimmy. We're going efter these Ruskies tonight, right?'

'We've got the drug boys and tactical firearms en route, but we're still leading. Any of this could compromise the murder inquiries. They still take priority.'

'Whit if His Highness decides different? He might want tae pop this off tae Special Branch, aye, or take the reins himself.'

'Come on, Brian. How long have you known the man?' Daley smiled. 'Of course he'll be in notional command, which goes without saying, but he'll never let go of this. It's another brilliant opportunity to shine in a big way. He'll leave us alone too, just in case there's a fuck-up and we end up with nothing. That way he can wash his hands of it and hang me out to dry. If we succeed, he steps in as the guiding light, and before you know it he's an ACC. QED.'

'A whit? Anyhow, you're right. I dunno whit I wiz thinking aboot. The hangover's still dulling my heid.' Scott busied himself tidying his desk. 'The last thing I need today is a lecture on how "a tidy desk reflects a tidy mind". It's OK fir him, he's got a battalion of wee lassies lifting an' laying everything fir him, if you pardon the pun.' He picked up a piece of A4 paper, and after squinting at it for a few seconds, rolled it into a tight ball, and despatched it neatly into a metal waste-paper basket.

Daley looked down Main Street. The grey skies and rain had given Kinloch an entirely different feel. The tenements looked grim: their dark slate roofs were slick with the downpour, and the buildings seemed to huddle in on the street itself. Daley had been impressed with the buzz about the town, but with the change of weather, the pavements and road were virtually deserted, with only the odd brave soul dashing out from cars to purchase essential items from the shops that lined the street. From where he was sitting, Daley could see a bored shop assistant surveying the dismal scene, arms folded, from her position at the window of the large jewellers that was the nearest shop to the police office.

It was now mid afternoon. He intended to wait for the arrival of Donald and the drugs and firearms units, and formulate plans for the arrival of the Latvians. Both he and Scott could carry firearms, and he had spoken to the station's armourer, who was also a shift sergeant and had shown him the small selection of weapons available. They had taken two sidearms and an automatic rifle. Scott had to have his firearm-holder's certificate faxed from headquarters, because, as was habitually the case, he was not carrying the document.

Daley picked up his mobile from the desk, and pressed 1 on the speed dial.

'Hi, darling. There seems to be a lot of excitement, you OK?' Liz's voice oozed from the phone.

'I'm sure you know about as much as me. Are you in the hotel?'

'Oh no. Mark arrived an hour or so ago – he's flying back tonight.' She paused in time to hear Daley sigh. 'Don't worry, darling. I told him I was staying. We're just having lunch. I'll be back at the hotel about four. Is that OK?'

'Sure, sure … Listen, Liz, things are pretty full on here. Maybe you'd be better going back up the road. I mean …'

'Don't be silly, Jim. After last night, I'm staying put.'

He could picture the wicked smile which was doubtless playing across her face.

Her voice became serious. 'I really feel we got somewhere last night, you know? I remembered why I married you, why I love you. Do you understand?'

He felt his heart soar. 'Yes, I do understand, and I feel the same. I'll try to make it down to the hotel about five or so. I don't know how long we'll have this evening, but I'll explain it all to you later, OK?'

They said goodbye, and as he put the phone in his jacket pocket, he realised that they really had made progress with their relationship. This was a chance to heal things amid all the chaos. All it had taken was a fading seaside hotel, a murder and this place – Kinloch. There was definitely something in the air.

The arrival of Donald was, if anything, more of a virtuoso performance than even Daley had expected. Three cars sped up a rainswept Main Street, windows blacked out, with the front vehicle sporting a flashing blue light and warning siren. The prime minister himself could not have made more of a splash. A splash literally, as the rain and gloom that had enveloped the town became ever worse, drenching policemen, the public and press alike. So bad was the downpour that a press conference, to be held in the early evening, had to be cancelled as the wet weather was playing havoc with the satellite up-links. In short, a feeling of impending doom was all-pervasive.

Superintendent Donald, after a quick briefing with his DCI, commandeered the wretched Inspector MacLeod's office, called on the senior sergeant now nominally in charge of the sub-division, relieved him of the onerous responsibility, and took full control of both the sub-division and the triple murder inquiry, quoting 'forces of extreme circumstance' as legitimacy. A well-groomed, watchful PR man never left his side, whispering into the great man's ear at every opportunity.

Amazingly, one of his first actions was to seek out DS Scott and envelope him in a manly bear hug. Much mumbling of 'Don't worry about yesterday', and 'Watch a master at work', followed by a hearty slap on the back and an assurance that Scott was a pivotal member of the team. And then, in a stage aside: 'Regardless of his deficiencies in PR, and as a human being in general.' This elicited a sycophantic laugh from his PR man, who reminded Daley of a cross between Tony Blair and Goebbels, such was his slimy air of threat.

To Daley, though, behind the closed door of MacLeod's office, he was less sanguine. With even Goebbels banished, Donald came straight to the point. 'Needless to say, Jim, we have a situation of the utmost seriousness on our hands here.' He looked heavenward, hands steepled in front of his face.

Daley wondered for a moment if he was in fact in prayer, but decided that even the consultation of the Almighty would be deemed unnecessary by his boss.

'A bloody bear trap for us all.' Suddenly the mask slipped, as he took the back of his hand to a tartan mug bearing the legend 'Clan MacLeod' and propelled it against a wall, breaking it into three neatly proportioned pieces. 'That little bastard. As far as I'm concerned, you can take the Highlands and all that's in it, and stick it firmly up his arse. I'll do it personally.

'Here's me thinking that all we have to do is send you down here to solve some dispute amongst the bottom-feeders who inhabit this godforsaken place, identify the murderer, and bag the plaudits and a little piece of empire at the same time. We'll all soon be working for "The Scottish Police Force", the way things are going, and a right bunfight it'll be too.' He stared morosely into the middle distance.

'What have we got now? A corrupt senior police officer, an international drug-smuggling ring, as well as a brutal murderer who takes pleasure in perpetrating the most unimaginable horrors. All life is here, or should I say death?' He looked past Daley and out of the window onto the almost post-apocalyptic scene outside. 'I can tell you this, James: we better hope we can round up these Lithuanians tonight and tie up all the strings, or we'll have Special Branch on us like a ton of bricks. Customs and the drugs boys are already getting territorial about all this, to say nothing of the crime squad.'

'They're Latvians, sir.'

'What?' Donald looked at Daley as though he was surprised by his presence.

'They're from Latvia, the guys on the fishing boat tonight.'

'Well, whatever.' Donald drew in a deep breath and pursed his lips. 'Whether they're Latvians, Lithuanians or Spanish hermaphrodites, we'll have to nail their arses to the wall, or we'll be going down the same road Hielan' Laddie's embarking upon, as we speak.' Two discipline branch officers had been despatched to interview the disgraced inspector. 'The Ruskies will be at home here at any rate. Can't be any grimmer in the gulag than it is in this dump, that's for sure.' At that, a gust of wind splattered a flurry of torrential rain against the office window.

'You're not seeing the place at its best, sir. This weather … It's quite nice when the sun's out.' Daley smiled neutrally at Donald, secretly enjoying the discomfort his superior was feeling at being involved so closely in such a complex investigation. 'What's the form for tonight? I know the support unit's on the way.'

'Oh, yes.' Donald took some notes from his desk. 'We'll have a team of six armed men from the unit, two representatives from Customs, and a DI and a DC from the drugs squad, along with a dog of some description, and I presume a handler, to search the vessel once we've subdued these bastards. Even the fucking Royal Navy's involved now. They're tracking the fishing boat. The Navy are going to block the head of the loch in case they make a break for it. Though just quite how they would effect an escape in a fishing boat, I'll leave to your imagination. We could, of course, have done all this at sea, but we want to find out if they meet anybody here, or en route.'

'There's something bothering me, sir.'

'*Bothering* you? The whole fucking thing's bothering me. What is it?' There was more than a trace of the old shift sergeant in Donald's tone.

'These guys are out on the high sea, and they've been up around Skye, yes?' Donald nodded his head. 'So, if we're working on the premise that one of this Latvian gang was responsible for our three murders, how does the fact that they're miles away when at least two of the murders were committed factor in?'

'Hit man, or one of their party sent on ahead. Could be an associate, or even someone involved with this Mulligan character. The possibilities are endless. Anyhow, I'm certain that these Russians, or whatever they are, will unlock the door to the riches of the truth.' He noticed the confused look on Daley's face. 'Hanson, my PR man, came up with that. Good, don't you think?'

'Truly inspired, sir. I better get on. Is there anything else?'

'No, Jim, off you go and get organised. We'll have a strategy meeting here at one – unite the various agencies. You'll be Officer Commanding, under my auspices of course.' He smiled beneficently.

'Of course, sir. Of course.'

The forensic teams had thoroughly swept *Russian Gold*. Only a small quantity of cannabis had been found, which strengthened the uneasy feeling that was gnawing away at Daley. If they were out on a drugs run, who were they meeting? The Latvians were nowhere near Kinloch at the time. It didn't make sense. Unless they were involved with some other supplier. Perhaps they were just running away, though Daley doubted this scenario.

Like Izzy Watson, the body of Janet Ritchie contained evidence of more than one sample of semen. Whether they came from the same partners had yet to be verified, however, Daley was almost certain that would be the case. Collecting and identifying samples was one thing, matching them to suspects was another.

Something he could not define was shouting at him, like someone trying to make himself understood from a great distance. The odd word could be made out but offered little in the way of understanding. That he was missing something, he was sure. The question of what that might be was perplexing his subconscious, distracting him during conversations, or when trying to work through other problems.

He needed to step back, if only for an hour or so, to get some perspective. With forensics doing their job, and while the rest of the team were involved in the daily grind of the investigation, he decided he could make some time to meet Liz. Scott opted to go to his room for a sleep, ahead of the late-night raid. They had agreed that Daley would wake him around ten, when they would go back to the station and prepare.

Daley had led many raids, mostly on the homes of suspected drug dealers or murder suspects. He had once stopped a train with a passenger on board whose suitcase was filled with cocaine, but he had never had to perform this task aboard a boat. He worried about the character of the Latvians. MacLeod had made no bones about the fact he reckoned them tough. In Daley's experience, though, anyone who came from the old Soviet Union or anywhere near it was suspected of being either ex-KGB, or Russian Special Forces. More often than not, they turned out to be gangs of opportunists, desperate to escape the grinding poverty of their homeland. The possibility that something more sinister lurked on the fishing boat en route to Kinloch was a possibility. He hoped they had the firepower to cope with any eventuality.

The two detectives cadged a lift to the door of the County Hotel, despite its proximity to the station. The rain was now torrential, thudding off the road and forming deep puddles; filthy water was gushing from a blocked drain into the gutter. At the bottom of the street, Daley could see that the loch was near to the edge of the pier, meaning a high tide swollen by the deluge.

'See ye later, boss, and mind and not forget tae gie me a shout at ten.' Scott waved as he made his way up the staircase.

Through the hatch, Daley could hear his wife's dirty laugh. He found her sitting on a bar stool, her long, tanned legs shown off to optimum effect by a short denim skirt and cowboy boots. Daley's smile was pure reflex.

She took a few moments to notice him, so engrossed in conversation was she with a tall dark-haired figure leaning on the bar, a small glass of whisky clutched in his veined hand.

'*Chief* Inspector, I hope you don't mind me passing the time of day with this bonnie wife of yours. Aye, it makes an old cop's heart glad.' He smiled at the detective.

'Good evening, Mr Bain. Be my guest. I'm used to men finding my wife excellent company.' He grimaced slightly at this as it sounded more accusatory than he had intended, and was glad to see Liz affect a mock pout in response.

'Why don't you have all these funny stories about your time in the police, darling? Lachie's been keeping me company. What else can you do in this weather?' She grinned.

He bent over her, briefly kissing her forehead. 'What do the good people of Kinloch do in weather like this, Lachie?'

'Drink mostly. Mind you, it doesna really matter what the weather's at for that to happen.' His Highland lilt – in contrast to MacLeod's – was easy on the ear.

Daley bought them a drink each: gin for Liz, a Talisker for Lachie and a pint of 70/- for himself. With the operation to coordinate in the early hours, he decided to limit himself to two pints of beer. He was pleased that Scott had opted for a lie down, as he reckoned that his wayward DS may have found it difficult to resist a hair of the dog, such had been the severity of his hangover and the nature of his day's work.

They sat at the same table near the back of the room that Daley had grown strangely accustomed to during his short stay in Kinloch. The bar was quiet, with only Mandy keeping busy restacking newly washed glasses onto shelves behind the bar. A log fire crackled in the grate near their table, which, along with the dark wood panelling and low lighting, gave the place a cosy midwinter feel. A sodden customer entered the room, shrugging off a heavy waterproof jacket that seemed to gush water like an open tap. He was ushered back into the corridor by the fussing barmaid and instructed to hang the offending garment over an old iron radiator. Daley looked on as steam rose from the coat, while its owner ordered up a half pint and a whisky chaser, rubbing his hands together vigorously in an attempt to set his circulation to rights.

'You certainly have sudden changes to the weather here, Lachie. It was like summer yesterday, and now it feels like winter again.' Daley put his arm around the shoulders of his wife, who nestled closer to him.

'That's the thing, sir, the joys of living on the mighty Atlantic seaboard.'

'Please, Lachie, call me Jim. You're a civilian now. I hear enough of that at work.'

'Old habits die hard. Ye'll find oot yersel' one day. Anyway, that's half that's wrong with the job these days. No one has any respect any more.' His face was thunderous, but soon broke into a smile. 'We had an old minister on Barra when I was a boy – Wee Free, of course – and I think I'm getting more and more like him every day.'

They laughed. It was strange how hypnotic a real fire could be. All three of them stared blankly into it for a few moments, until Liz broke its spell. 'Oh, weather permitting, I'm off on a photography trip tomorrow, out into the wilds.'

Liz had studied photography at college, and exhibited her work on a number of occasions. Her parents, disappointed that she hadn't opted for law or medicine, had actively discouraged her, and, disheartened by poor sales and distracted by becoming a policeman's wife, she had given it up and consigned her expensive Leica 35mm camera to the back of a cupboard, where it had stayed. The rise of digital photography, with its instant results, had reignited her passion. Now, armed with the Nikon Daley had given her for Christmas, she had produced some stunning results, mostly landscapes and seascapes. 'I noticed an advert in the newsagent's window, you know the one in Main Street?' They both nodded. 'Well, this guy does escorted wildlife trips, especially for photographers, birdwatchers, that kind of thing. I hope to get some wildlife pictures. Anyhow, I gave him a bell earlier, and we're heading out tomorrow about ten, if the weather's OK.' She held up both of her hands with fingers crossed.

'Is it that wee bugger Seanessy?' Bain looked inquisitive.

'Yes, that's him. I take it you know him?'

Daley was only half listening to the conversation, the weight of the inquiry preying on his mind, but he caught the name Seanessy. 'Is that the guy who lives in the cottage by the beach, near to where, well, where we …?'

Bain nodded. 'Aye, an unfortunate man in many ways he is too.'

Daley was surprised at the remark. He had considered Seanessy a harmless eccentric, nothing more.

'He had a bit o' a hard time teaching up at the school.'

'Oh, in what way?' Liz was all ears.

'Och, the kids used to give him a hard time. Nothing malicious, you understand.' Bain went on to tell them that his daughter had been taking her exams when Seanessy arrived at the school as a young chemistry teacher. He had an awkward, shy manner, and was excellent fodder for a classroom full of adolescents who could spot an insecure teacher at a hundred yards. Despite himself, he was prone to allowing his eyes to wander to the plunging necklines of female students, who – girls being girls – made sure their blouses were unbuttoned to the absolute limits of decency. 'They would all piss themselves watching this poor bastard clocking their tits. Oh, eh, pardon me.' He looked embarrassed.

Liz brushed it off. 'I'll have to watch myself tomorrow. Maybe I should wear a polo neck!'

'We got a complaint about him once. I went up to talk to him at the school. I felt sorry for him, really. Some wee lassie accused him of touching her up, but there was nothing in it.'

'Oh?' Daley looked at Bain questioningly. He didn't want Liz tripping about in the middle of nowhere with the local pervert.

'Och, something and nothing. We had a complaint from a town councillor, so we were obliged to take it further. It turned out that he'd been married, but his wife buggered off with a colleague. They had a young daughter too. I don't think he ever saw the wife again, at any rate.'

'Oh, poor guy,' said Liz.

'Anyway, out of the blue a few years ago, his lassie turned up. In her twenties by this time. She caused him all sorts of grief: drugs, drink, you name it. She took off after about a year or so. Not before she relieved him o' bags o' money, right enough.'

'Wayward daughters seem to be the order of the day down here,' Daley said absently, gazing into the sparking flames of the fire.

'Sorry, darling?' Liz touched his face with the back of her hand.

'Nothing, love, just miles away there.' He smiled warmly and kissed her fingers.

Bain carried on, oblivious to the scene of marital bliss. 'A couple of years ago he found out she died. Aye, in some squalid flat somewhere in Edinburgh. Drugs, of course. I think he took it badly. He's one of these do-gooders who think they can change the world with a bit o' kindness. He brought her back and buried her here.' Bain swilled his whisky. 'Can I be getting you both another?'

They both said yes, and the older man got stiffly to his feet, proceeded to the bar with his hands folded behind his back, and waited as Mandy served another drenched customer.

'He couldn't be anything else but a cop, could he, darling?' Liz was studying Bain's stance.

Daley nodded. It was true: once you had been in the police, or had been involved in any meaningful way with it, spotting other policemen was easy – even ones like Bain, long retired.

'What a sad story about Mr Seanessy. Poor guy.'

'Just you keep your hand on yer ha'penny, darling, and wear that polo neck.' Daley grinned as she punched him playfully on the arm.

Bain suddenly turned around. 'Spunky, that was his nickname. Aye, Spunky.' He chuckled, before turning back to order the drinks.

They spent some time discussing the changes that had taken place in Kinloch since Bain had arrived in the late 1970s. It appeared that locals had a fierce loyalty to their town, and despite the remoteness of the place thought there was nowhere like it; a kind of relationship to home and hearth that had all but disappeared elsewhere. This didn't surprise Daley, who had rapidly developed an affinity with the area. Like everywhere else in Scotland, alcohol and drug abuse took its toll, and in the words of Lachie, things hadn't changed for the better.

Daley wasn't sure how many times he had heard that trotted out. Every generation throughout history must have looked upon the behaviour of their progeny with a leery eye. Things weren't perfect by any means, yet the town had a kind of bonhomie, surely extinct in many communities in the twenty-first century.

'Having said all that, I wouldn't like to live anywhere else in Scotland.' Bain drained his whisky. 'Aye, and it'll be even better when you get this little mess cleared up, eh? It's all people are talking about at the airport. I even heard that the army were on their way to sort things out. Anyway, folks, I've enjoyed your company, and I hope I'll see you again.' He got up slowly. 'The best of luck to you tonight, *Chief* Inspector.' He winked at Daley, gave Liz a big smile and then left, assuring them that 'mince and tatties would wait for no man'.

Later, in the dining room, Liz asked her husband what was happening that evening. Daley paused. 'I can't really talk about it, Liz. I'm not trying to be difficult' – he shrugged – 'but it's nothing you're not used to.' He raised his eyebrows in contrition.

'All I'm concerned about is you.' Liz looked earnest. 'I don't know what it is, I've just got a weird feeling in my stomach. Know what I mean?'

Daley did, but decided that reassurance was the best policy. 'You know me – belt and braces – and I've got Brian with me. What could possibly go wrong?'

She smiled, but the strain on her face was clear. The rest of the meal was a quiet affair.

15

Tick. Tick. Tick. The wall clock in the CID room seemed especially loud, or maybe the tense atmosphere just made it appear so. Representatives from all the agencies involved in the imminent raid on *Koba* had gathered to discuss their strategy.

Representing Strathclyde Police were Superintendent Donald, DCI Daley and DI Paterson, who was in charge of the Tactical Firearms Unit to be deployed at the raid. HM Customs was represented by a wispy-haired Ulsterman called Tommy Shanks, whose angular face bore a permanently disgruntled expression, as though being in the Kinloch CID office in the early hours of the morning was absolutely the last place in the world he wanted to be. Lieutenant Philip Carter had just arrived via helicopter from the Royal Navy frigate *Sirius*; the warship was still trailing the Latvian vessel at a discreet distance. Harbour master Flynn sat nervously at the end of the table.

Donald, as chairman, was the first to speak. 'Welcome, gentlemen, and my apologies for dragging you all here at such an uncivilised hour. However, as you no doubt appreciate, we are facing a tricky set of circumstances.'

Here we go, thought Daley, watching his boss consult an impressively large pile of typed notes. 'We know from our friends in the Royal Navy' – he smiled at Lieutenant Carter – 'that the *Koba* is heading for Kinloch, and on current estimates should arrive at the harbour between three thirty and four. We will, of course, be in position well in advance of this time.' He discarded the top sheet of notes. 'Now, we all know the challenge. We are reliably informed that this fishing boat is a regular visitor to the port, and that her crew is involved with the supply and distribution of illegal drugs.'

At this, Shanks sighed. 'I think we're all aware why we're here, Superintendent. I think it would be more appropriate at this time to discuss who should be leading this operation. This is clearly a matter where HM Customs should take precedence.' He waved his hand at Donald in an imperious way that Daley reckoned he might regret. Vain, posturing and arrogant, Donald undoubtedly was: ill prepared, easily dominated, malleable he was not.

'I had hoped we could run this operation in an adult, non-partisan fashion. I see that's not going to be the case.' Donald removed his spectacles and glowered at Shanks. 'While I do not deny Customs have every right to be involved in the due process of the operation, the non-availability of support personnel, combined with lack of infrastructure in this area, excludes the possibility of command.' Shanks cleared his throat to speak, but Donald carried on. 'We came by the information about this boat as part of an inquiry which now concerns the brutal murder of three individuals. We have good reason to believe that an individual, or individuals, aboard *Koba* could well be involved with these events, if not directly responsible. Therefore, this operation will proceed as it began: police led.' He slapped the palm of his hand on the table to emphasise the point.

Shanks, though, was not to be put off. 'First, I find it highly irregular that you've chosen not to inform us from whom and from where this information came, and also, perhaps more crucially, when? We were only contacted in the late afternoon. However, it has been brought to my attention that you received the tip-off this morning. Had we been contacted then, we would now be in a position to have the correct infrastructure in place. Do you follow, Superintendent?'

It had been a long time since Daley had seen Donald go red in the face with anger, not since his makeover from being a crude, gruff, overweight shift sergeant, in fact.

'You listen to me.' Donald pointed his Mont Blanc fountain pen at the Customs Officer. 'I'm overseeing a triple murder investigation a hundred and fifty miles from my headquarters, an investigation which contains much sensitive and restricted information, as well as the possibility of a number of serious crimes. Too many cooks spoil the broth, in my experience. Do you really think I am about to hand over the reins at this crucial phase to an organisation more at home creeping about bonded warehouses, or getting my taxes wrong? If you're not prepared to go along with the command structure of this operation, you can fuck off. It's going ahead with or without you – is that clear?'

Daley saw the young lieutenant lower his gaze to the table in an effort to conceal his obvious amusement, while Shanks managed to look more waspish than ever. After a moment's pause, he made a dismissive gesture with his hand, then folded his arms as a silent indication that he reluctantly accepted.

From then on, the meeting progressed in the way Daley expected, with Donald firmly in charge and making all the decisions. The plan was simple: the Navy would track the fishing boat by radar into the harbour, while keeping an open communication link with the land-based authorities, who would be in position around Kinloch's second pier. The two access roads there would be closed, just in case any of the good citizens of the town was out for an early-morning stroll. The Navy would then send an armed security team in a RIB to seal off the loch, should the Latvians somehow get wind of what was going on and try to make a break by sea.

Lieutenant Carter spoke up. 'We'll have ten marines on the RIB, Superintendent, just in case things get a bit heated on the ground – nothing your men can't handle, I'm sure.' He smiled at Donald. 'We don't have any intel on this particular vessel, but some of these ex-Soviet gangs can be ruthless. If required, we should be able to deploy in three to four minutes. It'll mean revealing our position, but that won't matter once the trap's sprung, eh, gentlemen?'

He reached down, picked up a blue holdall from his feet and lifted it onto the table. He unzipped it and took out what looked like a pair of large two-way radios. 'These are satellite-enabled comms devices.' He looked around the table. 'They're intuitive – if the radio signal goes down or is blocked by defensive tactics and so on, they'll open up a local satellite channel with the command unit. In this case, *Sirius*. I suggest that the ground ops commander' – he handed one of the devices to Daley – 'and the overall commander retain these units.' The assembled police officers nodded in agreement. 'Of course, I'll be shadowing you closely, Chief Inspector Daley, so you might choose to give me control of comms – for naval communication at least.'

Daley was impressed with the competence shown by the young naval officer. He hadn't really appreciated just how often the Navy was now involved with crime enforcement issues, especially those involving drugs or armaments. Carter reminded everyone that international terrorism sourced a huge proportion of their funding from the sale of narcotics, the well-worn drugs route from Afghanistan overland into the former Soviet Caucasus region being a favourite. The defence of the UK coastline was the historic role of the Royal Navy; to them, the trade embodied the Armada of the twenty-first century.

Scott was in the car park smoking a cigarette. Daley gave him a brief summary of the meeting, while the pair stared up at the night sky. The weather had taken a turn for the better, though the temperature was only four or five degrees. Being city boys, they weren't used to seeing the firmament because of the amber glare of light pollution. Daley remembered his grandfather's passion for the heavens. On their trips away from Glasgow, he had shown him the different constellations, explaining how they moved across the sky. Daley had now forgotten most of it, though he thought he recognised certain patterns. 'I think that's Taurus, Bri. Just there, to the left.'

'Nah, nah, that's the Bear, Jim. Or maybe the Plough? Och, I'm no' sure. I wis brought up in Maryhill fir fuck's sake. The nearest we got tae stars wiz when Thistle were playing the Gers at hame – ye know whit I'm sayin' – or some bastard stuck wan on ye at the dancin'.'

Nevertheless, they stood, silently rooted to the spot for a few more minutes, with only the click-flare-click of Scott's gas lighter to break the spell. This was done more effectively when the security door swung open to reveal Superintendent Donald, swathed in an expensive black overcoat.

'You won't get any answers up there, lads,' he said through a mouthful of food. 'We leave in an hour, so we better press on with this general briefing. Everyone's ready.' He stared up at the sky. 'Ah, the Big Dipper – wonderful sight.'

Scott looked dubious. 'It's the Bear, is it no'?'

'Don't be ridiculous, Brian.' Donald turned abruptly and walked back towards the door.

'Aye, whatever you say, boss,' Scott said in a loud whisper so Daley would hear. 'Fuckin' Roger Moore, noo.'

'It's Patrick, Brian. Patrick Moore.' Daley enlightened his DS as they made their way to the briefing.

'Eh?' Scott was already disconnected, stubbing out his cigarette in a flurry of orange sparks.

The whole team now consisted of the crew of the Royal Navy RIB, a seven-strong police Tactical Firearms Unit, four armed CID officers, plus six uniforms and a DC charged with keeping the public away. Not that the townsfolk should be a problem: the plan was to keep the matter as low-key as possible, using the element of surprise as their key tactic.

Still, Daley had a heavy heart. Those involved in action on the pier were kitted out with the latest bullet-proof body armour over their civilian clothes, and had each been provided with a reinforced steel helmet by the firearms unit, which Scott was refusing to wear. The DCI though, was still not entirely happy. Sure, they had enough firepower to effect a small revolution, and had more support unit officers on their way from Glasgow to deal with any possible aftermath, but somehow he felt there was an element out of kilter – something he had missed.

He had discussed this unease with Donald, who had immediately deployed his arm-around-the-shoulder approach, assuring Daley that everything would be fine and hinting that he felt the DCI's fears were merely down to the added responsibility of a more senior rank. He would 'get used to it'. But Daley had learned to trust his instincts, and he was finding it almost impossible to rid himself of the leaden feeling of impending doom.

Maybe I'm just getting too old for this, he thought, as he shouted for a bit of quiet in the room full of police officers. Body armour was being strapped on, helmets secured, weapons being checked just one last time, and the radios and secure mobile phones being used by each officer monitored for serviceable quality, battery level and the like. 'We all know how we want things to progress. Our first priority, as always, is our own and the public's safety – please bear that in mind at all times. I don't want anyone to be too shy to speak up if they feel that something's wrong or want to draw my attention to possible problems.' At this, he looked at Donald, who seemed engrossed by something on his Blackberry. 'We embark in five minutes, so good luck, lads. Now, Superintendent Donald will say a few words.'

Despite thinking that his boss was not concentrating, no sooner had the invitation to speak left Daley's mouth than Donald was on his feet addressing the assembled personnel, or 'unit', as Donald now insisted on calling them. At his side, an expressionless Shanks looked straight ahead.

Donald having completed his hackneyed pep talk, Scott began struggling with the straps on his body armour as the room now emptied into three personnel carriers that would transport them all to their drop-off point behind a row of buildings located in front of the harbour. 'This fuckin' thing reminds me o' the ski jacket she bought me last Christmas – mind I telt ye aboot it?' Daley always admired the *sangfroid* of his DS, constantly distracted as he was by some seeming triviality despite the circumstances. 'I says tae her, fuck me, you'd need tae be Harry bastardin' Houdini tae get intae the thing, never mind get oota it.'

'I never knew he had a middle name.'

'Who?'

'Houdini.'

'Aye, very good, *sir*. Can ye no' make yersel' useful and strap me intae this contraption, in case Ivan the fuckin' Terrible wants tae take potshots at me.'

As Daley was securing a recalcitrant strap, he saw DC Fraser making his way towards them. Not yet trained in firearms, Fraser's job was to oversee the uniformed constables who were to be involved in sealing off the pier from the rest of Kinloch. He was wearing a dark ski jacket. 'Tell me, Archie, did you have any bother getting into that jacket of yours?' The young detective's answer in the negative was obscured by a stream of invective from DS Scott.

The night was cool, and a stillness had descended upon the sleeping town as the unit emerged from three vans, now parked nose to tail behind the local marine chandlers. Daley took a deep breath that smelled and tasted of the sea, which itself looked as black as ink, reflecting only the glow of the few lights bordering the harbour. In the distance, he recognised the pealing of the bell on the pontoons, the mournful sound adding an air of melancholy to the scene.

Quietly and efficiently, those involved in the operation gathered around the chief inspector, who, after a few words, sent them to their relevant positions. Radios were to be used only in emergencies, to keep the frequency clear for command-and-control purposes, and each officer was wearing a hands-free earpiece, so that no command could be missed.

Donald and Shanks remained in the station control room, gaining an overview of the operation by monitoring radio traffic and CCTV images from the town's system, the latter now trained on and around the second pier.

Fraser and his uniformed colleagues were positioned to the north and west of the second pier, the only road access points. Instead of the regulation fluorescent jackets commonly worn at night by police officers, they wore plain, black waterproof jackets. Not being in the front line, and only responsible for crowd and traffic control, they did not wear the bulky bulletproof vests. Fraser was stationed in the doorway of the last shop on the Main Street before the harbour, keeping a watching brief on the roads which converged near the piers.

Daley, Scott and Lieutenant Carter positioned themselves at the side of the chandlers, in a narrow lane between it and a two-storey office block. The firearms unit was placed at strategic points at the head of the pier, making sure no one would be able to make a break for the roadway. The four DCs who accompanied them were wearing bulletproof vests under black jackets with discreet police logos, their heads adorned by the navy-blue helmets reminiscent of those worn by World War II German storm troopers.

The tolling pontoon bell continued until only those with the sharpest hearing discerned another noise – a light, regular thud reminiscent of a generator in a basement. At 03:42 Carter's radio burst into life. Even with the volume low, Daley could make out what was being said.

'*Sirius* calling Carter. Over.'

'Go ahead. Over.'

'Please note that our quarry has entered the loch. Our Alpha Unit will shadow in approximately five. Over.'

'Roger. Out,' Carter whispered into the radio, and then to Daley, 'The marines are Alpha Unit, in case you haven't guessed.'

Daley nodded, and Scott raised his eyebrows as he removed his sidearm from the shoulder holster concealed by his jacket. 'Fuckin' sure I'm no' facing doon half o' the Red Army wi' jist my baton, whether they're retired or no'.'

The thud of the diesel engine grew louder. To their left, they could see the fishing boat making steady progress up the loch, bright arc lighting hanging from the rigging.

'It's a pity that dug couldna get here. It wid have been the very dab on that boat, supposing they're carrying drugs.' Scott was referring to the sniffer dog, which until an hour ago had been plying its trade at a huge drugs raid in Glasgow, and was now in the back of a van being driven by its handler to Kinloch.

'Can't be helped, Bri. With these cuts, we're lucky we can still feed the dogs we have, never mind get any more. Here, take this, and don't point it at me for fuck's sake.' He handed Scott the Koch automatic machine gun, as Lieutenant Carter looked warily on.

The vessel was now less than four hundred yards from the pier. As regular visitors to the port, the Latvians knew exactly where they were going to berth. They'd confirmed their arrival with Flynn earlier in the day. The harbour master was sitting anxiously in his office, ready to be of assistance.

'DCI Daley to all units.' He spoke using the hands-free throat mic. 'On my mark of three initiate strategy F for foxtrot.' This entailed DI Paterson illuminating the fishing boat with an enormous searchlight set up by his team. At this point, he was to shout instructions through a loudhailer in what he had been reliably informed was Latvian. The firearms team would board, then secure the vessel, accompanied by the DCs who were also equipped with sidearms. The marines aboard the alpha RIB would speed into the harbour under full power to assist if necessary.

Daley knew that the moments following the trap being sprung were likely to be the most dangerous. However, he took comfort from the professional conduct of Paterson and his fellow officers, as well as the reassuring presence of Carter's marines and the indomitable Scott.

He could now see the fishing boat manoeuvring around the end of the pier towards her designated berth. He would wait until the last minute to give the order: when the ropes were secured to bollards and the engine began to die. His men were well concealed, even from the crewman who would have to jump onto the pier to secure the ropes. So far, so good.

The tone of the engine lowered, and he could make out the foreign voices of the crew as orders were barked into the cool night. In the instant before he pressed the button at his lapel mic to give the order, he thought he heard another noise, a high-pitched buzz. However, unable to hold back for fear of confusion, he gave the go-ahead: 'Three, two, one – go, go, go!' Immediately, he saw the bright searchlight on the pier illuminate the scene and heard the sound of raised voices. Everything now happened in a blur of noise and adrenaline.

Daley took off, closely followed by Scott and Carter, the latter giving instructions to his marines to speed into the pier as soon as they could. Two tactical officers with automatic weapons were kneeling, fore and aft of the vessel, their weapons pointing towards the crew, who were standing on board with their hands placed on their heads – apart from the rope man, who was already being handcuffed, none too gently, by a Paisley DC.

The bridge of the fishing boat was illuminated, and Daley could see the man whom he assumed was the captain standing at the window, hands aloft, as police officers scrambled onto the vessel. The crew were subdued easily, no doubt fearful of the consequences of making a wrong move while being watched by a dozen heavily armed men. Flynn had told them that the crew usually comprised six men, though that number could vary by one or two. Daley watched as Paterson bounded up the gangway to the bridge, followed by two of his men. The figure on the bridge turned his back to the window and hastily put his hands on his head.

'DCI Daley to Paterson. Over. Update. Over.' Daley was breathless, quietly cursing his unfit state; DS Scott was beside him, his automatic weapon raised menacingly.

'Stand by,' barked Paterson.

From his position in the charity shop's doorway, Fraser had a clear view of both piers and their environs. He was slightly put out that he wasn't involved in the raid proper, but he knew that it was due to his lack of firearms training. It was hard to believe that in all the time he had been in Kinloch these serious crimes had been going on under his very nose. He had not suspected Pulse to be the den of iniquity it had proven to be, despite visiting the establishment a few times. Again, he felt gnawing doubts as to his suitability for a career as a detective eating away at his confidence. Was it possible that men like Daley and Scott had started out their careers in such an inept way? He thought it unlikely, and nor could he contemplate a future like that of his uncle, an unfulfilled drunk whose only boasts were contained within the confines of some hostelry and fuelled by the contents of a whisky glass.

He worried about his personal life too. The police force was not a career conducive to social interaction with the opposite sex. His only proper relationship, with a girl from school, had ended abruptly when he had joined up. He was no longer available to go out with their mutual friends at weekends, and felt uncomfortable if somebody even lit a joint. Eventually she'd accused him of always 'having secrets' and being 'obsessed' with his new job. She didn't realise he was being subconsciously assimilated into the world he had chosen. It was a journey she was not willing to accompany him on. Her name was Tina, and try as he might he could not seem to conjure up her face, nor bring back the warmth in his heart that she had kindled for a while.

Just then, he saw movement. A figure was slouching along the short distance between the pontoons and the east pier. Something was wrong. All the vessels moored at both piers and the pontoons had been cleared earlier under the excuse of the discovery of an unexploded World War II mine, and he knew exactly where all the operational officers were. He thought about alerting Daley, but reasoned that the man was most likely some inebriated yachtsman, inadvertently left aboard his vessel during the clear out. Still, the man was about to stray into a very dangerous situation. Fraser stepped out of the doorway.

Daley could see four men on the deck, now in various states of detention by police officers. There was one man on the bridge, and a crewman was lying on the pier with his hands cuffed behind his back. That made six.

'Bridge secure. The captain's taking me into the body of the vessel. Crew accounted for. Over.' At that, a scruffy man made his way gingerly down the gangway from the bridge, his hands on his head, preceded by an officer walking backwards in front of him, gun trained upon the Latvian. Behind, also wielding a weapon pointed in his direction, came another tactical officer, himself followed by DI Paterson.

The man from the bridge was shouting in broken English: 'We are fisherman ... land fish ... no problem. We have no problem, no?' He looked around, bemused at the sight of his crewmen, most of whom had assumed the prone position. They were wearing an assortment of torn oilskins, old jeans, filthy jumpers and baseball caps; apart from their swarthy complexions, they could have passed for any of the fishermen Daley had seen since coming to Kinloch. Back on deck, DI Paterson stood behind the captain as he opened a door which led into the body of the fishing boat.

Daley looked warily at the side of the boat, then decided he would have to make yet another nautical leap of faith. He grabbed the gunwale with both hands, arms stretched out over the inky void between the vessel and the pier. Judging the rise and fall, he heaved himself up, managed to get one leg over the side then propelled himself in a rolling motion onto the deck, to the sound of tearing fabric.

'That's another pair o' breeks away, Jim.' Scott grinned from below, as the DCI, dignity barely intact, got back to his feet with a curse.

Paterson's head poked around the door leading to the lower deck. 'It would appear that we have the all-clear, sir. No sign of a seventh crewman.' No sooner had he uttered these words than a distant crack sounded over the harbour, closely followed by another. It took no expert to recognise the report of a firearm. Instinctively, all heads turned to the likely source of the shots – the east pier, some seventy yards away.

'Code twenty-one. Man down. Repeat, man down!' The voice over the radio was panicked; Daley recognised it as one of the young uniformed cops. He was also aware of Carter yelling into his radio, as what sounded like an aircraft sped between the gap in the two piers.

More shots.

Daley jumped back onto the gunwale of the fishing boat, paused for a moment, then leapt down onto the pier, coming down so quickly that he had to take a couple of rapid steps forward, like a poor gymnast's dismount, to stop himself falling. Scott was at his side; together they made for the short length of promenade that separated the twin jetties of the harbour.

'DCI Daley to DC Fraser. Position, please. Over.' Daley shouted breathlessly into his throat mic. 'DCI Daley to any unit stationed at the' – he had to pause to gulp down air – 'bottom of Main Street with DC Fraser. Come in. Over.' Ominously, there was still no reply. Though his lungs were bursting with exertion, Daley was desperately trying to piece together what had happened. Paterson and his men had appeared to have the situation entirely under control:

the crew were rounded up and a search of the vessel with the captain was complete. Then he remembered the high-pitched buzz he had heard just before giving the order to spring the trap. It had been a small boat.

Scott was ahead of him now and getting further away despite being the older man. Suddenly his earpiece burst into life. 'Firearms being discharged. Officer down.' The voice in his ear was muffled, the words a rush of fear and adrenaline.

'DCI Daley receiving. More details. Which officer' – he swallowed more air – 'is down?'

Silence again, though from the corner of his eye he was aware of the movement of black figures heading rapidly up the jetty. Scott had reached the top of the pier with Daley following; then, without warning, he felt a weight land on him from behind, and momentarily his world went black.

His first instinct was to fight. He didn't feel fear, only the desperate need to get whoever, or whatever, it was off his back.

'Stay down, man! Stay down!' He recognised the young lieutenant's voice. More shouting now, urgent and insistent, like two people trying to make themselves understood across a busy street. Then, for a heartbeat, complete silence, followed by a blood-curdling yell and the deafening sputter of automatic gunfire.

Daley felt a hand with fingers spread wide hard on the back of his head. The pressure was pushing him down to the pavement. He was aware of someone at his side, also on the ground, getting to his feet. Looking up he saw Carter standing over him, offering a helping hand up while talking urgently into the large radio.

'Jim, Jim, get over here!' This was Scott, standing a short distance away at the head of the east pier.

Daley pulled himself to his feet with the help of Carter's outstretched hand, nodded his gratitude, and hurried over to his DS. He saw the look on Scott's face, the blood on his hands. 'Brian, have you been hit? How ...' He followed Scott's line of sight. On the ground a few feet away he could see someone lying on his back, legs wide apart, like a tired man who had just flopped down onto a particularly comfortable bed. Two men in dark clothing were standing around the recumbent figure; a third was kneeling.

On the breast of the black jacket, a deeper stain had spread, at its heart a gaping dark hole around which the blood was already congealing under the streetlight. The body was motionless, head turned to the side as though in repose, not flat against the cold concrete. Even under the ethereal orange glow the face was devoid of colour, the features standing in sharper relief. A strand of red hair curled onto the pallid forehead.

Archie Fraser was dead.

16

Throughout his career, Daley had felt nothing like the pain – the burden of responsibility – that now enveloped him as he stared, transfixed, at Fraser's corpse. All that life and promise extinguished, and worst of all, it was his fault.

Daley had seen many corpses, had often pondered whether any residue of consciousness remaining after death was a medical possibility. Could the brain still perceive, be aware, even though the heart had stopped beating? He remembered being on points duty as a young cop in Glasgow city centre during the run-up to Christmas. Shoppers hurried to and fro clutching bags whose logos spoke not only of their likely contents but also something of the individuals carrying them: a tall patrician figure with a small paper package bearing the name of an exclusive watch manufacturer; giggling teenage girls, arm in arm, huddled together like an amorphous entity, their bags proclaiming the latest and most trendy shops; a whey-faced middle-aged woman bearing the basic wares of a discount store. On and on they came: wet, cold, happy, sad, chattering, silent, fat, thin, bald, hirsute; man, woman, child – the whole world was here, or so it seemed. All caught up in the whirl of Yuletide.

So large were the crowds, policemen were stationed at every pedestrian crossing in the city centre in a vain attempt to keep some kind of order. The one was subsumed by the heaving mass that was the many; an entity in its own right. Red man – stop; green man – walk: the principle was simplicity itself. And, just in case the visually impaired, or just plain stupid, should happen along, a shrill, insistent beep provided audible indication of when it was safe to cross. This, though, proved too difficult a concept for many. Pitting their few pounds of frail flesh and bone against the hard heavy edges of hurtling traffic, pedestrians regularly took insane risks in a festive game of Chicken – a game that the overwhelmed policemen, mostly those wet behind the ears, and who stood for nine hours at a time, were trying to prevent.

Daley had been standing at one of Glasgow's most dangerous crossings, now long consigned to the city's history. An attractive blonde girl waited dutifully across the road in the company of a phalanx of fellow shoppers, watching the red man, who stood out against the gloom of the dull December day. In his mind's eye he could still see her in every detail: her faux fox-fur jacket and tight blue jeans tucked into knee-high boots. Then, things happened in slow motion. The crowd of shoppers began to move, like corn rippled by the wind. The girl stumbled forward, as though she had been pushed. To Daley's left, the giant shape of yellow, white and green that was a Corporation bus hurtled into view in a mechanical growl of diesel engine and sigh of air brakes. A teenage boy pushed past the pretty blonde girl, looking neither right nor left. He had a blue sports bag thrown casually over his shoulder and the red of his hair nearly matched that of the amber of the traffic signal.

He was unlucky. He stopped when he saw the bus. He was halfway across the road and the shock of seeing the vehicle hurtle around the corner prompted the moment of indecision that would kill him. The driver slammed on the brakes with a banshee wail, too late though to arrest the momentum of the vehicle. The youth was smashed into the roadway with a soft thud. The front wheel of the bus crushed his skull, bursting his brains out of his head like a squeezed pimple.

Daley looked down at his polished right boot and the white and red pulp that was dashed across it and up his trouser leg. He had never forgotten the sense of unreality that he had experienced during and after the incident – something he had never encountered before, or since, until now.

Back in the office now, Daley tried to piece things together. By what could only have been pure luck, a small dinghy had set out from the rear of the fishing boat, out of sight of the assembled police officers, moments before they sprung the trap. The buzzing Daley had heard had been the whine of the tiny outboard motor. Scott reckoned that the crewman in the dinghy had used the arrival of the larger boat to deflect attention from a proposed clandestine meeting with a third party. He had moored his small boat at the pontoons and was then disturbed by the noise created by the raid. In an effort to escape he had stumbled upon the tragic Fraser, whom he had shot twice at point-blank range in the chest, just before the marines, who had spotted the dinghy using night-vision gear, had a chance to speed into the harbour. It was they who had killed the Latvian.

It was a plausible theory, but something about it didn't ring true. There was too much chance involved. And, in Daley's experience, chance was a rarefied commodity.

Why didn't I make him wear a bulletproof vest? Daley asked himself over and over again. But the answer was simple: no one had expected Fraser, nor any of the uniformed officers manning the temporary road blocks, to be in any danger.

'The question is: who was this guy expecting tae meet? If it wiz Peter Mulligan, then we can hardly put them in the frame for his murder.' Scott waited for his boss to reply but got no response. 'Jim, you canna go on blaming yersel'. Nane o' us could have predicted that.' Still no reply. He tried a different tack. 'You fancy a coffee or something?' On seeing the blank look on Daley's face, he decided to get him one anyway, touching the DCI on the shoulder on the way past in a typical example of restrained West of Scotland male sympathy.

Police officers had been sent to Fraser's parents' home in Glasgow, and Daley resolved to call them once the news had been imparted. It was a task he was dreading. He couldn't get the sight of the broken figure lying on the pier out of his mind. If this was the price of the promotion he had so coveted, it was far, far too high. He was aware of the door being opened and didn't bother to look up, assuming it would be Scott. In fact, it was Donald.

'I know you're devastated, naturally. Though I barely knew the boy, it's a tragedy.' No response. Donald walked over to the window. Though only half past five, the sun was beginning to light up Main Street. Gulls, crows and a myriad of other birds contributed to the early-morning cacophony, which today somehow seemed so inappropriate.

'This may not be the best time, Jim,' the Superintendent spoke in a low tone, 'but for some time now, I've felt that your eye was off the ball, that you were distracted ...' He turned to look at the DCI, whose head remained firmly in his hands. Undaunted, he continued. 'Under these extreme circumstances, and if you have no objection, I have decided to take operational command of this inquiry.' He raised his eyebrows in an expression that demanded some kind of answer.

Daley felt the wheels in motion, the buttons being pushed, and despite being fully aware of it could not resist. 'So you swan in here with your platitudes and your empty sympathy.' He was leaning back in his chair, but looking anything but relaxed. 'Let me tell you something: for some time now I have thought you to be a thoroughly detestable man. Vain, arrogant, and absolutely unsuited to running an investigation of this nature. Your whole career has been predicated on the hard work of others. And if you think I'm going to hand the reins of power over to you, so that you can stumble along to who knows what conclusion, then blame me when you turn up fuck all – you can think again. There are four people lying dead, and I don't care if I have to leave the job and become a private investigator, I'll solve this case. Understood?'

Donald stood in silence with his back to Daley. He then turned on his heel and walked towards the door. 'OK, DCI Daley, this time you have it your way. But, remember this: a young man gave his life to this cause. Don't let him, or me, down.' He stared at Daley for a few seconds, then left, closing the door firmly behind him.

Daley ran his hands roughly through his hair. He knew that he had just been in receipt of the proverbial kick up the arse he needed to galvanise himself back into action. He picked up the phone from his desk and dialled the nightshift custody sergeant's internal number.

Donald reflected ruefully on the night's events as he got into his car. He would have to get a couple of hours' sleep, then face the inevitable press conference. The death of a young police officer, particularly under these circumstances, was bound to create yet another feeding frenzy. He certainly would not be leaving it to Daley and Scott; neither of them had what it took to appear competent in front of the media. Daley always looked fat, unfit and careworn, while his DS looked more like the criminals he was trying to apprehend than the highly effective, if unorthodox, detective he was.

Donald had always found Jim Daley a man full of contradictions: a talented sportsman who had let himself go, early, to seed; such a volcanic temper, yet a man who could be paralysed by over-sensitivity; a quick, intelligent individual, yet one who could, as again today, be easily manipulated. But, above all, he was one of the best police officers Donald had ever worked with.

Donald was in no doubt as to his own talents. He had always found the endless grind of a major investigation too much to bear. He quickly lost any sense of objective and became bored with the exhausting schedule of fact and procedure, and the eternal sifting of a grain of truth from a beach full of lies. No, he knew that his talents lay entirely in his ability to make people bend to his will with a casual comment or harsh word that would send them into a flurry of productive activity. He smiled to himself in the rear-view mirror, then turned the key in the ignition.

The persistent bleep of her husband's alarm clock was enough to rouse Liz from her slumber. She had asked Jim to set it for her, as she wanted to be up and about in plenty of time for her trip with Mr Seanessy. From what she could glean through the yellowing net curtains, the day looked like a huge improvement on the previous twenty-four hours or so – a return to a glorious spring, in fact.

She stretched and yawned, smiling at the sight of her husband's Patrick O'Brian novel and the fact that it didn't matter where in the world the couple found themselves, his side of the bed always looked the same: radio and a good book. He actually pined for the BBC when he was abroad, and would go to extreme lengths to receive the World Service, no matter where they were. She laid her head on his pillow, breathing in his smell. The last few days had reminded her of how things had been when they were first married. Despite the responsibilities of running a murder investigation, her husband seemed more at ease with her than he had been for a very, very long time. She supposed that being away from home and hearth threw people together more and that exposure to the unusual reinvigorated interest in each other. Anyway, regardless of the reasons, it was most welcome. At times like this, Liz was afflicted with gnawing feelings of guilt, like a drunk waking up in the morning remembering acts of intoxicated stupidity from the night before. The litany of her infidelities often played, unbidden, in her head. This, she reckoned, was a reminder of her own inadequacy, of her need to feel wanted in the most primal way, as though sexual intimacy would banish the demons of loneliness and insecurity that haunted her when her husband – the man she truly loved – immersed himself in yet another impenetrable case.

The knock at the door was quiet but urgent. Preferring to sleep naked, she reached for Daley's jumper, which would serve as an impromptu dressing gown. 'Hello! Just give me a second,' she called to her visitor. The reply she received was indistinct, but she could tell it was a woman. She pulled the jumper over her head, took a quick look in the long mirror, smoothed out the tangles of sleep from her hair and tiptoed across the cool floor to the door. 'Oh, Annie, how are you? Did I book a wake-up call? Sorry, I didn't remember. Jim ...'

The look on Annie's face made her stop speaking. 'Is there something wrong? It's not Jim, is it?' She felt panic strike at her heart and stomach, making her legs feel weak.

'Don't worry, Mrs Daley.' Annie's face was pale, and the look of uncertainty she bore was out of place with her habitual cheerfulness.

'Annie, tell me. What's happened?'

'I'm jeest telling you whoot a' the gossips are comin' oot wi' jeest noo.' She was in the room now, and had closed the door. 'There wiz some kind o' polis operation last night, doon at the quay. Did Mr Daley tell you?'

'I knew something was happening, but I never discuss my husband's work with anyone, Annie. I probably know less than you do.' Liz could feel herself becoming annoyed. She liked the genial hotel manager, but was in no doubt as to the major role she played in the dissemination of local gossip.

With a hurt look, Annie chose to continue, the words tumbling from her mouth in her hurry, in an effort to justify her visit. 'I'm jeest here tae tell you that everyone's sayin' that a polisman got killed last night, and I wisna sure if you were awake or no'. I ...'

Liz darted to her jacket. She fumbled her mobile from the inside pocket despite the trembling of her hands. She tried hard to focus on the screen: no messages, no missed calls. She began dialling a number, then realised it was the number of Daley's office in Paisley. 'What's the number of the police office here, Annie?'

Annie gave Liz the number. Liz decided to call Jim's mobile first. *I'm sorry. The person you are calling is not available, please try again later or ...* She hung up and dialled the number that Annie had just given her, and, after what seemed like an eternity, the call was answered. 'Kinloch Police Office, Desk Sergeant Williamson. Can I help you?'

She could hardly get the words out. This was the scenario that had been in the back of her mind when she first met and then fell in love with Jim. Only two years ago, one of his colleagues had been shot during a drugs raid. Liz had visited his widow, who sat in an armchair, behaving entirely normally, save for the fact that she refused to believe her husband was dead, convinced he was playing an elaborate hoax – a windup so loved by police officers. 'Can I speak to DCI Daley, please? It's his wife.'

The pause at the other end of the phone was excruciating, then, somewhat hesitantly, the voice returned. 'Yes. I'll need to put you on hold, I'm not sure if he's in the office at present.' The line clicked onto a musical hold sequence: Queen's 'Seven Seas Of Rhye'.

'Hi, darling, I'm sorry I haven't had a chance to …'

'Fuck!' she swore loudly. 'Fuck, Jim! I'm at my wit's end here.' Suddenly her mouth went dry, and no more words would come out. She felt as though something was trying to make its way from her chest into her throat. She started to sob convulsively.

'Liz, what's wrong? Are you OK?' Daley sounded really worried. 'Where are you?'

She did her best to control the spasm of tears. 'I've just … just been told a policeman was killed last night, and I thought …'

Daley raised his head to the ceiling and massaged his temples with his free hand. 'Listen, Liz, I can't say anything about what happened last night. You understand. It's been hard, OK?' He heard her trying to compose herself. 'All you need to know is I'm fine, and the danger's over.'

'Yeah?' she managed to squeak in reply. 'Oh *thank God*'.

Daley knew that, despite all her faults, Liz had a deep faith: not a structured or formal religious belief, just a basic faith in God, a supreme being, entity, something. He knew she prayed every night and he realised that her words came from the heart and were not some casual blasphemy.

Liz felt her breathing ease. Annie was sitting beside her on the bed, arm around her shoulder, and she felt comforted by the other woman's closeness. 'All I need to know is that you're safe and out of danger. Surely you can at least give me that?'

'I'm fine, really. I have a lot on, Liz. I'll call you as soon as I can. Things will be a lot clearer later today. Please try not to worry. Aren't you going on your photography trip? At least it's not pissing down.' He heard her sobs break into a throaty laugh. Calmer now, she told him what she had heard, and how fear had gripped her heart.

'I could come up, see you for a few minutes.' Liz's voice was now almost normal.

'I'd love that, darling, but I can't, not just now. Things are going to be full on over the next few hours. Just enjoy your trip, and I promise I'll keep my phone on, even on silent, OK?'

They ended the call expressing mutual love. Liz tossed her mobile on the bed and hugged Annie in silent thanks for just being there.

As Daley put the phone down, Scott appeared at the door looking grim. 'The captain of the boat is ready tae be interviewed, boss. Vassily, is his name: Vassily Demienov. He's an arrogant bastard an' all. What's the plan?'

Daley stayed silent for a few moments. He felt real anger. Every time he stopped thinking of something specific,

Fraser's boyish face filled his mind's eye. Every time he thought of it he felt his bile rise; the familiar lifting feeling he had when about to lose it. 'You and me, Brian. The emperor's gone for a lie down. Let's nail the bastard.'

Daley's face was devoid of emotion. Scott, though, knew that, inside, his friend was struggling to keep a lid on his hot temper, which he would have to try to ensure did not boil over.

The pair made their way in silence down to the interview room. Passing an open doorway, they saw a young female PC in floods of tears, being comforted by her colleagues. The left corner of Daley's mouth began to twitch involuntarily, and his eyes narrowed.

There was an overpowering stench of fish, and the fainter odour of stale alcohol, in the interview room. Vassily Demienov was leaning back, his ample frame filling the chair. His hair was dark and greasy, and he had a few days' beard growth. Pudgy hands were clasped across his plaid shirt, which strained to contain his bloated belly. He looked as though he was in his early sixties, though he had assured the desk sergeant he was ten years younger. In short, he was no stranger to hard living.

He appraised the detectives with bleary eyes as they entered the room. Scott went over to switch on the tape machine. but Daley asked him to wait. He took his seat and leaned over the desk that separated him from the Latvian.

Before Daley could speak, the fisherman began waving his hands. 'I have been here for over an hour, and I have had no coffee, or tobacco.' His accent was strong, like the classic movie interpretation of a Russian voice. 'Before I say anything I want to be fed and I want a cigarette.'

Scott could see that Daley was on the point of combustion, so spoke up quickly. 'You, my friend, are in Scotland now. If you'd told us you were a transvestite, we'd have sent out for a dress, or if you'd told us you were a heroin addict we wid have filled you full o' methadone. Fuck, we'd have got you a picture o' Stalin if it wid help you cooperate, but I'll tell you this: you've mair chance of flying tae the moon right noo, under yer ain steam, than lighting up a fag in a polis station. Let me assure you, I know. I've tried.'

Daley's face remained blank. 'I want you to tell me all you know about the man who killed my officer. I don't want any shit. I'm most certainly not in the mood, and you won't be seeing one scrap of food, or anything else, until you do. That clear?' He looked the captain straight in the eye.

The Latvian raised his eyebrows, then unclasped his hands, letting a long continuous sigh issue from his lips. 'Before you try to bully or threaten me, I will tell you this: I was in the Soviet army. I've been interrogated by the KGB and the FSB. I've been made to stand in a barrel of freezing water for two days, then thrown back into a cell covered in my own shit and piss. I have had my fingernails pulled out. I've even had electrodes taped to my balls. Let me assure you, there's nothing you can do that will scare me.'

'You've obviously no' been tae the Stewart Street CID office,' Scott quipped, silenced by a look from Daley.

'We have your boat, Mr Demienov.' Daley's voice was steady but menacing. 'So far, we have found nothing aboard, but I know why you and your friends were here. So, unless you're willing to help me, I'm sending the vessel to Customs, who will take it apart piece by piece, then hand you it back to you as a lorry full of wood. Do you understand?'

Scott was impressed. He knew Daley was furious, devastated by the loss of Fraser, yet he was still managing to conduct the interview without exploding, and judging by the look on the fisherman's face, he had located his soft spot.

It was the captain's turn to lean forward. 'You are the one who does not understand. How could you? Living here where you are even paid not to work, given houses, food put in your belly by your country.' Demienov was clearly an emotional man. 'My whole life is in that boat. It is my home as well as my place of business.' He sat back in his chair and stared down at his stomach. 'In my country we don't have people like you to defend us against the …' He uttered an unintelligible word in his own language. 'I think you call them parasites.'

'Explain.'

The fisherman flung his arms in the air. 'If I want to land my fish, if I want to repair my boat, if I want a visa from the local magistrate to allow me to leave home waters – all these things must be paid for.'

Now Scott took his turn. 'We've a' got to pay – everybody, everywhere. Whit makes you any different?'

'We don't pay a nice man with a briefcase in a government office.' He put his head in his hands. 'In the West, you think we have been liberated since perestroika. You are wrong. This is why I leave Moscow.' He was becoming more agitated. 'In the old days, if you kept your head down and put a few coins in the right pockets, you could get on with your life. I moved to Latvia. Who cared about Latvia? I bought a small boat and started to fish. Do you not see? There was law and order, like you have here. Now ... now it is different.'

'Give him a fag, Brian.'

'Whit? Fuck me, there'll be smoke alarms an' a' sorts goin' off. Are you sure, gaffer?' He didn't need to ask twice. He produced his cigarettes from his pocket and, flicking open the packet, offered one to Demienov, who grasped it desperately with filthy fingers. Scott lit the cigarette with his Zippo, then slid a metal wastepaper basket over to the man with his foot, to serve as an ashtray.

'Go on, please, Mr Demienov.'

'I am sorry for your loss, but it is not my doing. We are just fishermen. The man who is dead, I only know him as Kirov. We land him at certain places, he moves things about, he picks things up.' Demienov shrugged his shoulders.

'What things?' Daley asked.

'I never ask. Where I come from, it is better not to know.'

'You can guess, though. I can tell already that you are not a stupid man, Mr Demienov.' Daley studied the Latvian, going through the same mental processes that he always used when trying to form a picture of someone from whom he was attempting to extract information. People lied to the police: that was a given. Even seemingly upright responsible citizens would find themselves guilty of at least the sin of omission when faced with any kind of questioning. Mistrust of the police ran as deep in Govan as it did in Vladivostok; only the methods of investigation varied. He had already decided that Demienov was in essence an honourable man placed in an impossible situation. Daley was sure that the skipper knew exactly what Kirov – if that was the man's real name – was up to, however, he was powerless to do anything about it.

As if reading his thoughts, the Latvian spoke again. 'Every time I come to your country, I hear complaints from people. It's too cold. I pay too much tax. The TV is rubbish. The beer is expensive. I can't afford a new car. People should come to my country and find out what it means to have a complaint. Do you understand me?' The fisherman rubbed his sallow face and looked at the officers through weary eyes. 'I have always dreaded this day.' He sighed deeply, like someone carrying a huge burden. 'You hope and pray that you will get through it, that they will leave you alone. But in your heart you know that one day luck will run out, and everything you have worked for will come tumbling down.' He narrowed his eyes. 'A man is dead, a man from a strange land, who I don't know. It is my duty to help you. I am only sorry that it has taken me so long to come to my senses, be brave enough to do the right thing. I hope you can understand this, sir?'

Daley nodded silently.

17

Liz waited outside the hotel, perched on the windowsill. She could see that the bottom of Main Street was cordoned off with a mixture of blue-and-white police tape and the yellow do-not-cross variety. She shivered involuntarily, still feeling sick about the dead policeman.

Seanessy had arranged to meet her at ten, and he was already fifteen minutes late. She didn't consider this an auspicious start, but had managed to entertain herself by wondering just who the many people were who had said 'Good morning, Mrs Daley, fine day', and, more importantly, how they knew who she was. She was dressed sensibly – stout hiking boots over thick socks, a pair of navy-blue trousers – and carried a heavy fleece, just in case the weather changed. A tight-fitting round-necked T-shirt revealed the curve of her breasts and her slim figure. Her hair was pulled back in a ponytail and a pair of expensive sunglasses were propped on her head, while over her shoulder she had a backpack, specially designed to hold her camera and lenses, along with a bottle of water and the sandwiches which Annie had insisted on making for her before she left.

Liz leaned her head back, feeling the warmth of the sun on her face. It didn't feel possible that this was the same country as yesterday, never mind the same town. The driving rain and strong winds of only a few hours ago had given the place an entirely new aspect, and she much preferred today's conditions. Gulls soared in the blue sky, and the smell of the sea filled her nostrils. A cold hand grabbed her heart when she thought of the policeman lying on a mortician's slab, his days of feeling the wind on his face over for eternity. She removed her sunglasses and hair bobble, then shook her head vigorously, banishing the nag of mortality she felt.

She was redoing her ponytail when an ancient Land Rover drew up beside her. The driver leaned across the passenger seat and with some difficulty managed to wind down the window. 'Mrs Daley, I presume. Sorry I'm a tad late. Hop in.'

Liz took the backpack from her shoulder and grabbed her fleece in the same hand as she opened the passenger door to the Land Rover, which creaked alarmingly. 'Good morning, you must be Mr Seanessy. Liz Daley. Pleased to meet you.' She held out her hand for Seanessy to shake.

Her guide seemed slightly flustered, gripping her hand weakly. 'Oh, I say, I wasn't expecting anyone quite so attrac—' He paused. 'I mean, quite so young as yourself. I get a lot of retired people on my trips, you see. All a bit like me, you know, too much time on their hands. You can put your bag at your feet if that's comfortable enough. We'll take a drive to the car park at Machrie, then get the map out and try and work out the best places to take you. I'm so glad the weather's improved.'

Liz cast an eye over Seanessy, as he struggled to wrestle the stick into a forward gear. He was wearing a green waterproof jacket, though there was no obvious sign of rain. Liz had hers in a neat pack strapped around her waist. He was also wearing a pair of light-grey jogging bottoms that had seen better days, tucked into green Wellington boots, onto one of which was placed what looked like a puncture repair, more commonly seen on a bicycle tyre. His hair was plastered with some deliberation across his balding head. He was unshaven, rather than sporting a beard, and she noticed a trace of faded red in his short sideburns. The vehicle smelled vaguely of fish, and an ancient mobile phone slid backwards and forwards across the dashboard, depending on the direction of travel.

She began to wonder whether or not she had made the right decision in booking the trip, but reminded herself of the pleasantness of the day and the possibility of getting some great images of the local flora and fauna, something she hadn't done enough of recently.

'Would you like a mint?' Seanessy took a paper bag from the recesses of his waterproof, and offered it to Liz.

'No, thanks,' she said, feeling slightly queasy at the smell of the car and the thought of consuming something of such dubious provenance. 'I had a big breakfast,' she explained.

'Ah yes. I'm afraid I tend to skip breakfast as a rule – always starving by this time of the morning.' He managed to steer the vehicle and extract a small handful of mints from the bag, which he proceeded to place awkwardly into his mouth, missing with one, which rolled down his jacket and onto the floor of the Land Rover, destined to be lost amongst the detritus there. 'We'll be there in five minutes,' Seanessy mumbled through a mouthful of mints.

The deal was simple. In return for immunity from further prosecution of he and his crew, Demienov would undertake to tell Daley all he knew about what the gang, who had inflicted themselves on his vessel, were doing and had done. This would include those with whom he knew them to be in contact, local drop-off points and any information he had regarding their operation and structure within Latvia.

Daley knew that there was no little risk involved with an agreement of this type. He could not be sure that Demienov was not part of the organised crime gang who had targeted Kinloch, nor could he be sure that anything the fisherman said would be of any value. However, he was working on the instinct which throughout his career had worked better than any of the technical processes that had been hammered into his brain over the years. He would have to set the ball rolling by putting the proposition to Donald, who would then need to get authorisation from the very top.

Daley was desperate to bring those behind the murder of Fraser to justice. Despite the culprit lying dead on a gurney at Kinloch Hospital, he felt strongly that the wider organisation was like a cancer feeding on this small community and something that must be eradicated. However, he did not believe that the Latvians were responsible for the three other murders he was investigating; it was that instinct again. On reflection, the gnawing doubt had been there before the raid took place. Was it merely his self-preening arrogance that had led to the death of Fraser? Should he have handed the whole operation over to Customs or the drugs squad? Certainly, he had been urged by his boss to retain charge of a situation of which he was not the architect.

He now had four murders on his hands; probably two distinct investigations. Why was he so sure that the deaths of Watson, Ritchie and Mulligan were not connected to the drug smugglers who had killed Fraser? According to the Royal Navy, the Latvian fishing boat was nowhere near local waters when Mulligan and Ritchie were killed. They could have been murdered by accomplices of the gang, but Daley thought this unlikely.

'Apart from Pulse, and the involvement with the Latvians, Bri, there's some connection we're missing.' The two detectives were sitting in Daley's glass box, having left Demienov to sweat it out in the Kinloch cells. Donald was due back in an hour, and Daley was desperately trying to find something to justify his approach to the various deaths.

'I know what you mean. Why wid the Ruskies come intae port here if they'd jist killed their mates? They must've known that we'd have found the bodies by that time, Jim,' Scott said, swirling the coffee in his mug.

The DNA of all the Latvians, including the dead gunman, was being tested, along with that of all the regular male customers of Pulse. This would take time, with no promise of anything conclusive; part of the grind of the investigation, but you never could tell.

Daley's phone gave its internal-call ring. 'Sir, there's a Davie Fraser on the line to speak to you.' The PC's voice was strained; she had made the obvious connection.

Liz and Glynn Seanessy were standing in the Machrie car park studying an Ordnance Survey map spread over the bonnet of the Land Rover. He had donned a pair of old-fashioned thick glasses, and his hair was now flying up in strands in the light sea breeze. Already, on a rock in the small bay, Liz had spotted a colony of common seals basking in the spring sunshine. The sea made the air fresh and new, and with the sun on the back of her neck, she was beginning to enjoy her trip, despite her unusual guide and the state of his transport.

'I thought we could try up here first.' Seanessy was pointing at a location on the map with a chewed pencil. A small ridge was located behind the bay, from which she could take some good panoramic shots and possibly catch sight of a pair of golden eagles that were nesting not far away. Now there was an image that Liz would love to capture.

Seanessy pored over the map, then scratched at his behind, only stopping when he noticed the curl of disgust on Liz's lips. 'Eh, sorry, I'm afraid I'm not so used to company these days, especially of the female variety.'

Liz noticed that his ears had become very red. 'I'm the one who should be sorry. I'm too used to nagging my husband when he does things like that. Go on, scratch your arse whenever you want.'

Seanessy resumed his deliberations with an awkward smile.

'I canna believe it, Jimmy. He wiz a good lad, ye know? A bit o' a lassie when it came tae the bevy, but a good lad a' the same.' Davie Fraser sounded frail over the phone.

'I know how you must be feeling, Davie. I've not even been able to phone his folks yet. Everything's just been ...' He didn't get time to finish.

'Well, that wiz kinda why I wiz phoning, Jimmy.' Davie Fraser still used the diminutive with which he had addressed Daley when he was a young probationer. 'They've had that prick Donald on the phone, and Mary's quite upset.'

'How do you mean?' Daley could feel his hackles rise.

'Och, you ken that one. It wiz a' "noble sacrifice", an' "for the greater good" stuff. He's forgettin' I kent him when he wiz a two-shilling bully fae the slums. Fuck me, ye wid think ye were talking tae the prime minister noo, the way he goes on ...'

'You still there, Davie?' Daley was doodling with a pen on the large deskpad. Speaking to bereaved relatives was arduous at the best of times; even more so when you shared a past with them.

'I'm sorry, Jimmy,' Davie Fraser said, his voice breaking. 'I had a lot o' time fir the boy – like a son tae me, ye know? I mean, look at the state o' me noo. I can hardly walk the length o' myself, an' I know it's a' cos o' the bevy. I'm a fuckin' waste o' space. The boy wiz worth somethin', ye know?'

Daley agreed, but said nothing.

Liz and Seanessy were scaling the ridge that overlooked Machrie Bay. The climb was steeper than it had looked from the car park, and she could already feel rivulets of sweat running down her back. She wondered how Seanessy must be feeling; he was still wearing a waterproof jacket and now looked extremely hot. Despite this, he kept up a commentary on the visual pleasures of their trip; they had already seen numerous seabirds, small mammals and plant life, about which Seanessy seemed to be well informed.

'Ah, look, a heron. Beautiful bird, don't you think?'

'Yes, they're wonderful, so majestic in flight,' Liz replied.

He peered at the bird through a pair of old binoculars. 'They only nest in two places in the world, you know. Here and the African savannah. Incredible, isn't it? I've always thought of them as a little bit of Africa here in Scotland.'

After much exertion, they reached the summit of the ridge. Before them, at this elevated height, lay the full panoply of the bay. Immediately below, arable farmland gave way to patchy machair, then on to the sandy bay, fringed by the breaking waves of the restless Atlantic. In the distance, the islands of the Inner Hebrides loomed.

Liz looked to her left, training her binoculars on what seemed like the closest visible landmass. 'Which island is that, Mr Seanessy?'

'You're right to say it's an island, technically that is. However, it's a much larger one than the others.' He had that perambulatory way of explanation peculiar to the enthusiast. 'That is the wonderful island of Ireland.'

Liz looked again, amazed at the proximity of it. 'Wow, I can see a car! Look over there to the left – it's quite clear.'

'It's only twelve miles at the closest point, not far from where we are looking at the moment, in fact. That's the coast of County Antrim.'

The pair continued to take in the view for a few minutes. Magnified, the Irish coast looked blue. A lighthouse flashed white every few seconds, wavering through a heat haze.

'Of course that's still the UK we are seeing, but look there – to the right. Do you see that faint shape in the distance?'

'Yes, it's pretty clear.'

'That's County Donegal, in the Republic, a foreign country to all intents and purposes now. Where my grandfather came from, actually. We haven't strayed far as a family, come to think of it.'

Liz breathed in deeply; the mixed scent of land and sea was heady in the spring heat. 'If you don't mind, I'll get one of my lenses and try to get a few shots of the Emerald Isle,' she said, fumbling in her backpack and eventually extracting an expensive-looking piece of equipment.

'Be my guest. We've got all day,' replied Seanessy.

Liz looked up and smiled in response, but his gaze was cast far away, his expression unreadable. She busied herself attaching the lens, found her portable tripod, and then looked around for the best image.

Daley had just received a report from the pathologist: still no matches for the unidentified semen samples found on both Watson and Ritchie's bodies. They would have to consider extending the criteria from just the sample group in the local community. Action like this was always controversial: people became concerned about a Big Brother state. But a modern police force had to use everything it had to hand in order to catch criminals: that was the pay-off.

Forensic examination of Mulligan's cabin cruiser, *Russian Gold,* had proved more fruitful. SOCO had found a number of fibres not belonging to the vessel or victims; more work was being done.

Scott arrived back in Daley's glass world to let him know that Donald was back in the office after his 'doss', as the irascible DS termed it.

Daley walked along the corridor to what had been MacLeod's office to find Donald sifting through a mountain of paperwork which had been deposited on the hitherto immaculate desk.

'It's you, Jim.' Donald had been caught off guard, and he looked flustered at the DCI's arrival. 'Just getting down to some investigation of my own.' He furrowed his brow to indicate sincerity, which always had the opposite effect. 'Hopefully find what else this Highland rogue was keeping hidden. He's coming in later for an interview with discipline and myself. I wouldn't mind a few lines from you on what took place between you both, say in the next couple of hours?'

'So you're basically rifling through his drawers.' Daley's statement was flat, just the way he felt.

Deciding to ignore the remark, Donald changed tack. 'I've spoken to young Fraser's parents, thought I would take some of the weight off your shoulders.' Donald raised his eyebrows, looking, no doubt, for an expression of gratitude from Daley.

'I heard,' was his only response.

'They were upset, as is to be expected.'

'I'm going to call them myself, this evening.'

'I'm sure there isn't any need. I think I covered our response to the tragedy adequately. They'll get a letter of condolence from the chief constable, and of course the First Minister.' Donald smiled with satisfaction, as though, in his mind, the intervention of such exalted figures more than compensated for a dead son in a mortuary drawer.

'Please ensure that no one else talks to them before I get a chance to. Enough damage has been done already.' Daley was emphatic.

'Meaning what, exactly?'

'Meaning I've talked to another close relative, who thought that your call was disgraceful, that's what.'

Donald put down the silver quaich he had been examining and glared at Daley. 'Whatever it is that's eating you, please excise it by bouncing it off your halfwit DS, not me. I've still not forgotten that we have a growing number of unsolved murders, with no solution in sight. Neither have I lost sight of the fiasco that was the last press conference you and that fuckin' idiot presided over. If you've come to chastise me, think again, and get your head back into the job in hand.' He picked up the quaich and turned it over in his hands.

Daley ignored his boss's outburst. 'I need to extend the local DNA sample. Every man in the area between sixteen and forty. Is that possible?'

'Oh yes, it's possible, but is it *desirable?* These "human rights" things are a pain in the arse. Endless paperwork and ...'

'The Latvian skipper wants to do a deal on behalf of himself and his crew, in return for information about the drugs supply here. I'll need an answer to both these questions within the hour.' Daley turned on his heel and left the office, slamming the door in the process.

★

Liz had managed to capture some good images, including a stag, a hare, some fantastic landscapes, and even a distant, yet clear, shot of a golden eagle soaring high over the escarpment. She had enjoyed herself, though her guide had become more and more introverted as the trip had gone on, despite her frequent attempts at small talk. True to her nature, she decided to ask why. 'I hope everything is OK? Sorry if I've been blethering on. You must be used to this wonderful scenery, but it's such a novelty for me.'

Seanessy looked blankly at her for a moment. 'I apologise. Been a bit off colour today. I can't help thinking about these dreadful murders. I hear a policeman was killed last night, at least that's the local gossip.' He suddenly looked embarrassed. 'I'm not fishing for information or anything … I mean, I know who you are. I hope you don't think …'

'Not at all, it's OK. It must be such a shock to everyone, especially in a quiet little place like this.' She decided to change the subject. 'You were a teacher here, weren't you?'

'Yes, indeed, served before the mast for much longer than I care to mention. I always wanted to be a scientist. You know the type of thing: research, Oxbridge, a comfortable life as a don. Not to be, I'm afraid.' A shadow crossed his face.

'You can't complain about where you live now, though? It's absolutely glorious. You somehow never think that places as beautiful as this exist in Scotland. Do you know what I mean?' Her husband would have winced at the inflection in her voice.

'Yes, I suppose I have much to be thankful for.' Seanessy looked dreamy and preoccupied.

'Oh, wow!' Liz's shout made Seanessy jump. She was looking excitedly through her binoculars. 'I think I've just seen a whale out in the bay! Surely not.'

Seanessy took a look in the same general direction, just as the creature ejected a telltale plume of water from its blowhole hole. 'A minke whale, if I'm not mistaken. They're the most common here, though we occasionally get others. I've seen a couple of orcas, but that was further out, from a boat.'

'You have a boat?' Liz took her excited gaze away from the whale.

'Well no, not exactly. I have a loan of a small vessel from some local fishermen should the need arise. Helpful for spotting the more unusual. I bagged a Manx shearwater recently – the world's most travelled creature, you know.'

'That's fantastic. I would love to see a killer whale, or a Manx shearwater come to that. I have a friend who works as a picture editor for a wildlife magazine. I'm sure he'd be interested in unusual specimens like that. Maybe kickstart my career again.' She looked wistfully for the whale.

'Tell you what – if you're interested, I'll try to get the use of the boat tomorrow, if the boys aren't using it. Unofficially, you understand, I'm not licensed to conduct nautical tours, and neither is the boat for that matter, but I do have a maritime certificate. Just don't tell that husband of yours.' He grinned nervously.

'He's got more than enough to worry about just now. That would be fantastic if you could manage it. I'll pay the going rate, of course.'

'I'm sure we can work something out to our mutual satisfaction, Mrs Daley.' He gazed at her as she scanned the bay for another sight of the whale. Holding the binoculars made her white T-shirt ride up, exposing her flat tanned stomach.

Daley and Scott were discussing just how easy or not it would be to round up the entire target male group for DNA samples to be taken: *not* was the general consensus they reached. For Daley, it was all a bit like wading through treacle at the moment. He couldn't get Archie Fraser off his mind, and there was nothing worse than being emotionally preoccupied when trying to fathom a difficult case.

'I'm the same as you, gaffer.' Scott was chewing gum to stave off his nicotine craving. 'But if it's no' the Latvians who're responsible for our three murders, then who is?'

'I want to take another look at all the CCTV footage.' Daley stroked his jawline; he was badly in need of a shave. 'There must be something we're missing around the time Izzy left Pulse. How did she get from Main Street to the bay at Machrie? I'm sure there must be something on the CCTV.'

Scott looked at his boss wearily. He knew the man inside out. He could see how badly Daley had been affected by the young detective's death and how horrified he was – they all were – by the violent way that he and the other three victims had met their end. He also knew how this determination was most likely to manifest itself: painstaking reworking of all possible evidence, re-examination of all potential witnesses and those close to the victims – anything that would be likely to churn up a vital clue to break the case. It was quite unusual to have this amount of forensic evidence, and for it to have made so little difference. Yes, they had managed to expose an Eastern European gang doing a roaring trade in narcotics in this isolated community and who knows where else, plus a morally corrupt police inspector: that, though, was not the point. They had failed to come anywhere near to solving any of the three original murders, and to compound this failure had managed to lose a young colleague in the process. In short, Scott knew it was time to burn the midnight oil, time for his boss to become unbearably intense in a concerted effort to solve the crimes.

'Dae ye want me tae send oot fir pizza?'

Daley smiled weakly. Not for the first time, his DS had read his mind.

The Land Rover was hot and stuffy inside when they opened the doors. Liz could again smell the fruits of the sea gone bad. The old diesel engine rattled into life, then they began the short drive back to Kinloch. Though she was tired, she was in high spirits. The little excursion had seen her get some good images, and she now couldn't wait to get them onto her laptop and then Photoshop them into saleable work. She felt a sense of pride that she was, once again, doing something positive, something she knew she was good at, and something to make it worthwhile getting up.

'I hope seven's not too early for you? I have to fit in with when I can get the boat. It's a bonus that we can sail from Kinloch, and it'll probably take about an hour and a half to get to where we want to be. However, it's a stunning sail, especially if this weather holds.'

Seanessy changed gear, and Liz noticed how the sun had burned the back of his hands into an angry red, matching his forehead, unprotected by his receding hair. 'I love being up early, and thanks for today. It's been fantastic. I'm really looking forward to tomorrow. What do you think the chances are of seeing an orca?'

Seanessy turned his head towards her. 'Good, I'd say. It's the right conditions and time of year. They tend to come a bit closer to shore during the better weather. Our friends the common seals get a bit lazy in the sun, take their eye off the ball, and before you know it: *bang!* He thumped the steering wheel, making Liz jump. 'The orca is a highly intelligent creature, you know. They've developed a number of really effective strategies with which to capture prey.'

'I would've thought that swimming as fast as possible and having big teeth was all that was required.'

'A good start, but not enough for these killers.' Seanessy chuckled. 'Do you know, sometimes they hunt in pairs close to the shore? Recently, in Sweden, I think, a woman was walking her dog along the beach and spotted one about fifty yards offshore, jumping from the water and doing tumbles – you know, the way they do in these dreadful Florida shows?' Liz nodded for Seanessy to continue. 'Well, of course she went a bit closer to the water's edge to get a better look, and then from nowhere another killer whale launched itself out of the water, onto the beach, grabbed the dog, pulled it from her grasp, and waddled back into the water, quick as you like.'

'Really?' The story made Liz shudder.

'Oh, yes. To an orca, you see, a dog and a seal look much the same. They use that strategy all the time with seals. The poor things get mesmerised by the antics of the orca doing tricks and forget to look out for his mate slinking through the shallows with murder in mind. Clever, eh?'

Liz silently resolved not to walk too near the sea again.

The flickering images on the screen were from the five CCTV cameras that covered Kinloch town centre. The detectives had seen better quality footage, but it was monochromatic and mostly in sharp focus, which made a significant difference.

Daley was desperately going through all he knew about the murder victims: they were friends who moved in the same social circle; they all used illegal narcotics and were involved in the purchase and distribution of said substances within the community; and, lastly, they were all dead. Mulligan was from Glasgow, where background work by colleagues in the city had shown him to be a petty criminal with two charges of shoplifting, three breaches of the peace and a minor assault charge against his name. Hardly a Mr Big in the fetid world of organised crime. However, he did associate with a few key players, men whom police knew to be at the heart of Scotland's criminal underworld. Unfortunately, coming from the housing scheme that he did, almost everybody qualified under the 'associates' banner, so numerous were the criminals from that area. No direct connection could be found between Mulligan and any existing crime family, and how he had managed to fund Pulse remained a mystery.

18

The atmosphere in the County bar was so oppressive that Liz decided to retreat to her room. She was not in the mood to answer questions about the death of a policeman the previous night, not least because she knew less than her interrogators. In any event, she would never have dreamed of being so indiscreet concerning her husband's work.

The ever watchful Annie, seeing her plight, had supplied her with a menu and a large G and T, and told her to give her a shout whenever she wished a top-up, or an evening meal.

Liz tried to call her husband, but his phone was off. She left a message, then attempted to numb her mind with gin and some bad afternoon TV. She was marvelling at the prices of barn conversions in East Sussex when her mobile intoned its best approximation of an old-fashioned callbox ring.

'Hi, darling.' She could instantly detect the strain in her husband's voice. 'Sorry I've had the mobile switched off all day – been checking it though. How was your trip?'

She proceeded to ramble on about her excursion with Seanessy, anxious for him not to feel he had to make mention of the death of a colleague. During a brief lull in her tale, Daley interrupted. 'Keep this to yourself for the moment, love. It was Archie Fraser who was killed last night. Remember the red-haired lad who was in the bar the other night?'

Liz suddenly felt cold. Yes, she remembered Fraser: tall, slightly awkward. She had watched him looking at Jim, and she could tell that he held her husband in great esteem by the way he hung onto the older man's every word.

Though the call was brief, she was glad that he had taken the time to speak to her. She sensed both determination and exhaustion in his voice, but knew that this was nothing unusual when he was on a major investigation. Jim could survive on hardly any sleep for days on end when the hard yards were being covered. She knew him well enough to know that he would be mentally scourging himself because of Fraser's death, re-enacting the whole incident in his mind, trying to isolate what had gone wrong and what he should have done. He had gone on to tell her how he was going to come down to the hotel around eight, get a bite to eat and a couple of hours sleep, if he could manage it. She had advised him to stay away from the bar and take up Annie's offer of room service. After a pause, he agreed.

They were taking it in turns to examine the CCTV footage. Scott was at the screen now, with DC Dunn assisting, her sharp eyes and local knowledge adding perspective to what was being displayed. They were doing forty-five-minute shifts, as it was, literally, an eye-watering task.

Daley was in his office, brooding and calculating – not a mental count of numbers, more a studied equation of probability, combined with chance and vested interest. Someone had left a car magazine on his desk. He was flicking through it idly, like an existential *aide-mémoire*. Why had he not made it clear to Fraser and his team that they were only present to keep the public at bay and observe? He should have made it crystal clear that, unarmed as they were, intervention was not in their remit. How had the Latvian known to jump ship when he did? The Navy had been monitoring their radio and internet traffic for a period of hours before the operation was conceived.

He turned over a page on which the Jaguar XF was being displayed in all its smooth-lined, polished magnificence. It was then he knew the answer.

Flynn's car was visible on the pier, so Daley and Scott made their way along to his office. A wide-eyed Flynn looked at them when he answered the door.

'Good afternoon, Mr Flynn. Can we have a word?' said a businesslike Daley.

'Well, eh, of course. I was just going home – long night and all that. It won't take long, will it?'

'Oh, I don't think so,' said Daley, who watched the harbour master visibly relax as he showed them into the office. It was in its habitual state of untidiness, and there was no sign of Hamish sitting at the antiquated desk. The computer screen was still displaying the updating satellite weather map; beside it lay a half-eaten fish supper, still in the paper wrapping. The enticing smell of fish and chips made Daley's stomach rumble.

'Dae ye mind if I hae a chip?' Scott looked at Flynn quizzically.

'Of course not. Be my guest. You might as well finish it off. I've lost my appetite after last night's … Well, I needna tell you.' He looked at the floor, stroking his neat beard.

The three men didn't speak for several minutes. The events of the previous night were still viscerally recent.

'I thought I'd bring you this.' Smiling, Daley handed Flynn a magazine. It's got the new Jag XF in it.'
'Thanks, Mr Daley, thanks very much.' There were beads of sweat appearing on Flynn's brow, and it was only then that Daley noticed the smell of alcohol on his breath.

'Been havin' a wee dram, Mr Flynn?' Scott seemed to hone in on Daley's thoughts.

'I wisna goin' tae drive, gents, if that's what you're worried about. In fact, I wiz about tae call my wife tae come an' get me.'

'How much did you get for your scallop boat?' Daley's question came from nowhere.

Flynn now looked very nervous, his eyes flicking between the two detectives. 'I don't understand, why would you want tae know that?' His voice was wavering in tandem with his resolve.

'Eight and half thousand, I was told. Not a huge amount, eh?' said Daley.

'No, the trade around here's not what it wiz. It gave me an' the wife a wee lift though.' Flynn spoke quickly.

'The car that's sitting outside, what's it worth new? Forty-five, fifty grand?'

'I, well, I'd saved up, you know. I ...'

'Why did you do it? You're a decent man. You have a good job and a nice house. Why did you get involved with people who spread poison and misery?' Daley was standing in front of Flynn now, dwarfing him in his swivel chair.

'I don't know whoot ye mean,' Flynn shouted, panic in his eyes.

Something inside Daley snapped. He hauled the harbour master out of his chair by his collar and tie, and pulled him close. 'A young man died because of your actions last night.' Flecks of spittle landed on Flynn's face. '*You* tipped off our Latvian friend. *You've* been working for these scum – watching their backs, seeing they had a safe harbour – you little bastard.' Daley pushed Flynn back violently. He landed beside the old desk, hitting his head against a corner of it, making him yelp in pain. Daley towered over the whimpering man, but before he could strike him, Scott pulled Daley back by the shoulders.

'That's enough, Jim. Fuck's sake, man, this isna goin' tae bring the young fella back.'

Daley was shaking with fury, but he managed to control himself; Scott's intervention having cleared some of the red mist. 'Tell me how you contacted him. Now!' he shouted.

Flynn sobbed, the pristine collar of his white uniform shirt was now stained with blood. 'Mobile,' he whispered through tears, 'I called a mobile number.'

'Get the cuffs on him, Brian. I need some air.' Daley left the building, slamming the door on his way out. He breathed deeply in the salty air, leaning on Flynn's Jaguar. He looked through the dark privacy windows at the leather seats and the walnut finish, the creamy luxury of the interior. He cursed Flynn's greed: the owner of that car had cost Archie Fraser his life. Was that all it was worth?

Flynn was taken back to the office by Scott, who had called a van. Daley had another port of call: James Newell, who ran the RIB hire business from the pontoons. Daley had seen the vessel glide into the loch and deposit half a dozen camera-wielding tourists safely ashore. The area had been cordoned off for most of the day after Fraser's shooting; not that there had been much to find out, though the relentless master that was procedure had to be followed.

Two men were still working aboard the boat as Daley made his way down the pontoon. The bell was silent in the still air, and Daley recalled its baleful reports throughout the operation the previous evening.

One of the men was probably in his sixties; both were tall and thin with dark hair, no doubt they were related. Daley placed the younger man somewhere in his thirties, though trying to estimate the age of anyone between the ages of twenty-five and fifty seemed to be an increasingly difficult task these days. He wondered if it was something to do with his own advancing years, then dismissed the idea.

The older man on the boat eyed him over a pair of halfmoon glasses. 'Can I help you?'

'Are you James Newell?'

'Yes, and I take it you're Chief Inspector Daley.' Newell smiled. 'This is my nephew Rory.' He had seen Daley looking at the other man. 'He's up from the smoke for the summer to get some air in his lungs and work out what he wants to do with his life now the bank have dispensed with his services, eh, Rory?'

The younger man nodded.

Daley was invited aboard and he took Rory's offer of a hand up, over the side of the craft. He felt as though he was viewing himself from above, like some sort of hackneyed death scene from a hospital drama, and he was angry with himself about losing control earlier. For someone who dealt with death as part of his daily life, the murder of Fraser had had a profound impact. That, combined with the heavy tiredness he was experiencing, left him feeling that his mind was wandering, akin to being in a trance. In these periods, he often had the inspiration that led to solving a case.

The three shook hands politely. Newell had an easy manner, and had Daley not known he was an ex-naval captain, he probably would have guessed.

'Wedded to the sea, Inspector, that's me. Anyhow, what more could a man want than to ply his trade in such a beautiful part of the world, despite the hostility of some of the locals? I suppose you've already come across that?' He looked to the detective for an answer.

'Not really, Mr Newell. They're a very *interested* body of people in my experience, but I haven't come up against anything malicious yet. Apart from the obvious, of course.'

Newell shrugged his shoulders. 'That's probably because they see you as being from the same stable.' He went on to tell Daley that despite his parents being Scottish and having been born in Glasgow, his accent and manner had marked him down as an Englishman in Kinloch – a posh one at that. 'I'm not in the least bothered, of course, though some of them can be quite unpleasant. Water off a duck's back for me after being caged up in a submarine full of hairy sailors for months on end. And let me tell you, that breed doesn't suffer from the reluctance to speak out that afflicts the rest of the service. I'm sure I don't have to tell you anything about man management.'

After what was no more than an exchange of pleasantries, Daley informed Newell that what he wanted was any kind of rota or ships' logs covering the period of the murders. 'I'm not accusing you of anything, Mr Newell. I just have to cover all my bases. I already know about the movements of the fishing craft, but you and the rest of the visitors to the pontoons are still a bit of a mystery.'

'Well, worry no more, sir. As you've probably heard, I'm involved in the company that owns this pontoon. We keep records of all our visitors – well, the honest ones at any rate.'

'Honest ones?'

'An unwritten rule of the sea. If you moor somewhere, you do your best to find out to whom your harbour dues are paid. I'm not here day and night, so sometimes we get – let's just call them *visitors* – who come in out of the weather late in the evening and upon the arrival of a better morning, bugger off without parting with a penny. They are, I'm glad to say, in the minority.'

It turned out that Newell had an upstairs office in the same building that housed the harbour master. Newell junior removed something from an old grey Land Rover, while his uncle searched for his office keys. Once inside, the older man went in search of the register of vessels that had been moored at the pontoon during the relevant period.

Rory hadn't said much, so when his uncle left, Daley took the opportunity to quiz the younger man. He asked if Rory had known any of the victims. The detective thought he was being evasive when he did not answer immediately.

Eventually, Rory said, 'I did know one of the dead people, if the stories I've been hearing are right.' He had the same patrician mien as his uncle, thought Daley, as he sat languidly on a metal chair, one foot resting on a small table.

'What stories would these be?' Why could no one answer a straightforward question in a similarly straightforward way? This conundrum had pestered him throughout his career.

'The cop who got killed last night, I knew him – if it's the guy I've heard about, of course.' He continued to stare at Daley, his expression unchanging.

'I'm afraid I can't comment on that incident at the moment. Anyway, I was referring to the murders of Janet Ritchie, Izzy Watson and Peter Mulligan.'

Rory Newell snorted derisively. 'I don't know why you're bothering wasting your time on people like that. As far as I can tell, they're the scum of the earth, like most of the folk in this sorry shithole. I liked Archie though – good bloke.' He stared at Daley again.

'Why did you leave the bank, Mr Newell?'

As the policeman had planned, that had the desired effect. A shadow of annoyance passed over Rory's face. 'I wasn't aware it had become a police matter.' He managed a weak smile, but Daley could sense his anger.

Newell senior arrived back in the office, clutching three coffee cups, and with a red ledger tucked under one arm. He handed the beverages around, then took his seat behind a small desk, on which were placed a laptop computer, a telephone and a leather-bound Roberts radio.

'Is that an original?' Daley gestured at the radio.

'That set, Inspector, has been with me for forty-two years, and has been around the world at least four times. My guilty pleasure, you know? Addicted to Radio 4 now I've managed to settle down in the one place.' He smiled.

'Though why the fuck it had to be here, no one knows,' his nephew muttered, looking at the ceiling.

'Do you like the radio, Mr Daley?' Newell continued as though Rory had not spoken.

'Oh yes, a little passion of mine too. I just got my hands on a Grundig Party Boy recently, though, like you I still prefer Roberts. Owned by the Japanese now – how things change.'

All three sat in silence, as though contemplating the consequences of a classic British radio brand being owned in the Far East.

'I'm sure you don't need me, Mr Daley. I've got to get back home, get online and see if I can find a real job, back in civilisation.' Rory stood up suddenly.

'I take it you're under forty, Mr Newell?' Daley asked the younger man.

'Thirty-four.' His uncle didn't give him a chance to reply.

'In that case, I'd like you to volunteer at your earliest opportunity to go to the police office and have a DNA swab taken. Every man resident in the area will be taking part.' He smiled at Rory.

'If I must. Do you think you've got your man, officer?' He sneered at Daley. 'OK, Uncle Jimmy, I'm heading off to the hacienda. Goodbye, Inspector Daley. I'll provide my

DNA tomorrow, if that won't hinder your investigation too much. *Ciao*'.

'Don't let him wind you up, Mr Daley. I'm afraid he's very like my late brother: stupid. He had a good opportunity at the bank but he blew it. He tried for the Navy you know – didn't get a sniff, of course.' Newell looked into the middle distance.

The two men discussed the pontoon and the Newells' movements around the time of the murder of Izzy Watson. It transpired that they had been to County Antrim, acting as aquatic transport for a film crew making a documentary about the Giant's Causeway. The weather had caused a few problems, so they'd had to stay longer than intended. 'Flynn was in charge, nominally, of course. As usual, he was too busy chewing the fat with his fishermen friends than checking on my pontoon. I wonder where he is? His office is in darkness. It's an early dark, even by his standards.'

'Was your nephew with you on this trip?' Daley changed the subject.

'Look here, Mr Daley, I'm fully aware of how aggravating Rory is, but I can assure you he is no murderer. Beneath the swagger he's actually quite shy, and certainly not violent. His wife buggered off with one of his best friends just before he lost his job, tried to top himself.' Newell looked at the ceiling in the same manner that his nephew had, only moments earlier. 'That's why he's here. I hope you understand, and yes, to answer your next question, he was with me the whole time.'

Newell went on to show him the list of craft berthed at the pontoons around the time of the murders. Daley decided to take the register with him, Newell reluctantly agreeing to use a temporary log in the meantime.

He was aware of eyes on him, that primeval sense that man long ago forgot how to use properly. Even through the limited view of the bar's serving hatch, the good citizens of Kinloch were straining to get a look at the detective who had just arrested a well-known member of the community. Annie shouted a brisk hello, as he turned right before the reception, then up the staircase.

The steps always felt strange to Daley. They were less deep, wider than normal stairs, so, consequently, as you ascended you felt as though the effort being put in was not commensurate with progress. Maybe he was just tired. In fact, he was shattered. He'd had little sleep the night before, he was hungry, and his heart was sore – not in the sense of stress or medical pain – sore in that it represented the gauge of the soul, the prism through which was viewed all he had felt, seen, heard and subconsciously assimilated during his lifetime. Right now, the image of Archie Fraser was accompanied by an acute feeling of guilt. Some people were destined to strive all their lives for betterment, the march towards greatness of the truly ambitious: but at what price? Had Daley been a mere bystander, an operative put in place by another during the raid? Of course, he would have felt sad at the demise of any fellow officer. No doubt he would have said a silent prayer of gratitude that the man lying on the cold tarmac of the jetty with a hole in his chest was not him. However, he was the man who had put Fraser in the place that eventually led to his death. He was the man who had played so carelessly with a young life that was lost forever. For that reason, he felt no unspoken relief. He wished he could turn time on its head and swap places with the young detective. With his long experience he would never have exposed himself to harm, the way Fraser had so selflessly done. In the event that harm had come his way then so be it. There would have been no one to blame but himself and fate. There would be no pathetic, ashen-faced ghost haunting his thoughts and tortured dreams.

He found the door to his room locked. Before he could fumble the key from his pocket, Liz had opened it. She was wearing his favourite jumper and somehow seemed more tanned and beautiful than when he had last seen her. He suddenly remembered that she had been on her trip. He tried to speak, but finding words so hard to come by, and the mere presence of her so intoxicating, he simply fell into her arms. Automatically, he searched for her lips. They kissed passionately. When he pulled away, he could see disappointment flicker across her features. He pulled the woollen garment over her head, revealing the contours of her naked body. A loose wisp of hair fell over her face. They tumbled onto the bed, and made the frantic, desperate love of those spared the terminus of death.

19

It was five in the morning when Daley was roused from a fitful sleep. He had agreed to be back at the office around six to give Scott a break and some much-needed sleep. He switched the alarm off as quickly as he could, but to his dismay Liz began to stir.

'Get back to sleep, Liz. It's only just after five. Duty calls, I'm afraid.'

She sat up, breasts peeking over the duvet. 'No, no, it's OK. It's an early start for me too. Mr Seanessy's taking me out on a boat he's got from somewhere. I promised him I wouldn't tell you because I don't think it's strictly legal, but if I can get a shot of an orca he can steal the *Ark Royal* for all I care.'

Daley processed this information through a fuzz of sleepiness. 'Well, as long as he's competent at sea. How far out are you going?'

Liz yawned, arms outstretched. 'Huh? I'm not sure. I'm still tired, exhausted actually.' She smiled mischievously at

Daley, who was looking at his reflection in the wardrobe mirror.

'Do you think I've lost a bit of weight?' He moaned and drew in his stomach. As soon as he had opened his eyes, a melancholic gloaming had shaded the prospect of another day. Thoughts of Archie had immediately crowded his mind, but he was anxious not to show Liz how much he had been affected.

'Yeah, I think you have, you know – a bit. But you know I love you just as you are, don't you?' She looked up at him.

He smiled. She was heartbreakingly beautiful. He had often wondered if it was only him that could see her beauty. Maybe she was just another attractive woman to others. Was there really 'someone for everyone', as the song described? What song was that anyway?

'You're miles away, darling.'

'No, just thinking,' he said, knotting his tie.

She was silent for a few moments, then said quietly, 'I'm so, so sorry about Archie, but you can't blame yourself. It's not as though you, or anyone come to that, can legislate for something so horrible.'

He felt a sudden buzz of anger, a feeling with which he was acutely familiar. 'Look, just don't go there today, Liz.'

She bridled at his tone. 'That's your problem, Jim. You bottle up every feeling or emotion, and then when your head can't hold any more hurt or worry, you lash out. It's always been a problem in our marriage, you know?'

That fucking intonation again. He adjusted his collar and tried hard to keep quiet.

'And that's another thing – a perfect example. I talk, and you say nothing.'

The dam broke. 'You talk about what *you* want to, and when *you* want to.' He knew he was raising his voice, but he was in no mood to be lectured. Not today, not by her, not by anyone. 'And when it comes to freeing emotions, we all know how you liberate those.' He snatched his jacket from the back of the chair and patted the pockets for his mobile and keys.

Liz slumped back on the bed, staring resignedly at the ceiling. 'You know, I thought we were finally getting over this – this shit.'

The brief silence afforded Daley the perfect opportunity to administer his argumentative *coup de grâce*. 'Liz, just shut up, please. Just do what you always do – go and have a good time, enjoy yourself, whatever. I've got four people's deaths on my plate, one of whom was a fellow police officer … in my care. How could a dedicated pleasure seeker like you ever understand the burden of that responsibility?' Not waiting for an answer, he opened the door, exited, then slammed it shut, by way of punctuation.

Liz held her head in her hands and wept tears of frustration.

DC Dunn looked hesitant as Daley strode into the office, and he realised that his expression was probably thunderous, as he had been contemplating the argument with Liz during the short walk from the County Hotel. 'Yes, DC Dunn, how can I help you?'

'Something and nothing, sir, concerning Izzy Watson.'

'Right now I'm interested in anything. What do you have?'

Daley ushered her into his glass box. DC Dunn informed him that Izzy Watson had been mainly brought up by her grandmother, who was now in her eighties and living in a retirement home in a small village about fifteen miles outside Kinloch.

'Why are we only finding out about this now?' He was puzzled as to how they had managed to miss the victim's closest blood relative.

'Michael's mother mentioned it to me last night, sir. You'd already left for the evening, and I didn't think it significant enough to get you back in. DS Scott told me to wait till you were in this morning. Anyway, according to Mrs Watson, the old lady has dementia, and they didn't think we would want to talk to her.'

'Aye.' Daley was already distracted by two enlarged CCTV images on his desk. 'And you know what thought did, DC Dunn. Get me her details please, and give the home a call. We'll have to get somebody up there to see her. Where's DS Scott, by the way?'

DS Scott was in the station's audiovisual room. He had spent the night poring over hours of CCTV footage, looking for anything that didn't appear right around the time that Izzy Watson had gone missing. Just after three o'clock, as his spirits were flagging, he had had a small breakthrough. At 8:23 on the evening of her disappearance, Izzy had been caught on camera walking up Main Street, arm in arm with Janet Ritchie. As they were about to cross the road to Pulse, they stopped. Almost out of shot, a headlight and part of the front of a vehicle could be discerned. The two women had turned around, and Watson, breaking away from her companion, headed towards it. She was away for no more than thirty seconds, before she returned to her friend and they both entered the bar. Strangely though, instead of proceeding back up the street past the camera, the vehicle reversed. Scott had spent the whole evening trying to find a trace of it from other locations, but had come up with nothing. The poor CCTV coverage in Kinloch had been further exacerbated by two of the cameras being out of action. The vehicle had vanished.

The door swung open to reveal Daley carrying two mugs of coffee. 'I take it ye saw the pictures on your desk, boss?' Scott was scrolling absently through more CCTV footage.

'I did. A breakthrough, do you think?'

Scott played Daley the sequence showing Izzy Watson frame by frame.

The chief inspector took it in, then asked to see the clip another couple of times. 'At last, something to get our collective teeth into, Bri. Your IT skills are coming on by the way. I'm impressed.'

Scott took a slurp of his coffee. 'Aye, one o' they young geniuses showed me whit tae dae last night. I'm bloody cross-eyed looking at it, but it's a start.'

The pair watched the clip again, almost frame by frame. 'Apparently Izzy's granny lives in a care home near here, and we've only just been told. Great, eh? Still no sigh of her mother.'

'Aye, I heard. The woman's no' altogether wi' us though, is she?'

'You never know. We'll take a trip to see her later. In the meantime, let's concentrate on this motor.' The headlight and the corner of the wing of was frozen, tantalisingly, on the wide screen. 'Email that to forensics. Hopefully they'll come up with something by the way of make and model at least.'

Liz sat in the dining room of the hotel, at a small table for two. It was still early and the large room was chilly. She could hear a radio playing in the kitchen.

The girl who came to take her order looked like a sullen ten-year-old. No doubt having to work at this time of the morning was not conducive to smiles and good cheer, Liz reasoned. However, a little civility never went amiss. She stirred her coffee absently. The fight with her husband had put her off her stride. She was now starting the day with a heavy heart, something she had done far too often during the course of their marriage. She forced herself to look forward to her boat trip.

'Here's-yer-bacon-an'-eggs.' Liz marvelled at how the young waitress managed to run the words together while being able to judge exactly how hard to throw the plate so that it landed on the table and not on her customer's lap.

The email had been sent to forensics, and Daley had despatched Scott to the hotel for a rest. To begin with, his deputy had been reluctant to leave, but he'd been persuaded at the promise that he could return at lunchtime, when they would both visit Izzy Watson's grandmother.

'You know me, Jim. Two or three hours does me. I'll see ye soon.' He donned his jacket, fished in his inside pocket for cigarettes and lighter, then headed off.

Daley replayed the clip. The front of the vehicle was straight up and down, and he began to wonder if it was some type of van, but quickly resolved not to waste any more time on it. He'd leave it to the experts. He also decided to have a team meeting. It would be an opportunity to refocus minds. He sat at his computer and began typing out the course of the investigation as he had seen it. He thought he would begin the meeting with a short silence in memory of Archie Fraser. He regretted letting his emotions cause another ruction in his marriage. He pulled his mobile from his pocket and clicked on Liz's name.

Her mobile rang, but by the time she had searched through the clutter inside her insanely expensive and cavernous handbag, the ringing had stopped. She made to call him back, then changed her mind. He had behaved like a prick earlier, so she wasn't inclined to forgive him – not just yet, anyway. He could sweat it out a little longer.

She had finished her breakfast – deliberately not returning the forced smile of the grumpy waitress as she left the dining room – and returned to the room, where she filled her backpack with the items she would need for the day. A camera, lenses, bottled water, paper hankies, travel make-up kit (essential), mobile phone and a case to keep it dry, and a large bar of chocolate she had purchased the day before: all were packed neatly into the bag. She recalled Jim arriving home from a fishing trip to Oban, absolutely freezing, so resolved to tie a thick jumper around her waist. The sky was already blue; she could feel the windowpane warm in the early morning sun. With a pang of guilt at not answering Jim's call earlier, she decided to ring him while she waited for Seanessy outside the hotel.

Daley discovered that the images of the vehicle from the CCTV footage would not be analysed until later that day, as the unit was too busy with another investigation. It was now after seven, and he took the short walk to MacLeod's office in the hope that, by this time, it would house Superintendent Donald.

Sure enough, he was hailed by the familiar 'Come', when he knocked on the door. 'Jim, come in, come in. You're an early bird today.' Donald was particularly bright and breezy, which immediately rang warning bells in Daley's head. 'Now, first of all, I take it you want something from me?'

'I need forensics up the road to get a move on with analysing the CCTV footage we've identified as being of possible interest.'

'I see. How significant is this evidence, do you think?'

'If you take a trip along the corridor, I'll show you. Could be pivotal.'

'I will, but first I have to tell you that events have forced me to reconsider the tenet of the investigation.'

'In what way?' Daley could feel the mist descend.

'I'm bringing in the National Crime Squad. We'll have a meeting, of course, and I'll remain in charge overall, however, operationally speaking, we may have to restructure a bit.'

'Which really means that you have no faith in me to solve this.' Daley struggled to keep a lid on his temper.

'Not true, Jim, not true at all.' Donald was on the defensive, so Daley readied himself for a large dollop of honey, the habitual salve. 'As you well know, we have four murder investigations running concurrently, investigations that may or may not be connected; and one of which is the murder of a police officer. Add to that a major narcotics inquiry, with foreign involvement, and, well, we're swamped, Jim. You're not the only police officer under pressure from above here. Maybe now you've been elevated in the ranks, you'll come to appreciate the delicate position I find myself in from time to time.' He looked steadily at Daley, as though to underline what he had just said.

Daley played with a pen between his fingers, then, when he decided to answer, surprised himself with the even tone of his voice. 'I'm not concerned with the drugs investigation. If the NCS want to take that on, fine – we're probably too emotionally involved anyway. I want to remain at the head of the Izzy Watson investigation though, as well as those of Ritchie and Mulligan. They were definitely carried out by the same person or persons. We know there's a sexual element to the murders, as well as a level of brutality that's unusual. We haven't had much luck with forensic evidence yet, but I'm sure this CCTV footage is a breakthrough. Will you move things along with it up the road? Or are you content for the NCS to trample over everything before we take action on this?'

Donald passed his hand over his slicked-back hair, disturbing its hitherto shining perfection. Daley hadn't considered that his boss could be under the same pressure of scrutiny that he felt; he always supposed that Donald was too smooth an operator to be troubled by the highest echelons of the force. He thought he even detected a measure of strain on the face of the Superintendent.

'Sometimes, Jim, this job just gets to you – to us all.' He sighed. 'Yes, I'll give them a kick up the arse.' He stood up from his chair. 'On the subject of the NCS, I'm afraid I can't commit myself. They won't be here until this evening, and for what it's worth, they've been forced on me.' He removed his uniform jacket from a coat stand in the corner. 'Come on, show me this CCTV stuff.'

Liz was surprised to see Seanessy's Land Rover already parked outside the hotel. She pulled open the stiff passenger door, climbed in and sat down, arranging her backpack and camera on her lap with one hand while searching behind the seat for the safety belt with the other. 'Good morning, Mr Seanessy. On time today,' she said and smiled at her guide.

He smiled shyly in response. Liz noticed immediately that he was wearing different clothes. His scruffy assortment of multi-coloured waterproofs had been replaced by new-looking combat-style gear. The filthy Wellington boots he had worn the day before had been discarded in favour of upmarket hiking boots. It was her turn to smile to herself; it was clear that her guide had made an effort to smarten himself up.

They drove down Main Street, but instead of stopping at the pontoons as Liz had expected, they followed the road around the head of the loch, passing the shuttered Island Bar en route. 'I thought we'd be leaving from the pontoons,' Liz said.

'No,' said Seanessy cheerfully. 'Too much police activity there after the shooting. The boat's moored round here, out of the way – Kinloch's forgotten pier, old but still just about in use.' He stopped the car at the head of a small jetty surrounded by emergency fencing and warning signs. It looked old and decrepit, and a large section of it appeared to have fallen into the loch, as though a giant mouth had taken a bite out of the central portion.

'Oh, don't worry about these signs.' He could see Liz eyeing a notice about the pier's unsafe structure. 'Needs a bit of attention, but the main reason these warnings are everywhere is that the powers that be are in league with the owners of the pontoons. There's nothing to stop this place from being used, but it doesn't suit them. Fishermen use it all the time.' He held out his hand to help Liz out of the Land Rover.

Liz paused for a moment, feeling slightly doubtful, but she decided to place her faith in local knowledge. She removed her backpack and camera bag from the Land Rover. She could see only one vessel moored by the jetty, an old-fashioned clinker-built fishing boat, replete with a small wheelhouse on a single deck. It reminded her of the lobster boats she had taken trips on as a child when her family holidayed in Cornwall.

She followed Seanessy towards an old iron ladder positioned over the edge of the pier, which led down to the boat. The tide was low, so the climb down the ladder looked precarious.

'Best foot forward, Mrs Daley. Nothing to worry about. We better get going if we want to take advantage of the time we have.' Seanessy stood at the top of the ladder, adopting a beckoning stance. 'I'll take your kit if you want. Less cumbersome for you getting down, eh?'

Liz handed him her kit and, kneeling down, slowly placed one foot out behind her and on to the ladder, beginning her careful descent onto the small craft.

★

'I agree with you, Jim. This could be a break, at long last.' Donald handed Daley the images printed from the CCTV footage. 'I'll put a rocket under those lazy bastards up the road. Oh, by the way, if you're not going to charge this Camel Johnstone, we'll have to let him go. We've held him as long as we can.'

Daley didn't want to admit that he had forgotten all about Camel still being in custody. So much had happened in the last few hours, the young fisherman's incarceration had completely slipped his mind. He didn't think for one minute that Johnstone was guilty of anything apart from questionable morals and minor drug offences; he would have had him released before now if he had remembered. It was clear that even though he had had sex with Izzy Watson prior to her death, he had not been the last to do so. Their tryst had taken place at Pulse, when she had been very much alive.

'I'll attend to that directly, sir.'

'No, you have enough on your plate as it is, Jim. I'll deal with it.'

Daley was taken aback by this unusual generosity. 'Sir, we've also discovered that our original victim, Izzy Watson, has an elderly grandmother residing in a nursing home not far from here. It's worth a shot, even if she has dementia.'

'In this case, we need to clutch onto any proverbial straw, no matter how tenuous that straw may be.'

Their business concluded, Donald left. Daley reflected on how changeable the man was: when you expected him to be at his most obstructive, he would surprise with unlooked-for support, or even just a helpful word. Maybe Donald did feel the loss of the tragic Archie Fraser every bit as keenly as he did. Maybe there was just no fathoming the man.

Liz decided to occupy the rear of the vessel, where there was a narrow bench seat and where her view was only partially obscured by the small wheelhouse. Seanessy made his way heavily aboard; as he descended the ladder she could see that the soles of his boots were brand new. He was carrying a large backpack, which sagged from his shoulders, indicating that it contained something heavy. When he was safely on the deck, Seanessy placed the bag in the wheelhouse. He coiled the large rope that had secured the boat to a bollard on the jetty, and the craft began to drift off. She was pleased that he was busying himself with the vessel; because of the early hour she wasn't keen on engaging in forced small talk; in any case, she was more than happy just absorbing the beautiful scenery. She watched as a swan made serene progress up the loch not far from the vessel, its serpentine head moving slowly to and fro, taking in the sights and sounds of the watery environment.

Though the water was mirror-like, Liz was aware of a slight swell, which made the vessel rise and fall gently. She shivered momentarily as the sun was obscured by a small white cloud, perhaps foretelling a drop in temperature out to sea. She zipped up her fleece, just as something landed on the deck beside her with a thud.

'Put that on, please.' Seanessy said, handing her a lifejacket. 'You'd be amazed how many fishermen decide to do without them.'

The wheelhouse where Seanessy stood reminded Liz of the potting shed her father had built at the bottom of their garden. She watched as he bent down and lifted a little trap door on the deck, then, not without some effort, managed to fire the noisy engine into life. Clouds of smelly blue fumes puffed from a little chimney. Seanessy made his way back towards her. 'Have you managed to secure the lifejacket properly?' he asked, giving it a gentle tug. 'That'll do,' he said. 'We'll get on our way directly.' He made his way back to the wheelhouse, where he patted the backpack that lay at his feet beneath the ship's wheel, and then steered the vessel away from the jetty and towards the open sea.

Daley decided to make the short journey to visit Izzy Watson's grandmother by himself. He doubted whether she would be of much help, but you never knew what seemingly meaningless piece of information might solve a case. He repeated this mantra as he looked again at pages of interview notes taken by the rest of the team. He decided to do this for an hour or so until it was late enough in the day to go to the retirement home.

Dunn arrived with the car keys for the pool car. 'Sir, James Newell is at the front desk. He says he wants to talk to you urgently.'

Daley asked for Newell to be shown through to the interview suite. He held back for ten minutes or so, working on the old cop's premise that the longer someone had to think about something they wanted to get off their chest, alone, the more likely it would be for them to be honest. He left the CID office and ambled along to the interview room.

Once out of the loch and into the Sound, the breeze became more chilly and the sea much more restless. They were sailing almost parallel to a road which threaded its way amid a backdrop of fir trees and white sandy bays, reminding Liz of holidays in the Greek Islands. Come to think of it, she had been reminded of various vacations since she had arrived in this magical little place.

Seanessy was positioned behind the wheel. He had looked back at her a couple of times, slightly inclining his head in a gesture that she supposed was one of reassurance, or merely a check that she had not fallen overboard. Suddenly, she detected movement to her left. The grey arch of a porpoise shadowing the boat was unmistakable. Liz fumbled in the backpack at her feet, trying to find her camera.

'Have you spotted something?' Seanessy was making his way along the deck towards her.

'Yes, a porpoise, I think. Any chance of us stopping for a short while so that I can try and get a couple of steady shots?' She held up the camera.

Seanessy looked at his watch, then shrugged his shoulders. Presently the engine noise died away, and the chimney's belching ceased. Only the lap of water on the side of the boat was audible.

Liz struggled to align her camera with the area where she felt it most likely the porpoise would reappear. She focused on the water, taking her eye away from the small screen to check her surroundings. Seanessy stood by her side, wanting to help steady her on the deck, but not quite knowing where to put his hands.

★

James Newell was standing with his arms behind his back, looking at the painting on the wall of the interview suite. He turned on hearing Daley's arrival. 'Chief Inspector, thank you for finding the time to see me.'

'See me about what, Mr Newell? Please take a seat.' Daley gestured to a chair.

'It's about my nephew, actually. He appears to have done a bunk, buggered off, in fact, and taken my RIB into the bargain. I'm the last person to tell tales, Mr Daley, but I admit I've been concerned about him – his behaviour – especially in the light of recent events. And, of course, I need the boat back. Bloody inconsiderate, as usual. He's supposed to be up here trying to find something useful to do with his life.' Newell was plainly irritated, his jaw working furiously.

'OK. I'll have to investigate this as having a possible connection to our other ongoing inquiries.'

Newell nodded.

'I'm just making you aware, that's all. Do you know if he submitted to a DNA test?'

'Oh, I have no doubt that he did not. He is and always has been irresponsible. His father should've given him a kick up the arse years ago, instead of forking out a small fortune on private education and university courses he never had the gumption to finish.' Newell drummed his fingers on the table and Daley could easily visualise the naval captain that he had been, frustrated by some incompetent rating.

'How much fuel was on board, or would he have had access to before he left?'

Newell raised his eyes, calculating. 'I suppose enough for around a hundred nautical miles or so. She wasn't full, and he must have taken off well before the pumps opened up on the pier. So yes, his radius can be no more than a hundred nautical miles, maybe even slightly less.'

'How fast does your vessel go, Mr Newell?'

'Forty-five knots in the right conditions, just over fifty miles an hour. That doesn't sound much on land, but I can assure you that it's fast enough on the water.'

Using a rough reckoning, Daley tried to work out where he could be, given the fuel onboard. The possibilities were seemingly endless, but a little voice in his head told him that Newell junior's sudden disappearance was no random act of rebellion against his uncle. 'Who exactly was Rory friendly with here? He must've had some kind of social life.'

'Mainly the local fishermen, or the odd tourist he would go out for a drink with after we'd been on a trip. I'm afraid there's little on offer here for someone with Rory's tastes.'

'What do you mean by "tastes"?'

Newell said nothing and looked as if he was weighing up whether or not to say something.

'Please, Mr Newell, this is no time for misplaced family loyalty, I can assure you.'

Newell rose from his seat and took a few paces over to the opened window. 'All my life, Chief Inspector, I wanted to have family, settle down, you know. However, being a sailor for so long, that kind of life was never possible. It was never quite the right time.' He turned to look back at Daley, who was surprised to see tears in the man's eyes. 'I've always looked on Rory as the son I never had. Brought him home toys and the like from my travels, took him to the zoo, camping – that sort of thing. I really don't know what's happened to him. He was such a good little boy.'

'Meaning what? I don't have time for riddles, Mr Newell. If you have information for me you really must tell me now.'

'Drugs, Chief Inspector. Rory's life has been ruined by drugs.'

20

Liz's attempts to photograph the porpoise had presented her with problems she had not considered. Despite having a camera with all the modern stabilisation technology money could buy, the yaw of the boat meant that trying to focus on the creature and stay upright was virtually impossible. She mentioned this to Seanessy, who far from being put out by her problems, showed genuine interest.

'Now, I think I can help you there. Just around the coast, about a mile off Machrie Bay, there's a small outcrop of rock – a glorified skerry, really, and the very devil to get into – but an ideal spot for what you need. I mean, you're both off the sea and on it at the same time, if you get my drift.' He smiled affably at her. 'There's even a lobsterman's cottage there, handy for shelter or brewing up a cup of tea. I've used it a few times. Quite dramatic, really – you have the feeling of being at the power of the ocean.' His eyes took on a distant look. 'I keep a few creels there, just a hobby, you understand. It would take us about an hour to get there, if you'd like to go, that is?'

Liz thought for a few seconds. The island skerry sounded fascinating, and she might as well forget shooting any decent material from the vessel. 'How long do we have, Mr Seanessy?'

'Oh, don't worry, my dear – as long as we want. I've had a word with the fishermen, and I don't think they intended to do much today. A bit tied up with other things, you might say.'

'Well, if that's the case, let's go for it.' She put away her camera equipment as Seanessy made his way back to the wheelhouse. Within seconds the noisy engine was belching clouds of pungent black smoke as they chugged off again. Liz looked down at the sun's dappled reflection on the rippling wake of the vessel, and then raised her head to see Seanessy smiling at her from the wheelhouse.

Daley was about to leave the office when his phone rang. He instantly recognised Camel's voice.

'It's my brother, Mr Daley. He's fucked off with the boat. Aye, and oor stash o' money. I canna believe the little prick.'

Daley took some quick details, then told Camel to sit tight. He took a mental note of directions to the fisherman's home, deciding that he would take a look around there prior to making his way to the retirement home.

As soon as they had rounded the Point, the sea had become choppy. Liz felt quite nauseous, but tried to keep this fact from Seanessy, who kept turning round to check that she was OK. She hadn't seen anything more in the way of maritime creatures, but the number and variety of birds she had spotted was far in excess of what she could have reasonably expected on land. As she mused idly about this, a small ringed plover landed on the gunwale of the boat, head darting anxiously before it took off again. She swallowed back the bile in her throat and tried to focus on the photographic opportunities the island would offer.

Daley sat in the lounge of Camel's home. It contained none of the luxury items he had seen in Michael Watson's bungalow. An old sofa and two unmatched easy chairs occupied the centre of the floor, around the dual focal points of an elderly TV set and a coal fire, the surround of which would have been familiar to anyone brought up in a Scottish council house during the fifties and sixties. A drop-leaf table under the window was adorned by bits of old netting, a dented plastic buoy and a copy of the *Rangers News*.

'Sorry aboot the mess,' Camel announced as he bent down to pick up a discarded sweater from the floor. 'The auld yin works two jobs, startin' at five in the morning cleanin' offices, so she's no' feelin' too much like hoosework when she gets hame.' He looked at the policeman apologetically.

'Do you never think of doing some yourself?' Daley asked in return.

'Aye right.' Camel grinned. 'I'm happy enough wi' things like this. We just live here, it's no' a visitors' centre.'

Deciding not to argue the toss, Daley sat down. 'So how long have you lived here?'

'Always. I telt my mother we should've bought the place, but she said we couldna' afford it. So it's still a council hoose. Shite, eh?' Camel shook his head ruefully.

'So, Bobby. What's the story?'

'He's fucked off, Inspector. Simple as that.'

'How do you know he's not just off on a jolly somewhere?' Daley was processing the fact that this was not the first time in the day that someone had 'fucked off'.

'He's taken his clothes, oor boat and all oor savings. There's no way he's comin' back.' Camel's face was pale with anger. 'An' see if he does, Mr Daley, ye'll be investigating another murder. Know whoot I mean?'

Daley took Camel at his word. He detected no dissemblance, no attempt to confuse or divert. Families could be impenetrable, especially when involved in a murder investigation. Sooner or later, however, little fissures would appear and built-up resentment would break down the walls encompassing the united front. Daley had never been close to his family. He had a brother he never saw and a sister he couldn't stomach. Both his parents were dead, and any aunts, uncles or cousins were best left to their own devices. In fact, his cousin Malky was currently serving two years at Her Majesty's pleasure for theft and assault. Who needed family? His mind alighted momentarily on Liz and the fight they had had earlier. 'Can I have a look at Bobby's room?' He refocused on matters in hand.

Camel led Daley up a threadbare carpet to the first floor. There was a powerful smell of stale tobacco and fish.

In many ways the room seemed more suited to a much younger person; a child, in fact. Football posters adorned the wallpaper, which was covered in cartoon characters

Daley did not recognise. An old chest of drawers sat in one corner of the square room, an empty drawer open so much that it pointed towards the floor and looked in imminent danger of falling. Against the opposite wall stood an equally ancient wardrobe, one door of which lay wide open, revealing a bare interior. Beside a single bed, draped in a duvet with a football print cover, sat a flimsy-looking bedside cabinet. Daley opened the top drawer: it was empty save for three black plastic hoops about the size of a large bracelet, though nearly an inch thick. Daley picked one up and on examination found that the collars could be closed by means of two metal press studs at each end.

'What are these?' he asked Camel, who was still standing outside the small room with his arms folded.

'Jeest fastening braces for the creels. Helps attach them to the rope wi'oot havin' tae tie mega knots.'

'Why would your brother have them here in his room?'

'How dae I know? Probably jeest in his pockets or something. Whoot aboot it?'

Daley picked one of the collars up. 'I hope you don't mind,' he said to Camel as he put one in his pocket.

'Aye, whootever.'

'I can see that he's cleaned the place out. You didn't have any idea he was going to do this?'

'No. Mind you, I wiz kinda tied up at the time.'

Daley ignored the reference to the young man's incarceration and continued to cast his eye over the room. 'Does your brother have many friends?'

'Same as anyone.'

'But you'd say that you and he are close, like best friends?'

'Suppose so. We're brothers, Mr Daley, we're stuck wi' each other.' He looked around. 'Well, no' the noo right enough.' He gave Daley a wan smile.

'What about girlfriends?'

'What aboot them?'

'Has Bobby had many?'

'Are you tryin' tae say he's some kind o' poof or something?'

'No. I'm just asking if he's had many girlfriends. It's a simple enough question.' Daley's face suddenly took on a thunderous expression.

'Aye, OK, don't gie yersel' a heart attack. He's had a few.'

'But not as many as you?'

'He's no' got the patter. Anyway, whoot's this got tae dae wi' anything?'

'Just wondering. Would you say he's quite awkward with women?'

'He's no' the most confident guy, Mr Daley. If you had a faither like oors, you widna be very confident neither.'

'Was he hard on you?'

'He used tae get drunk an' beat the shit oot o' us. If that's whoot you mean by being hard, well, aye, he wiz.' Camel looked straight at Daley.

'Does your brother know Rory Newell?'

'Aw, if this is the queer thing again, you can fuck off,' Camel answered angrily.

'No,' Daley said, then paused. 'It's just that your brother doesn't strike me as the type of lad who does things on his own. He needs someone to give him a nudge, point him in the right direction – you, for example.'

'Are you sayin' that Rory Newell pit this in his heid?' Camel looked as though he had made his own connection. 'I telt Bobby tae stay clear o' that bastard. He's a right dopeheid, aye, an' a fucking smart arse tae,' he said more forcefully.

'Did he listen to you?'

'Nah, no' a' the time. We're brothers, Mr Daley, we spend a lot o' time wi' each other. We fa' oot tae, dae ye know whoot I mean?'

'So, when he's not got you to tell him what to do, he relies on Rory Newell. Is that it?'

'Mebbe. I don't fuckin' know,' Camel said quietly. 'Dae ye really think this bastard Newell has pit him up tae this?'

'Well,' answered Daley, looking around the room one last time, 'if he hasn't, somebody else has.'

'He's a bad bastard,' said Camel suddenly.

'Who, Newell? Why do you say that?'

'Just the way he treats folk, especially women.'

'And do you think he could persuade Bobby to do the same?'

'I'm no' saying any more, Mr Daley,' Camel replied sullenly.

The swell was heavy now. To Liz, it felt like being tossed in a blanket, as in some childhood game. She had been told that keeping your eyes on the horizon helped. As she squinted into the distance, contemplating asking Seanessy to turn the vessel back home, she spotted what looked like a sliver of land to her right. Just as she had seen it, Seanessy turned in the wheelhouse and gestured to her to look at the small island.

'That's us there – won't be long now,' he called over the noise of the sea, wind and echoing cries of birds. 'Be able to get a cup of tea at least.' He turned back to his steering duties, seemingly relishing everything about being at sea.

Men, thought Liz, as they began to turn in a slow arc towards the island.

He thought he had it: the break he had been looking for. The plastic collars in Bobby Johnstone's room. That was all it took.

He drove the car back into the town centre, stopping outside the County Hotel. In less than a minute he was hammering on Scott's door.

'Aye, a' right, a' right. Is there a fuckin' fire or something?' Daley could hear his DS shouting from inside. With the click of a lock, the door swung open. 'Here wiz me expectin' some wee blonde. Never mind. Come in.'

Scott looked bleary-eyed, but Daley was sure that he would forget his tiredness soon. He said nothing, merely threw the collar onto the unmade bed.

'What the fuck?' Scott yawned and picked up the plastic ring. It took him a few seconds, then it clicked. 'Oh, Jamie boy, well done! This matches the marks left by the restraint on Watson's leg. Where did you get it?'

'In Bobby Johnstone's bedroom. Looks like we might have missed the obvious from the start. Rory Newell was reported missing this morning, and now Bobby's done a runner too. What's the likelihood Newell's with him?'

'Aye, could be. It's too much o' a coincidence, the two o' them disappearing at the same time. And this thing' – he held up the collar – 'well, whit's the plan, boss?'

'We'll have to try and find them – with all the resources available.' Daley looked troubled.

'Don't worry, Jimmy. If it is them, I'm sure they've got mair tae bother aboot than intercepting your wife and thon Seanessy,' said Scott, yet again reading his boss's mind.

There was a small jetty on the ocean side of the island. The telltale fluorescent buoys bobbing nearby indicated the location of lobster pots, held within a shallow bay which opened out into the Atlantic. At the head of the small pier, in front of a low hillock, a dirt track led some fifty yards to a fisherman's cottage, the walls of which had once been whitewashed but were now a wind-blown grey, contrasting with the rust-red of the corrugated-iron roof.

'Wow!' Liz enthused. 'From the sea you wouldn't know this place was here.'

'Yes, it's an interesting natural feature.' Seanessy was uncoiling rope from the deck. 'Been here a long time, and hardly ever used now. All the pots here are mine. Not a good enough yield for the commercial fishermen. A couple of the younger lads use it, but not very often. When they're up to something not quite legal,' he said, winking at Liz.

'So you just kind of turn up here?'

'In a manner of speaking. If there was any fisherman serious about this little nook, I'd never have come here.' He was shouting above the noise of waves washing onto the shingle bay. 'I bought a small boat from an old seadog

I met when I first came here. Boat lasted one season. It was him who told me about this place.' He gestured over his shoulder. 'As I say, I'm left to my own devices in the main. Apart from having to clear up after the occasional clandestine party, that is. More than made up for by having this little bolthole.' He coiled the rope, then handed it to Liz.

It was all systems go at Kinloch Police Office. The Royal Navy, Coastguard and the police's own Marine Division were now deployed in an effort to find James Newell's RIB, which contained – so everyone reasoned – Rory Newell and Bobby Johnstone. Daley found it hard to believe that the mild-mannered Johnstone brother was a cold-blooded sadistic killer, or that he was somehow involved in international drug smuggling; it was much more likely that he had been coerced by Newell, with his veneer of urban sophistication and desire for the high life.

Scott's face was a mask of concentration as he passed on details of the craft and its possible occupants to yet another interested party. Air searches were being initiated using an RAF helicopter normally used for air-sea rescue. The Coastguard was aware of what was going on, but under strict instructions not to let it be known what was afoot, in case Newell and Johnstone got wind of it. The Navy was moving three ships – on exercise in the area over the last few days – onto the trawl. In some ways, the land-bound police officers felt somewhat impotent, despite being at the centre of operations with radio traffic from all the relevant agencies pouring into the control room at Kinloch. Superintendent Donald sat proudly at the hub of it all.

Daley had been amazed at the speed with which this had been achieved. It was little over an hour since he and Scott had returned to the office with the news that Newell and Johnstone were now prime suspects for the murders of Watson, Ritchie and Mulligan. Daley knew that Bobby Johnstone had an alibi for the time that Izzy had disappeared, but the brothers had been in Glasgow for little over eighteen hours, and accurately assessing her time of death had been difficult because of the condition of her body.

Daley opened the door of interview room one. James Newell was nursing a mug of coffee and staring into space. 'As you've been informed, Mr Newell, we're now actively seeking your nephew to help us with our inquiries regarding the recent murders, of which I'm sure you're aware.' Daley took a seat opposite the retired sea captain.

'How very like a police inspector you sound, Mr Daley.' Newell placed his mug on the table in front of him with no little resignation. 'However, I appreciate your candour. Though I still find it impossible to believe that Rory has been so ...'

'I want to go back to your trip to County Antrim. Are you absolutely sure Rory was with you all the time?' Daley unbuttoned his shirt collar, which was beginning to feel like a noose.

Newell thought for a moment. 'Despite Rory's feckless nature, Chief Inspector, he was not without his attractiveness to the opposite sex. Of course, when they got to know him properly things became very different. You saw him though: tall, well built, with a certain charm, I suppose.'

Daley said nothing, merely nodded at Newell to continue.

'He struck up a "friendship" with one of the film crew. At night, the pair of them were out and about. A couple of drams and it was off to bed for me; he was more adventurous.'

'Did he ever use the RIB alone when you were there?'

Newell looked at the table, as though he was reading something. Suddenly he looked up. 'Yes, as a matter of fact he did.'

This tiny outcrop of land was by far the strangest place she had ever visited. She felt as though she was seeing the sky through a lens, that she was enveloped in some gigantic glass bubble.

'On a stormy night, this place is quite remarkable.' Seanessy was standing beside her. 'The sea sprays off the pier and onto the windows of the cottage. I find it thrilling, really quite dramatic.'

Liz had always been comfortable at sea – on a boat. She had often tried to imagine what being in a lighthouse in a storm would be like: all at sea, yet still on land, no matter how vulnerable that land actually was. It must be the same here, though instead of a solid structure which had weathered generations of all the sea could throw at it, you had a broken-down fisherman's hut.

'Do you often stay here overnight?' Liz addressed Seanessy over her shoulder.

'Only when I feel the need to be alone. You know how it is. When one needs peace and quiet to get things done, away from the pressures of the world.' He gave Liz an unprepossessing smile. 'You'll have to walk over there to get a more panoramic view.' He stomped off in his new boots.

All bases were covered. As well as they can be at any rate, Daley thought. He was trying to think himself into their heads. If these killings had been motivated by drugs, then why the grotesque level of violence? After all, these men were no hardened criminals bent on sending messages of fear to those who would oppose them. He had found Rory Newell an arrogant prick, yes, but a sadistic killer? No. And Bobby Johnstone had looked more like a lost little boy than a man who could perpetrate such horrors. But, as he knew all too well, looks could be deceptive.

Logic dictated that the simultaneous disappearance of the two men was too coincidental for them not to be mixed up in the killings. The access to boats, involvement in the sex and drugs scene in Kinloch, as well as an acquaintance with the deceased, looked like a coalescence of circumstances that could not be ignored. Who else here would fit the profile?

Donald was busy consulting the force psychologist; Daley was trusting his instinct. Yet ... he couldn't shake off a persistent doubt, and neither could his grizzled DS. Scott was not behaving the way he did when the end of a difficult case was in sight. He had none of the insouciance of a policeman who would shortly be celebrating the cracking of a particularly difficult case. Daley knew how he felt.

'Sir, it's the old folks' home for you.' DC Dunn poked her head around the office door. 'They called my mobile for some reason. Will I fling them a deafie?' The young woman seemed as though a great weight had been lifted from her shoulders. The death of Fraser was still a raw experience that bore down particularly hard on the younger investigating officers. The revelations about Newell and Johnstone promised resolution and respite from this: a chance for everyone to move on.

'No. Tell them I'll call back in a few moments. Thank them for getting in touch and tell them I apologise for not coming when I said I would.' He resolved to go and see the old woman, if only as a courtesy.

Scott reappeared back in the glass box. 'It's a Land Rover in they photos from the CCTV, Jim,' he enthused. 'They're trying tae pin doon the colour up the road, but they reckon it's an older model, maybe late 1980s, early 1990s. I've asked a couple o' oor boys tae see whether they know of any examples here. What dae ye think the chances are?' There was doubt in his voice.

This was a rural area, so it made sense that more people would drive that type of vehicle. Of course, even if they pinned down the identity of the Land Rover's owner, it was still uncertain as to whether he was involved with the crimes or merely engaging in conversation. 'Who knows, Brian? Whoever owns it, I want to speak to them. We're treading water here anyway. Everything's happening out at sea, so we've nothing to lose, eh?'

'Aye, you're right again, compadre.'

It always amused Daley the way Scott managed to append so many designations to him in the course of a day, and in so many languages.

'A' this sittin' aboot's makin' me jumpy. I think I'll go an' gie the lads a hand.' Scott left Daley alone in his glass world.

'Wait!' shouted Daley. 'The Newells have a Land Rover.' Suddenly, all Daley could see in his mind's eye was his wife – out at sea and vulnerable.

Liz was sitting on a rock scanning the horizon. She had seen nothing of interest since they had arrived on the island and she was trying to remain stoical. Not losing heart was the key.

Seanessy was in the shack working at something with a hammer. She was aware of him peering from time to time over the small rise that lay between them. She was starting to feel hungry, but her backpack was in the shack where Seanessy had stowed everything to keep them 'safe', though safe from what, she wasn't quite sure. She decided to give it another fifteen minutes or so.

'I'm so sorry I've not had the chance to call in yet. Things keep cropping up, as you can appreciate ...' Daley was on the phone to the retirement home. 'Yeah, I should be there within the hour. Thanks again for your patience.' He put the phone down. The wheels of the machine were cranking along here. He checked for his mobile in the inside pocket of his jacket, then tried to remember where the keys to his pool car were.

Seanessy hastily exited the cottage as Liz walked past the small jetty.

'Feeling a bit peckish,' she shouted to Seanessy. 'Time for a bite to eat. My backpack's in there, isn't it?'

'Don't worry. I'll get that for you,' he said hesitantly.

Liz was only a few yards away now. She shrugged her shoulders. 'OK, thanks. I'll take a seat on the jetty.' She watched him go back into the small building. He was squeezing himself through the doorway, as though something was preventing the door from opening fully. Strange man, she thought. He was so keen to impress.

'Aye, well, you make sure you don't get up tae any nonsense wi' them auld folk. They'll fleece ye at a hand o' dominoes.' Scott was busy writing a report of his involvement in the case so far. They had what was thought to be a sighting of Newell's RIB off the Ayrshire coast, thirty minutes earlier, but the trail had gone cold. Daley had spoken to the officer in charge of the search, who was of the opinion that, assuming the men knew they were being pursued, hiding along Scotland's rocky coastline would be a relatively simple task. However, the sailor was convinced that time and patience were the key to flushing out the suspects. After all, they would have to eat, and the craft would need to be refuelled at some point.

Daley was well used to the waiting game: every policeman was. It was bred into the very bones of the profession. He surveyed the scene in the large CID office. Radio traffic involving the searchers at sea was being monitored by a feed through loudspeakers on the wall. Intermittently, Donald could be heard offering words of advice, or making banal enquiries. Daley was convinced that this was merely for show and that he was determined to appear at the heart of the chase, even though desk-bound in Kinloch. All the radio transmissions were being recorded as a matter of course, and Donald was making sure his involvement was to the fore – or appeared to be.

Daley left the office. Momentarily, he considered telling Donald where he was going but soon realised that to be a fruitless exercise as his superior was too busy in the pursuit of glory via the Royal Navy and the deep blue sea.

Liz sat at the edge of the water eating a smoked salmon and cream cheese sandwich. Seanessy was busy removing a coil of rope from the boat. He glanced at her and smiled momentarily. He seemed to relish the chores he'd set himself on the little skerry.

He passed on his way back to the cottage and said, 'Running repairs. Have to take every opportunity to get these things done when the weather is right.' He hurried back up the rough path as Liz pondered what 'running repairs' might require a length of rope.

The glint of the sea suddenly dulled as a cloud passed over the sun. Liz shivered involuntarily and noticed goose pimples on her forearms.

The road to the retirement home was winding and narrow. Hugging the coast, it was dotted with little bays resplendent with pure white sand. On the other side of the road rose a thick pine forest with little clearings occupied by houses or gateways to forestry tracks. He was listening to The Police song 'Every Breath You Take' and his thoughts turned to Liz. He remembered dancing with her to the song in a

Paisley nightclub. He tried to work out how many years ago it had been and failed. It seemed like a lifetime ago – and, strangely, someone else's lifetime. His world was so different, had changed so much in the last few years.

The signpost read FIRDALE. Daley slowed down and started looking for the home. DC Dunn had given him rough directions; there was the church on his right, then the village hall. By his reckoning, he needed to take the next right.

Liz spotted movement in the water to her right, coupled with the grey flash of wet flesh arching through the waves. 'Mr Seanessy! We've got a bottlenose, I think.' She put down her binoculars and bent down to find the dolphin on her camera, now rigged to the tripod.

She heard a muffled voice coming from the shack as she scanned the scene with her naked eye. There it was again, directly in front of her and about thirty yards from the shoreline. She aligned the camera to that area just as the dolphin reappeared, and with her left hand pressed the button. She missed the old automatic cameras, the whir of the shutter. It just wasn't the same with digital, the experience somehow lessened.

Liz was aware of footsteps behind her; the distracting presence of Seanessy while she was trying to concentrate hard on getting the short. There was a strange noise – a humming like that of the old fluorescent lights everyone used to have in their kitchens. She stood back from the camera in order to examine the source of the sound.

Wouldn't it be typical for something to go wrong with the equipment just as she was about to …

She felt a sharp pain in the small of her back, like a sting from an insect or the prick of a needle. A split second later, her body began to convulse in pain, the like of which she had never felt before. She was falling but could do nothing to stop herself. Her limbs would simply not obey her mental commands. Even her eyes were blurred. Her vision was shot through with sparks and flashes. She fell to the ground heavily. And her world went black.

Daley was led down a carpeted corridor by a young care worker who chatted amiably as they walked. She told the detective how hard they worked to let residents feel that they had their own space in the home; each had a patio door leading out onto a communal garden, which they could access at any time of the day or night, unless of course they had medical problems where this was inadvisable. 'Mrs Sneddon's a fine old woman.' She intoned this with a more sing-song accent than prevailed in Kinloch. 'A bit confused at times, because of her condition, you understand, but otherwise really nice and friendly … It's so sad to see them getting worse, you know, kind of losing who they are. That's a terrible way to end your life, don't you think?' She looked at the policeman, her face tinged with sadness.

Daley nodded, recalling how his own grandmother had gradually lost her sense of self after three massive strokes. He would go to visit her with his mother every Sunday in the geriatric ward of the local hospital. Not a pleasant, bright place like the one he was walking through now: it had been cold and stank of antiseptic, age and shit. Rows of old people in various stages of decline lined the sides of the ward in metal-framed beds, each with a small bedside cabinet on which a tray and a plastic glass were placed, alongside the few meagre possessions they were permitted to retain. Everything was impersonal, stripped of any kind of homely familiarity. Those who were lucky enough to be visited regularly by friends and relatives boasted vases of fresh flowers by their beds; many, though, lay alone day after day, often too frail to make the short walk down the corridor to the toilet and having to suffer the indignity of shitting in a cardboard potty, with only curtains pulled hastily around the bed for privacy.

He could remember how sometimes the nurses would neglect to close those drapes sufficiently; the look of shame on the face of one old man, as he squatted on the bed trying to go, his hand held by an impatient nurse, her lip curled in distaste. He would always come away from those visits with the vague impression that those like his grandmother, who had lost so much of herself, were actually the lucky ones. Not for them the parade of indignity as they lay alone watching the large clock on the wall inexorably tick down what remained of their lives. Where there was no sense, there was no feeling, as his mother often said, fighting back tears as they left.

This place was different. Paintings lined the walls of the corridor: local scenes, or the paint and crayon creations of children, all adorned with names and ages. Easy chairs and bookcases filled with popular romances and well-known thrillers lined the corridor.

The nurse stopped at a door marked with the number ten and a small nameplate that read MRS M. SNEDDON. She cleared her throat and knocked on the door lightly. 'Madeleine, it's the policeman I was telling you about.' She turned the handle, opened the door and poked her head through the gap. 'Ah, you're decent. Is it OK for Mr Daley to come in?'

A muffled 'yes' prompted the young nurse to open the door wide and then step back to let the detective enter.

A thin woman sat in a high-backed chair, with a woollen patchwork blanket over her knees. The room was bright and airy. French windows, slightly ajar, opened onto a garden which was reaching full bloom. The scent of newly mown grass and flowers filled the space with a glorious aroma. No stink of shit or lack of privacy here.

'Hello, Mrs Sneddon.' Daley remained standing, despite the nurse's indication that he should sit on the couch. 'Do you mind if I take a seat?'

'Nah, son, be my guest.' Her accent was Glaswegian.

He sat down, and looked out of the French windows. 'Lovely view you have here, Mrs Sneddon.'

'Aye, no' bad, no' bad. Ca' me Madeleine, by the way, son.'

'Would you like a cup of tea or coffee, Mr Daley?' said the nurse.

'Yes, please, coffee if you don't mind. It's the only thing that keeps me awake, Madeleine. Do you know what I mean?'

'Ye canna beat a nice cup o' tea, son. No, I love ma tea, dae I no', Maggie?' She lifted her head towards the nurse. 'Make sure you gie the constable wan o' my special biscuits noo.' She held up a bony finger by way of making her point.

'You know why I'm here, Madeleine?'

Momentarily she looked confused, then realisation spread over her face. 'The wee lassie … whit's her name … och.' She shook her head in frustration.

'Isobel. Izzy.'

'Aye, right enough. Izzy.' She shook her head again and looked at him with a resigned expression. 'I hope yer no' going tae tell me she's been plunkin' the school again. She's a wee rascal, so she is.'

Daley knew that the staff had told Mrs Sneddon what had happened to her granddaughter, but that she didn't seem able to accept or retain the information.

Maggie handed him a mug of coffee. 'Do you take sugar?'

'No, just milk, thanks.' He patted his stomach by way of an explanation and grinned at Mrs Sneddon. 'Watching my weight.'

'Away wi' ye.' Madeleine looked animated. 'Yer a braw-lookin' young man, right enough.' She let out a cackle, then coughed asthmatically. 'A' these skinny malinks ye see the day. Sure the constable's just lovely, Maggie?'

'You'll take a biscuit though?' Maggie offered him a tartan tin containing small shell-shaped biscuits. 'You like them because they've got the same name as you, eh, Madeleine?'

They chatted about the home, Madeleine telling him how much she liked the place. Daley took a couple of the biscuits, recognising them from his trips to France, and looked around the room as he took the first sip of his coffee. In a display cabinet were some framed photographs, mostly black-and-white, though some in colour looked like old school photos.

'Would you mind if I took a look at some of your photographs, Madeleine? Is there one of Izzy?'

'Aye, son, carry on. She's in a couple right enough, though how they managed tae get a photo o' her at the school, I'll never know. She's never there.'

Daley got up awkwardly from the couch, mug of coffee in one hand, the remaining biscuit held in his mouth. He scanned the pictures from left to right: an old black-and-white posed image of Madeleine as a young woman, bearing a strong family resemblance to her granddaughter. Two men wearing flat caps and football scarves giving thumbs up to the camera, one smoking a pipe. Another grainy image of a young man in a World War II army uniform. The two more recent photos were at the end of the line. He had dipped his biscuit in his coffee and had just taken a bite when his heart sank.

He was so shocked that he dropped what remained of the biscuit on the floor. It was a typical school photograph: a group of about twenty children – some sitting, some standing – flanked by a teacher. Seated at the front, arm in arm and both laughing, were two girls, one looking side on at the other. The girl in profile had her hair up in a ponytail. The other girl was strikingly pretty. She stared at the camera, her dark hair tied into two bunches by red ribbons. They were young but instantly recognisable: Janet Ritchie and Izzy Watson. On the left-hand side of the class photo stood the teacher. He was wearing what looked like a green jacket, a white shirt and an orange tie knotted badly and hanging askew over his paunch. His hair was red and brushed in wisps over a balding pate. Despite the passing of years, Glynn Seanessy was unmistakable.

335

Daley thrust the mug onto the cabinet and reached for his mobile phone. He pressed 2 on his speed dial. 'Brian, we're wrong. It's Seanessy … and he's got Liz.'

Daley was in his car now. He drove at speed away from the retirement home, the gravel chips on the driveway popping under the car's wheels. He felt the same sensation of disorientation that he always experienced at times of extreme stress: his face was hot and sweaty; he felt queasy. He felt as though he was on some kind of hellish rollercoaster, unable to do anything to stop the feeling of falling, spinning out of control. At times like this he spoke to himself. Focus, take the overview, stop being subjective.

For some reason, he remembered the day his mother died. She had been ill for a long time, and when the hospital had contacted him to say that her condition had worsened during the course of the previous night, being used to such calls he hadn't rushed to the hospital. He had taken a quick shower and grabbed a sandwich before he left. The look on the face of the nursing sister when he had eventually arrived required no articulation. His mother was dead. In the infinite universe of time, he would never see her again.

He dragged his mind from these melancholy reminiscences and tried desperately to concentrate on the matter in hand. He was surprised just how hard he found it to concentrate. Liz. For some reason he couldn't visualise her face. All he could see was the hideously violated body of Janet Ritchie sprawled across the table in the *Russian Gold*.

His mobile rang. 'Jim, where are you?' It was Scott. The sound of his voice managed somehow to strengthen his resolve.

'I'm just heading out of Firdale. I'll be with you in twenty minutes or so.' He checked the time on the dashboard clock.

'No. Listen, Jim.' Scott's voice was insistent. 'We know what boat he's in – it's the Johnstone boys'. They lend it tae him for sightseeing.' Daley remembered the small lobster boat he had seen at Machrie Bay. 'We just found out when we were trying tae get a number on Bobby Johnstone. That's not all.' Scott sounded breathless. 'It was sighted about three hours ago near a wee island called Abb's Skerry. I got a hold o' Camel, and he says that yer man Seanessy has some lobster pots in the bay there. There's an auld fisherman's cottage tae – dilapidated apparently – but he remembers Seanessy askin' fir the boat tae take some wood and stuff o'er there tae dae some repairs. Are ye still with me, Jim?'

'Yes, I'm here. What's the plan, Brian? I'm desperate here.' Daley could hear the plea in his own voice.

'I've got Camel wi' me. He thought Bobby had taken the boat, didn't think tae mention Seanessy sometimes uses it. We're just waitin' for the lifeboat tae get under way ...'

'So I better get a shift on.' Daley had stopped the car at the roadside, but was now pulling away.

'Nah, hang on! You're nearer where you are. Camel says tae get yersel' doon tae the harbour at Firdale and get someone tae take you oot tae this place. He says there's a wee shop on the quay an' they'll sort ye oot. OK, Jim?'

Daley was already turning the car in the middle of the road to head back into Firdale. 'I'll bell you when I get to the pier, Brian.' He threw the mobile on the passenger seat and gunned the car towards the village harbour.

Liz opened her eyes. She couldn't remember anything for a few seconds, such was the pain she felt. Trying to get up, she realised that she could not move her arms. She fought the urge to scream, trying to control her breathing. It was so gloomy she could barely see. Diffused light was coming through a tiny window, curtained by what looked like a filthy hessian sack. The room reeked of damp fish and a nasty chemical smell.

Managing to turn her head, she saw that her arms were spread out on either side of her, each tied by the wrist to a rusty metal headboard. What looked like a large belt encompassed the bed and her lower limbs, leaving her only able to move her head forward by craning her neck. A cold shaft of fear pierced her mind, almost making her cry out. She fought the impulse. Her whole body was aching.

Her eyes were assailed by bright light, as the door to the shack swung open.

Daley sped through the village of Firdale. He remembered looking at a map of the area before he had left the office, so he knew the village was spread along a main road which led down to the harbour. His mind was a riot. He was trying to think like the detective he was, but he could not get the image of a lifeless Liz from his thoughts. He had seen so much death – so much gruesome death – that it had become his default response. When he heard of people he knew dying, he automatically pictured their greying corpse on a gurney at the mortuary, chest roughly sewn up after a post mortem. He heard himself whimper as he steered the car down an incline, the sea now visible through buildings and trees.

At the bottom of the hill, straight ahead, he could see two small boats tied up alongside a pier and a shop with an old Esso sign. He parked the car and ran to the shop. A bell rang above his head as he opened the creaky wooden door. It was like Aladdin's cave: shelves of groceries lined two walls, while the floor space in the middle was taken up by items as diverse as a large box of cabbages and a small outboard motor. An array of wares hung from hooks in the ceiling, including a child's mountain bike, a spade, a mop and a camping stove. The place smelled like those he had visited with his grandparents when on holiday as a child: a heady mixture of detergent, fruit and vegetables, engine oil and polish. At the end of the crowded space sat an old-fashioned counter, glass-fronted and framed in stout oak, the varnished wood worn bare in places by age.

'Can I be helping you, at all?' A disembodied voice came from somewhere behind the counter. An elderly man stood up. He was wearing a faded barge cap and a thick blue fisherman's sweater, which he rubbed his hands on absently. 'I've lost one of my bloody contact lenses again and I can't see bugger all. His voice had much more of a Highland quality than that of Kinloch, like the young nurse from the care home. 'You'll have to come a wee bit closer. I like to see the colour of my customers' eyes before I ask them to part with their money.'

Daley approached the counter, fishing in his jacket for his warrant card. The man took a step back at this, as though he was expecting the detective to produce a firearm from his pocket. 'It's OK, sir. Detective Inspector Daley.' He brandished the ID. 'I have to ask you for your help, It's an emergency.'

The shopkeeper examined the warrant card, squinting through one eye with his other closed. 'Aye, well, I'll have to be taking your word for it, officer. You could be Reggie Kray for all I know.'

'I have to get access to a boat, and someone to sail it, now. We have a very serious situation at Abb's Skerry. Do you know where I mean?' Daley was doing his best to present a calm façade, while his heart pounded in his chest.

'Abb's Skerry, eh?' The man scratched his head under his cap. 'My grandfather used it for creels. I dinna think anyone does now though. Would you be having a cup of tea, or something stronger perhaps? You seem a bit overwrought.'

'Listen, Mr … I'm sorry, I don't know your name.'

'Munro, Anda Munro. Say your piece, officer. I'll help you if I can.' He realised something serious was afoot.

'Thank you, Mr Munro.' Daley gave him a brief summary of what was happening, omitting names and the fact that the person who was in danger was actually his wife.

'A dreadful carry on, altogether. I knew there were problems in Kinloch – aren't there always? – but this is serious stuff indeed. C'mon with me and I'll see what I can do for you.' He lifted a hatch at the end of the counter, the polished brass hinges squeaking in protest, and stepped out, then replaced the heavy hatch gingerly. 'Damn near took my head off with this thing a number of years ago. I've got the measure of the bastard now though.

'Under normal circumstances I'd be able to take you there myself, but unfortunately our boat is beached at the moment. My brother has her over at McConachie's slip.'

Daley cursed inwardly.

They headed for the edge of the pier. The water was low; the tide, according to Munro, was on the turn. Daley thought he recognised one of the vessels, but wondered how he could. A cloud covered the sun, turning off the glistening sparkle of the harbour and casting a distinct chill over the scene. He was desperately trying to keep things together; his mind, though, kept up a loop of gut-churning images – murder scenes he had witnessed in the past.

An unmistakable face appeared from the wheelhouse of one of the boats, an old-fashioned craft that looked in much need of repair. Hamish grinned at the two men above him on the pier. 'Aye, m'boys, fine day for it. No?'

'Ah, Hamish. This man is a police officer. His name is …'

'Mr Daley.' Hamish removed the pipe from his mouth. 'And how can I be of help tae you the day?'

Munro turned to the policeman, his hand cupping his mouth. 'He has the sight, Mr Daley,' he said. 'Sounds like a damned fool half the time, but mark my words, he's as wise as an owl.' Munro looked back down to Hamish with a forced smile.

'Hamish, I'm desperate. I need your help.' Daley looked imploringly at the old fisherman, as Munro turned towards him, surprise etched across his face.

'You're acquainted with this reprobate already?'

'Oh, yes,' said Daley. 'Our paths have crossed quite a few times in the last few days.' He suddenly remembered his arrest of Flynn and, knowing the men to be friends, wondered how the old man would react to him. 'I need you to take me to Abb's Skerry right now.'

'Aye.'

'You'll be reimbursed for your fuel and your time, of course,' said Daley, for want of anything better to say; he was already working out how to get onto the vessel.

'You better get aboard, Mr Daley. It'll take us aboot three quarters of an hour tae get there, wi' steady steaming, you understand.' He moved to the side of the boat and offered his hand to Daley.

The policeman eyed the jump with trepidation, but time was of the essence. He leaned forward, grabbed Hamish's hand and jumped onto the craft, which lurched to the side as he landed heavily on the deck.

'I'm thinking you're built mair for the land than the sea, Mr Daley,' Hamish announced in a puff of pipe smoke before disappearing into the wheelhouse.

'All right, Mr Daley. I wish you safe passage,' Munro shouted from the pier. 'I'm afraid you're stuck with this bucket. The fishing fleet, such as they are now, are all at sea, and there's no sign of anyone aboard this vessel here.' He nodded at the boat tied up next to Hamish's. 'Is there anything else I can be doing for you?'

'No, thanks, Mr Munro,' said Daley, then changed his mind. 'Actually, would you be able to lend me some kind of jacket or something?' He remembered his trip on the lifeboat and the chill he had felt while at sea, despite his survival suit.

Munro dashed back to the shop, before returning with a red garment wrapped in a clear plastic bag. 'An excellent seagoing fleece, Mr Daley' – he tossed the package at the detective – 'water-resistant an' everything, an' a snip at a hundred an' twenty pounds. Do you have the cash on you, or will I open up an account?'

'An account please, Mr Munro. We are in a hurry.' Daley couldn't quite believe what he was hearing.

'Aye, very good. I hope you have a life jacket for the chief inspector, Hamish?' he enquired cheerily.

'Why?' Hamish's head poked out from the wheelhouse. 'What will it cost if we have to buy one fae you? A thousand pounds? Don't you be worrying, Anda Munro, you've made all the money you will out of us today. Now, get back in your shop an' keep countin' yer fortune. And think on forbye, there are nae pockets in a shroud.' All the while, Hamish was moving nimbly around the small vessel, having grasped the urgency of the situation.

Munro's reply was drowned out by the loud rumble of the boat's engine firing into life in a cloud of blue smoke. He untied the rope that was securing the craft to a stubby bollard and threw it onto the deck at Daley's feet. 'God speed, Mr Daley,' he shouted, loudly enough to be heard over the engines, and waved languidly as the small boat turned from the pier and headed out of the harbour into the open sea.

Just as they neared the mouth of the harbour, Daley's mobile rang. 'What's happening, boss?' Scott's voice was loud and clear despite the rattle of the boat's engine.

Daley informed his DS that he had found a vessel and was now en route to Abb's Skerry, a journey that Hamish reckoned would take about forty-five minutes.

'Aye, well you'll be there before us.' Scott sounded concerned. 'The weather's closing in, a real sea haar. It's not safe for the helicopter, and we're waiting for the lifeboat. She's towing a boat back into Kinloch. The upshot is I'm not sure when we'll be leaving. But I'm told it'll only take aboot an' hour when we do get going.'

'We'll need armed officers on the boat, Bri.' Daley was trying to visualise what he was about to face without thinking of Liz, a task that he was finding impossible. 'I'll have to work things out on the hoof.'

The answer from Scott was garbled. They had just left the mouth of Firdale Bay and the mobile signal was rapidly disappearing. He could make out Scott's plea for him to be careful, then the connection was broken. He checked the screen: NO SIGNAL.

'Can I use your radio, Hamish?' Daley shouted to the sailor.

'Well, that's a wee bit tricky, Mr Daley.' Hamish rubbed his chin with a grimace.

'Meaning?'

'I'm no' big on people interfering with my movements. There's aye somebody tryin' tae tell you whoot tae dae o'er the airwaves. Dae ye ken, Mr Daley?'

'You mean you've no radio, Hamish,' said Daley in a resigned tone.

'No.' Hamish was being canny. 'We've got wan, it's jeest no' workin' very weel, at the moment.'

Daley stared ahead. What was that saying he had first been made aware of in anger management? We are where we are. How appropriate.

In the distance he could see where the blue sky ended. It was as though a giant wad of cotton wool had been left on the horizon; there was no way to discern where the sea ended and the sky began. Daley remembered his history – when sailors were genuinely afraid they would sail off the edge of the world – and thought if anything had happened to Liz, this would be a cruelly apt metaphor.

21

Seanessy leaned over Liz, his face in hers. His breath was foul, and she could count the individual blackheads that peppered his bulbous nose. The shack had become even gloomier inside, and despite her predicament she reasoned that the weather outside had clouded over. What time was it now?

'What are you thinking about, you whore?' Flecks of spittle sprayed into Liz's face; her stomach churned in revulsion. She remained silent. 'Wondering what's going to happen to you, I've no doubt.' Seanessy grinned maniacally, displaying a mouthful of uneven yellow teeth. 'First, we're going to have some fun, you and I. Fun. The kind of fun you would never have with someone like me. Look at me, you bitch.' He grabbed her chin, pulling her face in line with his. She had to blink his spittle from her left eye.

He took something from his trouser pocket. She gasped as he bent over her, a Stanley knife brandished in her face. 'You're just like them all. Young or old, you're all the same, eh?' His eyes looked as though they were on stalks: bulging, the pupils mere pinpricks. 'Nice when you're little girls: happy, funny, pretty – all you want to do is play at being mummy,' he snarled, still gripping her chin so that she couldn't move her head. 'Then you start to bleed, and we all know what you think about then. Time for a change, pretty one.' In one swift movement, he let go of her face, grabbed the neck of her T-shirt and slit it open with the sharp knife, revealing the white of her bra against her tanned skin. He grabbed her left breast and began to knead it roughly.

Liz closed her eyes tightly. This was her – every woman's – worst nightmare. For the first time, she realised what was going to happen: she was going to suffer, and then she was going to die.

The weather had worsened. Within a few minutes of leaving Firdale, a thick mist engulfed them. Daley could barely see from one end of the boat to the other; the scene that had seemed wide open and infinite had now been reduced to a patch of black oily water with hardly a ripple on the surface. The strangest thing was the silence. No squawk of gulls, rush of wind, or crash of breakers onto the shoreline. Nothing. It was like being enclosed in a tiny bubble of life on a silent ocean. Despite the expensive fleece, Daley shivered with cold. Only the noise of the engine was audible, and even it appeared deadened.

'This will slow us up a wee bit.' Hamish's voice at his shoulder made him start. He turned round to face the old sailor. The smell of pipe smoke had replaced the stench of diesel, and any sea tang was now strangely absent.

'How the hell do you know where you're going in this?'

'It's no' a case o' jeest knowing where you are, Mr Daley, mair a case o' feelin' it.' His face creased into its habitual slit-eyed smile.

Daley looked at him. Despite the desperate nature of the situation, the older man remained utterly unfazed, almost serene. 'You do know what's at stake here, Hamish? This is more than a case for me now. If he harms her ...' The meaning was implicit.

Hamish sucked on his pipe a couple of times, and just when the detective thought he was not going to answer, he spoke. 'In life, Mr Daley, all we have to hold ontae is the certainty of death.' His eyes were bright blue and at their most piercing. 'If she's deid, you'll know – even if she's in pain, you'll know. But I'll tell you this, Chief Inspector, if a' you can dae is picture her lying deid on a mortuary slab, then deid she'll be – aye, as sure as ye killed her yersel'.' His gaze was unflinching. 'That Englishman wrote aboot there being mair things on heaven an' earth ... well, let me tell you: it's no' jeest heaven an' earth, it's in the mind tae.' He removed the pipe from his mouth, still staring at the policeman, and casually tapped it on the hull of the boat. Such was the stillness, Daley could hear the fizz as the spent ash hit the water.

Hamish turned on his heel and headed back towards the wheelhouse. Daley looked back out to sea and remembered making love to Liz in the hotel room. The warmth, the smell, the very touch of her filled his senses. Suddenly he felt a calm resolve, as though he had been emboldened by the old fisherman's words.

Liz was aware of a thumping noise on the wall of the shack, which made Seanessy stop what he was doing and listen. She was breathing heavily, and despite herself was crying silent tears of fear and humiliation. Her tormentor had sliced into her bra, exposing her breasts, and he was devouring them visually as one would an expensive meal, actually salivating at the prospect of having her.

He's going to rape me, she thought. Her mind was still working, though in a random, intermittent way. Subconsciously she was calculating the possibility of survival despite the sickening realisation that while others knew she was on the boat trip with this man who had turned out to be the monster of her worst nightmares, nobody knew where they were going and certainly not that they were on this strange island.

Seanessy stared at her for a few seconds more, then abruptly left. She was aware of a dull thud. Her situation precluded speculation as to its source. Instead, she pulled, tugged and strained at her bonds, a cause she knew to be futile, though she knew she had to try something – anything – to fight back, to remove herself from this hell.

The door creaked open again, the leering figure of Seanessy framed in the doorway. 'Very appropriate weather, don't you think?' He walked towards the bed. 'Even if that big brave husband of yours and his grubby little sidekick have realised what's happened to you, they'll never find you in this.' He sat down awkwardly at the end of the bed. Liz could feel the thick strap that held her legs fast loosen slightly as his weight made an impression on the filthy mattress. She jerked her leg, hoping that she could free herself. To no avail: Seanessy caught her limb with both hands, so tightly that she cried out in pain. 'You're going nowhere, Mrs Daley. Time you had a little rest, I think.' He fumbled in the pocket of his jacket. 'Now, I have things to attend to, and it will be better for both of us if you spend some time out of harm's way.' He produced a hypodermic syringe, removed the needle cover and squirted some of the fluid into the air. 'This will help you get some sleep, keep you fresh so to speak. Not many bonuses to being a chemistry teacher – apart from knowing the effect of particular substances on the human body.'

'You mad bastard!' Liz heard herself say this as though she was listening to a recording of her own voice.

In one quick movement he grabbed her pinioned arm, feeling along her forearm with his fingertips. 'Ah, the joys of being slim and fit, Mrs Daley.' He smiled at her. 'Never hard to find a vein when you need one.' He thrust the needle into her arm.

Liz felt a wave of nausea, rapidly followed by an overwhelming tiredness. She slipped into unconsciousness.

Seanessy waited a few more seconds, then slapped her. The strong sedative had had an almost immediate effect. He began to untie her bonds, all the while taking in the swell of her breasts under her ripped T-shirt. Again, he began to salivate.

Daley crabbed his way towards the wheelhouse. 'Any idea how we're doing, Hamish?' He looked on as the doughty

350

skipper raised his head and seemed to sniff the air. Daley had no idea where they were, and was not encouraged by the paucity of instrumentation available to Hamish. From the little he knew of life afloat, he could discern no radar, no clever electronic device that could help them navigate through the enveloping murk.

'Did I ever tell ye aboot my grandfaither, Mr Daley?' Hamish addressed him with his level gaze.

'No, I don't think you did.' Daley's heart sank at the thought of some hoary old tale, but recognising that this man held the key to saving Liz and that they probably couldn't go any faster, he decided to listen to the story with as much enthusiasm as he could muster.

'Don't be worrying.' Hamish displayed his unnerving talent for reading others' thoughts. 'I can talk an' navigate at the same time.'

Daley smiled, despite himself, and nodded for the older man to proceed.

'He was a fisherman, like myself, you understand.' Hamish took a draw from his pipe. 'He volunteered for the Russian Convoys – a hell o' a thing tae volunteer for if ye ask me – but there ye are, he wiz aye a thrawn auld bugger.' He sniffed the air again distractedly. 'Tae cut a long story short, they were sunk by a torpedo in the Baltic. My grandfaither an' a few others managed tae scramble intae a lifeboat afore they froze tae death. Jeest a wooden boat wi' a pitiful sail an' an even mair pitiful sack full o' basic rations, maist o' it ruined by the sea.' He fixed on Daley with his blue eyes. 'Nae such thing as a compass, nah, nor radar eithers – the auld fella navigated them safely tae the shore, aye, safely tae the shore,' he repeated, 'jeest wi' whoot he had up here.' He proceeded to tap his temple with his right forefinger.

Daley raised an eyebrow. 'Some feat, Hamish. I hope you've inherited the same talent.' He smiled encouragingly at the old man. 'I suppose he went on to sail on more convoys?'

'No. He didna.' Hamish shook his head. 'Unfortunately his instinct fir the shore didna run tae jeest whose shore wiz whose, if you get my drift, Mr Daley.' The detective looked confused. 'Ended up sailin' them right intae German waters, aye, right intae the hands o' the Nazis themselves.' Hamish looked at his fingernails, a look of regret on his face. 'Spent the rest o' the conflict in a prisoner-o'-war camp.' He paused for a few moments, then looked up with a beaming smile on his face. 'Still an' a', Chief Inspector, things could've been worse – they could a' hae been drooned.' He pursed his lips, signalling, Daley thought, the pride he felt in his grandfather's nautical prowess.

The policeman said nothing, peering desperately through the fog. Suddenly his mobile burst into life, the theme from *The Sopranos* somehow amplified by the mist.

'You'll be gettin' a signal fae County Antrim,' Hamish announced with a nod of his head.

'Brian, what's happening? We're ploughing on, but this fog's a bastard.'

'We're jist aboot tae leave, Jim.' Scott's voice was surprisingly clear, and again it raised Daley's spirits. 'We should be at the island in about an hour, yer man tells me. It's a' doon tae the weather. Where are you?'

'Eh' – Daley glanced at Hamish – 'kinda hard to tell at the moment. Just get going, mate.'

'Don't worry, boss.' Scott could hear the desperation in his friend's voice. 'We're going tae sort this oot, trust me.' Daley could hear voices in the background. 'I'll need tae go, Jamie. Keep the faith, man.' Daley smiled at the use of the phrase his DS normally reserved for a poor Rangers game.

Seanessy held the knife in front of his face, examining the blade carefully. It gleamed, polished by the sharpening process. Things hadn't gone as well as he had hoped – they never did in his experience. People refused to conform to his idea of how things should be, how life should be conducted. He drew a finger gently along the blade, drawing a bubble of blood, which turned into a small drip. He watched as it spattered onto the dirty wooden floor and wondered how long it would take for his life to drip away at this rate of flow. He knelt down over the recumbent unconscious figure, taking the back of the knife in both hands. He positioned the knife at the middle of the neck, just touching the white skin; immediately a red line of blood streaked across the length of the implement. An involuntary twitch began in one of the muscles on the bare shoulder. He pushed down, his full weight behind the blade. Blood spattered his face, hands, chest and trousers. The body underneath him shook in the spasms of death throes. Another gush of blood, then there was a snap. The eyes opened, but the light behind them was already gone.

Without warning, Hamish shut off the engine. Daley turned to see him listening, his head cocked to one side, eyes closed.

'Can you hear that?' he asked the policeman, as he removed something from his pocket.

Daley listened intently, but could hear nothing other than the muted lapping of water against the side of the boat and a distant hissing noise. He clambered over to see Hamish holding a small compass in a wooden frame up to the light. 'Thank goodness! For a minute there I didn't think you had any instruments to sail by at all.' Daley looked hopefully at the old fisherman.

'Been with me noo for over fifty years. My first skipper gave it tae me. Handy when you're caught up in a pea-souper lake this.' He sniffed the air, eyes closed again. 'From now on,' he said quietly, 'ye might consider keepin' the voice doon.' He nodded into the gloom. 'We're no' far off the skerry.'

Daley peered over the prow of the vessel. He could see nothing: no shadows, no breaks in the water, nothing at all to indicate they were nearing land. 'How do you know, Hamish? I can't see a thing.'

'Aye, well, you see,' the old man mused. 'Whoot you're no' takin' intae account is the fact that ye need tae use a' yer senses, no' jeest yer eyes. Dae ye no' hear that swish in the distance?' His voice was barely a whisper.

'Yes, I can.' Daley closed his own eyes, better to hear the hissing noise he had detected a moment ago.

'That's the surf drawing off the shingle bay at Abb's Skerry. Either that or we're on the coast o' Islay, which wid be a bugger, indeed. I canna stand Islay.'

Daley's heart leapt into his mouth. If Hamish was correct, he was within a few yards of Liz. He mouthed a silent prayer of hope that she was there and still ... still alive. He shuddered. 'How, or should I say where, do we land?'

'Noo, that's a matter o' tactics. I kinda thought that wid be your concern, Mr Daley.'

Daley thought for a few moments. He had to get onto the small island, but he didn't want to alert Seanessy. This was no easy task: first, he couldn't see the lie of the land, and second, he had no manpower apart from himself and the old fisherman, whom he could not put at risk.

'I'm no' blaming you fir the harbour master, Mr Daley,' Hamish whispered apropos of nothing. 'I knew fine he wiz up tae nae guid, wi' the big car an' a' the fancy holidays. I wid never hae pit him as a drug dealer though, no, not at all.' He shook his head in disbelief.

'I'll not even ask you how you know that,' Daley admonished. 'We've other things to worry about at the moment. The lifeboat won't be here for at least another half hour, and if we can get onto the island unseen, we'll have the element of surprise in our favour. At the moment, that's all we have in our favour. How well do you know this place?'

Hamish squinted at the chief inspector, rubbing his nose with the back of his hand while sniffing loudly. 'This place hasna been used regularly since before they had engine power. In the old days, when ye had tae sail or row, whoot wi' tides an' winds an a' that, ye could be stuck here for a good while. It's a great place tae get the big lobsters though, the deep-sea kind. They shelter in the wee bay ...'

Daley interrupted the tale. 'That's all very interesting, Hamish, and if we get through this I'll buy you a bottle of the best malt whisky there is, and you and I can talk about it until the cows come home, but at the moment I really want to catch a murderer and save my wife's life.' He had raised his voice at the beginning of that statement, but recalling Hamish's warning, his voice was back to a whisper by the end.

'Noo, if I'm right, we're at the back o' the island. There's a wee inlet, nae mair than a pond, ye understand.' Hamish was holding his hand to his mouth in a conspiratorial manner. 'We can likely pit in there, under cover o' the wee hill. Yer man'll no' see ye fae the cottage, unless o' course he's no' in the cottage an' on top o' the hill, in which case we're ...'

'Right, Hamish.' Daley stopped him in his tracks. 'We'll ... I'll just have to take my chances.' He looked back into the fog. 'I don't suppose there's much chance of this clearing soon? I can't see it holding up the lifeboat, mind you. With all that equipment they have at their disposal they could get to the moon and back.'

Hamish took his pipe from the pocket of his dungarees. 'Aye, nae bother for them, Mr Daley. No' so funny fir the vessel comin' in the other direction wi'oot a' the gadgets. No. Campbell will no' be able tae make headway wi' any speed in this jeest in case he hits something.' He struck a match on the bulwark of the vessel, cupping the tiny flame expertly in his fist as he applied it to the pipe, while making a noise not unlike a fish out of water in an effort to set the tobacco aflame.

'I'll say this for you, Hamish, you're not scared to give anyone bad news, eh? Get me as close in as you can. I'll just have to make it up from there on in.' He slapped the old sailor on the shoulder. 'You better put that pipe out, man; you can smell it at two hundred paces.'

'Aye, you're right enough, Chief Inspector.' Hamish took the pipe from his mouth and tapped it on the side of the boat; its glowing contents disappeared into the sea. 'I'm letting her drift in. The swell's in oor favour. Hopefully yer man'll no' hear a thing, an' I can manage tae steer her where we want to go. I want you tae keep an eye oot on the bow. My eyes are no' whoot they used tae be. Jeest raise yer hand if ye see any sign o' land, an' we'll take it fae there.'

Seanessy didn't like the way things had gone; not that things hadn't gone wrong before. No, this time it was different: he had been forced to kill before he'd had the chance to exploit the situations he'd created. All the careful planning and subtle persuasion involved in luring someone unsuspectingly to their death had been spoiled. Like cooking the perfect meal, and being able only to eat half of it.

He looked across the small bay. It would take keen eyes to spot the headless corpse submerged beneath the still water, one of the legs attached to a large weight by a rope and a rubber cuff around the ankle. It had taken him a long time to work out the best way of disposing of a body. They could be killed at any time, of course, then kept relatively fresh, or at least kept from polluting the air with the foul stench of decay, by employing this method.

He cursed himself for the mistake he had made with the body of his first victim. The cuff had not been strong enough to hold in the swell. He had searched the small coastline of the skerry to see if the woman had been washed up on its rugged shore, but to no avail. It had led to a pathetic attempt at extortion and more death. In a way he had enjoyed the torturing and killing that day, despite the unexpected nature of the circumstances. He had resolved then and there to be more spontaneous, less deliberate as to the identity of his victim: that was how he had stumbled upon the policeman's pretty wife, or rather she had stumbled upon him. The improvised nature of the situation had added an unexpected frisson of excitement to her capture. Yes, things had gone wrong, but the world was an uncertain place, and it didn't do to be overly concerned with the perfect execution of a plan. He smiled at the memory of how dismissive the big detective and his sidekick had been of him when they met. Dismiss me now, gentlemen!

The air was beginning to clear. More of the bay was visible. It was time to put the next part of his plan into action. He picked up the bag of tools at his feet and strode back towards the shack. First, he wanted to fix the corrugated-iron roof of the lean-to at the side of the cottage, where he stored his fresh meat. He fished inside the bag, bringing out the nail gun he had brought especially for the task.

The boat edged forward on the swell. Daley peered into the grey mist. He thought he could see shadows. He turned, lifting his arm as Hamish had instructed, and the old man made his way forward.

'We're close tae the shore, Mr Daley,' he whispered. 'Better prepare yersel' fir a wee bump. Here, can ye try and fend us off any rocks wi' this.' He held up a gnarled-looking oar to the detective. 'Shouldna be much o' a bump in this sea, and mebbe we'll be lucky an' get right ontae the shingle. That's whoot I'm aiming fir, anyhow.' He made his way back to the tiller as Daley kept watch intently on the bow, the oar poised.

Daley could see something ahead now – a bay with a pebble beach. Again, he held up his arm, looking round at Hamish, who nodded enthusiastically. Even though they were not under power, the beach seemed to be rushing towards them at some speed. Daley braced himself against the gunwale for the inevitable impact.

As it was, they seemed to glide onto the shingle. Like a car suddenly moving across a gravel drive, the noise was sudden and brief. They stopped quickly, the vessel lurching to one side as they came to rest. Daley looked down, to see that they were three quarters of the way beached, with the stern of the craft still in the water.

Without reference to the old man, he laid his impromptu fender carefully at his feet and jumped over the side of the boat, levering himself over the bulwark of the vessel as though he was clearing a fence. He landed heavily on the shale with a dull thump, nearly toppling over, though he managed to keep his feet. As he looked up, Hamish spoke to him from the deck. 'Now you're in charge, Mr Daley. At the top of that little knoll you'll get a grand view of the whole island, just about. If you can see for the mist, that is, though I think it's clearing.'

'Thanks, Hamish.' He hoped they hadn't alerted Seanessy. If he was even here. Daley's heart was pounding. 'I want you to stay here. If you see the lifeboat, tell them what's happening.' He turned to face the small hillock, dropping to his hands and knees.

'Very good, Mr Daley.' Hamish watched the detective scramble up the hill, crouching so that he wouldn't appear silhouetted against the skyline should Seanessy actually be at the cottage.

Seanessy loaded the nail gun. The lean-to adjoining the shack was his larder; the place he kept his dead meat – for meat was all they became – and the place he did his butchery. He had killed his first victim there only a short time ago. He looked at the door. The big padlock was lying on the grass where he had left it before securing the corpse in the bay. No need to lock it now.

An old wooden ladder was propped up against the wall. He decided to secure it before attempting any repair to the roof. He placed the nail gun on the grass beside the padlock, then put his foot on the bottom of the ladder. The rungs were worn, but not dangerous. He pushed down on it, ensuring that the ladder gained purchase in the rough soil. It seemed firm, though he decided it would be best to climb to the top, just as a test, before he went up with his tools. He climbed carefully, noting that the mist was clearing. There was a tiny patch of blue showing through the gloom.

Daley reached the top of the hill. His trousers were already torn at the knee – one of his new pairs too, he mused. He cursed his lack of fitness. His legs were stiff, and his back ached after having to climb the small incline. He couldn't recall ever having been so nervous. He forced thoughts of Liz to the back of his mind. The mixture of rage and fear he was experiencing was like a completely new emotion. All his senses were intensified: the ground smelled richly of wet earth; the tang of the sea was so sharp in his nostrils that he could taste it; the swish of the swell receding from the shale beach behind him sounded like distant thunder, over the pounding of his heart in his ears. Then he saw him.

Seanessy looked across the slanted corrugated iron. Two large nails had come loose in a recent storm, causing a bulge between the roof and the top of the wall through which rain had poured, leaving part of the earthen floor within the construction damp and cloying. The roofing material was old, but still thick and robust. He passed his hand over it, deciding the nail gun would make short work of the job. He paused briefly, then made his way back down the old ladder.

Daley watched the man scale the short ladder and examine the roof. He was literally only fifty yards away; the proximity made Daley hold his breath. He recognised Seanessy immediately, although he looked different to the shambling eccentric he and Scott had encountered on the beach. He seemed more severe – evil, almost. Daley realised this was absurd; it was his gut reaction to the horrors he had perpetrated. He now felt certain Liz must be here. His chest ached with fear, and he could feel beads of sweat on his brow.

What am I going to do? He was alone. He had to get to Seanessy and subdue him, while not putting Liz in any danger. He had to keep a clear head and be optimistic – a mantra, he realised, he had picked up from Donald. He watched as Seanessy descended the ladder and went into a little shack. Taking a deep breath, still crouching, he scrambled over the top of the hill, and began to slip and slide down the muddy slope. He was heading for the rear of the cottage, all the time keeping his eyes on the building in case Seanessy appeared. He reasoned that he had the element of surprise, and that the retired teacher would be no match for him physically. He shortened his stride as he reached the back of the cottage, minimising the sound of his footfall. He leaned against the wall in order to catch his breath, which he drew as silently as he could. Please God, let her be in there. Please God, let her be safe.

The walls of the cottage were cool and damp, the salt smell of the sea here replaced by a musty odour of age and decay. He began to make his way slowly along the wall, in the opposite direction to Seanessy. He could hear no sound, nothing to indicate that Seanessy was busy inside, that he was inside at all. He edged to the corner, gripping the stonework with his fingers. He could hear nothing, so he decided to be bold and take a look.

He could see the bay now. The mist had cleared. There was no sign of Seanessy. If Seanessy had seen or heard him, he must surely make a move. There were tools strewn about the front of the building, and among them was Liz's backpack. His blood ran cold. The emotions he had been fending off welled up inside. This man – this monster – had his wife. He tried to apply the lessons he had been taught in anger management to stave off the blinding rage he was now feeling; ultimately he knew it would be futile. He was beyond caring about the consequences: his only goal was to save Liz.

He heard a high-pitched whining, and in the split second he turned to face the direction of the noise, he saw a figure, arms outstretched, holding something before it. He just had time to lift his arm to protect his face when the flash of something caught his eye.

His head felt as though it would explode as he felt something hit his arm. Instinctively he fell to the ground. He landed heavily, banging his head and feeling his chest start to convulse as he struggled to breathe. Agonisingly his lungs would not inflate; it felt as though he was being crushed in a massive fist. He saw a figure loom over him. Seanessy. His body arched as his torturer triggered the taser, sending the crippling voltage along the wires now embedded in his arm. His right hand spread involuntarily, as though he was forcing his fingers to span. The pain was now excruciating.

'Now, now, Inspector Daley, I'd expected so much more from you.' Seanessy looked down at him. 'Your airhead wife – yes, an easy conquest. I'd thought you were going to be an altogether tougher nut to crack.'

Daley heard the whine beginning to rise in pitch again. He felt a certain surprise; despite the pain and convulsions he was suffering, he had remained conscious and was fully aware of what was going on around him. And he could move his leg. He knew the whining noise was the weapon rearming another charge.

With all the strength he could muster he kicked his leg out, catching Seanessy on his knee and knocking him backwards. With huge effort he managed to force his right hand to work. This arm was trapped under him because of the way he had fallen, which meant fortuitously that his hand was only inches away from the wires inserted into his left arm. He strained, little bursts of light exploding in his vision. The rubberised coating of the jacket he'd got in Firdale had somehow reduced the voltage of the taser. He ripped the wires from his arm with a cry, then leaned heavily on his right arm, determined to be able to stand and face his attacker.

Suddenly Seanessy looked panicked. He had fallen backwards and had dropped the weapon, which was squealing now on the ground beside him. He was groping at a small pouch that was attached to the waistband of his trousers, while at the same time trying to force himself off the ground with one arm in much the same manner as Daley.

The detective managed to get to his knees, and with the very last strength he had left, forced his large frame forward on top of the older man, who was still struggling with the pouch. Both men gasped simultaneously. Daley felt his muscles loosen – the enforced cramps the taser had initiated were fading – though he knew his body was still not entirely his to command. He managed to pick himself up and straddle his opponent.

He could see the fear in Seanessy's eyes. Daley lifted his arm, ready to send a fist into Seanessy's face. 'Where is she, you sick fuckin' bastard?' It was almost as though someone else was shouting. As his fist connected with Seanessy's face he felt a sharp pain in his left thigh. Looking down, he grimaced at the sight of a hypodermic syringe sticking proudly from his leg. He tried to lift his arm to dislodge it, but could not. A smile spread across Seanessy's face. Then Daley lost consciousness.

22

He came round abruptly, like someone being thrown into a pool of cold water when fast asleep. Strangely though, he was unable to move. He could feel – he knew – he was being dragged. He could see the blue of the sky showing through the evaporating haze of mist, but despite every effort he could not move so much as a muscle. Without warning he was thrust roughly to the ground, his head bouncing off a hard surface. Whatever he had been drugged with dulled the pain, but his eyes still pricked with the tiny lights he associated with being concussed.

Seanessy's face was above him. 'I thought a city boy like you would appreciate drawing his last few breaths of sea air.' He was grinning insanely at the detective, a wisp of hair flopping over his eyes, his freckled face lobster pink. 'Oh, and you might like to take a last look at that bitch of yours.' Daley felt himself being pulled up by the hair. He was facing a tiny harbour; they were on what seemed to be a little jetty.

'Look down there.'

Daley felt his head being thrust forward, a hand clasping the back of his neck. The water in the bay was clear, the sunlight reflecting off the sandy bottom. Daley tried to focus. There was something, something in the water. It was a body. He recognised arms moving gently in the swell, like seaweed on the tide. The drugs had made his sight blur, but he could see enough to know that the body had no head. He retched, unable to expel the vomit from his mouth. He felt himself being flung back onto the hard surface of the jetty, again banging his head, the force of it sending vomit splattering from his mouth. Images of the floating corpse, Liz's face and Fraser's body lying on the pier at Kinloch all flashed through his mind.

Someone was speaking to him. The words were hard to understand at first, but gradually he began to make them out as his head cleared. 'I have her head, you know. It's back at the cottage. Do you want me to get it?' Snot was flowing from Seanessy's nose, insanity written all over his features.

Liz. Liz was dead. Daley could hear his own scream – half anger, half fear – echoing around the bay.

'I was made a fool of all my life by *idiots*, cretins who weren't fit to lick my boots.' Seanessy's rage was volcanic, palpable even through Daley's drugged and diminished senses. 'Standing in front of *imbeciles*, trying to impart some knowledge to them as they called me the most awful names and laughed at me.' Daley could smell the tang of the sea mixed with the stench of his own sick. 'And those snooty bastards – like your stupid wife – taunting me with her big tits and tight jeans. Me! Their intellectual superior!

Even my own daughter became one of them: useless, ruined with drugs, profane.' White spittle was caked at the corners of his mouth. 'Now they're all dead, and soon, very soon, you will be too.'

Daley saw Seanessy reach behind his back. The silver flash of a large blade filled his field of vision; it was like an old butcher's cleaver, with two improvised handles at either end, covered with electrical tape – a hand-held guillotine. He struggled to make his limbs move, to do his bidding: nothing. He was paralysed. Having come into contact with so much violent death in his career, he had always wondered how the victims felt at the point of extinction. Did your life really flash before your eyes, or was the fear of imminent death such an all-encompassing, visceral experience that it excluded everything else? He knew the drugs were affecting him – the fact that he couldn't move bore witness to that – but now that he knew he was going to die, he felt a strange detachment as to his own fate. What hurt, what gnawed away at him, was the thought of his beautiful wife having met with this grim end. He had failed her as a husband, as a human being, and even as a police officer.

Daley stared up at his executioner, silhouetted against the patchy blue sky. He could smell the overpowering stench of stale sweat. Seanessy was straddling him, the cleaver held between both hands, like someone about to force down an explosives detonator. Beads of Seanessy's perspiration dripped onto Daley's face.

'I'm not in the habit of despatching conscious victims, Mr Daley, but I want you to feel the pain of death for both you and your whore of a wife.' He leaned back on his heels and raised the blade in front of his face. Daley could only feel his fingertips clawing uselessly at the rough surface of the pier. This was it; he was going to die.

There was a noise – a metallic snap – followed by a dull impact, like the sound of an axe biting into a damp log. At the same moment, a shaft of sunlight glinted through the dispersing mist, highlighting Seanessy's face in grim detail. His right eye had exploded in a shower of blood and gore, replaced by a sharp metallic point. He didn't scream, didn't even move. His mouth gaped open, whereupon a torrent of blood oozed over his bottom lip and down his chin. Still upright, straddling the detective, he dropped the blade, which landed heavily on Daley's chest, causing him to exhale sharply. Slowly, like a building being demolished, Seanessy's lifeless body fell forward, his forehead catching Daley on the chin. Above them, another figure was silhouetted against the sky: Hamish, a nail gun in his fist.

'Aye, I'm sorry I let things go so far, Mr Daley. It's jeest you'd said that you'd be takin' care o' everything. I wisna sure whether or no' ye had a master plan on the go, that I couldna fathom. I take it ye need a hand?' He smiled down at the recumbent police officer.

'Off ... Get this bastard off me,' Daley managed to whisper. 'He killed Liz.' He felt a sob rise from his throat.

Hamish rubbed his chin. 'No, he didna,' he said. 'She's up in the cottage – oot for the count, right enough, but no' deid. I checked her pulse myself.' He walked to Daley's side and, sticking his boot under Seanessy's body, kicked it aside. A loud klaxon sounded. The lifeboat roared into the tiny harbour. 'Here's the cavalry, Mr Daley. Aboot as much use as a ha'penny watch.' The large orange and blue lifeboat was entering the tiny harbour.

23

Daley had never attended so many funerals in such a short space of time. Judging by what had been found in Seanessy's cottage, they were lucky not to be attending many more. Pictures of schoolgirls – their faces circled in red pen – from throughout his time as a teacher in the local school plastered the walls. The smiles of the two dead girls were almost obliterated by thick black crosses. They had been the unlucky ones, or was it that the others had been lucky?

A criminal psychologist reckoned that Seanessy had bottled up his resentment over decades, that the dam had simply burst when he retired. It seemed likely that his hatred of his mocking adolescent pupils had been heightened by the debauchery and premature death of his own daughter. Whatever the truth was, it had died with Seanessy on Abb's Skerry.

Izzy Watson's funeral was first. Her widowed husband Michael had shaken Daley by the hand, his blond-haired son hanging on to his father's trouser leg. The child looked wary and sad, as though he grasped something of what was going on. Daley mumbled the usual platitudes, hoping he was showing the correct level of empathy. In truth, he had spent every day thanking God that Liz had survived her ordeal at the hands of the deranged Seanessy. She had bravely insisted on accompanying him to the burials of the other victims as a show of solidarity with them and their families, and an unspoken offering up of thanks for her delivery from evil. Daley looked at her now. No signs of the torment she had gone through were visible, bar a small scratch on her cheek, even now fading under the adroit application of make-up and the brief passage of time. His heart swelled with love and relief. She was still subdued, didn't have the old spark in her eyes, and he knew it would take time for her to recover, if in fact she ever did.

The next day, it was Janet Ritchie's funeral. MacLeod was at the service, accompanied by two prison officers. He had been remanded in custody after a speedy investigation by the discipline branch, instigated by Superintendent Donald, who himself was present at this service. Daley was sure that he had only attended to see MacLeod's shame, however, he decided to say nothing. Officially, Daley was still on sick leave, but he had kept in touch with Scott and the rest of the team. They had remained in Kinloch to tie up the loose ends of the Seanessy case and launch a serious investigation into the drug-smuggling ring responsible for Fraser's murder. Daley frequently found his mind wandering to the circumstances surrounding the killing of the affable young DC. In fact, he found it hard to think about much else.

★

It was the morning of Bobby Johnstone's funeral, and Daley was back in the CID office at Kinloch. He had been the headless corpse floating in the tiny bay of Abb's Skerry. His head had been recovered from the lean-to shed where they had found Liz, unconscious and half naked, but alive. The place had looked like a butcher's, and it had been obvious that the young fisherman had been killed that day, most likely as Liz lay next door.

'It's like wading through custard here, Jimmy.' Scott was chewing on a fried-egg roll, the yolk of which was dribbling down his chin. 'There's nae doubt aboot it, they're a tightknit bunch doon here an' no mistake. Still, I've no' had tae go shoppin' wi' the wife fir nearly three weeks, so every cloud …' He shrugged, then cursed as some yolk landed neatly in the middle of his tie. Instantly, Daley remembered Archie Fraser and, unusually, could think of no witty remark.

He had spoken to Camel briefly after the service, offering him his condolences. The normally chirpy young man was withdrawn and sullen. To be expected perhaps, as he was still under investigation for his purchase and use of illegal drugs. It was obvious that he saw Daley as the enemy as well as the man who had failed to save his brother.

Daley was about to leave the office when Donald appeared, a vision in sharp creases and gold braid.

'Can I have a word with you, Jim?' Donald was affecting his most gushing tones.

'All right.' Daley looked pointedly at his watch. 'Liz is down at the County having a drink with Annie and the staff, and we'll be driving up the road soon.'

'I will only take up a moment of your precious time.' Donald already had Daley by the arm and was steering him towards the door, his smile positively unctuous now. 'Quick chat, then you can hit the road.'

They walked in silence along the corridors of Kinloch Station to the office that had once belonged to the disgraced Inspector MacLeod. Donald waved Daley towards the visitors' chair as he removed his cap and placed it carefully on the coat stand. 'Now,' he said, adopting an expression of consolation, 'how are you both getting on after your ... ordeal?' He leaned forward in his chair, and for a brief moment Daley thought he was about to clasp his hand in a gesture of sympathy.

'You know how it is, sir. It's taking a bit of time. Liz is doing OK. She's my priority at the moment.' He left a pause in the conversation by way of emphasis.

'Absolutely. You do the right thing.' Donald stroked his chin, a thoughtful look on his face.

'If you have something to say, sir, I would appreciate that we get on with it. As I mentioned, we've got a long drive ahead of us.'

'Quite so, Jim, quite so.' Donald opened a file on his desk. 'You've been off sick since the incident?' He looked at Daley who nodded. 'Mmm.' More chin stroking. Just as Daley was about to interject, Donald closed the file and patted it in a gesture of finality.

At last, thought Daley.

'I'm going to be blunt, Chief Inspector.'

Suddenly Daley was full of trepidation.

'I can't afford an asset like your good self to be idle for much longer. It's the usual madhouse up the road, and I know you're fully aware of the extra manpower we've had to divert here.' He raised his eyebrows as Daley nodded silently, fully aware that an announcement of some import was forthcoming. 'I want you to spend some more time down here. Let's call it a temporary transfer.' He smiled guilelessly.

'Ah, at last we have it, sir.' Daley threw his head back in disgust. 'I fully realise that we're pushed on all fronts, but I'm not about to up sticks and leave Liz on her own at home, while I become the friendly neighbourhood sheriff in perpetual residence at the County Hotel.'

'As usual, Jim, you are jumping to conclusions – strange for such a gifted detective.' Donald stood, giving the impression of an edict from on high. 'And as far as your accommodation is concerned, I am quite prepared to let you rent a home of your choice, within reason of course, with the expectation that your wife will accompany you on your, let's say, mission, here.' More smiles and raised eyebrows. The deed was done.

Abba's 'The Eagle' blasted from the car's speakers as they drove alongside a truly stunning shoreline. Islands glowed blue above a darkening sea as the light faded and changed colour into dusk.

Liz had said very little since they had left Kinloch, and Daley was anxious to find the best time to articulate Donald's idea. He really had no clue as to how she would react, a feeling that he had made clear to his superior. She had suffered the worst moments of her life near Kinloch. He didn't know if he should ask her at all.

'Are you OK, darling?'

She was playing absently with a strand of hair. She turned to him and smiled.

'I need to run something past you, Liz.'

Shades of purple adorned the sunset that was now framing the distant isles.

24

Donald was behind the wheel of his new Audi, top of the range and paid for, largely, by his generous car allowance. He was wearing his number one uniform, complete with white gloves and service medals.

The church where Archie Fraser's memorial service had been held was only thirty minutes from his home in the leafy suburbs to the north of Glasgow. He was enjoying the familiarity of the route, as well as a childlike pleasure in driving this car – his new toy. The humid clamour of a cloudy July day was expelled from the vehicle by the climate-control system, and he relished the drama of Beethoven's *Ninth Symphony* issuing from the car's Bose speakers. He had spent a long time listening to classical music, trying to develop a taste for something he now regarded as a social necessity. After many months of struggle, he had come to prefer this sea of sound and emotion to the prog-rock bands he had so admired in his youth. Like everything else in his life, he had worked hard at it, and now he could impress those who travelled with him by being able to name the music being played on Radio 3 or Classic FM, long before the presenter had seen fit to enlighten the audience. He was particularly fond of Beethoven, though he was developing a taste for Wagner as well.

His attempts at learning a foreign language were coming along well too, as were his piano lessons. He had made it plain to the tutors of both subjects that he wished to gain only a fundamental knowledge of their subjects, enough to be understood in this new tongue, and to be able to play a simple piece that would be easy to learn, while sounding impressively difficult to the untrained ear. His progress on both fronts made him smile.

The smile quickly disappeared from his face as his mind scrolled back to the cool reception he had received at Fraser's service. The late DC's father had refused to shake his hand; he reflected how like his son he was, with faded red hair and awkward manner.

One man who had needed no introduction was the lad's uncle, though even he had been shocked by the pitiful figure Davie Fraser had become. The ex-cop had sat motionless in his wheelchair during the whole service, his emaciated body leaning to one side and his white shirt highlighting the yellow tinge of his skin. He had brought to mind Donald's own father, who had killed himself with drink: that same jaundiced complexion brought on by a rapidly failing liver. They could do more these days, though why bother in Davie Fraser's case, he knew not. He thought that his ex-colleague would have been better employed asking the minister to reserve him a funeral slot, rather than his slurred attempts at insults. It wasn't his fault that the nephew had as few brains as the uncle, walking into a highly dangerous situation wide-eyed and unprepared. Why should he reproach himself for the failings of others? After all, he couldn't hold the hand of every cop under his command. The job required common sense, and in his opinion, Archie Fraser had displayed none whatsoever.

He had been momentarily diverted by the fetching figure of Liz Daley. How it was possible for her to look so alluring in her plain black dress and hat, he did not know. She bore little signs of the traumatic experience she had so recently been through, apart from perhaps being a little paler than normal. He had read the report on her ordeal with great interest. Though he found it hard to admit to himself, he had been aroused by her plight, trying to picture how she would have looked, half naked and chained to the filthy bed in that shack on Abb's Skerry.

The sight of her lumbering husband had brought him back to reality. He was wearing a suit that looked at least two sizes too small, as usual, and his paunch hung over his waistband. He still bore marks of assault on his chin and carried himself stiffly, the result of the muscles he had torn trying to fight off the effects of the taser. Donald admired his skills as a detective – even his humanity – but he still saw the DCI as being weak-willed, unable to, or unwilling to, achieve the potential he undoubtedly possessed. One look at his thickening waistline was confirmation enough.

Donald turned the car into his street, then drove the few yards to his large Georgian home. The pebbles on the driveway crunched under the eighteen-inch alloy wheels as he parked at the side door of the house. The exultant soar of the orchestra was suddenly extinguished as he turned off the ignition.

He was about to open his door and leave the vehicle when he heard his mobile ring. Noting the name on the screen with a raised eyebrow, he spoke: 'Good afternoon, Sergei. I can only imagine that you have an urgent reason to contact me this way.' A frown spread across his face as he heard the familiar bells of the small Latvian town tolling plaintively in the background.

Acknowledgements

Thanks to my lovely family for putting up with me. And to Hugh Andrew and Neville Moir at Birlinn; to my editors Alison Rae and Julie Fergusson who have helped make this book what it should have been all along; to the late Angus MacVicar who never forgot he told me to be a writer; and my late mother and father, Alan and Elspeth Meyrick.

And to the people of Kintyre – your support has been wonderful.

About the Author

DENZIL MEYRICK was born in Glasgow and brought up in Campbeltown. After studying politics, he pursued a varied career including time spent as a police officer, freelance journalist and director of several companies in the leisure, engineering and marketing sectors. Denzil lives on Loch Lomond side with his wife, Fiona.

Hello from Aria

We hope you enjoyed this book! Let us know, we'd love to hear from you.

We are Aria, a dynamic digital-first fiction imprint from award-winning independent publishers Head of Zeus. At heart, we're avid readers committed to publishing exactly the kind of books we love to read – from romance and sagas to crime, thrillers and historical adventures. Visit us online and discover a community of like-minded fiction fans!

We're also on the look out for tomorrow's superstar authors. So, if you're a budding writer looking for a publisher, we'd love to hear from you. You can submit your book online at ariafiction.com/we-want-read-your-book

You can find us at:
Email: aria@headofzeus.com
Website: www.ariafiction.com
Submissions: www.ariafiction.com/
we-want-read-your-book
Facebook: @ariafiction
Twitter: @Aria_Fiction
Instagram: @ariafiction